THE
DARK KINGDOM
BOOK ONE

KINGDOM OF DARK SOULS

JACI MILLER

Solitary Pen Press

Kingdom of Dark Souls
The Dark Kingdom : Book One
Endless Sea Universe
Copyright © 2022 by Jaci Miller
Solitary Pen Press
Cover Design by Miblart
Editing By Tiffany White at Writers Untapped
*written and edited using The Chicago Manual of Style and the Merriam-Webster dictionary
Map design by BZN Design Studios

Print ISBN: 978-0-9988069-9-0
eBook ISBN: 978-0-9988069-8-3
First Edition: 2022

www.jacimiller.com

CONTENT WARNING

Kingdom of Dark Souls is an adult romantic fantasy set in a medieval and brutal world of warring kingdoms, stolen thrones, dark magic, and treachery. Acts of violence, blood, war, and some sexual encounters are included in these pages. Please enter the realms with caution.

ALSO BY JACI MILLER

THE SCRYING TRILOGY

The Scrying

The Hallowed

The Arcana

Sign up for our newsletter www.jacimiller.com and receive a short story
from the world of The Dark Kingdom

To all those who rise from the darkness.
And to Jen who always pulls me from mine.

THE
ENDLESS
SEA

ISLE OF HADDES

VALLEY OF SOULS

CITY OF RAVENIA

BRAE

KINGDOM OF RAVENIA

ZION

MISTENVALE
THE KINGDOM OF THE ELVES

GOLD COAST EMPIRE

BIZANG DYNASTY

WARNEX KINGDOM

REALM
OF THE
SHALLOWS

HOLY CITY OF KASMIRE

GOLDEN CITY

PURITY BAY

SHIMMERING COAST

LAND OF THE SEVEN KINGDOMS

CONTINENT OF EXILE

KINGDOM OF DARK SOULS
THE DARK KINGDOM: BOOK ONE

ENDLESS SEA UNIVERSE

PROLOGUE

The Kingdom of Ravenia, on the continent of Exile

Pleas for mercy echoed throughout the castle as invading forces assaulted and butchered servants and guards. Along with the hundreds of Gold Coast soldiers who'd sacked the city hours before, Queen Evinna suspected a handful of Ravenia traitors existed within the castle walls as well.

She grimaced at the gut-wrenching sounds. *Their betrayal will be judged when they meet their maker, their punishment just.*

The screams grew louder and more visceral as the air filled with the clash of metal and the cries of battle.

"Quickly," she said to the woman standing behind her. "You must go, now."

"Your Highness, please come with us." The woman's red-rimmed lilac eyes shone with tears as she clutched a small dark-haired girl in her arms.

"I cannot leave my people."

"But the king is already dead," the woman said, her voice strangled with grief.

"All the more reason not to flee."

The queen's face softened as she stroked the little girl's head. Wide blue eyes full of fear burrowed deep into her own. "I'm sorry I will not see you past your fifth year, little one." She turned back to the woman holding the trembling child.

"This is my fate, Kelena, but it isn't yours nor can it be hers. If I run, they will hunt me, and she will never be safe. They must be made to believe the Ravenia bloodline ends tonight."

"But your brother will protect you."

Queen Evinna stiffened momentarily and then put a gentle hand on the woman's shoulder. "You have been in my employ since I married King Ryguard. You left your home and family to ensure I was not alone in a strange land, but the time has come for you to go home, for both of us. You have my gratitude and my trust. I beg of you, keep her safe."

She pushed Kelena toward the bookshelf at the back of the chamber and pulled on the iron sconce to its left. The bookshelf swung inward to reveal a hidden passageway. The queen bent and kissed the small child in Kelena's arms.

"My brother must keep her hidden until it's time for her to know the truth, but not before she comes of age. Do you understand?" The queen reached around her neck and removed the pendant she wore. "Make sure he gives her this on her twenty-first birthday." She handed the bauble to Kelena and tucked a small white note into her trembling palm. "There will come a time when the lands will once again be besieged by unfathomable darkness and destiny will call to her. This will give her a chance."

"What is it?" The light of the torches caressed the small vial at the center of the pendant, and the red liquid inside glowed in response.

"A part of our past and maybe the only way these lands will ever find peace again. I don't have time to explain further but this pendant will one day need to be with the one for which it is intended."

Kelena nodded as tears flowed down her cheeks. Her eyes flicked back to the large bed where another smaller dark-haired girl slept. Through pursed lips, she asked, "Are you sure about this, Your Highness?"

The queen's face crumpled as she followed Kelena's gaze. "I've seen the future, and I know the terrors it holds. This is the only way. I hope I'm right in my choice."

The child in Kelena's arms began to whimper. "Mama."

"Go," the queen said, her heart wrenching. "My brother is waiting for you beyond the western wall." She pushed them into the shadows and closed the entrance.

"I will make sure she knows how brave and strong her mother was," Kelena said as the bookcase settled back into place.

A pounding on the queen's chamber door sent her scurrying back to the bed.

Quickly, Evinna woke the other little girl and pulled her into her arms.

Shouts echoed from the other side as the frenzied thumping increased and the thick wooden door began to splinter.

Fully awake, the child trembled, clinging to the queen in fear. Evinna looked down into the little girl's terrified blue eyes.

"Although you will never know it, little one, your sacrifice is of great service to the Crown and the future of Exile. Because of you, Princess Vallaria will live and one day seek retribution for our deaths. She will return to Ravenia and claim her rightful place as its queen, and when she does the lands will run red with the blood of those who betrayed us. She will forge a new beginning for this kingdom, and peace will be our salvation."

Soothing the frightened child, a single tear slipped down her cheek. "I'm so sorry. If there were any other way—"

The chamber door continued to splinter as the invaders pummeled it with their weapons, but an incessant tapping on the window's glass pane drew her attention away from the inevitable.

It was the ravens. They sensed the upheaval in the kingdom and had come to protect the family bloodline, the Ravenia bloodline.

She turned, catching the eye of the largest bird as its beak tapped ferociously on the glass pane.

All is lost my friend, but she is safe. You must leave the kingdom only to return when a Ravenia once again sits on the throne. She will need you more than me.

The huge bird ceased its pecking and blinked glossy black eyes at the queen. Stretching its wings wide, it cawed. A guttural sound rose above the screams, echoing through the night sky. With a final tap on the glass, the raven turned and flew into the night. The others followed. Mournful cries rang out, signaling the tragedy afoot.

As the ravens retreated, the castle stilled. The sound of frantic footfalls faded as the door to the queen's bedchamber broke, scattering fragments of wood across the stone floor.

Three soldiers entered outfitted in the red and gold colors of the Gold Coast.

Behind them she saw the bloody bodies of her royal guards.

The city had been sacked and the kingdom lost, and now she must forfeit their lives for destiny to prevail.

Queen Evinna stood, clutching the child tight to her breast, and calming her with a gentle rocking motion. The little girl sensed the danger and began to cry. One of the soldiers, tall and muscular, the right side of his face scarred from battle, crossed the chamber. Blood dripped from his sword and left a gruesome trail as he dragged the tip along the stone floor. The metal screeched as it met resistance and she cringed holding the little girl even tighter.

The soldier lifted his sword, menacing hate visible in his eyes. The black steel shimmered in the firelight as something rippled unseen from cross guard to point. Queen Evinna recognized the substance entrenched on the blade.

Dark magic. They came prepared to kill even one who is almost impossible to kill.

"No more will the kingdom of man be tarnished by the blood of elves," the soldier yelled as the other two nodded their heads and raised their swords in solidarity. "Tonight, King Ryguard's bloodline will be washed from these lands forever."

Lavender irises never left the man's gray ones as she pulled back her shoulders in defiance. "Sleep little one and know you are loved," she whispered in the child's ear as she turned her small tear-stained face away from the threat. "Your life will be avenged in time."

With brutal coldness, the soldier's lips contorted into a wicked grin, and he thrust the broadsword forward impaling both her and the child on its thick, sharp blade.

SHEETS OF RAIN POURED FROM THE DARK SKIES, BUT IT DID NOTHING TO muffle the terrifying screams echoing from the castle. The old crone watched from the shadows of the city below, her face hidden by the hood of the dark cloak wrapped tightly around her frail shoulders.

The cold deluge soaked through her garments and washed torrents of mud over the toes of her boots, but she was oblivious to the discomfort. It was her burden to bear witness to this terrible fate, for her destiny was inexplicably entangled with those whose paths would cross in a distant future, when the battle to seize control of a darkening world began.

Tired eyes, which had seen much in a lifetime, lifted toward the sky.

The ravens circled the castle. Swooping black silhouettes whose frantic cries mixed with the thunderous sound of the rain. They sensed the danger. The time of the ravens would end this night. Evil had taken the castle and would quickly find its way through the entire kingdom and beyond. An age of darkness would rise from the ashes and the Kingdom of Ravenia would see much despair in the coming decades.

The old crone huddled deeper into the shadows as the fires

burning in the castle ignited the night sky with slashes of orange and billowing black smoke.

Tonight, Ravenia would become a dark kingdom forged in blood, betrayal, and death. In time its fate and that of the rest of the continent would depend on the destiny of one. But for now, the old crone could do nothing but watch and wait. For those destined to carry the omens of the world were forbidden to interfere with the catalyst that hearkened those prophecies forward.

Only when the time was right could a harbinger cross through the barrier and appear to those who were marked and deliver the message that would change the course of fate forever.

I
VALLARIA

Sixteen years later—Mistenvale, the Kingdom of the Elves

It was the morning of her twenty-first birthday, a day she'd longed for since she was old enough to understand what it meant, and one Vallaria hoped wouldn't end in regret.

A thin mist hovered inches above the ground. Wispy tentacles swirled over the toes of her boots as she walked toward the training grounds. She loved this time of the morning when the streets of the elven kingdom were quiet, and the purple and orange rays of dawn peeked through the uneven crests of the surrounding mountains.

The coolness of the dewy air felt good on her skin, and she closed her eyes. A soft cooing echoed through the treetops as their leaves rustled in the waking breeze. She glanced up to see a group of small yellow birds flitting back and forth as they darted in play.

She walked down the hill toward the barracks as the sun rose over the mountain's pinnacle, washing the kingdom in a glistening light. Dewdrops glinted on leaves, and the mist dancing at her feet became awash with shimmering golden light. Mistenvale shone with vivid colors and succulent smells and all the beauty of the elements.

A prickling sensation crawled up her skin. The air was cool even though the morning sun warmed the earth, an indication winter was almost upon them.

Vallaria slowed as she reached the entrance to the training area. Her hand clasped the hilt of her sword as she stood in front of the massive iron gates. With a big inhale she pushed back her shoulders and entered.

She wasn't two steps in when the silky taunting voice of Riva broke the morning stillness.

"Oh look, the half-breed orphan made it on time today."

Deep mauve eyes glistened with disgust as Vallaria's nemesis pulled her lips back into a sneer. The elf was dressed in white leather, as were the two who stood behind her, Jale and Darnica. The color symbolized their status. All were kin to the enchantment elves, the purity sect of the race. They lived by the old code of magic and resented outsiders. To them, Vallaria was worse than an outsider. She was the product of the joining of two races, blasphemy in their eyes. Although the blood of the elf ran through her veins, she was mortal, without magic, and tainted by the weakness of humankind. She was everything they feared and despised, and Riva and the others never let her forget how lowly she truly was. Only out of respect for the king had the elders not banished her from the kingdom long ago.

"Sorry to disappoint, Riva," Vallaria hissed, tired of the all-too familiar greeting.

"Watch your tongue when you speak to me." Riva's long silver hair cascaded like a silky waterfall over her shoulders as she stepped forward, placing the tip of her dagger under Vallaria's chin. "Know your place, orphan. The king may favor you, but it is the elders who advise him. Do not push me."

"Or what?" From behind came a calm, controlled yet authoritarian voice. Faelin, the king's daughter stepped in beside Vallaria.

Riva smiled and stepped back lowering her blade. "I don't think you need to concern yourself with this matter, Faelin."

Although her gaze was steady, Vallaria could see a minuscule twitch of Faelin's forefinger as it lay atop her sword's pommel. "I suggest you three head to your stations and begin your morning training before Commander Cyran finds another reason to make you clean the armory's weapon cache again."

Jale reached forward and grabbed Riva's arm. "Let's go." His strong grip tugged her backward, and she whirled glaring at him as she shook off his hand. "One of these days the commander will put us together in the ring, half-breed," she said.

Vallaria clenched her fist. "Then I look forward to that day."

The elf stiffened but kept her mouth shut as she shot Faelin a look of disdain. The three enchantment elves turned and strode off.

"Why do you antagonize her?" Faelin asked.

Her eyes were full of disappointment, but Vallaria didn't care. Over the years she'd grown accustomed to the frowns and disapproving looks the elves gave her, but the constant abuse from Riva and her minions had reached a peak, and she was no longer willing to put her head down and take it.

At least not anymore, not when freedom was within her grasp.

Adrenaline raged through her blood, and she turned her attitude to Faelin. With a tone expressing her displeasure, she said, "I didn't need you to come to my aide."

The elf paused, "It was not your aide I was coming to."

Without waiting for a retort, Faelin walked away. "Come," she called over her shoulder.

Sulking, Vallaria followed her to a nearby station. The area was large and surrounded by a tall iron fence. Anchored into the right wall was a weapon stand boasting polearms, swords, bows, and other paraphernalia. To the left, a row of targets hung on wooden posts. The king's daughter was a skilled marksman. It was a rare occurrence when she missed the mark with her crossbow. Vallaria had never mastered the bow, preferring the weight of steel and a sharp blade in her hands.

"Shall we spar?" Faelin said.

It wasn't a question but a directive. Her actions at the gate had consequences. Faelin would not hold back.

Drawing her sword, Vallaria took her stance at the center of the open area. Clouds of dust appeared as she shuffled her feet in the dirt, waiting for Faelin to lunge. The elf did not disappoint. Without warning her sword swung upward in a lethal arc, leaving a mere second for Vallaria to react before the blade would have sliced her leather chest plate.

Metal clashed as their swords met. Faelin's skill was on full display as she drew back the blade and immediately thrust it forward. Vallaria whirled, the edge of the steel missing her by inches. With every swing of Faelin's sword, Vallaria ducked, weaved, or blocked the blade, always on defense.

Without a word, Faelin showed her disapproval.

"She deserved it," Vallaria said as she blocked another blow.

"Who?" Faelin asked her voice calm and her expression passive.

In a fit of rage Vallaria lunged. Faelin sidestepped her attack, spun, and pushed the hilt of her sword forward. It connected with a thud against Vallaria's jaw, the impact sending her sprawling into the dirt.

Faelin circled. "Anger makes you weak Vallaria because it overloads your senses and leads to mistakes. You need to learn to control it, or you will find it difficult to exist outside the kingdom's borders if one day you choose that path."

Faelin reached a hand down to help her up, but Vallaria swatted it away. Scrambling to her feet, she picked up her sword from where it lay and dusted herself off. Her anger had ebbed, instead replaced by the all-too familiar sting of humiliation.

The warm coppery taste of blood filled her mouth, followed by the throb of a split lip. She spit out the offending substance and sheathed her blade, keeping her eyes lowered.

"I think that's enough for today."

Faelin walked toward the gate but stopped halfway. Without turning to look at Vallaria, she said, "I know you've struggled to live within our culture, but soon things will change. I hope you're ready to learn that which you've long desired to know."

Without another word, Faelin retreated leaving Vallaria with an aching jaw, a bruised ego, and an overwhelming sense she would soon come to regret this day.

2

VALLARIA

B right blue eyes scanned the countryside, and for the umpteenth time in as many years, Vallaria wondered exactly what lay beyond the horizon.

Perched on a limb in a stately ashen tree growing atop the highest hill in Mistenvale, she was able to see clearly in all directions. But it was not the cerulean blue sea to the west drawing her attention; today it was the dark stormy skies brewing over the northeast that called to her.

Many an afternoon had been spent in this tree dreaming about the lands beyond the borders of Mistenvale and wondering if out there, in the kingdoms of man, was where she belonged. Other than the nightmares and a few cloudy memories of a distant past, the elven kingdom and its residents were all she'd ever known. She'd lived with the elves since she was five as a ward of the great King Elvander Ildaria. Besides a few excursions in a small boat to a deserted island to the north, Vallaria had been forbidden to leave the kingdom.

That was until today.

Today, the day she reached her twenty-first year and came of age, *whatever that meant,* was the day King Elvander promised to tell her of her past and give her the freedom she so desperately desired. But after all the years she'd longed for this day to come, now it was here, and she dreaded the answers the king might provide.

Vallaria rubbed her jaw where the pommel of Faelin's sword hit. Irritated she thought about this morning's events. Like all the other times, she'd handled it poorly, allowing Riva and her cohorts to goad her into losing her temper.

Would she ever learn?

Tears teemed in her eyes as their jeers rang in her ears. As the offspring of the elders, the revered, they'd always made sure Vallaria understood exactly what they thought of her. *Narcigni,* is what they called her behind her back, meaning 'one who's impure.'

Angrily she wiped at the tears and turned her gaze back to the distant horizon.

The chattering rustle of the ashen's leaves filled the air as the autumn breeze picked up. She pulled her leather coat tighter and leaned back onto the tree's massive trunk as memories of the past surfaced.

Her childhood had been innocent enough. She'd been too young to truly understand the significance of her life when she first arrived in the kingdom, but as she got older, and the whispering of the elves grew louder, it became apparent she didn't belong. This tree had been her solace for many reasons. A place to call her own away from the steely pitiful stares of the elves.

Vallaria tugged on her long, black braid. She'd been nine when she finally realized how different she looked from the inhabitants of Mistenvale. She'd been playing with a group of young elves, and one had commented on the funny brown dots on her face. In response, the others laughed. Confused and hurt she'd run to her rooms and cried for hours before King Elvander came to give her the hard truth: she was not one of them—not really. Although her mother was elvenkind, her father was human. Which essentially made her neither. An outcast, a half-breed who possessed neither magic nor the ethereal beauty of the elves. An orphan with no family and no purpose.

Her stomach clenched as she thought about the significance of that moment while her fingertips grazed the smattering of freckles along the bridge of her nose. She looked like her father, at least that's what the elven king said. Black hair, alabaster skin, brilliant blue eyes that flashed when she was angry, which was often, especially when the king refused to go into detail about her parents, their deaths, or anything about how she came to be a ward of the elves.

"All in good time, little one," he would say before he'd tilt her chin upward so their eyes met. "Patience is a strength that one day you will need, so master it now."

Her fingertips dug into the rough bark as she remembered how many times in the past years he'd given her enough information to appease her. But over those years her lack of identity had left her even more alone. Her carefree childhood turned into a tumultuous adolescence, which morphed her into a rebellious young adult. In her late teens, she'd caused more trouble than she was probably worth, and it had widened the divide between her and the elves, many of which didn't even try to conceal their contempt anymore. Yet through it all, the king had never wavered in his commitment to her, only providing kindness, patience, and a stern lecture when needed. It was another piece in the cracked jigsaw puzzle of her life —why would a powerful ruler care about an unimportant half-breed orphan like her?

She questioned him about this often and always it was the same answer: "In time you will understand, Vallaria, patience."

A rustle in the brush below caught her attention. Two fluffy fox cubs wrestled in the long grass. Their playful mews attracted the attention of their mother, who gently nudged them back in the direction of their den.

Vallaria's heart tightened as she watched the cubs obediently follow the elder fox home. Often, when she was alone, she thought of her parents, envisioning what they looked like and who they were.

What her last name might be? Another secret the king refused to disclose. She was just Vallaria—a pathetic orphan.

She sighed as the last cub disappeared into the tall underbrush.

With what little she did know she figured her mother was most likely close to King Elvander, an advisor possibly? Why else would he take in her orphan child? But it was her father she spent most of her time daydreaming about. The human who'd stolen her mother's heart. Was he a merchant, a warrior, a farmer? How did they meet? Over the years she'd romanticized her parents, their relationship, and even their deaths. It was easier to build images of them in her head than have them remain two black voids in her memory. They'd been happy once, the three of them, she was sure of it.

Tears filled her eyes as the emptiness inside expanded.

Riva was right.

She was impure, ugly, and unwanted.

"I thought I might find you here."

The calm voice tinged with a hint of cool exasperation was so familiar Vallaria didn't need to turn around to know it was Faelin. It also didn't surprise Vallaria she'd come looking. After Vallaria's outburst this morning, and chaotic display of swordsmanship leading to the butt of Faelin's sword connecting unceremoniously with her chin, she'd half expected another lecture.

"I didn't know you would be looking for me or I would have left word," Vallaria snapped, slightly irritated there was nowhere in Mistenvale she could be truly alone.

Ignoring the brash tone, the elf replied, "No need. You are not hard to find."

She felt instantly ashamed of her childish behavior. The king's daughter had watched over her since she came to Mistenvale, always ensuring she didn't find trouble, and if she did, promptly getting her out of it. Faelin had even saved her life once, using her shield magic to protect Vallaria from injury or worse. Years ago, after unseasonably heavy rain made the path down the side of the cliff to the beach treacherous, Vallaria had slipped and fallen over the edge. For a moment she seemed suspended in the air as the veracity of what was happening escaped her. Then she began to fall, her screams echoing behind her. The beach, a hundred feet below, hurtled up to meet her at a perilous speed. Suddenly, she slowed as an invisible energy cocooned her. Looking to the top of the cliff, she saw Faelin, arms pointed down toward her, lips moving. Vallaria landed softly on the warm sand below, no worse for wear. She'd been ten at the time and the incident garnered another visit from the king to explain the magical powers the elven race possessed. Although she didn't fear their magic, she'd been more cautious of them ever since.

Effortlessly, Faelin climbed the ashen tree and sat on the limb right below Vallaria. "Winter will be upon us soon," she said, her eyes searching the dark sky grumbling on the distant horizon.

"By us, you mean the northern kingdoms?"

The elf nodded.

Mistenvale was close enough to the balmy south so whatever winter season they experienced was nothing more than a cool, crisp autumn. Warm air from the sea swirled inland from the west and the mountain range surrounding its remaining borders kept out the snow that settled over other distant kingdoms. The kingdom of the elves, nestled in a secluded valley, was far removed from the kingdoms of man.

A distance Vallaria felt more than anyone.

"Why does that matter to us?" she asked, trying desperately to move the conversation toward what Faelin was not saying since she couldn't remember the elf ever before being concerned with the changing seasons.

"There is meaning in everything. Something which affects one will inevitably affect another sooner or later. Nothing remains unblemished or untouched by darkness. There is always a coming storm."

Vallaria rolled her eyes. When Faelin engaged in small talk or riddles, it usually meant she was avoiding a subject she thought might upset her. Faelin was her mentor and her best friend, but sometimes Vallaria found herself resenting the elf for being so perfectly frustrating and for treating her like a fragile human. She also suspected Faelin knew more about her past than she let on. She was the king's daughter, after all, and at times it felt somewhat like a betrayal.

"And what storm do you speak of?" she asked as her eyes flitted over the elf's features. Swept off her face and pulled tight at the temples into multiple braids, Faelin's long silver hair cascaded down her back in sheets of thick strands. Smooth pearl-colored skin tinged at the cheeks with a peachy hue, highlighted her high cheekbones and sculpted face. Faelin's perfectly pointed ears were bejeweled with small silver hoops, and as she cast her lilac gaze toward her, Vallaria was reminded once again of how striking their race truly was. A pang of jealousy raked at her stomach, and she silently chastised herself as her gaze drifted back to the churning sky in the distance.

"Father wishes to speak with you this evening," Faelin said, ignoring the question.

Vallaria's heart jumped. Was King Elvander finally going to fulfill his promise?

Before she could ask Faelin a question, her excitement abated as she caught the pained expression on the elf's face.

"What is it?"

A shadow darkened her friend's features. "What if the future was already written? Would you want to know what it held?"

A chill crept up Vallaria's spine at the elf's odd query. Although it seemed innocent enough, it was the way Faelin asked it and the way her voice wavered ever so slightly that unnerved Vallaria.

"I don't know," she answered, her mouth suddenly dry. Faelin's usually calm demeanor seemed to crack, and at that moment, Vallaria wasn't sure she wanted to know the origins of such a strange question. "Why?"

The knot in her stomach tightened as she stared at her friend.

Without another word, Faelin slipped off the limb, barely making a sound as her feet hit the ground. The familiar coolness in her voice and the unyielding gaze returned. "I'll see you in the throne room later. Don't keep the king waiting."

With a curt nod and a strained smile, Faelin disappeared down the trail, leaving Vallaria alone and once again shrouded in uncertainty that her twenty-first birthday would be anything but regrettable.

3

VALLARIA

Lanterns, silver flames flickering methodically beneath the beveled glass, greeted Vallaria as she exited the forest path. She loved this time of night when twilight wrapped everything in a tranquil calm. As the sun set the city sparkled with the glow of a hundred lanterns, throbbing pools of light dotting the paths and bridges. When she was small and had first arrived in Mistenvale, the nightmares had begun. King Elvander, hearing her crying in her room late at night, would take her small hand and walk the lantern-lit pathways until the residuals of the nightmares had vanquished and all that remained was a wide-eyed child gazing in wonder at the enchanted world in front of her.

It was also the only time in her young life when she didn't feel lost.

After Faelin left the ashen tree, Vallaria spent the remainder of the day walking the beach along the western coast. The sound of the sea calmed her nerves. If King Elvander granted her permission to leave the kingdom, she'd be free to travel anywhere on the continent, *or beyond*. But as the sun dipped in the sky and the surf broke on the ragged edge of the shoreline, spraying cold sea water across her bare feet, a panic had risen.

Would she be able to exist beyond these borders? Where would she go? Would she know how to succeed in the broader world? By the time she'd traversed the forest path back to the city she'd almost convinced herself that staying with the elves was not such a bad idea.

Voices broke through Vallaria's thoughts as a group of enchantment elves, books in hand and long white robes sweeping across the stone path, rounded the corner by the fountain and walked directly toward her. Instantly she shivered, lowering her eyes in hopes they would ignore her, but she could feel their steely gazes as they passed. Their essence, heavy with magic, swept over her like an angry wave.

Pulling up the hood of her coat, she quickened her pace. Their whispers of displeasure reached her ears, but she ignored them and kept moving. Another few hundred paces and she'd be home.

"Blessed evening, Vallaria," said a deep and familiar voice.

The lump in her throat lessened as she lifted her eyes to the leader of the elven army. "And to you, Commander," she said.

Thaneil Cyran, was one of a handful of elves who treated her with respect and made her feel like she wasn't a burden to their kind. He was also the one who'd trained her to fight. Although her sword skills were almost as good as Faelin's, she lacked the grace and precision the elves innately had. When she sparred with Faelin she felt awkward and clumsy, but in the past few years it had only fueled her desire to improve.

"I'm sorry I missed you this morning. An important matter needed my attention. How was your training?"

"Uneventful," Vallaria responded, sure the commander had already heard about her altercation with Riva.

"Was it?" A sly quirk at the corner of the commander's mouth indicated she was correct. "Will you be attending tomorrow?"

She nodded in affirmation, thankful the commander stayed silent on the matter. Vallaria had attended his training sessions regularly for the past eight years, filling his time with annoying non-stop questions and childish frustration when her lack of talent overwhelmed her. It had taken a long time for Vallaria to gain the skills she needed to impress Thaneil, but eventually, through hard work and sheer determination, she had.

"Good, I have something for you."

"For me?"

"For your coming of age."

"You didn't need to get me a present."

His violet eyes, shades darker than Faelin's, flickered with amusement. "That to which I refer already belongs to you."

Before she could inquire further, the commander laid a closed fist across his chest and bid her good evening. With brows knitted she watched as his tall form retreated, waiting until the shadows swallowed him before continuing home.

Within minutes of her encounter with Commander Cyran, Vallaria rounded the corner of the castle and entered the grounds through the side gate. Hurrying across the lush dew-covered lawn and into the reaching shadows, she felt a prickle creep up the back of her neck. Slowing her steps, her eyes searched the gloom. Perched on the threshold of the kitchen door was a large black bird. Its head turned toward her, and she was met with a piercing stare. Her breath hitched. Other than in her dreams she'd only seen a raven in Mistenvale once, shortly after she'd arrived in the kingdom. She'd been so young, but she remembered the moment vividly. She and Faelin had been playing in the far meadow when suddenly a group of birds, their feathers the blackest of pitch, landed in the tree above her head. While the others strutted and preened in the branches, one, larger than the rest, had stared directly at her, its watchful eyes never blinking. Vallaria had never forgotten how that raven's unyielding glare made her feel—uncomfortable as if it knew something about her she didn't. When she'd asked King Elvander about the black birds later, he told her they were ravens and once were revered in a far-off kingdom.

Since that day she'd never seen one again, until now.

As she neared the entrance, the large bird lifted its wings, cawed, and flew off. An uneasy sensation scuttled down her skin as the raven melded with the pitch black of the night sky. Hugging herself, she hurried through the kitchen door where she was met with the delicious aroma of dumpling stew. The homey smell soothed her nerves and soon the raven was forgotten.

"There you are," said the female elf who hovered over the hearth. "I was wondering where you'd gotten to."

Vallaria placed a hand on the shorter elf's upper back, leaned down, and gave her a small peck on the cheek. "Nowhere special, Kelena."

"There is no such place, my child. Everywhere in this world is special and has purpose. You would do well to remember that. Now sit—you must be hungry."

Vallaria's stomach growled as she sat at the large oak table and watched with affection as the woman busied herself, scooping stew into a large bowl. Kelena was like a mother to Vallaria. As a nurturer, elves gifted with calming magic, she'd been Vallaria's anchor during her younger years and a compass when her world became more chaotic in the later ones. Kelena had also been her real mother's confidant, spending many years at her side, which helped make Vallaria feel closer to the parents she couldn't remember.

Like the rest of the elves, Kelena did not divulge much about Vallaria's family. "Your mother was strong and brave, like you, little one, but you have your father's quick temper and thirst for adventure." In the past when Vallaria begged Kelena to tell her more, the elf would smile, squeeze her hand, and say, "Be patient. There will come a time when all will be revealed."

The tightening in her chest returned. Tonight that time had come.

Kelena placed a bowl of steaming stew in front of Vallaria and ripped a chunk of bread from a freshly baked loaf. "Will you see the king this evening?"

"He has asked for my presence. Do you know what he wants?" Vallaria asked hoping for some confirmation that King Elvander would indeed fulfill his promise to her this night.

"It is not my place to speculate. The king is wise; you will do best to listen to what he has to say."

After dinner Vallaria changed into a white shirt, green velvet tunic, and matching pants. Her hands shook as she pulled on knee-high boots, and a sheen of sweat appeared on her upper lip. What if the king told her something horrible about her past? Was that what Faelin referred to when she'd asked Vallaria if she wanted to know what the future held?

Suddenly the room was too warm, the air too stuffy, and a suffocating dread lay thick around her. With trembling hands, she reached for the doorknob, inhaled a deep cleansing breath, and stepped into the hallway. Whatever she learned tonight, good or bad, at least she would gain a past and an identity.

Tonight, Vallaria would become *someone*.

4

VALLARIA

A heavy silence seeped under the large oak doors as Vallaria stood outside the throne room. The guard to her left ignored her, his eyes instead focusing on something invisible at the far end of the hall.

She reached out and touched the door handle but pulled back quickly as if her fingers were seared by the iron. Her weight shifted back and forth from one foot to the other as she rubbed sweaty palms on her pants.

It was a rare occurrence, entering the throne room. Not because it was off-limits but because it was the one place where she felt truly unworthy. The grandeur of the room made Vallaria uncomfortable, but it was the room's energy, the unseen regal essence swirling in between its walls, that made her feel insignificant. Haunted by the memory of the kings and queens who came before Elvander, the throne room reeked of power, stature, and opulence—all the things the elven race embodied but none of which she possessed. The throne room reminded her of the distinguished legacy of the elves, which only magnified the lack of her own.

Why did the king have to pick the throne room to meet?

Fingers tightened around the strand of beads in her hand. The small balls dug into the flesh of her palm. Wincing she looked down at the prayer beads she held. They had been her father's, the only thing she possessed belonging to him. Kelena had given them to her years ago when she first started teaching her about man's religious way of thinking. Although the elves did not believe in man's gods, King Elvander had agreed to allow Vallaria to learn the differences between the two races. Man's belief in the gods was what often defined their decisions, their actions, and their consequences, and it helped Vallaria understand the man she would never know. Her father's beliefs and his beads had become a big part of her upbringing. Kelena had been methodical in her teachings, and although immersed in the elven traditions, Vallaria was thankful she had something of her own to identify with.

In the darkest of times, her gods were always there to listen. And in her hour of need she felt their presence, a comforting aura that wrapped itself around her.

Twisting the prayer beads in her hand she studied them like she had a dozen times in the past. They weren't much to look at, a mix of brown wooden beads and others fashioned from amber glass. They were haphazardly strung onto a thin piece of leather, the knot adorned with a piece of flat silver metal stamped with the letter R. Kelena never told her what the letter stood for, just that it was a symbol of her father's presence.

"The king is expecting your arrival." The guard's voice jolted her from her memories.

His words were not a reminder but a blunt admonishment that she'd been standing fidgeting in the hall for far too long. The guard's brows furrowed as he tipped his head toward the doors.

Suddenly Faelin's voice echoed through her mind. *Don't keep the king waiting.*

With her heart thumping, she grasped the handles and pushed the heavy oak doors open. When they swung inward and she crossed the threshold, her eyes fell on the magnificent white quartz throne at the front of the room where King Elvander sat, Faelin at his side. With every step, the click of her boot heels echoed off the vaulted ceiling. *Too loud.* The king's gaze was intense and suddenly she was overwhelmed by a desire to run. For so long she'd wanted this moment of revelation to arrive, but now that it had a numbing fear struck her. Maybe living in her obliviousness was better. Swallowing the lump in her throat, she forced one foot in front of the other, each step heavier than the one before. Her eyes darted around aimlessly as she tried to calm her erratic breathing.

The vast throne room yawned before her. Thick white stone pillars covered in dark green vines stretched up to a slat-wood ceiling. Besides the tall throne sitting on a raised platform, there were tables and seating lining either side. Large wooden chandeliers, candles lit, hung from the rafters and vases, perched on tall iron stands, held beautiful white flowers, their perfume imbuing the air with a pungent sweetness.

Vallaria had always found this room intimidating, not because of its size or grandeur, but because one could sense the haunting echoes of centuries of elven history. King Elvander, his father, and his father before him, all sat on that throne, ruled from this opulent room, waged war on the kingdom's enemies, and partook in diplomatic missions. It was the legacy of the Ildaria bloodline that spanned hundreds of thousands of years and one that would continue when Faelin took the throne.

When Vallaria reached the dais, she bowed. "King Elvander, you wanted to see me." There was a slight tremor in her voice. She clenched her fist around her father's prayer beads and cleared her throat hoping the next time she spoke she'd sound confident and relaxed.

Slender fingers caressed the ends of his long silver hair as the king's lavender eyes assessed her. Vallaria shivered under his gaze. The king had been her surrogate father since she was a child, but this was not the first time she'd stood in front of the great elven king and felt unimportant in his presence. His dark gray armor shone like brilliant diamonds, and his gossamer cape wound around him like a seductive emerald-green snake. Three large rings adorned his fingers, each one holding a large colored jewel that matched the ones embedded in his circlet. He was an imposing figure, especially when his presence was amplified by the resonant history of the throne room.

"Vallaria it's good to see you." The smile he gave her was genuine, even though a weariness dulled his eyes, a hint something burdened him.

Maybe he was exhausted from his trip. The king had recently returned from a journey across the Endless Sea to an ally city on the continent of Brulle that traded in elven weaponry and fine fabric. But Vallaria suspected that not to be the reason. She'd never seen the king tired; in fact the elven race as a whole never seemed to succumb to the fatigue she often felt.

"How was your journey?" she asked politely.

"Uneventful."

Vallaria noticed the king's eyes flit to Faelin and suspected his response was not entirely the truth. Vallaria didn't understand the complex relationship between the elves and man, just that it had been strained for decades. The elves kept to themselves and out of mankind's affairs unless Mistenvale was threatened. Since she'd come to live with them, she'd only seen the elves leave the kingdom to cross the seas to Brulle for trade. Only once had they left their borders to journey across the lands to the east, to kingdoms far beyond the horizon, but Vallaria never understood why.

She shifted her stance and waited.

"I never told you I had a twin sister, did I?"

Vallaria's eyes widened at the king's revelation, and she quickly glanced to Faelin, who nodded in confirmation.

His eyes flashed with the shadow of a memory, and he continued, not waiting for a response. "Her name was Evinna, and she was beloved by all. Her existence was a source of good in our kingdom and the world beyond. She had a kind heart and believed the kingdoms of elves and man could live in harmony with one another, even after so many centuries of bloody battles, deceit, and mistrust. It was her one desire for Exile to embrace peace."

"What happened to her?" Vallaria asked, although the unease that sheathed her skin in its grip suggested the answer might not be one she wished to hear.

The king shifted on the throne, leaned forward, and placed his hands on his thighs. His eyes locked on hers. "She was murdered."

The word seemed to vibrate throughout the massive room, like an agonizing scream from the past. Vallaria stood, mouth agape, unable to speak.

King Elvander continued. "Far to the northeast there is a kingdom known as Ravenia. It was once a powerful and respected kingdom ruled fairly by a beloved king and queen. But darkness lurked in the shadows, and eventually it came and took everything. It claimed the life of the king and the queen and seized the throne for itself, turning the once majestic lands into a dark kingdom. My sister, Evinna, was that queen. Her husband, King Ryguard, was human. It was the first marriage of its kind: a union between two different races and based solely on true love. Unfortunately, not all accepted it."

Vallaria's mind was wrought with confusion. Why was he telling her this? What did her past have to do with the king's twin sister? Bile rose in the back of her throat as a thought came to her. Was her past connected to Evinna's death? Did her family have something to do with it?

The king stood and walked down the steps to stand in front of her. His eyes shimmered, and for a moment, Vallaria thought she was going to see the stoic, unemotional veneer, so prevalent in the elven race, slip. His skin was cool as he took her shaky hands in his. "I made a promise to you long ago, and tonight I intend to fulfill that agreement. You want to know who you are? Where you came from and why you were fated to live among the elves, in a life not your own? Now is the time for truth."

Vallaria found it difficult to breathe. The king's words wound tight like a vice around her, each sentence leading her to a fate which for years had escaped her. A cold sweat covered her skin as she waited for him to continue.

King Elvander's gaze locked on hers. "Your real name, the name you were given at birth, is Serifine Vallaria Ravenia. King Ryguard and Queen Evinna were your parents. You are my kin and a princess, the heir to their throne, and the rightful ruler of the Kingdom of Ravenia, a kingdom wrapped in darkness since that fateful day and doomed to exist under the rule of a cruel queen. That is, until the time its true ruler came of age and could make claim to the throne and challenge the dark queen's rule. That ruler is you, and that day is today."

The room began to spin and a noise like a pounding sea exploded in her head, blocking out whatever words King Elvander spoke next. She took an unsteady step back, wrenching her hands from his. She was vaguely aware of her father's prayer beads slipping from her hand and clattering on the stone floor at her feet, but she paid no heed. Somewhere in the distance, Faelin's voice called her name, but Vallaria couldn't answer, for blackness had already laid claim to her consciousness, pulling her down into its dark oblivion.

5
FAELIN

The king paced back and forth in front of the throne, hands clasped behind his back as Faelin entered the room. He paused as he heard his daughter's footsteps.

"How is she?" he asked.

Deep lines marred his forehead, and his eyes reflected the concern for the pain he'd caused Vallaria. "She's awake and in her chambers but refuses to speak to anyone. Kelena has advised we give her some time."

The king nodded. "Kelena knows best. Although Vallaria's heritage is most definitely not what she expected, she is of royal blood. I am confident she will come to terms with her destiny and the responsibility it carries. She must."

Faelin sensed the uncertainty surrounding her father's statement. For years they'd known of Vallaria's destiny and the burden that would eventually be thrust upon her shoulders. What they hadn't known was how she would react.

Faelin gripped the hilt of her sword. "Tell me again about Evinna's vision."

King Elvander and his sister were mystics and had the ability to see the future; although interpreting their visions presented a challenge—for things were often never as they seemed.

Her father sat heavily on the throne, his shoulders slumping forward. "The visions began before Vallaria was born. As you know, Evinna saw her own death." He paused, and a dark shadow crossed his face. He still carried the wounds of her loss. "Although my sister realized this to be her fate, her daughter's wasn't as clear. There has always been a haze of uncertainty around the visions pertaining to Vallaria."

Faelin noticed the same flicker of a memory flash in her father's eyes that she'd seen before when he spoke of Vallaria's birth. And again, she felt there was something he refused to speak of—more to the story. Possibly a secret he kept for Evinna? Whatever it was it troubled him deeply.

The king continued, "She sacrificed everything to ensure Vallaria's safety and to give her a chance to regain the throne. She was haunted by the visions of the darkness that would permeate these lands. The wars that would destroy kingdoms and the evil that would turn everything to fire. But most of all she was haunted by the prophecy."

The urgency straining the king's voice gave Faelin pause. "You too have seen something," she said.

Her father nodded. "Exile has begun to show signs of its coming ruin. Skirmishes between smaller kingdoms have occurred and it will not be long before the Gold Coast feels it necessary to intervene, to quell any uprising, it sees as a threat. The uneasy peace Exile has seen for decades will be no more. The emperor is ill and upon his death his son, Darrius, will ascend, and war will soon follow. If Queen Cereli retains the throne, the world will burn, and blood will saturate the lands."

"And if Vallaria sits on the throne?"

King Elvander shook his head. "The future is still not defined with respect to Vallaria's rule. I'm afraid now she has come of age the haze of uncertainty around her destiny will only increase. But Evinna saw the world as it would be if the throne did not return to the Ravenia bloodline. Every decision my sister made from that moment on was to ensure Vallaria's well-being. She was adamant Vallaria must rule Ravenia, so we must do everything in our power to ensure that happens. If her destiny is to be queen, then it must be fulfilled. Otherwise, I'm afraid nothing good awaits us in the future."

Again, the dark shadow of a tortured memory flitted across the king's face.

"What are you not telling me, Father?"

"Whatever do you mean?"

Faelin had never demanded anything from her father, but if she were to risk Vallaria's life and possibly her own, she would require all the knowledge he possessed about the past. "Every time you speak of Vallaria's birth and Evinna's sacrifice, there seems to be something missing. A piece of a puzzle that your sister did not want anyone to know but you."

Taken aback the king's eyes darted across the empty room toward the door. "There is nothing in Vallaria's past that will do you any good in the future. You will do well to stop thinking there is."

Her eyes blazed with defiance. "You ask me to risk my life without knowing why."

"You know all you need to." King Elvander's voice was tight, and his hands clenched the arms of his throne. "I promise you, Faelin, if there is anything I know that you do not, it is because sometimes knowledge is detrimental to the task at hand. If, and when, the time comes I will ensure any information required will be forthcoming."

His dismissive tone indicated this part of the conversation was over. Knowing when not to push the king, she steered the queries back to Vallaria's destiny. "Are you sure it's wise not to tell Vallaria about the prophecy? Her birthright is connected directly to it, is it not? And it's the reason she must sit on the throne of Ravenia."

The prophecy Faelin spoke of had been whispered through generations for centuries. But Evinna had seen something that connected it to Vallaria. It foretold of a mortal child born of royal blood who would one day harness the power of the ancient mages and bring magic back to the lands. There was a time, long ago, when magic and those who possessed it were commonplace in the lands. The mages: frost, blood, fire, and shadow, helped rule Exile and many a king relied on their gifts as much as they did their own armies. Kingdoms rose and fell under a mage's power, and for a time magic dominated all facets of life. But then magic began to die and those able to wield it slowly disappeared. Men, their arrogance unchecked and determined to reign supreme, turned on the remaining gifted, slaughtering them in cold blood. Full of bloodlust and power, the kings turned their eyes to the mages. Once revered in the kingdoms of man, they suddenly became the enemy. The kings, threatened by the mage's powers, hatched a plan to eradicate the remaining mages. The final slaughter from which the prophecy was born came at the hands of the Gold Coast Empire and their allies and took place in the Valley of Souls. It is said the valley's soil is still saturated with the blood of the mages, and their wailing cries echo in the misty fog that permanently embraces the valley in its cold, relenting grip.

"Faelin, are you listening?" her father asked.

Casting aside the memory, she said, "Sorry. You were saying?"

King Elvander frowned. "Vallaria has been burdened enough for one night. Anyway, the one whom the prophecy speaks of is ambiguous. We can't know for certain of whom it speaks."

"But Evinna thought it referred to Vallaria. Was convinced of it in fact. And you also must believe Vallaria is the last mage or you wouldn't part with the stone."

Quickly he cast his eyes down to his hands and scowled. "If Vallaria is the one, we will know soon enough."

"And then what?"

"Then we will have to be ready for how the prophecy unfolds." A heavy silence surrounded the king as his eyes penetrated his daughter's. "Magic was not meant to be wielded by humans. Its power is too much of a burden and will eventually consume them, driving them mad or worse. If Vallaria is the one the prophecy speaks of we have to assume the magic may ultimately overwhelm her as the ancient magic of a mage is even more potent."

"Even though she does not possess our magic, she is half elf and our blood runs through her veins."

"That may be the only thing that saves her."

"And if the ancient magic is too much for her to handle?"

King Elvander sighed. "Then it must be stopped."

Faelin's skin crawled at the hidden meaning behind her father's words. "You mean *Vallaria* must be stopped."

"Yes."

The words of the ancient prophecy rang in her ears. The last line suddenly meaning something more nefarious than the elders' interpretation. *In time, frost will cover the lands, dousing the fires of evil and leaving in its wake a world encapsulated in a cold silence. A silence echoing the ancient magic that will once again be reborn to rule the lands.*

If Vallaria was the last mage and the ancient magic consumed her, the future of Exile would be at risk. A frost mage's power could destroy the kingdoms if left unchecked. Vallaria could very well become the darkness that destroyed the world, not the one whose magic saved it. The world could revert to its very beginnings: an icy darkness where nothing existed. Faelin's pale skin crawled with the enormity of her next thought.

Which means the elves will be destroyed as well.

Her father's eyes stared deep into hers as he said the words she dreaded. "If Vallaria succumbs to the ancient magic, only you can stop her. That is *your* destiny. You too are tied to the fate of the crown of Ravenia." He forced a smile. "But I know it won't come to that, for you will find a way to protect her. With you by her side, Vallaria will take back the throne and, if the prophecy comes to pass, will learn to control the ancient magic."

"How can you be sure?"

"Because I trust in my daughter's strength and wisdom. You will ensure she prevails."

The light in the throne room began to dim as a sudden rush of blood pounded in her head. Instinctively, her shield magic wrapped itself around her, caressing her skin with its warm, soothing embrace. Somewhere in the back of her mind she expected this day would come. The day her father would expect her to fulfill her duty as his heir and safeguard their kingdom by protecting another.

Faded memories filled her mind. Images of a face from the past. Deep purple eyes locked on hers as the executioner lifted the sword that would end his life. She'd fought those who held her, cursed the emperor, but it was the scream raging from her lips as his head was sliced from his neck that haunted her to this very day. He'd been betrayed by those who called themselves allies and by the one who claimed his love. And then, in his final moments, she too had failed him.

"I know you are thinking of him, Faelin." Her father's voice, calm and low, dispersed the memories back into the darkest corners of her mind. "You are not responsible for his death. Baladril understood what he'd done and accepted the consequences. He could have saved himself; his magic was powerful. He didn't require yours. His sacrifice stopped what could have been a war between the elves and man. One that would have ended in bloodshed, death, and a continent on the brink of destruction. He made his choice, and he would not want you to carry the burden of his death for all these years."

Her father stood and walked down the steps. "One day you will lead our people. How the world looks then will depend on Vallaria and the prophecy. It is your destiny, as the future queen of the elves, to ensure the survival of our race." His face softened. "Let the past go, daughter, or the future may be lost."

6
VALLARIA

Two days had passed since Vallaria fainted in the throne room. She refused to speak with anyone, barely ate, and cried herself to sleep each night. King Elvander and Faelin tried unsuccessfully to get her to open the door. Even Thaneil had knocked softly, stating he'd missed her at training and wanted her to know that her coming-of-age gift still waited whenever she was ready. Kelena had tried soothing her through the thick wood of the door, but even elven magic could not dispel the raw emotions that ricocheted through her. Nor did she take comfort in speaking with her gods. Although she clung to the prayer beads, she hadn't been able to bring herself to pray. And because of that, she found herself wrapped in a deafening silence, no longer able to feel their comforting aura.

After placing the beads on the bedside table, she walked to the window and leaned against the cool stone.

Coming of age.

Those words had taken on a new meaning in the past few days. For years, when King Elvander referred to it as a way to dissuade her from inquiring about her past, she'd always assumed he meant "when she was older," but now she understood the significance of the term. She was a princess, and her twenty-first birthday was the day she would ascend to take over the throne. The day she would come of age to rule a kingdom.

Her stomach lurched at the prospect, and she closed her teary eyes, savoring the cool breeze blowing in through the open window. Night had fallen and the air was heavy with the scent of floras. Off in the distance, amplified by the darkness, she could hear the thunderous rhythm of the waterfall. She was surrounded by familiarity, but nothing seemed normal. Her lost past had come roaring back and abruptly everything had changed.

The parents she'd idealized for so long were nothing like she'd pictured. Her made-up images of them now lay shattered in her mind. They were a king and queen murdered for their throne. And she, not a poor orphan, but heir to a stolen kingdom. This reality was anything but what she'd expected.

Vallaria opened her eyes and gazed out the window, surveying the shadowy elven realm. Lantern light glowed in the distance as cadenced chants echoed toward her. The enchantment elves were performing a ritual, providing gifts to the universe in order to balance the consequences of magic. Although the elves were magical beings, all magic had a cost. This was the one thing King Elvander made sure she understood. *Magic is not to be trifled with. It's a power much greater than us all, and it can only be wielded properly with respect, humility, and an understanding that it cannot be used selfishly. For it will take much more than it gives.*

For centuries the elves had lived in harmony with magic because they had a deep understanding of the magical properties of the elements from which they drew their powers and respect for the consequences of its use. The enchantment sect of their race ensured the cost of their magic was neutralized by replenishing these elements. Vallaria didn't fully understand how they did this, but the ancient code of magic, which they subscribed to, was older than the elven race itself.

The tenor of the chant rose and Vallaria squirmed. *Tonight, they are most likely trying to cleanse the earth of my existence.* An uncomfortable laugh escaped her lips at the absurd thought. It made more sense now why the elders hated her so. She was not only a *narcigni* but a royal one. A disgrace to their perfect race.

Her thoughts turned to Riva. *Does she know?*

Biting shivers prickled her skin, and she shook the thought away. "I don't care what Riva thinks of me," she said in a whisper to the empty room.

She closed the window and hooked the latch, pulling on the handles to ensure it was locked tight. She lit two more candles, the yellow glow chasing away the remaining shadows from the corners of her room.

Last night the dream had come. It was the same one she'd been having since she was a child.

She was in a grassy meadow. A warm summer breeze wafted around her.

Sunlight danced off the surface of a small pond.

She twirled in a circle, arms wide, and giggled.

Vallaria. Her name, a faint whisper on the breeze.

When she stopped twirling and turned toward the voice, no one was there, only her reflection in an unseen mirror. Pale blue eyes. Black hair blowing in the wind. White dress embroidered at the neck. Small hand waving.

To the left of her reflection, perched on a tall stone was a large raven black as night. Its inky eyes tracked back and forth between her and the image in the mirror. It cawed out a warning, its shrill voice marring the tranquility of the bright sunny day.

The sky began to darken, and turbulent gray clouds appeared to swallow the sun, and with it, the warmth of its rays.

She shivered and reached out, but her reflection did not mimic her movement. Instead, it turned toward the bird, blue eyes darkening, black hair tangling, lips contouring into a frightful grin. The white dress became soiled and tattered and a single bloody teardrop fell down her cheek.

Vallaria's blood froze inside her veins, cold and raging, as she stared at the horrific reflection of herself. A silent scream bubbled up inside, and without warning the image in front of her shattered into a thousand pieces, disappearing like mist until there was nothing left in the grassy meadow but her and the snow-covered raven, its round eyes blinking methodically.

She'd woken in a cold sweat with no understanding of the dream, only that it felt extremely real. And after seeing the raven above the castle door the other day, it was difficult to believe the recurring dream was just a trick of her subconscious.

A tap on the door startled her.

"Vallaria."

Faelin's voice was no longer soft and calm. This evening the edge of frustration was back, and suddenly Vallaria felt like a small child who'd been scolded. She walked to the door, her trembling hand hovering above the sturdy bolt lock. "Are you alone?" she whispered.

"Yes."

Vallaria had a complicated relationship with Faelin. In awe of the beautiful and flawless elf for most of her life, her jealousy had reared its ugly head. Since she was a child she'd longed to be like the king's daughter, but as she grew, she began to ache for her own identity. And now her yearning had become reality—she was Princess of Ravenia, orphan and kin to King Elvander and Faelin.

How had it all gotten so complicated?

A lump formed in her throat as she slid the bolt back and turned the doorknob. The door swung inward, and the candlelight illuminated Faelin's perfect skin causing it to shimmer with a silky sheen. Her kohl-rimmed eyes held a look that Vallaria knew all too well, and her pursed pink lips confirmed it. The elf had given her time to come to terms with the news and now she had more to say.

"Come in," Vallaria said, stepping aside.

Faelin had pulled her long silver hair up into a high ponytail that swung back and forth as she strode into the room. She wore loose pants, a long tunic, and pointed slippers—casual attire. The dark green of the fabric highlighted the soft peach tones in her skin, making her even more stunning. In her hands she held a dusty old leather tome that she placed on the table at the back of the room.

"You can start with this one, but there are plenty more in the castle archives."

"What is it?"

"The documented history of the continent of Exile and the lands of Brulle. It goes back about a thousand years. That should cover enough so that you understand the intricate history connecting the seven kingdoms that still stand today. There is much outside our borders, and part of your training before you leave Mistenvale is to understand as much about those lands as you can."

"What if I don't want to leave?"

The elf raised a perfect brow. "You have wanted nothing else for years."

Vallaria sat heavily on the edge of her bed. "Things have changed."

Faelin narrowed her eyes. "Have they? Or maybe it is you that is afraid for things to change."

She came to sit beside Vallaria. "There comes a time when each of us is challenged, pushed to do something we don't want to do or assume we cannot. That time has come for you. Do you really want to hide within these walls and pretend nothing has changed, or would you rather embrace your destiny, whatever that may be?"

Vallaria shook her head. "I'm not sure I can."

"I have known you almost your entire life, and although you are headstrong, impertinent at times, and often act before you think, one thing you are not, Vallaria, is a coward. You do not run away from a challenge, you run toward it."

Vallaria leaned forward, placing her elbows on her knees. "And what am I running toward this time?" she asked. Her pale blue eyes shimmered with the candle's flickering flame.

"Your legacy. A throne that was stolen from you and a kingdom that needs your leadership."

In a small voice she asked, "Why did you not tell me, Faelin?"

"Tell you what?"

"Who I was? Our connection. My legacy. Why did you and the king wait until now?"

"There was no reason to tell you before you came of age. It would have been dangerous and irresponsible to reveal your truth when there was nothing you could do about it. Until a couple of days ago, you were too young to rule a kingdom. Even if you wanted to, the laws of your land would not allow it. There was no advantage to putting you at risk for something you could not yet attain."

"I don't know how to rule a kingdom."

Faelin smiled. "No one really knows how, but you are of royal blood. The confidence of a ruler is within you—you just have to find it."

"And what if I don't want it?"

"I'm afraid you may not have a choice." The tone of Faelin's voice indicated to Vallaria there was more to her statement.

Vallaria stood and turned toward her friend. "What do you mean?"

The elf leaned back, her eyes sparking. "The time has come for the Kingdom of Ravenia to once again be ruled by someone of Ravenia blood. Darkness has seeped into these lands, skirmishes are breaking out, and loyalties are being tested. The future is bleak, war is on the horizon, and without an alliance with the elves, the kingdoms will fall to the Gold Coast Empire or burn until there is nothing left. For the elves to intervene and try to stop the inevitable, we can only align with the Kingdom of Ravenia, a pact made by the marriage of your father and mother."

"Then why do you not give allegiance to Ravenia's current ruler?"

A shadow crossed the elf's face as her upper lip curled in fury. "Because the queen that sits on the throne is the very one who overthrew your father and had your parents murdered. She is the reason your life was taken from you. Queen Cereli Damask is aligned with the Gold Coast Empire and would never unite with our kingdom. She created the dark kingdom with blood and treachery and has ruled it ever since as its dark queen. Ultimately, her interests lie only with herself. There is no alliance to be had."

A blustering roar filled Vallaria's head. *Queen Cereli Damask.* The name reverberated through her mind, mocking her. A faceless enemy in an unknown world. "How can I hope to challenge someone so powerful?"

"While the king and I will help you as much as we can, in the end it will be for you to figure out. It is what a future queen does."

Faelin's flippant answer prickled at Vallaria, and a sudden surge of anger bubbled inside.

"What would you know about it?" she spat. "You are a king's daughter, heir to a powerful kingdom. You won't have to fight for anything."

Faelin whirled, her eyes blazing. The emotion displayed by the normally stoic elf was so out of character it startled Vallaria, and she stumbled back a few steps, afraid of what the elf might do.

"Do you think I wanted this?" Faelin seethed. "We don't get to choose our destinies, *Princess.* We must make the best of the ones we are fated to live. My father is the most revered and powerful king to ever lead our race, and one day I will have to follow in his footsteps. Do you think I can live up to that? Do you think there will not be those who challenge my authority or whisper behind my back about my shortcomings?"

The elf clenched her fists. "Don't be so selfish. Nothing is easy for any of us. Now stop pouting. You have moped in this room long enough and it is time to grow up and accept your lot in life. Your mother sacrificed everything for you. Many of us did and still will, all so you can reclaim the throne of Ravenia and rightfully rule as its queen. Unless you accept your legacy, even with all its challenges, your parents' kingdom will never be whole, and Exile will crumble under the ruthless power of Cereli and the Gold Coast Empire. Is that what you want? To hide among the elves for the rest of your days and watch your parents' legacy be destroyed?"

Vallaria opened her mouth to respond, but Faelin had already turned and strode to the door.

"I will meet you in the morning at the training grounds." Faelin's stern words were not a request but a command. "You have learned much in the years you've trained with Thaneil and me and your weapon skills are excellent, but now you must learn what it's like to be a queen. It is time to become who you were meant to be so you can avenge your parents' deaths by taking back the Kingdom of Ravenia."

Her last words resonated like a hammer through the room, and Faelin walked out slamming the chamber door behind her.

A suffocating wave of shame wafted over Vallaria as she stared at the closed door. Faelin was right: the time had come for her to grow up and stop feeling sorry for herself. She had the identity she so badly wanted, even if it wasn't the one she'd created in her mind. Now it was up to her—did she crumble under the weight of her destiny or claim it and embrace all that came with it, the good and the bad?

7
VALLARIA

The edge of the blade barely missed Vallaria's cheek as Faelin swung it quicker than she'd anticipated. Spinning, she adjusted her weight and thrust forward before Faelin had a chance to bring her sword level for another blow. The tip of her blade nestled neatly against the smooth skin of Faelin's neck.

Vallaria smirked as a trickle of blood slid down her friend's skin.

"Nice move, Princess. You're getting faster," Faelin said as she pressed two fingers to the nick, infusing it with healing magic until it disappeared leaving nothing but a thin trail of dried blood.

A muscle twitched in Vallaria's jaw, and her gaze darkened. Through clenched teeth she said, "Don't call me that." With force, she drove the end of the sword's blade into the soft earth and kicked at the dry ground.

Ignoring the outburst, Faelin tossed back her silver hair, tilted her head, and raised a perfectly sculpted brow. "What shall I call you then? Especially when you become queen."

"Vallaria, always Vallaria and I'm not a queen yet."

"But soon we begin the journey to reclaim what was taken from you. And if successful you *will* be a queen."

Vallaria's heart pounded in her chest, not from the exertion of the fight but rather from the magnitude of the improbable task that lay before her. Claiming back the throne from the murderous woman who'd killed her parents and stole their kingdom would be anything but easy. It had been almost two weeks since King Elvander had told her of her past and its legacy. Since then Vallaria had learned much about the evil queen who held Ravenia hostage, the dark magic she wielded, and how the once great kingdom had crumbled under her severe rule. Queen Cereli was a formidable opponent with unscrupulous allies, loyal advisors, and an army and royal guard who'd long forgotten their allegiance to the Ravenia bloodline. Although the elves had secretly infiltrated the kingdom and were providing support, Vallaria's destiny was her own, and she'd yet to come up with a plan as to how to gain access to the castle in order to kill the queen.

"Well I'm not a queen yet," Vallaria repeated.

The shrillness in her voice made her wince, and she cast her eyes down to stare at the dust, which had collected on the toes of her boots. As angry as she was at the death of her parents and her stolen life, it was not fair to take it out on the elven king or his daughter. They had done nothing but be kind and protective, giving her the best life possible under the circumstances.

Faelin swung her sword up and into the sheath at her hip in one fluid motion. "You have spent countless hours in the past weeks training with me and the elven army. And devoured every tome and scroll in the archives pertaining to the history of the kingdoms, magic, and the art of war. Do you no longer want that which you have desired for so long? To leave the kingdom and see what is outside our borders?"

"I did. I do, but it's a bit more complicated now, don't you think." Although confident in her fighting skills, she feared the unknown dark magic the queen possessed. How did one battle an agent of darkness, a sorceress who could call upon the dark entities that existed beyond this plane?

"Is it?" Faelin asked, seemingly unaware of the limitations Vallaria possessed.

Vallaria stared at her friend, the familiar irritation rising inside. The elves, her mother's kin, were so infuriatingly superior. Even though she'd lived with them since she was five, she'd never gotten used to their unemotional demeanor. It was unsettling to be around people who rarely expressed outrage, overt affection, or any other type of human emotion, nor could they empathize with any who did. "I'm not ready."

"And you never will be." Faelin's eyes flashed with irritation. She'd grown impatient with Vallaria's indecisiveness. "Destiny does not wait for one to be ready, Vallaria. When it comes, one must react or be swept under, only to drown in one's own providence."

"I think I've had enough for now," Vallaria said haughtily, pulling her sword from the earth and sheathing it. "I need to prepare for the journey."

The elf's irritation abated as she recognized Vallaria's anger and her intent to end the conversation. "I look forward to accompanying you back to Ravenia."

Vallaria sighed dampening her temper. "Are you sure you want to come? You owe no fealty to my kingdom and to put your life at risk is asking a lot. Mistenvale is your home, and one day you will rule your father's kingdom."

"That day is thousands of years away."

"And one I will not live to see." Vallaria laughed uncomfortably.

Faelin shook her head, not acknowledging the sarcasm in her statement. "Unfortunately, the impurities in your blood do not afford you an extended life."

By impurities Faelin meant the human blood that also ran through her veins. The weak side of her that dominated whatever elven traits she may possess. And the reason the enchantment elves despised her so.

Pushing her insecurities down, she gave Faelin a lopsided grin.

"Then you are most welcome to ride to Ravenia with me tomorrow while I can still draw a breath."

Faelin's eyes narrowed. "Riding toward danger is not amusing, Vallaria. One day your lack of discipline or your stubbornness might just get you killed."

Vallaria understood Faelin's warning. The elf had seen the final days of war and lived through the peace in the centuries after. Now, as conflicts began to spring up across the continent, Vallaria recognized the future elven queen would do whatever it took to ensure her kingdom remained and her people were safe.

"If that is the will of the gods then let it be my fate."

"I'm not sure even your gods can help you this time."

Vallaria frowned and turned away. "Maybe not." The emptiness returned as her mind recalled the silence she'd experienced over the past couple of weeks. Her gods had always guided her, but now she felt alone. Ever since her past came to light, she could no longer feel their presence. Had they abandoned her?

Exiting the training grounds, she could feel Faelin's cool stare follow her, but she didn't look back—she couldn't. Faelin was right: she was pig-headed and lacked the discipline so prevalent in the elven race. Why did her gods burden her with such an obscure and dubious future? Maybe this was a test. Perhaps it was the gods who'd designed her destiny and if so, was it not her duty to answer no matter the cost?

While she pondered these questions, Thaneil Cyran, the elven commander, approached her. "Vallaria, a moment of your time?"

She nodded and followed him into the barracks and down the hall to the commander's chambers. "I did not feel it right to give you this, as previously intended, a few weeks ago because you struggled with the news of your legacy. But since you are leaving for Ravenia soon, I believe there is no better time."

He reached into a cabinet and pulled out a sheepskin bundle, placing it upon the wooden table to his left. "For you," he said as he unfolded the sheepskin to reveal its contents.

A deftly crafted elven sword lay in the middle of the fur. Vallaria could feel the commander's eyes upon her as her fingers brushed the smooth, cold steel. Her hand grasped the hilt and lifted it from where it lay. The blade was long and thin and the sword extremely light. Symbols were etched into the blade's steel and the softest leather covered the grip. At the top of the pommel was an engraved E. Vallaria recognized the similarities to a sword she had seen many times before—*King Elvander's.*

"It was your mother's," the elven commander said. "The sword was retrieved from where she'd hidden it in the castle at Ravenia a few years after her death by one still loyal to your family. I have safeguarded it ever since, waiting for you to come of age."

Blue eyes sparked as she locked them on the commander. "You knew I was Queen Evinna's daughter?"

He shrugged. "I suspected. You may not look like her, but you have her tenacity and her deftness with a sword. King Elvander confirmed my suspicions a few years back and then swore me to secrecy."

She ran a shaking hand ran through her long black hair, still damp at the temples with sweat. "Is this why for all those years you were so patient and attentive with my training? You, like King Elvander, were grooming me for what was to come." Her eyes widened as she looked down at her mother's sword. "Is my destiny so important?"

Commander Cyran moved closer, his long silver hair hanging in three low braids. Dressed head to toe in black, he was an imposing figure, which both his tall stature and dark brows elevated. "Many have sacrificed for a future of peace but none more so than your mother. Unfortunately, darkness has found its way back into this world and soon you will find yourself confronted by it. You are born of two races. Royal blood runs through your veins. Whether you accept it or not, your destiny was important the day you were born, but now only you can determine the path it takes."

Vallaria gripped the hilt of the sword tighter, knuckles whitening. Her lips pursed as she stared at the blade. Her mother had sacrificed her own life in order to save hers. Did she not owe her at least as much? "Thank you, Commander."

Thaneil nodded. "A future queen should have a blade worthy of her stature. And one not yet stained with the blood of her enemy. Your mother's sword is the perfect one to rule a kingdom with."

"Yes, it is."

Vallaria's blue eyes brimmed with tears. In a few days her journey would take her to another kingdom, a dark kingdom. A kingdom that called to her in the nightmares infiltrating her sleep the past few nights. After all these years she would return to Ravenia, her true home, to claim her lost past and confront the woman who'd betrayed her family.

The grip on her mother's sword had tightened to the point her knuckles ached, but she welcomed the discomfort.

Vallaria would seek vengeance for her parents' murders and the ruination of their once happy kingdom. She owed it to their memory and to all those who suffered because of their deaths. But what that vengeance looked like she did not yet know.

8

FAELIN

The elven steel glinted in the rays of the late-day sun that hovered stubbornly over the distant mountain peaks.

Faelin admired its craftsmanship.

The blacksmith had forged a dagger worthy of a future queen.

"You did well, Yandril," she said, her eyes roaming over the intricate detailing he had meticulously carved into the blade. "Vallaria will be pleased."

The towering elf nodded, his eyes full of pride.

"Thank you," Faelin said, handing him a bag of gold and wrapping the dagger carefully in a swath of sheepskin.

She hurried to the royal edifice to show her father the gift she would give Vallaria at the gathering this evening. Footfalls echoed around her as she hurried through the entry hall, nodding at the guards she passed.

"Father," she called as she burst into the throne room, the new dagger tucked under her arm.

The king sat atop his throne, his face a mask of worry. Something burdened him. He still looked the regal ruler dressed in robes of forest green with gold brocade trim, but a heaviness weighed him down; she could see it in the slump of his shoulders and the shadow that darkened his lavender eyes.

"What is bothering you?" she asked as she came to stand in front of his throne. "Have you seen something?"

King Elvander was prone to visions, like his late sister Evinna. Their ability to see into the future was a rare gift few in their race possessed.

He looked at her with eyes full of worry and shook his head. "No."

"Then what troubles you, Father?" She lay the bundled dagger at her feet and took his hands in her own.

"I fear fate has burdened you as much as it has Vallaria."

Faelin fixed her stare on him. "You know I am happy to be by Vallaria's side as she begins this journey."

"That I do, but it is a burden nonetheless and one that may have no end."

Her father meant for her to stay by Vallaria's side long after she'd taken the throne. A new queen in a new world would need an advisor, someone who understood the rules of man and someone she could trust with her secrets and her life. Mistenvale would always be her home but for the unforeseeable future, her destiny lay beyond its borders. "I'll be fine."

"I have no doubt." The king smiled, but his expression grew somber. "Promise me you will not leave her side. She will need guidance and possibly protection. The ways of man are at times unpredictable, and I fear I have not adequately prepared her for the world that lies beyond our border. Besides her stubborn nature, I fear her naivety might be her downfall."

"Vallaria is strong, smart, and skilled with a blade. Maybe too much of an inciter like her father," she quipped, "but certainly able to take care of herself. While she lacks knowledge about the kingdoms that lay beyond the horizon, I have confidence this limitation will rectify itself quickly once she experiences the lands of Exile first-hand. Vallaria is a quick study, and I have no doubt she will adapt and learn how to navigate effectively within the world of man."

"I do not doubt her capabilities—"

"Then let me alleviate your worries. I give you my solemn word, I will not leave her unattended."

The king nodded. "Thank you. I will feel better knowing you are by her side. You know what men are capable of and have seen them at their worst. Especially when they submit to their darkest desires. With the worlds of man fracturing and the scent of distrust tainting their kingdoms, Exile is not a place for the weak or unprepared. Although one of Thaneil's men would have been a suitable traveling companion for Vallaria, I feel more at ease that you have agreed to go instead." Eyes of lavender crinkled at the edges as her father smiled. "I also know you crave adventure that is not found in Mistenvale. You have a wandering spirit, just like your mother." His face softened at the mention of his wife. "Although it will break my heart to watch both of you go, I will feel more secure in my decision knowing you are together. Besides, two women riding alone through the dark kingdom will be less threatening and thus less suspicious."

"I'm not sure that will matter. The rumors coming out of Ravenia say Queen Cereli has become increasingly distrustful of late. All strangers are being viewed with suspicion."

King Elvander nodded and rose from his throne. "I have no doubt. The dark magic she wields has been draining her for years; it was only a matter of time before paranoia set in. Unfortunately, that only makes her more dangerous and erratic."

He stepped off the dais and walked to the table at the edge of the throne room, where a pitcher of wine stood waiting. "Would you like a glass?" he asked, pouring the red liquid into a silver goblet.

"No, thank you."

He took a long sip before turning back to Faelin.

"We must also discuss the other part of Vallaria's destiny."

"The prophecy," Faelin stated. "The foretelling of the rise of the last mage."

"Yes. I think it prudent for us to go over things again, in case Evinna was correct and Vallaria is the one the prophecy spoke of. As Vallaria's guardian, you need to know what to look for—so you can recognize the signs that indicate its passing."

Faelin walked to where her father stood as he continued.

"Parts of the prophecy have already come to pass. The kingdoms of man grow restless, on this continent and the next. Alliances are breaking down, and conflicts are erupting where none existed before. Alagarn has also confirmed ravens have been seen around Ravenia."

Faelin lifted a brow. Alagarn was elvenkind. A spy loyal to her father who under an illusion had been hiding in plain sight for years as one of the queen's royal guardsmen. "The ravens haven't been seen in the kingdom since the king and queen died."

"No, but it is foretold they would be one of the signs heralding in the frost mage's return."

"Which is another indication Vallaria may be the one prophesied. The ravens of Ravenia are loyal only to the Ravenia bloodline."

"Yes." King Elvander placed the goblet of wine back on the table, closed his eyes, and began to recite a part of the prophecy. "*When the winter winds scorch the lands, the blackest of birds will once again soar in the dark skies, their sorrowful cries becoming the messenger hearkening the return of the cold mage of old. A moon, white as snow and cold as winter will hang low in the sky, its light a beacon revealing the last mage and the magic hiding within.*"

Opening his eyes, the king breathed deeply. "Winter will soon blanket the lands, and if the prophecy is correct, the frost mage's magic will be revealed during the time of the ice moon."

Faelin frowned. "Another ice moon so soon?"

Her father nodded. "I have only seen three in my lifetime. But two coming so close together is suspicious."

"Do you think they're connected?"

The king's slender fingers absently played with the large rings adorning them. "Maybe, but what that connection is I have not deciphered."

The last ice moon had appeared shortly after Vallaria arrived in the kingdom. The unearthly moon so white and so large hung low in the sky for days, its edges almost grazing the treetops. It had cast an eerie glow from one edge of the continent to the other. Flakes of ice drifted from the heavens, and their descent caused a haunted echoing din as they fell to the ground. Faelin stiffened. It had also been the last time she'd seen her mother who'd left Mistenvale a few weeks later on healing mission to the eastern side of the continent. She'd never returned, and it was months later that her body was discovered in a shallow grave near the northeastern coast. After her death, nothing had been the same.

Faelin, hands shaking, drew in a deep cleansing breath. And now another prophetic moon was set to rise.

Recognizing his daughter's discomfort, the king quickly changed the subject. "You will not be completely alone in your endeavor. Alagarn believes many in the royal guard and the army are still loyal to the crown of Ravenia, even though they do the bidding of Queen Cereli. He's confident once Vallaria regains control of the throne, those guards and soldiers will swear a covenant to her. The individuals completely loyal to Queen Cereli are either from the Gold Coast or assassins from the Kingdom of Zion and can be easily dispatched once power transfers back to the rightful queen."

The king took a step forward, his gaze hardening. "A word of warning daughter. Overthrowing the dark queen will be no easy task. The future is not yet written, and the sword of destiny has two edges to its blade. Do not take anything for granted, or we all may find ourselves feeling the sting of that blade."

Faelin nodded, knowing her father's words, although seemingly forthright, always had a deeper meaning.

The creak of the throne room door drew her attention as a guard stepped into the room. "Sire, she's arrived," he said, bowing slightly at the waist.

"Thank you. Send her in."

Curious, Faelin turned to her father.

"I've invited Vallaria to join us. She needs the stone if we are to ascertain if she is the one the prophecy speaks of. I thought it best to give it to her in private and not at the festivities this evening."

9
VALLARIA

allaria had not been back to the throne room since she'd fainted almost days prior. Déjà vu set in as she stood in front of the heavy doors and waited for the guard to announce her arrival, her father's prayer beads rolling between her thumb and forefinger. The beads felt heavier now, weighted by the realization that although she had prayed continuously over the past few days, she still felt the aching silence from her gods.

Where had they gone? Why did she not feel the aura of their presence anymore?

The beads pressed into her flesh as she gripped them tighter. She could not dwell on the god's absence—she must have faith that they would return when she needed them most. In the meantime, she had other matters that required her undivided attention. Mainly, her journey to Ravenia tomorrow.

Over the past few days, she had plenty of time to think about what her destiny meant for the future, and in some ways, she'd made peace with the burden laid at her feet. But it was her discussion with Kelena that made the anxiety of her newfound identify and the task ahead less daunting. Kelena made her see not only the importance of her parents' legacy but also that her past did not define who she would become.

"Your parents were more than a king and queen, Vallaria," Kelena had told her. "They were two individuals who truly cared about each other and the people they ruled. During their reign, the kingdom thrived, and the people were happy. All that has changed, I'm afraid."

"And I am the only one who can make the kingdom like it was before."

The elf's eyes shifted, and she grasped Vallaria's hands. "No one expects you to return the kingdom to what it once was, sweet girl. And your parents would not expect it either. With you as its queen, Ravenia will become the kingdom it was meant to be under your rule. Don't place a burden upon yourself that no one expects you to carry."

But how could she not when everyone kept telling her how wonderful her mother was? How could she ever live up to her memory?

The guard nodded to Vallaria as he exited the throne room and placed a closed fist across his chest and bowed slightly. "The king will see you now, Princess."

Vallaria winced at the formal moniker most in the castle deemed it necessary to use now. "Thank you," she said, her voice barely a whisper. It hadn't taken long for the rumors to swirl through the kingdom about her true identity. Most had accepted it without question, but the enchantment elves still scowled at her when she passed. She did not expect them to ever accept her fully.

Again, she walked through the throne room doors, but this time it was different. This time she was a princess, much more than an orphaned nobody. Pulling her shoulders back, she walked confidently toward the king and Faelin, who stood waiting on the dais at the far end.

"It is good to see you looking like your old self, Vallaria. I suspect you are well?" The king's gaze flashed with mischief even though the tone of his voice conveyed concern.

"I am well," she responded more at ease in his presence.

"I realize the information I provided you may not have been what you expected concerning your past, and for that I am sorry. But your lineage is one you should be very proud of."

"I'm not sure everyone would agree with you," she said thinking of the cold stare she received from Riva this morning when she passed her and Jale in the courtyard.

As if the king could read her mind, he said, "The elders and their kin do not define our race, Vallaria. It is true they are purists, but even they realize and embrace the importance of your existence, even if they refuse to acknowledge that fact to you."

Vallaria smiled. Her fingers still fiddled with her father's prayer beads, and the soft clacking sound drew the king's attention.

"I see you still carry your father's beads."

She nodded. "Yes."

"And now that you know your father was a king, do those beads and your gods mean anything different?"

Vallaria hadn't really thought about it. Since Kelena had taught her of the beliefs of man and their pantheon of gods, she'd found herself curious about the beings they revered so much yet could not see or hear. Man's beliefs differed so much from the elves who did not worship anything other than the powers of the elemental world. To them, man's gods were a foolish concept but nonetheless it was one she had, over time, become completely vested in. It was because of that Vallaria chose not to disclose to the king that she felt her gods had abandoned her.

"The gods are still in my heart and my mind, if that is what you are asking. And I assume my father would have followed their guidance during his rule."

"And you would be correct. Evinna, your mother, often spoke of the king's devout loyalty to his faith. I suppose in a way you must admire one so fervent in their beliefs, even if they are unequal to yours. So, I am glad you have found some form of solace in something we could not give you."

She shifted her stance. "From everything I hear, my parents were the type of rulers one could only hope to emulate." A sadness infiltrated her words, and she gripped the beads tighter.

"This is true. Ryguard and Evinna were a formidable and much-loved duo, but you will be a ruler of your own making." The king glanced at Faelin as he shifted on his throne. "You must understand Ravenia is a very different place now. Do not leave Mistenvale with a false sense of security. You have been sheltered here and your concept of the outside world is not yet fully realized. Once you leave these borders you will learn much. Keep your mind sharp. You are quick with a blade but often too curious for your own good. Out there it is your intuition you must rely on; you cannot lose focus. Nothing is as it seems in the lands beyond. Remember, shadows can sometimes hide the darkest of truths."

Vallaria nodded. King Elvander had explained to her in the past how shadows could hide things. "I will be vigilant. But if my destiny is to sit on the throne of Ravenia, and I am meant to take back the crown, then the truth will prevail, even in the darkest of shadows, would it not?"

The king's eyes narrowed. "The kingdom will do well under your governance, Vallaria. I do hope your gods see fit to bless your journey, but if not, my hope is destiny will." He stood and stepped off the dais. "One more thing." He reached inside his armor and removed a small ice blue rock holding it out toward her in his palm.

The edges sparkled with light. Not as though the stone's surface reflected the light but rather as if it expelled its own light from within.

"A gift," he said.

The sparkling blue light undulated as it flickered. It was mesmerizing, and Vallaria was instantly taken with its beauty.

Curious fingers grazed the stone, but as flesh touched its surface she instantly pulled back. Although the throbbing glow looked warm, the rock was unexpectedly cold. "What is it?"

King Elvander turned it over in his palm. "This is an elemental stone known as an ice crystal. It is very rare, found only in the ice glades located in the far north of the continent of Brulle. Long ago the ice glades were the homeland of the frost mages."

During her time with the elves, Vallaria heard many a story about the time of the mages, when magic was abundant in this world and mages were revered by kings for their powers—and then betrayed because of it. But the time of the mages had long passed, their life and death relegated to the annuals of time.

"What is it used for?"

He held the ice crystal aloft between forefinger and thumb. "Legend has it that when mages still roamed the earth, crystals like this, harvested from the four corners of the world, increased their elemental powers. A conduit if you will."

"It's beautiful."

"And it's yours." King Elvander handed the crystal to Vallaria.

"Are you sure you wish to part with something so treasured?"

The king nodded. "There comes a time when everything must find its true place in the world." He pointed to the crystal. "I believe that belongs with you now."

She gazed at the stone in her palm, the cold burning a numbness into her flesh. "I shall cherish it."

His hand squeezed hers. "Word to the wise: I would keep it hidden. Superstitions run deep within the heart and head of man. The emergence of an elemental stone after all these years might bring more trouble than good. And would certainly draw the attention of Queen Cereli."

"I will ensure that no one knows of its existence outside this room."

The king leaned in. "May your gods be with you," he whispered before turning and walking out of the throne room.

Goosebumps flared on her skin as she watched him disappear, his emerald cloak swirling majestically behind him.

I have no idea where my gods are.

Faelin placed a gloved hand on Vallaria's forearm. "I'll see you this evening at the gathering."

"I'll see you then," Vallaria said, tucking the mage stone into the pocket of her tunic. After leaving the throne room, she hurried toward her chambers. The gathering tonight would lessen the time she had to get her affairs in order, and she still needed to finish packing. An unexpected sadness engulfed her, for she suspected it would be a long time before she laid eyes on Mistenvale again.

The trek to Ravenia would take approximately two and a half days. If all went well, she and Faelin would be in the heart of the kingdom before the next full moon.

When Vallaria reached the door to her chambers, she hesitated, her hand on the door handle, as the gravity of the daunting quest before her loomed. Although Faelin would be by her side, she was essentially alone. All the king could offer was a meeting with his spy, Alagarn.

Of course, he has a spy in Ravenia, she thought, recalling the conversation with King Elvander, Thaneil, and Faelin the other week when this was revealed.

"The queen believes the Ravenia bloodline ended long ago, so we have that as an advantage, but we also have Alagarn," the commander said as he laid out maps of Exile and Ravenia.

"Who is Alagarn?" Vallaria had asked.

The king's eyes sparked. "I've had an elf inside the castle since before your mother died. Evinna had visions of her demise, so we knew of the overthrow before it happened."

"And you couldn't stop it?" Vallaria asked, her eyes narrowing in confusion.

"Just because you have the knowledge does not mean you can affect the outcome. Rather, it gives you time to prepare for the inevitable. The insider is one of my generals and is currently a captain within the dark queen's royal guard. He will assist you as much as he can."

"How will I recognize him?"

The commander rolled out the map of the kingdom and pointed to the city of Ravenia. "A meeting will be set prior to your departure. Alagarn is disguised under an illusion and therefore will look no different from any of the other royal guards in the queen's employ. But he will be the only guard that knows the answer to your question."

"And what is this question?"

"Will you live for the true queen of Ravenia or die for a false one?"

"And the answer?"

"I will live and die only for the true queen."

The king picked up one of the metal pieces that indicated the elven army and placed it near Ravenia's borders. "The elves cannot intervene in the politics of man, not until their alliance with Ravenia has been renewed with you as its queen. Alagarn will help you as much as he can, but if he is found out the queen will have him hung for treason. You must be prepared to carry this burden on your own."

"Is it possible to gain access to the castle through work?" Vallaria had asked. "Could Alagarn help me get a job in the kitchens or as a chambermaid?"

The king glanced at his commander, a twitch playing at the corners of his mouth. "It's possible I suppose."

"A position where those who undertake them become invisible to those in the castle with stature. A job like that would allow me unfettered access to the castle and time to find a way to get near the queen."

"I will send word to Alagarn at once," the king said. "But make sure if you are going to breech Cereli's sanctum, you know the land-scape and all the players."

Heeding the king's advice, she'd spent the following days preparing for the journey. She'd studied the annuals in the library, practiced her fighting skills relentlessly, and learned all she could about the Gold Coast and the other smaller kingdoms aligned with the dark queen. Unfortunately, there remained not one kingdom in Exile that still held allegiance to her parents. After the insurrection, Cereli had ensured all aligned with her, or they were ruthlessly crushed.

The one thing Vallaria did lack was specific information on the magic Cereli wielded. As she walked to her chambers, she recalled a conversation on that subject she'd had with Faelin only days before.

"There's not much to know. Most is speculation. What we do know is that she manipulates a dark magic that's not of this world," Faelin had said. "It comes from another plane, one where ravaged souls lay trapped in purgatory for an eternity. Queen Cereli is mortal and therefore unable to use the magic she possesses without consequence. There are rumors the dark magic she wields may be consuming her and driving her mad, fueling her paranoia. We also know through Alagarn her staff is the conduit. Without it, she may be vulnerable, but I fear parting her from it will be difficult."

Impossible is more like it, Vallaria thought as she pushed open the chamber door and stepped over the threshold.

A fire burned brightly in the hearth. The flickering flame danced across the gleaming steel of her mother's sword that lay on the table in front of it.

Her heart clenched and she sighed.

This was her destiny, unwanted or not. Although it would no doubt be fraught with peril and obstacles impossible to overcome, she'd made her decision to try. She owed it to her parents' memory, to King Elvander and Faelin, and all who had made sure she would survive until this day.

But most of all she owed it to herself.

Vallaria sat in the chair and stared at the crackling fire. Whatever challenges her gods deemed necessary and no matter how dire the cost, her parent's legacy must be regained.

The crown of Ravenia did not belong on the head of a usurper.

The kingdom and its people deserved their rightful queen.

10
VALLARIA

The celebration had already begun when Vallaria walked into the courtyard gardens. The air carried the sound of music and the whispers of conversations, which drifted toward her as she searched the grounds for a friendly face. Lit by small glass lanterns filled with fireflies, the fountain gurgled at the courtyard's center. Strings of wildflowers hung around the perimeter, swinging in the breeze.

Kelena stood at the back near the banquet table.

With her head down Vallaria weaved her way toward the back. The deeper she moved into the crowd the more she felt eyes upon her and heard the whispering increase.

"Princess Vallaria," she heard from her left. Turning toward the voice, she saw a male elf bow as she passed, then another. Suddenly, a path opened in front of her as elves parted to let her through, bowing as she passed.

The surrounding air became thick, and she found it difficult to breathe against the increased pounding of her heart. Just when she thought she may faint she felt a firm hand on her elbow, guiding her quickly past the elves to the safety of Kelena's side.

"Thank you, Thaneil," she said, inhaling deeply, attempting to slow her heart.

The commander nodded, a flicker of mischief in his eye. "There is much you will need to get used to being of royal blood, Princess. But at least you can relax into anonymity once again when you leave the kingdom in the morning."

He walked away, and she turned to Kelena, her back to the many eyes still upon her. "For so long I wanted to know who my parents were, who I was, but this was not what I expected."

"And what did you expect?"

"To be someone, but not this kind of someone."

Cocking her head, Kelena asked, "And what kind of someone is that?"

"Someone who people bow to."

The elf smirked. "If it makes you feel better, it is probably more difficult for them to bow to you."

Vallaria frowned. "No, it doesn't make me feel better." She glanced over her shoulder relieved to see that most had gone back to their own conversations. "Why do they have to bow to me, anyway?"

"You are an Ildarian. Regardless of your mortal parent, you are still a daughter of the royal bloodline."

"So, because of my mother, they must accept me now?"

"In a manner of speaking, yes. Acceptance is more a concept in the outside world. The elves stick to a more rigid hierarchy and centuries of tradition. You carry the blood of the royal family, and that is the only thing needed to gain at least the appearance of respect."

"So they still despise me."

"They don't understand you. Your parents' union was the first of its kind and very much not tradition. The enchantment elves are purists, as you know, so mixing bloodlines—"

Kelena didn't need to finish the sentence; Vallaria was painfully aware of how the enchantment elves felt about her.

"Did they treat my mother differently after she married my father?"

"In some ways, I suppose. The few times she returned to Mistenvale, she was always greeted with the respect her lineage dictated, but there were always the whispers and the looks of disenchantment. But your mother was proud and strong, and she never once let it bother her. She loved your father deeply, as she did you. That's what mattered."

"Am I interrupting?" Faelin asked as she glided up to where Vallaria stood, her back still facing the gathering.

"Not at all," Kelena said. Patting Vallaria's arm, she said, "I'll see you in a bit."

As Vallaria watched her walk away, something suddenly occurred to her. Turning to Faelin she asked, "Why don't they bow to you?"

"Who?"

"Everyone, anyone." She gestured to the many elves in front of them.

"I'm not their queen."

"But I am not their queen either."

The corners of Faelin's perfect pink lips quivered. "I wouldn't get used to it. It's a one-time thing."

"I don't understand."

"Ceremonial. Do you see them bow to my father every time he walks through the kingdom?"

Vallaria's mind wandered back through time. She'd never really thought about it before. She'd been so young in the beginning, and when she did begin to understand their ways, it had become commonplace and much had faded into the background. "That doesn't explain why they salute me and not you."

"Their respect for your stature is new. This is the first time they are interacting with you as a member of the Ildaria bloodline. It is a sign of respect and acknowledgment. It won't continue. The same respect is given to me. I have been saluted and bowed to in the past, at milestones in my life, unimportant in the scheme of things. When I become queen, things will be different, as it will be for you in your kingdom."

A sigh escaped Vallaria's lips.

"Enough talk of protocol. Come, I have a gift for you." Faelin waved, indicating for Vallaria to follow.

They wove their way through the elves. Vallaria kept her eyes downcast until they reached the farthest fountain where a small gazebo, adorned with small firefly-filled glass lanterns and colorful flowery vines, stood. At its center, on a small table, was a bouquet atop a sheepskin bundle.

"For you," Faelin said.

Carefully, Vallaria picked up the bouquet of small purple flowers, lifting them to her nose and inhaling deeply. The scent was subtle but fragrant.

"They are morning dewdrops, and they only grow in the cold snowy peaks of the mountains. They were your mother's favorite."

Tears welled in Vallaria's eyes. Even the smallest amount of information about her parents was monumental.

"Morning dewdrops are the oddity of the botanical species. They flourish in cold climates and lose their vibrant color and scent if warmed past their tolerance. In elvish, they are known as *Vallaricium*."

"My mother named me after a flower."

"She did—but not just any flower. One that is strong, beautiful, defiant of the norms, and relishes being different. Your mother named you well."

With a heavy heart Vallaria placed the bouquet to the side and turned her attention to the sheepskin bundle. "What is this?"

"A gift for a future queen."

The sheepskin had been scented with sage, and as Vallaria unwrapped the cloth, the fragrance wafted upward, embracing her in its calming, cleansing scent.

When she unfolded the last corner, an exquisite dagger appeared nestled at its center.

It was about ten inches in length from tip to pommel. The blade was thick but narrow. The cross guard splayed out like two dark iron wings. The grove or fuller at the blade's center was carved with runic symbols. The grip was wrapped with the softest of leather straps, and when she held it in her hand, the dagger felt almost weightless.

The blade glinted.

"It's gorgeous, Faelin."

The elf moved around to the other side of the stone table. "Yandril is an exceptional blacksmith. He crafted this to my specifications perfectly." She pointed to the runes on the blade's fuller. "From fear comes strength, from strength comes victory."

Vallaria held the dagger aloft. "I will cherish it forever." She looked at her friend. "Thank you for all this. You didn't have to."

"My father and I have been to enough gatherings outside the kingdom to know how important man's traditions are. Your twenty-first birthday may not mean much to us, but it is an important milestone in the life of one who is heir to a mortal throne. And for that we felt it appropriate to honor a tradition that your parents would have if they were still here. I'm sure there would have been more pomp and circumstance surrounding your day of ascension in Ravenia, but we did our best."

Vallaria could not even imagine what her life would be like if she'd grown up in Ravenia. A princess and heir to the throne. But before she could ask Faelin any further questions, she heard a familiar voice.

"Well, well, Princess Vallaria Ravenia. How quickly you've ascended."

Riva, Jale, and Darnica sauntered up to where she and Faelin stood.

"Riva, it is so good of you to come this evening," Faelin said, her eyes flashing a warning.

"We certainly did not want to miss Vallaria's send-off. Who

knows if we will ever see her again?" Riva said as her lips spread into a sneer.

Darnica raised an eyebrow and cast a quick glance at Faelin before taking a step back behind Jale.

Without warning Riva grabbed Vallaria's forearm and pulled her close, whispering in her ear, "Your new status changes nothing, Princess. Although I must adhere to my oath to protect the Ildaria bloodline, know that I do it unwillingly. You will always be a *narcigni*," she hissed. "A half-breed, unclean, and unworthy to carry the royal blood of the elves."

Vallaria's voice rumbled from her lips, low and guttural. She wrenched her arm away from Riva and glared. "Your approval means nothing to me. The enchantment sect of your race live in an antiquated illusion of how the world and those in it should be. Your allegiance is to King Elvander, not me. If you have a problem with my new status, take it up with him."

When she stalked off, she glanced at Faelin, whose face, other than a raised brow remained an expressionless mask. Once past the elf Vallaria smiled—at least this time Faelin's eyes didn't reflect a disappointed gaze.

HOURS LATER THE GATHERING WAS WINDING DOWN AND MOST HAD retreated to their homes. Faelin had left with Thaneil to check on their horses and weapons for tomorrow's departure.

Vallaria stood in the dark, eyes skyward, cherishing the solitude.

Millions of stars lay scattered across the late-evening sky. Tiny pins of light twinkled in a pitch-black canvas. When the full moon added its silvery glow across the elven lands, it was the most serene and fantastical sight she'd ever witnessed.

It was one of her favorite things about Mistenvale, the quiet haunting beauty of its nighttime heavens.

I wonder what the sky beyond these borders holds.

She'd observed the angry gray skies on the distant horizon for so long, she assumed this beauty would end the moment she left the kingdom.

"Know if you need me, I will always be under these stars, waiting."

Vallaria jumped at the voice. She hadn't heard King Elvander come to stand beside her. *Nothing new.* The elven king moved like water as it meandered down a riverbed—silent but with purpose.

She smiled up at him. "These tranquil night skies will be the thing I will miss the most."

"I won't take that to heart."

"You know what I mean." Standing beside the powerful elven king, Vallaria, so used to the familiarity of him and Mistenvale, again questioned her decision to leave. So much uncertainty lay beyond the kingdom's borders. For her the world of man was a vast unknown, and she would be remiss to think otherwise.

Although the king and Faelin had faith in her, she herself was riddled with uncertainty. Her destiny may have been written, but that did not always make it absolute. She would have to outsmart the dark queen without alerting the army or garnering the attention of the royal guard. With so much stacked against her, the only advantage she had was her anonymity—the entire Kingdom of Ravenia thought Princess Serifine dead.

King Elvander put a firm but gentle hand on her shoulder. "Your mother made sure you were safe so your destiny, the crown, and the future of Ravenia could be yours. The path you are about to embark on will not be an easy one, but it is the correct one. You must trust your instincts and let those who are no longer with us guide you."

She smiled, knowing he was speaking of her mother.

The elven king looked down. "There is something else that troubles your mind."

Tears welled up in her eyes as she blurted out, "Why can't I remember them? My parents. Why are the memories of my child-hood prior to Mistenvale so fuzzy?"

"If there is one thing I've learned from my long existence, it is that the minds of man are complex. Your mind has a way of protecting you by blocking out painful and traumatic events. Some-day, when you are ready to handle that pain, your mind will give those memories back to you."

"And what if I can't bear to see them?"

"It is not only the good that defines us and builds our strength but also the bad. Weakness comes from fear, fear of the unknown, and fear of thy self. I have faith that one day if those memories return, you will have the strength to bear them." The king moved closer so their shoulders touched. "Until that time I will bear them for you."

Vallaria laid her head on the king's shoulder. "Do you remember the first time I crawled onto your lap?"

The king smiled. "I dropped you to the floor."

"You were so startled by my actions that you immediately stood and I slid right off." Vallaria laughed.

When she was a child, she hadn't understood that the elven race didn't show affection the same as those from the mortal world. Although still stiff in his mannerisms, the king had become more accustomed to her affection over the years and learned to show her some back.

"It was not my finest moment," the king said.

"But I remember it."

King Elvander nodded, seeing her point. "And some day you will remember them as well."

"I spent my life creating an image of them in my head. Wondering how they looked, what they did, who they were, and how they died. I guess somehow it gave me a sense of comfort and purpose."

"And now?"

"Now reality has shattered the illusion, and I am left facing a staggering truth. One I am not sure I'm prepared for." She lifted her head and looked up at the man who raised her. "Why do you believe I can do the impossible?"

The king took her by her shoulders and with a gentle voice said, "I believe you can do the impossible because you are your mother's daughter."

II
VALLARIA

The fateful day had arrived.

Vallaria was to meet Faelin at the city gates by late morning. The horse the commander brought over early this morning was saddled and ready to go, and she could smell the vestiges of breakfast floating into her room.

Staring at her image in the mirror, she turned back and forth, pulling uncomfortably at her clothes. Faelin had given her an outfit of elven armor to wear, and Vallaria was not yet used to how restrictive it was. The woven black leather and metal bodice was tight, the corset-style belt had too many buckles, and the wrist wraps were difficult to lace up. The only thing that was the least bit comfortable were the knee-high leather riding boots to which she had strapped the sheath that held her dagger. Her long hair had been braided down the middle of the top of her head, leaving the sides loose.

She tugged at the leather strap across her shoulder while she scrutinized her reflection. Grumbling to herself, she grabbed her sword in its sheath from the table and buckled it around her waist, securing it with an additional strap around her upper thigh.

"I look ridiculous," she'd said last night in response to Faelin's demand she wear the armor.

"We are entering a world that is dangerous, even if people don't know who you truly are," Faelin had countered. "This armor will protect you. It's been woven with silver and steel by the finest craftsmen in the city. It's made to look unremarkable so we won't stand out. You must wear it."

The smell of salted meat filled her nose as she left her bed chamber and entered the kitchen.

"There you are," Kelena said as she bustled around the kitchen. "Sit."

A plate of food appeared before Vallaria as the elf said, "Eat, I'll be right back."

She ate in silence, savoring every bit. It might be a long time before she had food this good again. Kelena had packed provisions for them, but it was nothing as fancy as her homemade breads and salted meat.

Vallaria shoved another piece of sweet bread into her mouth as she got up from the table and grabbed her pack. "Kelena! I have to go!"

Footfalls echoed through the house and within seconds Kelena hurried around the corner and into the kitchen. "Sorry," she said. "It took me a while to find this." She held up a large red knitted ball.

"What is it?" The ball unwound as Kelena shook it out. It cascaded toward the floor, and Vallaria saw it was a cloak.

"It was your mother's traveling cloak. I made it for her when she first agreed to marry your father and move to Ravenia." She held it out toward Vallaria. "It's yours now."

Taking a step forward, Vallaria took the cloak from the elf. The wool was soft and plush. Its color the deep red of a full-bodied wine. The front of the cloak was short, sitting just above the bottom of the breastbone. It swept over her upper arms and then flared out, lengthening into a trailing cape that reached mid-calf.

"Put it on. Let's see if it fits." Kelena wrapped the traveling cloak over Vallaria's shoulders and latched it with the buckle at the front. After smoothing the wool fabric over Vallaria's shoulders, she took a step back. "Perfect, like it was made for you."

Vallaria smiled and looked down. It fit well and was oddly comfortable. The stretch of the wool allowed for unimpeded movement and the sides were far enough back as to not interfere with her sword.

"Thank you, Kelena. It's beautiful. I will cherish it deeply."

"There is something else." She dug into her tunic pocket and pulled a sparkling silver pendant on a long chain from her pocket. "Your mother gave me this on that fateful day and told me to give it to you on your twenty-first birthday." She held it up by the clasp. The necklace dangled in mid-air, sparkling in the morning sun that shone through the window. "Your mother never took this off. It was a gift from her father. She was adamant it must pass to you."

Vallaria's gaze dropped to the pendant Kelena held in her fingers. It was an oval-shaped locket. Its exterior was a lattice cage of metal vines and leaves. It reminded her of the plants that climbed the south wall of the kingdom. A small vial filled with a dark crimson liquid was nestled inside, and it sparkled as the pendant swung. "Why?" she asked.

"Evinna did not say, only that it was part of the Ildarian family legacy and the only way the lands of Exile may find peace in the future."

She passed the trinket to Vallaria and again reached into her pocket, this time pulling out a small white card. "She also left you this."

Vallaria unfolded the note card, and two perfect lines of script written in black ink materialized.

> *As it once was before the kingdoms forgot,*
> *Blood of three royals, one pure, two not.*

Her brow drew downward, and she tilted her head. "What does it mean?"

A shrug raised Kelena's shoulders. "I do not know, and your mother did not elaborate. She said the adage would make sense when you needed it to."

Vallaria tucked the note into the pocket of her satchel and placed the long thick chain around her neck, tucking the locket under the layers of her leather bodice so it lay directly against her skin, just above her heart.

"Thank you," she said, hugging the elf. "I am going to miss you terribly."

Kelena drew back, holding Vallaria by the upper arms. "We will see each other once again, of that I am sure. But until that day, know I will always be here." She placed her index finger on Vallaria's heart.

Tears stung at the edges of Vallaria's lids, and before she could change her mind, she grabbed her bags and hurried from the house.

As she crossed the familiar streets of the elven city, the elves that were out watched silently as she rode by. Although their expressions remained passive, Vallaria had no doubt that many would not miss her unwelcomed presence in their world.

From the corner of her eye, she saw an expanse of white. A group of enchantment elves, the elders, watched her ride by from the shadows of their temple. Numerous sets of purple eyes followed her path through the city toward the gate.

They definitely won't be upset to see me go.

She glanced over her shoulder as she rounded the corner. Thankfully, Riva and her cohorts were nowhere to be seen.

The rhythmic clop of the horse's hooves soothed her mind and she found herself being lulled into the memory of last night.

The dream had come again in all its familiarity and dread. Only this time a minor detail was different, and Vallaria could only assume her subconscious had infected it with the anxiousness she felt at leaving the kingdom and journeying into an unknown world.

She'd been in the same grassy meadow, the raven ever present. Her name came to her on the breeze and then the reflection of a little black-haired girl appeared before her. They stared at each other, so much alike. The sky turned dark, and the reflection of the little girl did too, tattered clothes, messy hair, her sweet face contorted by anger. Suddenly, the cold came surging through Vallaria's veins, uncontrolled. The twisted reflection of herself shattered, fragmenting into a white snowy dust that covered everything.

The same but different.

Somewhere behind the familiar images in the dream there'd been a flicker, something that didn't belong. Like a slit in a canvas that opened up to let you see behind the painting. The flicker had been fleeting, only a second before it was gone, but it revealed to Vallaria another place behind the meadow. A place dark with fear and death that reeked of a suffocating loneliness. And as she was pulled from the dream, an unfamiliar voice whispered from that dark place—*I see you.*

Vallaria shivered as the vivid memory ignited a chill over her skin. She pushed the memory aside and squeezed her knees gently into her mount's flanks causing it to elevate its gait into a trot.

"Good boy, Siron," she murmured to the gelding as she stroked its neck.

The city gates appeared before her as she turned the last corner. To her surprise both Commander Cyran and King Elvander were waiting with Faelin, who sat atop her white mare, Krest.

"I didn't realize you were both coming to see us off," Vallaria said as she came to a stop beside them.

"A surprise," the king said, waving his jewel laden hand around.

Vallaria laughed at the king's awkward reference to the human world. Surprises were not a part of the elven culture. Faelin had told her once that the concept would no doubt lead to an untimely death if anyone tried to surprise an elf.

"Well, I appreciate the gesture.' Vallaria dismounted. "But why did you really come?"

"To ensure we give you as much aid as possible before you leave our borders." The king glanced at Thaneil. "Although I cannot physically help you claim back the Ravenia throne, I would be remiss if I did not at least provide you with as much as I can to ensure your success."

A crisp wind blew strands of Vallaria's long dark hair across her face. With a steady hand, the king's slender fingers pushed it off. "You may look like your father, but you are fearless like your mother."

Vallaria felt a flutter in her chest as he invoked her mother's memory.

"She would be proud of the strong, independent woman you've become.

A lump formed in her throat, and she swallowed with difficulty, trying to dislodge it. "I will do my best to make you both proud."

"That is all I can ask." The king's gaze dropped, and his fingers slid over the edge of her red cloak. "Kelena gave this to you."

"Yes."

"It looks good."

"Father, we must go if we are to make the canyon before nightfall," Faelin said, her horse stamping the earth with its hooves. "Winter approaches and the light of day is becoming shorter."

The king nodded and turned back to Vallaria. "The Kingdom of Ravenia is the largest kingdom in the north and much of its land is uninhabited. Since Queen Cereli took the throne, the kingdom has fallen into darkness. More and more thieves and worrying sorts roam the lands freely, torturing and killing citizens, stealing livestock and crops, and terrorizing smaller villages. There are many dangers you will face outside our borders, Vallaria. You must remain vigilant and listen to Faelin, for she knows these lands better than any. Do not think you know more than you do because of what you've read in books. Promise me."

"I promise."

The elven commander stepped forward and helped Vallaria back into the saddle. "Understand your enemies and always watch each other's backs." Thaneil glanced quickly at Faelin, who nodded in acknowledgement. "A word of warning, Vallaria: do not make this quest about revenge. It is not about what you lost but what you can gain. Killing the dark queen is a means to an end, *not* the objective. Her death will not bring your parents back. It is only one piece in a bigger strategy game. Do you understand?"

"Yes," Vallaria said, her throat constricting.

The commander's voice softened. "You will avenge their deaths by restoring their legacy."

"And if I do defeat the dark queen and take the crown, what then?"

"Our allegiance to your father still stands as long as one of Ravenia blood sits on the throne. Once you make claim to the throne you can be certain your enemies will align against you behind the Gold Coast Empire. It will not be long before your kingdom will once again be threatened. Light the beacon at the top of the highest spire and the elven army will come."

"And what of the Ravenia army and the royal guard? Will they stand with me?" Over the past week Vallaria had also considered where the loyalty of the fifteen hundred plus men who served in the kingdom's army and guard would fall if she claimed the throne. The commander had explained many bent the knee to the dark queen after Ravenia's overthrow instead of losing their head for treason. But so many years later, no one could truly know how many remained secretly loyal to the dead king.

The commander's gaze narrowed. "Unfortunately, I do not have an answer, although Alagarn seems to think it a possibility. It is certain those who hail from the Gold Coast Empire or the Kingdom of Zion will not welcome you. Once the dark queen is dead and you wear the crown our hope is those who served your father may be willing to serve the true heir of Ravenia.

"Unfortunately, your word will not be enough to convince any of your claim," King Elvander said. He reached out and grasped her hand. "The Ravenia army, the royal guard, and all the kingdom's citizens have long believed the rightful heir to King Ryguard's throne, Princess Serifine, to be dead. There is only one way to convince any who may still be loyal to your parents that you aren't an imposter."

He gently turned her arm over and pulled up her shirt sleeve, exposing the soft, pale skin of her wrist.

"This may help to convince them you are the true heir to the Ravenia throne."

With a wave of his hand, he undid an illusion that hid a part of her identity. Within seconds a blood red shape began to appear on the inside of her wrist—

raven wings.

She'd seen this image in many of the tomes she'd studied in the library when researching the history of the kingdoms of Exile.

It was the mark of the Ravenia royal family. An identifier magically inscribed into the Ravenia bloodline by the blood mages of old, ensuring all babies born of royal descent were easily distinguishable.

Vallaria stared at the mark, and her mind once again drifted to the monumental task ahead of her. *It was the proof she needed to sway them if she stayed alive long enough to ask any for their allegiance.*

12
FAELIN

Faelin's eyes of lilac rimmed in black kohl looked down on the kingdom of elves from the edge of the bluff. Quietly, she surveyed her surroundings one last time, unsure when she would ever see her home again.

Mistenvale was hidden away from the rest of the world. A place of peace and stability separate from the everchanging realms of man. Bordered on one side by the expansive cerulean sea, the vale lay nestled behind a tall, craggy mountain range surrounding it on the other. Its seclusion was the reason the elves could forfeit their allegiance with the kingdom of men without repercussions. Although there hadn't been a need for allegiances since King Ryguard's death.

Or Baladril's.

Faelin's hand tightened on the reins as his face floated through her mind. It was an image she could never scrub from her memory, that moment their eyes locked seconds before the blade met his throat. She'd thought about the look in his eyes for years, never fully understanding what she'd seen. It wasn't fear or hate, not even confusion. No accusation or plea for help—his eyes seemed void of anything but acceptance, something she found difficult to equate with the finest commander the elven army had ever seen. Baladril would never admit or accept defeat, not for anything. But he had— *for her.*

The late morning sun rising over the mountain peaks cast a kaleidoscope of reds, yellows, and oranges across the crystal clear blue sky. Its rays warmed her skin and thankfully Baladril's face faded back into the recesses of her mind.

She sensed Vallaria move in behind her. "It's breathtaking."

"You've never seen Mistenvale from this vantage point. The entirety of the kingdom laid out in full view."

"No."

Vallaria had been somewhat of a captive in the elven kingdom most of her life, strictly forbidden to venture outside the city gates without accompaniment. Faelin had been the only one to take her farther, but it was always to the small isle to the north, never toward the borders that merged with the kingdoms of man. The risk would have been too great. For any to discover an heir to the Ravenia throne was still alive, it would have meant war. A war that would have been bloody and senseless without Vallaria being of an age to reclaim the throne. Dire sacrifices had to be made. It had cost them all something.

The jagged edge of the sea merged with the white sand of the shore as the early-morning rays twinkled playfully on the surf.

Faelin breathed deeply, the salt air filling her lungs.

The tips of the mountains, still covered in early winter snow, rose stalwart in the distance. Towering waterfalls thundered into crystal clear pools. Flowers in a myriad of colors dotted the brilliant green landscape. Arching trees, lush with large leaves, their boughs dipping gracefully to the earth, cast whimsical shadows across the green velvety carpet of the forest. Birds sang cheerful songs as they flitted throughout the vale.

"In many ways I will miss it," Vallaria said.

"Will you?" Faelin turned her gaze toward her friend. Without waiting for an answer, she turned Krest away from the vale and toward the border. "Let us ride. We will camp at the edge of our borders tonight. Tomorrow we will enter the mountain pass into Ravenia. It will be about a two ride from there."

A sadness shrouded her as they left the bluff behind.

Mistenvale was Faelin's home, but Ravenia beckoned. It was time for the princess of Ravenia to return to her homeland, and Faelin intended to ensure that happened without incident.

———

THEY GOT TO THE CANYON AT THE BASE OF THE MOUNTAIN PASS LATE IN THE day after a half day's ride. Faelin raised her gaze as she led her horse down the narrow path into the gulch. A fiery red and purple sunset exploded behind the mountain peaks, but on the far horizon dark clouds churned in the skies over Ravenia, looking more volatile the closer to the dark kingdom they got.

"We will make camp in the canyon tonight. It is unwise to traverse the mountain pass in the dark, so we will resume our journey in the morning."

"Is the pass unsafe?"

"Not in the way you think."

Vallaria dismounted. "What do you mean?"

"The mountain pass is the only thing that connects the realms of elf and man. Many think it is haunted by the fallen spirits lost to the wars between the two."

Darkness shrouded the yawning mouth of the pass, and Faelin saw Vallaria shiver. "There is a small pool at the far end of the canyon. Take a bucket and fill it for the horses. We will refill our water skins in the morning before we leave."

Vallaria didn't move.

"Before we lose what little daylight remains."

Turning, she asked, "Do you believe the pass is haunted?"

"Spirits are everywhere, Vallaria. Death is a part of life and when that life passes on death remains."

Shaking her head, Vallaria snatched the bucket and mumbled, "I don't even know what that means."

The corners of Faelin's mouth quivered as she watched Vallaria walk away. There was much Vallaria needed to learn of this world, but for now her focus must remain steadfast on the task at hand. Once she became queen, there would be plenty of time for her to learn the rest.

A while later, Vallaria returned. The horses were glad for the cool, fresh water and the apples and oats Faelin had given them. Huddled over the fire, she watched the white beans begin to bubble, waiting a few minutes before scooping them out and handing a plate to Vallaria.

"Were my parents good people?" Vallaria blurted out.

"Why would you think they may not be?"

"That's not an answer."

Faelin dished out beans for herself. "Yes, your parents were good people. Evinna was kind and caring and believed in the goodness of man. You father was revered and respected. He was tough but a fair ruler. The kingdom prospered under their rule and so did its people."

"Then why were they killed?'

The plate of beans in her hand suddenly became of the utmost importance, and Faelin turned her attention to it, hoping her silence would suffice. She'd always thought Vallaria had a right to know the real reason her parents were killed, but her father thought it may tarnish their memory. But she couldn't, in good conscience, let the princess ride into Ravenia to overthrow the reigning queen without knowing the reasons behind what she'd lost. King Ryguard had chosen love over what was best for the kingdom, and it had cost him everything. It had cost *Vallaria* everything. Yet again, man's emotions had instigated a fall from power.

"Faelin, please. Your father would not answer me when I asked. What did they do to deserve such wrath?"

Sighing as the heaviness of the truth pushed down on her, she answered with reluctance. "Your father entered into an agreement with the emperor of the Gold Coast Empire to marry Cereli Damask of House Sand Serpent. An arrangement that would align the two most powerful kingdoms in Exile. Unfortunately, your father met Evinna months before the marriage was to take place. You know the rest."

A shadow darkened Vallaria's features. "My father went back on his word."

"Your father fell in love."

Faelin sensed the tension emanating from Vallaria. She was struggling to process the information and the implications of what her father had done. Although she couldn't remember him, he was nonetheless her father and his actions had caused the downfall of a kingdom. Faelin had been there herself once, watching someone she cared about die for his actions while she was helpless to stop it. Baladril had kept too many secrets, and it had cost him everything and her almost as much. Like her, Vallaria may never make sense of her father's decision, nor the consequences suffered because of it.

"Are you saying their deaths were revenge for a broken heart?"

"I'm not sure Cereli ever loved your father. It was a marriage of convenience. Marrying your father was her way out of the Gold Coast, but because of his disloyalty she was looking at a future of servitude. One of many wives to whichever nobleman her father decided to marry her off to. Humiliated maybe, angry definitely, but heartbroken, I doubt."

"So my parents' deaths were senseless? An act of blind vengeance?"

Faelin shook her head. "Cereli Damask is not a stupid or fragile woman; she found a way to revenge her honor, get out from under the emperor's oppressive rule, and establish her power in the world. Your parents' deaths were very much calculated."

"She sounds evil."

"You would be well not to underestimate her. Even without her dark magic she is a formidable opponent."

The fire crackled as Faelin tossed another log onto it.

"There is another question your father refused to answer," Vallaria said.

"You know curiosity is not a trait elves nurture," Faelin said, rolling her eyes. "But you always were annoyingly inquisitive."

"It's about the child."

"What child?"

"The one who was killed in my place. The one Cereli thought was me. Who was she? What was her name?"

Faelin stiffened. The question was familiar as she'd asked it of her father many times to no avail. "I don't know."

"Please, Faelin."

"Why is this information of importance now?"

Vallaria's ice blue eyes widened, and her jaw clenched. "A child died so I could live. It's a sacrifice worthy of a name, do you not think?"

"She was an orphan under an illusion to look like you. I was never told any more than that. I'm sorry, but I have nothing more."

Nodding, Vallaria shoved the last spoonful of beans in her mouth and wiped her lips with the back of her hand.

"Tell me more about Ravenia, then."

"What do you wish to know?"

"King Elvander told me of its past greatness under my father's rule, but he was always vague when describing its current status."

"Father does not like to infer too much about Ravenia's affairs. It's been a long time since he's entered its lands."

"But you have."

"Not for a while."

"Then tell me what you do know. How has it changed under the dark queen?"

Faelin hunched forward, her eyes reflecting the dancing flames. "Over the years, the Kingdom of Ravenia has fallen into despair. The sun never shines over its lands, instead a perpetual gray cloud base churns overhead. The earth yields little harvest, most of which is paid to the castle for taxes, and the people are starving, barely able to survive on the scraps of food the queen has her royal guards dispatch quarterly. The darkness that rules the kingdom has infected the entire land but the closer to the kingdom you get—" Faelin hesitated. "What is not dead is dying, and any light or spark of hope the citizens had has long been extinguished under a tyrannical rule. Ravenia has more than earned its *dark kingdom* moniker."

"Why do they stay? The citizens?"

"Where would they go? They are poor and hungry and most of the other kingdoms have aligned themselves with the Gold Coast and Ravenia, paying gold and bounties to confirm their loyalty. Fear has captured what little independence and fortitude the smaller kingdoms had. There is nowhere for Ravenia's citizens to run. Only Kasmire remains autonomous. Hidden behind their walls, they rarely interact with the other kingdoms and certainly would not intercede in another's affairs."

"Kasmire?"

"The holy city. A small but mighty kingdom located to the southeast of Mistenvale. In all the centuries of its existence, its walls have never been breached, although many have tried."

"And it has never aligned with the Gold Coast or Ravenia?"

"A holy city nor its kings ever show favor to any, for in their eyes, their god is above all and therefore everyone else is equal to each other."

Vallaria frowned. "I must have missed the books in the library that detail Kasmire."

Shaking her head Faelin said, "The only time pen is put to paper in reference to Kasmire is in creation of the holy scrolls, and none of those have ever been outside of the holy city's rectory. Any writings found in the other kingdoms of man are merely speculation."

"You've been to the holy city."

Faelin's mind drifted back to another time. "Only once."

Seemingly done with her interest in the Kingdom of Kasmire, Vallaria shifted her line of questioning. "How far is the Gold Coast Empire from Ravenia?"

"About a five-day ride. Why do you ask?"

Vallaria shrugged. "Just curious as to how long I would have if I'm discovered and Cereli calls for help."

"Rest assured, the dark queen will not call on the Gold Coast army to dispatch a mere girl. She will happily take care of you herself." Faelin lay back on the blanket. "Enough questions. Get some rest. We have a full day of travel tomorrow."

"Do you think it's possible for me to take the throne back from Queen Cereli?" Vallaria's voice was small and unsure.

Faelin sighed. "There are no assurances in life, Vallaria. The best you can do is try and hope fate will favor your outcome."

Silence hung between them as she watched Vallaria ponder her words. Eventually the princess lay back on her blanket and closed her eyes.

Faelin stared at the shadows dancing on the canyon walls, and her father's voice echoed in her head. *We must prepare Vallaria as best we can and hope she finds the path she is meant to follow and not the one that will lead to all our destruction.*

Sitting up, Faelin glanced at her friend. "There is something else. Someone who could challenge your claim to the throne."

"Who?" Vallaria asked, her eyes springing open.

"Queen Cereli has a son. Prince Zander Damask."

Vallaria leapt to her feet and cursed. "Why did your father never mention this prince? Or you? It seems like an important piece of information."

"Father believes too much information breeds indecision and therefore he tends not to be as forthcoming."

Vallaria placed her hands on her hips and pursed her lips, glaring at the elf as she continued.

"It was not deemed necessary at the time because its importance is debatable."

"How so?"

"Prince Zander left Ravenia when he was a young boy and has not been seen or heard from in years."

"Where did he go?"

"Initially back to the Gold Coast, but his whereabouts since have only been speculations. Some say he sailed across the seas to the continent of Brulle to escape his legacy and its future responsibilities. They believe Prince Zander has no interest in ruling the Kingdom of Ravenia. He does not desire power or want the crown. Others say he captains a ship in the emperor's navy. A few even think he's dead."

"Well, if he's dead he won't be much of a threat."

Faelin narrowed her eyes at Vallaria's sarcasm. "Do not underestimate fate, Vallaria. If the prince is alive, I have no doubt that eventually your paths will cross."

"Why would you think that?"

"Because he will either want the throne or want to avenge his mother's death."

Vallaria's brow raised. "Good point. Let us hope Prince Zander stays exactly wherever he is—lost to the ages. It's a complication I can do without."

"Agreed."

Vallaria tugged at the pocket in her armor. "The stone seems colder."

Faelin's gaze flicked to her friend's hand as she pulled the elemental stone from where she'd hidden it. "I'm sure it's the night air that makes it seem so."

"I guess," Vallaria said, turning the crystal over in her palm and then putting it back in her pocket. "Is there anything else you need to tell me that your father may have intentionally forgotten?"

"I don't believe so."

"Goodnight, then."

"Sleep well," Faelin said, turning her back to Vallaria. Once again she watched the shadows sway across the canyon walls. In the back of her mind, she could feel a subtle vibration that hadn't been apparent before.

It was the elemental stone.

13

VALLARIA

Sleep did not come easily, and when it did, Vallaria tossed and turned, agitated by the nightmare that infiltrated her slumber.

She was back in the meadow, but she was alone aside from the raven who sat high in a tree screeching out a warning. A flicker caught her attention, and once again she was drawn to something beyond the pasture. Although this time it did not disappear—it grew. Like a rip in fabric, the meadow before her split, showing her a world behind this one. Her heart thumped and the raven screeched louder, but she took a step forward anyway.

The rip widened, and she found herself no longer in the green meadow but instead surrounded by a dark wood, the trees dead and misshapen. They creaked and groaned as the wind pushed their limbs back and forth, a chorus of death singing around her.

She stepped through a gap in the tree line and found herself at the edge of a swamp. The water was black and oily, thick like tar. Bubbles rose to the surface and immediately popped, spitting the greasy water in multiple directions. At the middle of the swamp was a knoll, a hill of black dirt covered in brown reeds and patches of dead grass. At its center stood a familiar figure. Dressed in white, her long black hair blowing in the wind, was the little girl—her reflection. Only this time it was not a mirror image—the girl's back was toward Vallaria.

Vallaria. Vall-arrrria.

A strange voice called her name, drawing her attention away from the knoll. When she looked back, the little girl was gone. Her heart pounded and her hands trembled as Vallaria searched the dark swamp for her. But she was nowhere to be seen. She took a step forward and the toe of her shoe kicked something. Laying at her feet, the tips of a crown stuck up from the muddy ground. Its gold was tarnished and the jewels dull and cracked, but somehow she knew it belonged to her. When she stretched her arm toward it, a bloody hand snaked out and grabbed her wrist. She screamed as a face emerged from the swamp.

It was the little girl, but this time her bright blue eyes had been replaced by large black globes. Vallaria screamed again, desperately trying to pull her arm from the girl's grasp, but it was no use. The black waters came up to greet her as she was pulled headfirst into the inky tomb.

Vallaria woke with a start and reached for the dagger she'd tucked under the corner of her blanket. The remnants of the nightmare crept cold across her skin. Nausea threatened to overwhelm her as her belly tied itself in knots and the night's chill wove itself around her.

She shivered and pulled her wool cloak tighter around her shoulders.

A noise echoed through the darkness, a distance swishing noise.

Alerted to the sound, Krest and Siron snorted and pawed the ground.

"Easy," Vallaria whispered as she stood.

The fire had burned down to red embers, and what little glow they cast barely breeched the near darkness.

Vallaria looked to the right. Faelin's form lay still with her back to the firepit.

How can she not hear that?

The swishing noise grew louder as whatever came toward them drew closer.

Her eyes searched the darkness, finally landing on an obscure shadow. It swayed in time with the noise, moving the darkness to the side as it came closer.

Gravel crunched under what Vallaria could only assume were feet.

She gripped the dagger tighter, squinting into the dark. The shape took form, morphing from a blob of black to the silhouette of a person: a person draped in a long black cloak that trailed behind, sweeping over the canyon floor.

Vallaria's voice lay silent in her throat when she tried to call out.

The shadowy figure walked toward her, and the stone in Vallaria's pocket burned ice cold, the leather between its surface and her skin doing little in way of protection. Shifting uncomfortably, Vallaria searched the dark hollow of the hood, trying to make out the face beyond the shadows.

The figure stopped and raised a gnarled finger in Vallaria's direction, and a raspy voice pierced the darkness. "Only death and despair come to those who wear a crown drenched in the blood of innocents."

And then the figure was gone.

Seconds later, a hand clasped her shoulder.

Startled, Vallaria whirled, the blade of her dagger arcing until its tip was nestled against skin. The clouds blocking the moon passed and the canyon was momentarily saturated in a silver glow.

Vallaria stared into lilac eyes.

"Nice move, princess," Faelin said, raising a brow as she pushed the blade from her neck.

"Faelin, what are you doing sneaking up on me? I could have killed you."

A frown marred the elf's perfect skin. "I awoke and you were standing over here, staring into the dark. I called your name, but you didn't respond." Faelin glanced into the dark canyon. "What did you see?"

Her brow furrowed. Faelin hadn't heard or seen the cloaked figure. "Nothing, I thought I heard something, but it was nothing."

"Dawn will break in an hour or so. We might as well pack up and be ready to enter the pass at first light," Faelin said.

Vallaria nodded. She wasn't sure she could sleep again anyway. Her fingers grazed the stone in her pocket. The cold had dissipated, and the surface was now only slightly cool to the touch.

Maybe there was nothing there. Maybe she'd dreamt all of it.

After feeding and watering the horses and eating a breakfast of cornbread and salted meat, Vallaria finished tying the bedroll to the back of Siron's saddle.

"The trek through the pass will take us a quarter of the morning," Faelin said as she adjusted the sword at her side. "It will be a tedious ride, and we may at some points need to walk the horses, but once we're through and enter the grasslands of Ravenia, we should be able to make up time. From here it's about a two-day ride to the city gates. We will time it so we enter the city of Ravenia at night. It's better that way. The less eyes upon the strangers, the better."

"And what about you?" Vallaria asked, gesturing to Faelin's ears and eyes.

"What about me?"

"Are you going to ride through Ravenia as the future elven queen for all to see?"

"Don't be absurd. If I did that, the dark queen herself would meet us at the city gates."

Without another word, Faelin whispered an incantation as she moved her left hand slowly over each ear. Vallaria watched in awe as each pointed tip morphed into rounded curves. Her hand moved to her eyes and then slid through the air over her hair. When she was done, a green-eyed blonde mortal stood looking at Vallaria. Although

Faelin looked exactly as she always did, the magic she engaged changed the perception of all who viewed her. She would now look no different than any other human traveler in the kingdom. Illusion was a powerful elven gift.

"Satisfied?" Faelin said.

"I don't think I will ever get used to that," Vallaria responded.

Faelin mounted her horse and adjusted the crossbow on her back. "Are you ready to see your homeland?"

Vallaria's gloved hands shook as she took Siron's reins. "As ready as I'll ever be."

For all her feigned bravado, Vallaria was glad she had Faelin at her side. The future elven queen was Vallaria's only true friend in Mistenvale, and if the dark kingdom was as bad as King Elvander suspected, then Faelin's experience and knowledge of its mechanisms may come in handy. And if need be, so would her proficiency with a crossbow. And if things went awry, they may find her elven magic useful.

Newly illusioned green eyes locked on hers. "You better pray to your gods, Princess, for we will need all the help and guidance we can get." Digging her boot heels into Krest's side, Faelin took off at a trot toward the opening of the mountain pass.

Wrapped around Vallaria's hand were her father's prayer beads, and she squeezed them as she looked toward the heavens. A stormy sky rumbled in the distance and flashes of angry lightning split the sky.

I'm not sure praying to my gods will do us much good.

14

FAELIN

The trek through the mountain pass had been as Faelin assumed, laborious. A rockslide blocked the trail halfway through and they had to find a secondary route, a treacherous narrow ledge that slowed their progress by hours.

As they galloped through Ravenia's outskirts, rocky outlands morphed into fertile green pastures. Small farms dotted the rolling hills and sheep grazed in clusters on the highlands. Even under a tumultuous gray sky, the lands farthest from the city still cultivated a false sense of tranquility. But deeper, under the external wrappings, Faelin could sense the darkness—the heavy scent of fear and hopelessness.

She closed her eyes, remembering the last time she'd passed this way. It had been many years ago when the princess was but a baby. She'd come with her father for Vallaria's celebration of birth, a merriment that had lasted three days. The entire kingdom had been invited. Peasants and noblemen alike graced the gardens of the castle to welcome their future queen.

It had been a different time and a different kingdom.

Ravenia had been such a happy place then. Full of goodwill and abundance, with rulers who cared for their people. But then—

A piercing scream disrupted Faelin's thoughts, and her eyes flew open in time to see Vallaria charging toward a small farmstead in the distance. "Vallaria," she called, but the princess didn't slow.

"Damn it," she muttered.

Her mare reared as she dug boot heels into its flanks and chased after the fleeing princess. *Where the heck does she think she's going?*

Another scream filled the air as Faelin reached the barn and jumped off her mount. Vallaria had pressed herself up against the wall, her head tilted as she listened to the voices inside.

"Shut up, wench." A male's voice echoed from the interior.

"What do you think you are doing?" Faelin hissed.

Vallaria shrugged and pointed to the darkness that encased the inside of the barn. "Someone needs help."

"So you thought it was your job to provide such assistance?"

Vallaria pulled the dagger, Faelin had gifted her for her birthday, from her boot sheath. "It's the right thing to do."

The elf raised a brow. "It's not the right thing to do if you don't know what you're doing." Faelin tensed as that familiar frustration toward Vallaria surfaced. "You've been out in this world for a day, and you're already acting irrationally. You're supposed to follow *my lead*. How am I supposed to protect you if you act without forethought?"

"I never asked for your protection," Vallaria said before slipping through the barn's doorway and disappearing into the shadows.

The defiance in her tone was one Faelin had heard before, every time she'd intervened in an altercation between Vallaria and Riva. "I don't need your protection or your pity," Vallaria would say through clenched teeth before stomping off. It was at these times Vallaria showed her naivety for how the world—and friendships—worked.

Swearing under her breath, Faelin took the crossbow from her back, cocked it, and followed Vallaria into the outbuilding.

The scent of fresh hay filled her nostrils.

Her eyes adjusted to the shadowy interior, and she saw Vallaria just ahead, back pressed against a barn support beam, and the dagger, its blade gleaming in the dim light, gripped firmly in her hand.

Faelin's eyes narrowed, and she shook her head, silently warning Vallaria not to be rash.

Grunts echoed, followed by nervous laughter and the sound of a female crying. Faelin pressed a finger to her lips as they rounded the stalls lining the large barn. Only two were occupied, but the old mares cared little about what was happening around them, content instead to nibble on their hay buckets. A double door at the back of the barn was flung wide open and the gray light of late day flooded in, dispersing the shadows and highlighting the scene playing out in front of them.

"Save some for me," a male voice said.

Two men. One lay on top of a young woman in a mound of hay, the other, younger, stood over them fondling himself as he watched. The woman's skirt had been lifted above her waist, and her legs splayed wide. She struggled beneath her assailant. Faelin's gaze drifted over the nauseating scene, and she was surprised to note that both men wore the uniform of Ravenia's royal guards.

A third man, older and presumably the farmer of the property, lay face down on the barn floor a few feet away. A gash on his head still bled, pooling on the floorboards, but the slight up and down movement of his back indicated he was still breathing.

The young woman cried out again as the man on top of her continued his assault. In response he slapped her hard across her cheek.

"Shut your mouth," he roared. "Let me finish in peace."

The younger guard laughed.

Before Faelin could lift her crossbow, Vallaria leaped from the shadows and clapped her hand over the young guard's mouth, placing the blade of her dagger at his throat. Irked, Faelin stepped from the shadows into his field of vision, her index finger placed against her lips, warning him to be silent as she pointed the crossbow at his companion's head.

Vallaria kicked the grunting guard in the leg.

"I'll be done in a minute. Wait your damn turn."

Vallaria kicked him again. This time the toe of her boot slipped between his pimply ass cheeks. Faelin grimaced as the man yelped and rolled off the young woman. His ruddy face paled as he glanced between the two women, surprised to see Vallaria with a blade at his companion's throat and Faelin with a bolt aimed at his head. He scrambled to stand, then grabbed at the trousers bunched at his feet.

Faelin stepped forward, lowered her crossbow, and grasped the man by his throat. He grimaced but stood quiet in front of her, desperately trying to cover his shriveled manhood with his hands.

"Why are you here?" she asked, giving his throat a squeeze.

The man Vallaria held whined.

Faelin turned in his direction.

In that split second, the older guard slammed his arm down on hers, pulling her hand away from his throat. He slipped a small knife from a hidden pocket in his sleeve and swiped at Faelin, catching her in the cheek with the point of the blade. A warmth tickled her cheek as she brought up the heel of her boot and connected with his midsection before he could swipe at her again. He gasped in pain, doubled over, and clutched his stomach before his pants, still bunched at his ankles and restricting his movement, brought him lurching to the floor in a heap.

In one precise movement the crossbow landed on the barn floor and Faelin unsheathed her sword, pointing it at the cowering half-naked guard at her feet.

"Shall we try this again?" she asked, wiping the blood from her cheek with the back of her hand. After allowing him to stand and pull up his trousers, she nodded toward the other guard, indicating he should move beside his companion.

While they stood shoulder to shoulder eyes downcast, Faelin circled them, dragging her sword along their middles. Without breaking pace, she said. "Vallaria, could you please check on the well-being of the farmer?"

A few moments later, after assessing his condition, Vallaria said, "He's unconscious but breathing. The gash on his head has stopped bleeding. It looks worse than it is. Nothing a few stitches from his daughter's sewing kit won't close."

Faelin's gaze shifted briefly to the young girl, who huddled in the corner of the barn. Faelin came to face the older guard and stopped, pushing the tip of her sword into the toe of his boot.

He winced.

"What is your name?"

The man spit in her face.

Vallaria took a step forward, but Faelin raised her hand to stop her.

She wiped the sit from her face. "I see your manners are still misplaced."

With the speed of a barn cat, Faelin lifted her sword straight up, catching the elder guard under the chin with the butt end of the pommel. The man's head snapped back, and blood began to seep from the corner of his mouth.

The young guard beside him began to cry.

Faelin's gaze flitted to him. "And what is your name?"

The man, looking like he was about to faint, stammered, "Johansson."

"Okay, Johansson. What are you doing this far away from the castle?"

The young guard's eyes flicked to the older man. "We are collecting taxes owed to the Crown, ma'am."

"Are you?" Faelin looked toward the young woman. Tears streaked her face as she huddled in the hay, desperately trying to cover her breasts with her torn dress. "And is this how your queen expects you to extract such payment from her subjects?"

The horrified look on the face of the young guard was answer enough. Faelin had no idea what the dark queen would think or if she would even care but it was apparent the guards didn't know either. What was apparent was how terrified they both became when she mentioned the queen.

They are more afraid of her than my sword.

Faelin's eyes darkened with disgust. "You didn't answer my question."

Both guards paled, and the one who hadn't gotten a chance at the young woman shook violently before blurting out, "It wasn't my idea."

The older guard, face still ruddy from his recent exertion, shot him a dirty look. "Shut your mouth, boy."

Faelin glared at the older man. Without warning she grabbed him by the balls with her gloved hand.

He winced and groaned.

"Being vulnerable to someone else is humiliating, isn't it? Especially when you have no power to fight back."

Her hand tightened as a surge of unwelcomed emotions flared. Anger at the royal guards who stood before her. Resentment at Vallaria for putting them in this predicament. Sorrow that the world outside Mistenvale had become so broken.

Guilt that she couldn't save Baladril.

The corner of her mouth twitched. Annoyance at herself for allowing the memory of that day to control her.

In front of her, the guard's eyes filled with tears and his face reddened. "Please, don't," he gasped, sucking in air as the pain she inflicted inflamed his lower regions. The younger guard took a step back and involuntarily covered his manhood.

Faelin released his genitals. "I think it's time you apologize to the young lady."

15

VALLARIA

Vallaria had fought Faelin many times in the arena and watched her battle with hardened warriors in training but never had she seen the elf exert her skills in actuality. It wasn't her exceptional fighting abilities or tactical acumen that Vallaria witnessed when dealing with the royal guards—there was something else. Her demeanor had changed as well. She became cold, hardened, lacking any emotional intensity. Her calm, calculated movements were finite, leaving little room for error.

Although the elves experienced emotions, they were not driven by them. They rarely showed them, and it was even rarer for an elf to express elevated emotions. In the past Vallaria had seen Faelin disappointed, angry, even upset at times, but never had she seen her lose control or allow the emotions to control her.

No outbursts.

She thought about how many times she'd lost her cool at Riva or the king, thrown her sword, or kicked the earth. Over the years she'd cried uncontrollably, raised her voice, and had verbal meltdowns. Never once had there ever been any return outburst from an elf. They always remained calm, cool, and collected. Even Riva managed to make Vallaria feel small without raising her voice or her fists.

King Elvander, Thaneil, and Faelin had all told her at one time or another that emotions were a weakness. That this was man's greatest downfall—being driven by his emotions. And in her first day outside the kingdom, she had proven them right.

Upon hearing the scream, she'd run headlong into a situation she knew nothing about and was ill-prepared for. Her emotions had overruled her instinct. Her desire to prove herself had overshadowed her critical-thinking skills. She'd acted only out of a sense of superiority, and it could have gotten them in big trouble or worse if the guards had not been otherwise preoccupied.

A clap of thunder erupted overhead, and a large bolt of lightning split the sky in two. The dark clouds opened up and rain poured down, soaking the lands in seconds.

Taking a few steps back into the barn, she waited for Faelin to finish tending to the farmer.

A few moments later, the elf stood beside her, green eyes cast to the sky.

"How are they?" Vallaria asked.

"The scars on the outside will heal long before the ones on the inside." Faelin stood still, her pale skin shining with the mist from the rain that pummeled to the ground.

Vallaria shifted her stance and leaned against the barn door, waiting. She could sense the elf had much more to say.

"Is this how it's going to be?" Faelin asked.

"What do you mean?"

"You, running off toward danger without forethought of what you may find when you get there."

"They needed our help."

"A fact that is not in dispute, but in order to help, you must first be able to do so ably." Faelin turned to look at her. The disappointment radiating from her eyes made Vallaria feel ashamed. "What if there had been more guards or they'd seen us coming and ambushed us as you ran headlong into the dark barn?"

"I didn't think. I reacted."

"That is the type of behavior that will get you killed out here. Your naivety with regards to the realms of man already put you at a disadvantage. If you do not learn to control your impulses, you will not get very far in your quest for the throne."

"You're right. I'm sorry."

"I don't want you to be sorry. I want you to listen, learn, and always be aware that in this place danger is around every corner, even if you can't see it. You are not immune from the violence or from the bad people who exist in Ravenia because you are unknown. You must sharpen your instincts and learn to modify your approach. You are not in Mistenvale anymore."

Faelin walked out into the rain. "Don't fail me again, Vallaria."

Her words were a gut punch. The world of man had tested her, and she'd failed.

While she watched the elf walk to the farmhouse, Vallaria realized if she were to rule as queen, she would need to hone her instincts. But more than that she would need to be more ruthless and a lot less emotional.

She would need to be more like Faelin.

"COME IN QUICKLY, BEFORE YOU CATCH YOUR DEATH OF COLD." THE farmer's daughter, whose name was Ivina, beckoned at her from the open door as Vallaria ran through the downpour. She'd changed out of her torn dress, replacing it with a dark blue skirt and white blouse over which she wore a gray apron. Ivina's cheeks were flushed and her skin pale, but when she smiled, it was warm and inviting.

She reminded Vallaria of Kelena, and her heart clenched at the memory of the elf who'd helped raise her. *What would she think of my reckless actions?*

"Can I take your cloak?" Ivina asked, pointing at the soggy red wool around Vallaria's shoulders. Shaking the rain from her hair, she took off her mother's travel cloak and handed it to her.

"I'll place it by the fire. It will dry quickly."

"Thank you," Vallaria said, stepping farther into the room.

Faelin sat at the small kitchen table and she joined her.

"How is your father?" Vallaria inquired, her eyes searching for the man.

"He is resting, thank you. The cut was minor, and I was able to patch it without much difficulty. I think his pride is hurt more than anything."

Ivina shifted uncomfortably, and she leaned forward, lowering her voice. Her eyes welled with tears. "My father was knocked unconscious before the men—" She straightened and stuffed her hands in her apron pockets. "I would appreciate if you didn't tell him what you saw."

Vallaria opened her mouth to object, but Faelin reached over and placed a hand on her arm, silencing her.

"Of course. If that is your wish, we will not speak of it again," the elf said as she shot Vallaria a firm look. Releasing her arm, she stood and walked toward the fire where a large black cauldron hung. "It smells wonderful. What is it?"

Ivina smiled. "My mother's stew. I hope you like it."

"I'm positive we will and again thank you for putting us up for the night."

"It's the least we can do. Anyway, no one should be out in a storm like this, especially at night. You can't see your hand in front of your face, what with the rain coming down in blinding torrents. No, it is much better for you to resume your journey tomorrow."

"Where is it you're heading?" The voice was gruff, worn by age and years of hard labor. Vallaria turned to see the farmer, his shock of gray hair rumpled, standing in the bedroom doorway. A white strip of cloth wound around his head, marred by a small stain of blood.

"Father, you should be in bed."

"I'm fine, Ivina, stop fussing. I owe a debt of gratitude to these fine ladies."

"You owe us nothing," Faelin said.

"Well, that is a matter of opinion." The farmer nodded and shuffled to the table where Vallaria sat, indicating Faelin should join them. "And what of the two guards?"

Faelin sat at the table and clasped her hands together. "They won't bother you again."

Vallaria glanced at Faelin, but the elf did not return her gaze.

The altercation in the barn ended quickly. The royal guards had been completely castrated, metaphorically speaking, by Faelin. Despite their disgusting behavior, Vallaria was surprised when Faelin let them go.

Pulling the silver coin from the older guard's pocket, she'd said, "If I see you anywhere near this farmstead again or hear you've touched a woman without her consent, I will find you and make sure you don't see the start of a new day. Do we understand each other?"

The guards nodded and without another word or backward glance, they'd hightailed it, as fast as their steads would run, back toward the kingdom.

The farmer, sensing Faelin's conviction, turned to his daughter. "Get the whisky, Ivina. Our visitors deserve a stiff drink along with a hot meal." He shifted his bulk in the small wooden chair and looked at Vallaria. "So what luck brought you to my doorstep?"

"We were journeying past."

And where might you be heading, if you don't might the inquiry?"

"To the city of Ravenia."

The warning in Faelin's eyes stopped Vallaria from saying anything else.

'To the city, you say."

Vallaria nodded, noticing the look of concern that passed quickly between the farmer and his daughter, and knowing Faelin saw it as well.

"Is there a problem?" Faelin asked.

The farmer turned his weary gaze back to her. "Not a problem, really. You will be heading into the heart of the kingdom during a trying time is all."

Faelin tapped her long fingers on the tabletop. "What do you mean by that?"

"I'm surprised you haven't heard. Most of the kingdom and many outsiders will be in the city." He leaned in and lowered his voice. "Queen Cereli is executing a traitor in a few days. It will be quite the spectacle, I fear."

The farmer leaned back and crossed his arms in front of his barrel chest as Ivina placed steaming bowls of stew in front of them and a plate of bread at the table's center.

"Who is she executing?" Vallaria asked, noticing a pinched expression briefly mar Faelin's face.

The farmer shrugged and took a mouthful of stew. "Who knows? Someone from inside the castle walls. This is the third one in as many months. Rumors have been circulating that the queen has become increasingly paranoid and no longer trusts anyone save her royal guard commander and a few close advisors."

"Why is she so mistrustful?" Vallaria asked.

"I don't know much more. We are quite isolated here at the edge of the kingdom, but we hear things. People speculate that the queen is going mad. You know, the dark magic and all."

"Dark magic?" Faelin asked.

Vallaria frowned hearing the elf's question. Why was she pretending to not know of the queen's powers?

The farmer eyed Faelin. "Where did you say you were from?"

"We didn't."

Ivina shifted uncomfortably and, with a shaking hand, reached for the whisky, pouring more into her father's cup. The farmer pulled on his beard as his eyes flicked back and forth between his two guests.

"Well, there are stories, that harken back to the time of the overthrow when King Torrsen and Queen Cereli stormed the castle and stole the throne from King Ryguard and Queen Evinna. Sad day that was."

Vallaria's breath hitched when she heard her parents' names. Hearing the story from someone other than an elf made it all too real. "Did you know my pa . . . the Ravenia family?" Emotion cloaked her voice as she blurted out the question before she could stop herself.

The toe of a boot kicked her under the table, and she realized Ivina and her father were staring at her with quizzical expressions.

"Are you all right, Vallaria?" Ivina asked.

"Yes, sorry—please, you were saying?" She faked a smile and uncurled her fingers, which had become white knuckled from the grip on her spoon.

The farmer grunted. "Where was I? Oh yes, sad day. King Ryguard and Queen Evinna were fair and honest rulers, and the kingdom was a much different place back then." The farmer raised a callous hand and rubbed the bandage that covered the stitches his daughter had sewn into the gash on his forehead. "After their deaths, rumors swirled about Queen Cereli's dark magic. She carries a staff, you know. Awful thing, the glass at the top churns with black smoke."

"You've seen it?" Faelin asked.

"Once, long ago." The farmer coughed and took a sip of his whisky. "They say it's the dark magic she discovered when she disposed of the bodies."

"The bodies?" Vallaria repeated, her voice cracking.

"You really don't know much about the stories, do you?" the farmer said shaking his head.

"We haven't been to these parts in a long while." Faelin cast Vallaria a sidelong glance.

"You know Queen Evinna was elf kind. Queen Cereli hated the

elves. Blamed them for almost everything. Although she eventually gave King Ryguard a burial in the royal plot, she did not want her kingdom tainted with the blood of elves, so she disposed of them like garbage."

"Them?" Vallaria's heart began to pound and the room suddenly felt extremely warm.

"Queen Evinna and her daughter, Princess Serifine." He frowned. "Are you all right, girl?"

Vallaria felt nauseated.

"She's fine. Please continue," Faelin said.

"Like I said, she didn't want them in the kingdom, but she couldn't throw their bodies anywhere. They were elves after all, and she was fearful of King Elvander. People say she took them where they would never be found—the tar pits on the Isle of Haddes."

Vallaria tried to swallow the lump that had formed in her throat, but her mouth had no moisture. The images from the dream last night roiled through her mind. *The black oily water, the smell of death and decay. Could it be the same place?* Her stomach lurched as a sweaty heat rose on her skin.

"What about the dark magic?" Faelin asked, redirecting the farmer's story.

"Oh yes. After Queen Cereli came back from the Isle of Haddes, she was different."

"In what way?"

"Well, the staff for one thing. She had it made almost immediately and is never without it. Then King Torrsen died unexpectedly. After his death, the queen grew crueler and cared less and less for her subjects. Townspeople say she brought a darkness back from that unholy place and is tainted by it herself. You know they call her the dark queen?"

"I do," Faelin acknowledged. "You seem to know a lot about Queen Cereli."

The farmer leaned back in his chair. "I used to work in the city of Ravenia long ago. Blacksmith. But after the overthrow and Ivina was born, I thought it best to get as far away as possible. I may live a simple life, but I have connections still. And even out here on the edges of the kingdom rumors find their way. Anyway, it's all stories and hearsay mostly. All I know for sure is the queen does not take kindly to those that betray her, and the consequences are severe."

"Executions?" Faelin said.

"Yes, and very public. Everyone fears the queen."

"What is the Isle of Haddes?" Vallaria asked, finally getting her voice back.

Faelin turned her head. "It's a small island off the most northern tip of the continent. It's a place of death. No one goes there. To my knowledge no one has for centuries."

"Because its cursed." The farmer slammed his fist on the table.

Vallaria jumped.

A ruddiness covered his face and a small dribble of saliva slid from the corner of his mouth. "It's a place where darkness rises from the unholy places and pilfers the land of its life. No one goes there because they would never return. Except Queen Cereli did. What does that tell you?"

The farmer's statement rang in Vallaria's ears. What had she gotten herself into?

Faelin cast Vallaria a withered look. "It's getting late and we have a long journey ahead of us tomorrow." She stood. "Thank you for the warm meal and the drink. Your company and your hospitality are much appreciated."

The farmer smiled. "It is the least I can do after what you did for us." He squeezed his daughter's hand. "I wish I could offer you more than the barn to sleep in, but at least it will be dry and warm."

"The barn is fine; we would be sleeping under the sky otherwise."

Faelin grabbed her crossbow from where it lay against the wall and opened the door.

Vallaria reached out a hand to the farmer. "Thank you."

The older man took it, cocking his head as he narrowed his eyes.

"You look familiar. Are you sure our paths have not crossed prior to this day?"

"I'm sure." Pulling her hand away, she shook her head. "I haven't been in the kingdom since my childhood." As she walked out the door, she could feel the curious stare of the farmer follow her.

But they say I look just like my father.

16

FAELIN

The light was bleak and dark rain clouds collected overhead as they left the open farmlands and entered one of the small villages located outside the city of Ravenia.

Faelin pulled up her cowl and frowned.

A storm was coming.

She missed the sunny warmth of Mistenvale.

"Let us stop here for a few hours, get something to eat, and water the horses. This is the village of Brae, and it is only a few hour's ride from here to the city gates, and I would prefer to enter the city of Ravenia after dark."

After leaving the horses and a few pieces of silver with the blacksmith, Faelin and Vallaria wandered down the muddy streets toward the tavern. Most of the buildings were unlit, some boarded up against the coming winter. Many were dilapidated. The candles in the streetlamps cut a small hole in the surrounding darkness, but the town reeked of desperation. It had been a long while since she'd travelled through these parts, but nothing was the same. It was like the lands had been drained of life and the people of joy.

Darkness seeped through this land at will because of Queen Cereli Damask.

Few people were out on the streets and those that were dared not look at the strangers in town.

"They look scared," Vallaria said.

Before Faelin could reply a small voice spoke from the shadows. "Spare some coin, ma'am."

She stopped and turned to see a small girl no older than eight huddled under the eaves at the end of an alley. Her coat was tattered, her dress frayed and full of holes. Patches haphazardly placed, covered the hose encasing her spindly legs. Dirt streaked her small face, encircled by a tangled mess of red hair that she tugged at, as she looked up in misery.

Faelin stooped down and took the girl's hand. The skin was rough and cold. Turning it over so the small palm faced up, she asked. "Where is your mother?"

The little girl pointed into the dark alley. "Mama's sleeping."

"Tessie, where are you, girl?" a hoarse voice cried as a woman stumbled from the dark. She took one look at Faelin with her long blonde braid, green eyes, and black leather outfit, sword strapped to her hip, and grabbed her daughter, pulling the little girl back into the folds of her skirt. "I don't have any money and I don't want no trouble."

Faelin raised her hands shoulder height. "There is no trouble here."

"Who are you?" the woman asked.

Tessie stared up at Faelin with big brown eyes. "She's pretty."

Behind her Vallaria suppressed a laugh.

Raising an eyebrow, she said, "We are just passing through on our way to the city."

The lady eyed them with suspicion. "Attending the execution, are ya?"

"What do you know of the execution?"

"Nothing more than it has become a regular occurrence. The

queen's been a might paranoid of late. Best to stay out of her way, I say."

"Do you know who is being executed?" Faelin asked.

"Someone she deems a traitor, I suspect. Could be anyone." The woman wrapped her arms tighter around her daughter. "No one is safe from her wrath these days."

"This is her doing, isn't it? The queen." Vallaria's blue eyes scanned the meager town and its unhappy, starving residents.

"The queen cares little for us," the lady said, her eyes filling with tears. "Our lands are no longer fertile, yet she sends her guards to take more than half of the meager crops we sow each year yet taxes us on the full harvest. Our cows and chickens produce less because they don't get the feed they need. And now winter is upon us, and we don't have enough food to see us through to spring."

Vallaria came to stand beside them. "Is it like this everywhere across the kingdom?"

"Nothing is good anymore. Not for a long time," the woman confirmed. "Even those in the city are not as fortunate as they once were."

"Do you have somewhere to go?" Faelin asked. She'd seen other villagers sitting on benches, in alleyways, and on doorstops.

The woman shook her head as more tears rolled down her cheeks. "Lost my husband last year to sickness and our farm shortly after. The royal guard claimed the land under a tax seizure. The crops died and now the land sits there unused. The house is boarded up. I've been there on occasion, but it's filled with vermin. I work at the livery stable and the tavern, and every few days I make enough to get us a room, a hot meal, and a bath."

Faelin eyed the filth caked onto the woman's exposed skin. *It's been more than a few days.* She reached into her satchel and extracted a handful of silver coins, placing them in the woman's rough and calloused palm. "Get some food and a warm bed for a few nights."

The woman stared at the money in her shaking palm with wide eyes. Thanking Faelin for her generosity, she tucked the silver into the pocket of her soiled apron. With her arm draped protectively around her daughter, she led them back into the shadows to collect their things.

"The kingdom is dying and so are its people," Vallaria said, rubbing the back of her neck.

Faelin sensed her anguish and ire. "You must heed Thaneil's warning. This is not about vengeance. Not for your parents' deaths and not for them." Her head tilted toward the mother and daughter as they walked down the muddy street, a tattered blanket around their shoulders. They disappeared around a corner, and Faelin's mind wandered to the past.

During a time when man still accepted the help of elves and magic was not feared, Faelin would sometimes go with her mother to small villages like this one providing care and medicine to those in need. Her mother had been a prolific healer. Gifted with the power of intuition and blessed by the magic of their people, she was skilled at herbalism and elixir brewing and healed many outside their realm. Her mother believed it was her duty to help mankind, even after Baladril's execution when the elves distanced themselves from the human realms. At the time of her death, her mother still believed in the good of man.

I wonder what she would think of them now.

"Faelin." Vallaria's tight voice roused her from her thoughts. "The queen deserves to die for what she has done."

Faelin lifted her chin and cast Vallaria a stern gaze. "The queen may deserve much, but nothing good ever comes from a dark, vengeful heart. It will be wise for you to remember that."

JUST AS THEY REACHED THE OUTER GATES OF THE CITY, THE NIGHT SKY cracked with streaks of lightning and a thunderous roar. Faelin watched as Vallaria squirmed in her saddle as Siron reared, spooked by the volatile night and the shadowy wall looming before them.

Rain began to fall. The storm was upon them.

There was no turning back now.

The princess of Ravinia had come home. Soon Vallaria would be judged on whether she was worthy of the destiny laid out before her.

Faelin could still feel the vibrating hum of the mage crystal in Vallaria's pocket. As they passed through the gates and into the city, the elemental magic pulsating through the rock grew stronger. She pulled her hood farther over her face as the cold rain plummeted down upon them. Her eyes drifted to Vallaria as she rode beside her, the bluish glow of the stone barely visible through the fabric of her heavy cloak.

A massive crack of lightning streaked through the sky, igniting the darkness with a pale white hue, and drawing Faelin's gaze to the high peaks of the castle towers in the distance. She gripped the reins tighter.

If the dark queen doesn't kill us, the powers of the last mage just might.

17

VALLARIA

Under the hiss of the pouring rain, Vallaria could make out the echoing sounds of the city's underbelly as they passed along the mostly deserted streets. The rhythmic clop of horse hooves as they hit the cobbled stones, shouts echoing from the darkness, and the screeching creak of signs as they blew in the wind all filled the spaces behind the unmelodious thrum of the rain.

While she followed Faelin, a shiver caressed her skin and she shrunk deeper into her cloak. The city was no less depressing than the small village on its outskirts.

The outer gate had been manned by two guards, and Vallaria remained silent, her eyes downcast, as Faelin explained who they were and why they were in Ravenia.

"Just passing through on our way to the docks on the west coast. Need to rest the horses for a day or two and then we will be on our way."

The guard, grim-faced had nodded. "The Rosewater Inn is at the far end of the main street. You will find lodging there."

They passed along the deserted streets heading toward the inn. The hair on the back of Vallaria's neck prickled. Her blue eyes scanned the street, but no one was about except a drunk passed out in a doorway.

Why then do I feel like I'm being watched?

The clay and stone buildings glistened under the lamplight as they passed. Slick with rain, the walls and roofs reflected the dim light and enhanced the glow the lights cast along the street.

Shivers erupted on her skin, and from the corner of her eye, Vallaria saw movement. She adjusted her gaze up toward a streetlamp, squinting against the candle's blaze as it flickered in its glass sphere. Sitting quietly at the lamp's peak was a large black bird. It returned Vallaria's gaze, then shook its feathers, spraying rainwater off its back. The raven cocked its head, its dark stare penetrating. Without warning it screeched, tapping its long talons on the metal post. Its eyes followed them as they passed and then without another sound it spread its wings and flew deftly into the stormy night sky.

It was the second raven she'd seen in as many weeks.

Vallaria watched it disappear. Although she was sure Faelin must have seen and heard the raven, she made no reference to its existence.

Suddenly, Krest came to an abrupt halt in front of her and the elf raised a hand indicating silence.

Vallaria could tell by the tilt of her head Faelin was listening as she stopped Siron and waited. The elf must have heard something behind the ambient sounds filling the night air. Vallaria closed her eyes, trying to hear anything other than the tedious hiss of the rain, but it was all she heard, and all she felt was the chill of its touch.

"What is it?" she whispered loud enough for Faelin to hear as the elf scanned the street.

Using the back of her hand, Vallaria wiped the water from her eyes. Through the rain a mix of scuffles and cries reached her ears. Digging her boot heels into her horse's flank, she followed Faelin, who was already trotting toward an alley up ahead in the direction of the noise.

When she peered into the shadowed alley, Vallaria could make out three figures. Two silhouettes were large and menacing, the other small and cowering.

Something was amiss and Faelin had sensed it.

She dismounted, tied her reins to a hitching post, and followed Faelin into the alley.

The drumbeat of rain drowned out their footsteps.

Vallaria pulled her mother's sword from its sheath as Faelin readied her crossbow. The weight of the blade felt comfortable in her hand but as she walked slowly down the alley toward the figures, an uneasy sensation crept over her skin.

Could she use this sword on another?

The slick stones of the building thrust a damp cold through her clothes as she pressed her back against the wall. Keeping to the shadows, she continued to follow Faelin deeper into the alley. They neared, and Vallaria could make out two men and a small boy. Inching closer, she heard their voices over the thrum of the rain.

"You're a bloody thief," one man said as he poked a knife at the small boy. "And thieves end up with their throats cut in dark alleys."

"I didn't steal nothin' from you." The boy, shaking, shrunk away from the man.

"Ya did. I was in the tavern enjoying my ale and suddenly my money pouch was missing. You took it, and I want it back, ya filthy little shat."

The man grabbed the small boy by his coat and hefted him up against the wall. "Maybe we should run him through and be done with it, Horace."

"Or maybe you should let the boy go before you regret it." Faelin was about ten feet from the men, and as they turned, surprise marred their faces.

"This ain't none of your concern, wench," the other man said as he rubbed the raining drizzle off his ruddy face and unkempt beard. He was tall and slim, and his pants were too short.

"Oh, but it is," she responded. "Two grown men picking on a small boy doesn't seem quite fair."

"And what you gonna do about it?"

The glint of metal caught Vallaria's eye as Faelin raised her crossbow.

The man took a step back.

"My friend here is an expert marksman," Vallaria said, tightening the grip on her sword and taking a few steps forward. "Unless you would like to find out how good her aim is, I suggest you let the boy go and walk away." Her eyes searched out the small face pinned to the wall. Wide-eyed, he stared directly at Faelin.

The man holding the boy released him and turned to face them. He was a stout fellow, mostly bald, wearing a tattered leather coat, and when he leered Vallaria noticed many of his teeth were missing.

He flashed his blade at them. "Maybe I'll cut both your pretty faces and leave you in the alley for the rats to feast upon."

"Do you really want to do that?" Faelin asked.

"That and much more, girlie," he said, grabbing his crotch to make his point.

"Wrong answer," Vallaria heard Faelin say seconds before the trigger of the crossbow clicked and the bolt pierced the burly man's left eye. His body trembled slightly before it collapsed in a heap on the saturated ground. The blood running from his mangled eye pooled with the rainwater and flowed in a stream of red down the cobblestones.

The slender tall man stood staring in shock at the body before coming to his senses and running.

Vallaria inched toward the body and squatted down. With the bolt protruding from one eye and the other staring blankly at the stormy sky, she discerned him to be dead, but she felt for a pulse anyway.

"Did you need to kill him?" she asked, glancing up at Faelin. "We are supposed to keep a low profile. Your words. How in the gods is killing a man accomplishing that?"

Faelin cast Vallaria a stern gaze and hoisted the crossbow onto her back. "Sometimes plans change and things you hadn't intended happen." She lowered her voice. "If you think getting to the queen will be easy because of a carefully constructed plan, you are more naïve than I thought."

Faelin walked to where Vallaria squatted and yanked the bolt from the man's socket.

Nausea rose in Vallaria's gullet as the eyeball made a squishy pop as it fell from the bolt's tip and landed in a bloody puddle.

"Wake the gods, Faelin!" she yelped, jumping to her feet.

Disgusted, she turned her attention to the boy, who huddled in a corner, trembling. He looked so small and vulnerable, and she guessed he couldn't be more than nine or ten years of age.

"Are you well?" Vallaria asked as she walked over and bent down to give him a quick once-over. An old scar cut across his left cheek and small abrasions marred his dark skin. His clothing, nothing more than tattered rags, clung to his small frame. His tall leather boots were worn and a part of one sole had cracked.

"Those men won't bother you again," Faelin said, glancing down at the body.

Vallaria took the boy's small hand and helped him up. "Come, let's get you warm."

They walked from the alley, and Vallaria pulled a wool blanket from her sleeping roll, wrapping it around the shivering boy.

He smiled, an innocent toothless grin that made him look even younger.

"Do you have a name?" she asked.

"Pax," the boy whispered.

"Well Pax, we are going to have to get you out of these wet clothes before you catch your death. Where is your home?"

His eyes got big as they flitted back and forth between Vallaria and Faelin. He shook his head and pulled the blanket tighter around his small frame.

"He's a street urchin, Vallaria."

Torrents of water ran down the streets and gushed into the muddy gutters and overstressed drains. Light from the streetlamps blurred by the rising fog flickered weakly in the dark night. Apart from the odd drunk, not a soul roamed the streets. It was a nasty night. No one should be without shelter in these conditions, not in the Kingdom of Ravenia. A chill had begun to settle in her bones as the dampness penetrated her cloak. She looked down at his small vulnerable face.

My parents would have never let this happen and neither will I.

Vallaria scooped up the small boy and put him on the horse.

"Then he shall stay with us for the night."

Faelin raised a brow but didn't object. "The inn isn't far."

ONCE SHE HAD PAX WRAPPED IN ONE OF HER TUNICS, TUCKED INTO THE warm bed, and the fire roaring, Vallaria turned her attention to Faelin, who moments before had walked into the room.

She pursed her lips and crossed her arms. "Are you sure the queen won't send the guards to investigate the dead man in the alley?"

"I'm not sure of anything the queen may or may not do."

"And what about the other man? The one who ran away. What if he says something?"

"I doubt he will. No one wants the attention of Queen Cereli. Certainly not with the executions piling up at her whim."

Faelin's calm nature irritated Vallaria. She'd put a bolt through the eye of a stranger without pause and seemed completely unfazed by any consequences that may be forthcoming. The elves' stoic and aloof demeanors often irked and baffled Vallaria—and today was no different. Within her long life, Faelin had seen and done many things. She was worldly, an exceptional warrior, and one day she would be a great leader. Maybe it was time for Vallaria to stop judging and instead take note.

Resigned, Vallaria changed the subject. "Did you see the boy's ear?"

"You mean the lack of one?"

Vallaria cringed at how easy it was for Faelin to lack empathy. "Yes."

"I've heard of this practice. Many of the street urchins steal food, clothes, necessities, but occasionally they steal money. Money that belongs to the Crown. The dark queen has always ruled her kingdom with a firm hand, believing a quick judgment and severe consequences are just. Mutilating a thief, especially a child, sends a strong message. Unfortunately, the poor only steal to survive, hence, although the punishment is rendered, no lesson is learned and the cycle continues."

Vallaria looked back at a sleeping Pax. "Queen Cereli did that to him?"

Faelin shook her head. "Never does the blood of innocents touch the queen's hands. All punishments come at the hands of her royal guard commander, whether they be mutilations or executions. He is a vicious man who delights in inflicting pain on others and apparently has no qualms when it comes to children."

"You know him?"

The elf unbuckled her sword and placed it on the table. Jade eyes turned back to Vallaria as a shadow crossed through them. "I have run into him over the years." Before Vallaria could inquire further, Faelin lifted a perfectly sculpted brow and said, "It is also rumored that he bathes in the blood of his victims, but I am not convinced that has any truth to it."

Whatever the truth, wariness of any close to the queen was pertinent. *Learn the landscape and the players,* the elf king had warned, *before you enter the queen's domain.* The royal guard commander may provide the most hinderance to her plan, so once inside, watching him, knowing his schedule, understanding his mindset would be paramount. If she couldn't get by him, there probably wasn't much hope in claiming back the throne. But if she caught his attention, she may very well end up a victim of his specific brand of cruelty.

"By the way where did you go?" Vallaria asked.

Faelin had left moments after they'd procured lodging and was gone for a good part of the hour. "We are to meet Alagarn after sunrise tomorrow. I went to retrieve the message of confirmation that my father had notified him and that the meeting was a go."

The elf's composure cracked slightly.

"What's wrong?" Vallaria asked.

"There was no message."

Behind Vallaria, the fire popped and crackled, startling her. "What does that mean?"

"It could mean one of many things. My father's contacts were unable to reach him or Alagarn was unable to get a message to the proposed spot without being detected. . . ." Faelin trailed off.

Vallaria's grip tightened on the chairback she leaned against. "What do we do?"

"Nothing changes. We go to the proposed meeting spot in the morning like planned."

"And if Alagarn does not show?"

"He will."

Although Faelin's voice remained steady, the furrow of her brow left Vallaria with uncertainty.

"Do you think I can do this, Faelin?"

The elf frowned. "Do what?"

"Take back the crown, the throne, revive the kingdom, regain my family legacy." She sighed. "All of it."

"You have done all you can to prepare. It is not enough to be good with a sword, you must also be knowledgeable about the world you intend to infiltrate. Tactics come from a sharp mind," Faelin said, tapping her temple with a forefinger. "You have studied the tomes and scrolls in Mistenvale's library, you have listened to my father and Commander Cyran, and you have accepted my help, for the most part."

A slight pause followed Faelin's last statement.

For much of her life Vallaria had fought against Faelin and her help. Caught in a world not her own, she'd always tried to prove her worth among a race much more skilled and worthy than she. *And don't forget the chip you've carried on your shoulder. The one you built up over years of frustration and anger. You blamed Faelin for most of that as well.* It was easy to blame her friend, and sometimes the king, because in her heart she knew they'd never abandon her. Up until the past few years she'd been more of a pain in Faelin's side than anything.

"It is now up to you, Vallaria. Although I will be by your side, only you can choose the destiny that will prevail. You must believe in yourself. To win the war, you must first win the battle." The elf turned her gaze toward the window, where the rain coated the glass like a waterfall. "But even then you must remain wary, for it will never truly be over. If you are to be queen, you must be prepared to do what's necessary to keep the crown and your kingdom. There will always be enemies at your doorstep, and if you don't remain vigilant, you'll eventually find yourself impaled on the end of a blade, or worse, your head on a pike for your subjects to see."

Faelin's words rang of personal history. Although the details of her parents' murders had never been discussed, Vallaria had overheard Thaneil speaking to the king one night. They had been discussing her destiny and the alleged curse that hung over the Ravenia name since her father's betrayal and subsequent death. Superstition was still strong in these lands, and the commander worried the curse would not be broken even if Vallaria retook the throne. The door to the great hall stood ajar, and as Vallaria stood in the shadowy hallway, she heard the commander say, "King Ryguard's head remained on that pike for almost a fortnight, and a blade tainted with dark magic impaled your sister. The curse is strong in that kingdom. Do you not believe it will find its way to Vallaria?"

Before Vallaria heard the king's answer the echo of footsteps had driven her from the door and back to her chambers.

"Are you listening, Vallaria?" Faelin said, tapping her fingers on the table.

"Sorry. You were saying?"

"Heed my words: complacency and weakness are not traits that will see you have a long rule."

Vallaria nodded. Faelin was right. No one could deliver her the crown, and no one could guarantee she keep it. Faelin, King Elvander, Thaneil, and the king's spy were only devices to help her succeed, but only she could ensure her legacy survived, that she survived. She would need to ascertain what type of queen destiny meant her to be and then become worthy.

Tomorrow would be the beginning of a new age for Ravenia and for its rightful ruler.

18

CERELI

City of Ravenia, in the Kingdom of Ravenia known as the Dark Kingdom

Yelin Barro walked into the throne room as he always did, with an air of overt importance. Dressed in a gaudy tunic the color of smelted gold and tasseled satin slippers, he hurried toward her. His greasy black hair, slicked away from his bronze skin, shone under the torchlight. When he entered, he pulled his face into a ridiculously large smile of pearl white teeth under a heavy black mustache.

Queen Cereli shifted on her throne as he scurried forward and stopped at the foot of the dais. Someday she would send him back to the Gold Coast and out of her sight, but until then she put up with his extravagant attire and arrogant attitude because he was a valuable asset. Yelin Barro was someone who kept his ear to the ground and had an uncanny way of gathering information.

"Queen Cereli, you look lovely this morning," said Yelin as he leaned into a deep bow.

"Obviously you have something to say, Yelin. Rise and tell me what it is. I assume it has something to do with my son?"

Yelin's lips curled into a sneer. "Your Majesty is very perceptive."

"Out with it," Cereli said, slamming her fist on the arm of her throne. The headache had been raging since before sunup, making her tolerance for the imperious little man limited. "You insisted you needed to see me before I spoke with Zander. I hope this is not a waste of my time."

Lowering his voice, her advisor leaned in. "There have been rumors that have recently made it to my ears. A shocking speculation that I feel Her Majesty should be aware of."

"What information have your little mice whispered in your ear now?"

Yelin's lips pursed into a thin line.

Cereli smirked. The little man didn't take kindly to her referring to his network of spies as mice. "You are trying my patience," she said, rubbing her temple as the pain in her head flared. "What is it you wish to divulge?"

Dark eyes darted back and forth. "It seems there may be some truth to your suspicions about Darrius Mensah. His father, the emperor, is gravely ill and the magi do not expect him to live much longer. Whispers have made it across the lands that infer once Darrius becomes emperor he plans to put a king on the throne of Ravenia."

Cereli leaned back and scrutinized the small man. "This is not news. Darrius Mensah has never approved of his father allowing a woman to rule. And it certainly isn't alarming to find out he will attempt to do it quickly." Her eyes narrowed. "What is it you are not telling me?"

Yelin fidgeted and his voice lowered even more. "What *is* alarming is *who* he plans on putting on the throne and *who* he's apparently been plotting with for months."

Her advisor had her attention now. "And you know this man's name?"

Yelin straightened and smoothed out invisible wrinkles in his tunic. "As do you, Your Highness."

"And who is this person that threatens my crown?"

"Your son, Prince Zander Damask."

The queen began to laugh. "Absurd, why would Darrius choose to replace me with someone who is already in line for the throne?"

"It seems Darrius has discovered the impending nuptials of your son to the princess of Kasmire. An alliance which could affect his power greatly should it stand. You know the holy city has been unchallenged for centuries, an impenetrable kingdom full of gold and riches, with a steadfast ruler and a specialized army of military might. Darrius fears an alliance between you and the king of Kasmire would considerably lessen the power of the Gold Coast Empire, for it affords you a way to break free from its hold."

Cereli's face was a mask of seething fury as she glared at Yelin. Zander was against the arranged marriage, but to side with Darrius to spite her . . . This union was the only way she could keep Ravenia from Darrius's clutches and Zander understood that. Once he became emperor, Darrius would try and dethrone her. The alliance with Kasmire would double her army and provide a holy sanctuary to Ravenia.

Pain flared behind her eyes as she digested Yelin's intel. Zander's betrayal was alarming. She'd misjudged her son apparently.

A voice in her head whispered. *He's more like you than you thought.*

He's not!

Zander was born into privilege—and he was a boy. Because of his gender society saw him as superior. She, on the other hand, had to claw through an oppressive culture for everything she'd gained.

And do some unspeakable things.

Yes. And she would be damned if a man, any man, would take it away.

"So my son is a traitor?" Cereli asked, her breath hitching.

Yelin's chubby forefinger brushed at his mustache. "I'm not sure the young man even knows the part he plays in Darrius's game. I suspect Zander is merely a means to an end, my queen. The holy city is one stronghold the empire has never been able to breach. It has always been a jewel that Darrius desires. With Zander on the Ravenia throne and married to the princess of Kasmire, the holy city would become part of the empire. Once the holy king dies, of course." Yelin's dark eyes flashed as he eyed the queen.

His revelations shook her to the core, and her hands trembled as she tried to calm the raging blood that reared through her veins. Darrius Mensah was a sadistic man who cared little about anyone but himself. He already envisioned himself a god, and once his father died and he ruled the empire, he would have the means to make it a reality. With both Ravenia and the Holy City of Kasmire under the Gold Coast's rule, he would be unstoppable.

I'm running out of time.

She gripped the arm of the throne as another searing pain tracked through her skull. "Zander has never shared my desire to rule. He spends little time in the kingdom and when he is here, he hides his identity. The people of Ravenia don't even recognize their own prince when he is in their midst. Why would he want this now? To betray his own mother?"

Yelin cocked his head and pressed his mouth into a firm line. "My sources have not been able to confirm the young prince's motive, my queen. Perhaps it is merely personal?"

"What do you mean by that?" Cereli's voice crackled with anger.

"I do not wish to offend, but your relationship with your son has somewhat frayed over the years." Yelin stood to his full height and tugged at the bell-shaped cuffs of his tunic. "Even with all your good intentions, maybe your son prefers the familiarity and warmth of his homeland to all of this." His hand swept around indicating the cold stone walls of the throne room.

Her eyes narrowed. She detected the sarcasm in Yelin's statement. He'd never approved of Cereli allowing Zander to adventure across the continent and sail the open seas to lands afar. He had often advised her to rein him in and ensure his loyalty to her cause and to her kingdom, but she couldn't. Secretly she harbored resentment toward her son. Every time she looked at him she saw his father. The way he paused before answering. The subtle way he pushed the hair off his face. The way he held his sword and cocked his brow. Over the years he'd become a painful reminder of everything she'd lost and all she'd sacrificed. Having Zander gone was much easier than having him here.

Yelin Barro cleared his throat. "While Zander's betrayal is surely a shock, Your Highness must remember who is manipulating him and why."

"There is more to Darrius's plan, than stealing my throne?"

'It is all about the holy city, Your Highness. Darrius does not just desire bringing it into the empire's fold. He desires the crown. To rule Kasmire."

"But if my son weds Princess Aerilla, he will be next in line for the throne of Kasmire. Without any male heirs, Zander would be the son King Tirus Amorian never had. And once the king is dead, Zander will essentially rule two kingdoms."

"True, but Darrius will move quickly once the holy king is dead. Tirus is old, and it won't be long and with Zander on his side—"

"What are his plans?"

"I'm told he intends on taking King Tirus's youngest daughter, Aria as another wife. Through Zander's abdication and without a male heir, Darrius will become next in line to the throne of the holy city, thus absorbing it, its military, and all its wealth into the Gold Coast Empire. With the holy king dead and Zander as a loyal ally, there will be no one left to challenge him. Once the emperor of the Gold Coast is also the king of Kasmire, the smaller kingdoms will have no recourse but to pledge their allegiance to the empire, and other than Mistenvale, Darrius Mensah will control most of the continent."

Cereli's breath hitched. Darrius would take the holy city without force, without bloodshed, and then with a combined army of over five thousand strong, the other kingdoms would have no choice but to acquiesce or be destroyed. And then he would—*be a god*. Her dark eyes turned back to her advisor. "And what of Zander? How will this end for him?"

"That I can only assume, my queen. But as a reward for his fidelity and his obedience, I suspect your son will continue to rule Ravenia as a figurehead for the empire. After all, he is next in line and the people will accept him more readily than another outsider over-throwing its rightful leader."

The queen's fury roiled as she glared at the smug little man. His words were carefully chosen, but she understood the dual meaning. Once she secured her throne and routed Darrius Mensah, Yelin Barro would be sent packing back to the Gold Coast with or without his spiteful tongue.

He continued without acknowledging the displeasure that shad-owed her features. "Prince Zander will have great power as part of Darrius Mensah's inner circle. And if he stays in line, his life will be coveted, but if he does not, I have no doubt Princess Aerilla will find herself a grieving widow."

A wave of nausea flowed over her as the dark magic swirled in her blood. Her head pounded and she closed her eyes, desperately trying to regain control.

Her own son! Betraying her for the empire that killed his father!

Suddenly the gloom behind her closed lids darkened to pitch black, and a face she'd seen before rose in her mind. A woman with long white tangled hair and sickly pale skin floated toward her. Her eyes were large globes of black and blood dripped from the corners. The apparition pulled her black lips into a hateful grin as her tongue slipped over the edges of pointed teeth.

Cereli's mind filled with a voice not her own. *But he doesn't know who his father is, does he? Or what happened to him. You kept that from your son. Another lie.* The voice grew louder. The edges of its tone sharper. Taunting her. *Your secrets will be your undoing.*

In her mind, the apparition flew at her, a piercing scream shat-tering the vision. Her eyes flew open and she gasped for breath as the headache exploded.

Within seconds Yelin was at her side, his face contoured into a mask of worry. "My queen, are you all right?"

"No one will take my crown," she hissed, clutching the throne for support as the vision and pain subsided.

She leaned back and waved her hand. "Leave me."

"Your Highness—"

"LEAVE ME!"

Taken aback, Yelin leapt off the dais, bowed, and scurried out.

Cereli sat for a moment, hands shaking. The apparition had been clear, but the voice in her head did not belong to the specter.

No, it was her own voice she'd heard in her mind.

Glancing at the globe on her staff, which leaned against the throne, she noticed the dark smoke inside it churning erratically. A warm trickle slipped down her cheek and she wiped at it, her fingertips coming away stained with the oil of the black tear. The vision was getting stronger and the darkness that fueled her magic more erratic.

The closer it came to the rise of the ice moon and the prophecy, the more difficult it became to control her connection to that place. The place where it had all begun.

"*There will come a time when the ghost princess haunts your nightmares and your waking hours. As your destinies converge, so does the magic that binds you both.*" The harbinger's words reverberated through her mind.

The woman in white must be an omen.

The ghost princess was coming.

Picking up the goblet of wine from the table beside the throne, she stood and heaved it across the room. "Aargh." It was bad enough that the ghost princess was portended to try and take her kingdom, but now her own flesh and blood had turned on her as well.

She snatched up her staff and strode from the room. Things had changed, which meant plans needed to as well. It was imperative she find Tagar immediately.

Zander's betrayal could not stand.

———

CERELI SWEPT THROUGH THE CASTLE, IGNORING THE QUESTIONING EYES FROM the guards and servants. She was to meet with Zander within the hour and only had a short period of time to amend her already meticulous-laid plans. Bursting through the doors of the guard commander's rooms, she was met with a startled yet curious gray stare.

Tagar rose from his desk. "Queen Cereli, what is it that brings you to my humble quarters? It is not yet time to leave for the execution."

"I have had a conversation with Yelin. He provided me with some disturbing information."

Tagar's lips flattened and his eye twitched. There was no love lost between the two men. The commander thought the flashy advisor untrustworthy, loyal first to himself, second to the Gold Coast, and then Ravenia. Yelin, in turn, thought the royal guard commander abhorrent and barbaric. Both men deemed the other unworthy of Cereli's attention yet begrudgingly understood to her the other was invaluable.

Until they weren't. She tried to ignore the little voice that always reminded her men in general could not be trusted. That at their very core they still thought themselves the superior species regardless of their diminished capacity in her court.

The commander walked around to the front of his desk and leaned against the thick wood, crossing his arms across his black tunic. "And what did Barro say to get you so upset?"

"He informed me that Zander is the betrayer in my midst. He is working with Darrius to take Ravenia from my rule."

Tagar's eye twitched again while his bronzed face remained a blank slate, the subtle tic exposing the irritation swirling inside him. His arms dropped to his side and he clutched the edge of the desk until his knuckles turned white.

"Yelin plays both sides. He can't be trusted when it comes to the Gold Coast," he said.

Although they were all, at one time, loyal to the Gold Coast, she and Tagar had made the choice to walk away, but Yelin was forced to come to Ravenia. A wedding gift from Emperor Silvalas. A token of his willingness to let her reign without his interference if he had eyes within the castle to report back to him. Fortunately, Cereli understood where Yelin's loyalties lay better than the emperor—its why she kept him close. Yelin would always do what was best for *Yelin* first and foremost.

She began to pace.

"Trust his word or not, I cannot risk a coup when I am so close to gaining the upper hand." She walked back to her royal guard commander and placed her hand on his cheek her finger tracing the long scar beside his eye. He stiffened under her touch.

She leaned in, her lips meeting his. His eyes closed and he groaned.

Her hand dropped to his chest, and she pulled back. "Zander must be taken care of." Tagar's heartbeat quickened and she smiled. "We are so close, my love, and once we have the dagger, nothing can stop us. We will not need my son, or the king of Kasmire's allegiance. We will take the holy city for ourselves with an army so powerful nothing and no one will be able to stop us."

The commander pulled her back into him and kissed her again, his tongue ravaging the inside of her mouth as his large hands grappled with her skirts. He bent her over the desk and she gasped as he thrust himself inside her with a ferocity that mirrored the dark and vicious man existing within.

Tagar Garrate was an unyielding brute who relished in the cruelty and violence he inflicted on others. Over the years she'd witnessed his dark side. It often left a trail of blood leading straight to her door. He was the reason she was able to escape the Gold Coast and conquer Ravenia. He kept her secrets, warmed her bed, and killed for her without question. The royal guard commander only had one weakness—*her*. And it was a power she used to her advantage.

Tagar shuddered behind her, and with ragged breaths he whispered in her ear, "If the death of your son is what you desire, consider it done, my queen."

Cereli smiled. Sometimes it was too easy.

19

ZANDER

Zander was set to marry Aerilla, the princess of the Holy City of Kasmire, in the spring—an arrangement his mother had negotiated to ensure an alliance with the oldest kingdom on the continent of Exile. It was scheduled to coincide with the princess's twenty-first birthday, the day a Kasmire royal ascends to adulthood. Like Ravenia, Kasmire had a similar requirement that no heir may govern until he or she reached the legal age of twenty-one. The only difference between the two kingdoms was only a male heir may ascend to the throne of Kasmire. Like the Gold Coast, the holy city was rooted in a patriarchal hierarchy. Since King Tirus had no sons of his own, his only choice was to marry off his eldest daughter and allow her husband to reign in regent in the hopes she'd bear a son who would ascend to the throne and continue the family dynasty.

He sat heavily on the chair next to the window and stared across the city, still shrouded in a thick mist from the heavy rain the night before.

He didn't want to reign, not Ravenia, not Kasmire, not any kingdom. But his mother didn't care. It was his duty as a prince to adhere to custom and therefore she'd done everything in her power to ensure Prince Zander would be Princess Aerilla's husband.

Although his mother's endgame was unclear, building power against Darrius Mensah and the Gold Coast was paramount. Her paranoia had grown over the past few years and many of her alliances had become suspect in her eyes. Having the holy city and its military within her purview brought the balance of power over to her favor.

She needed it and therefore him.

Zander lifted his left leg onto the chair arm and slouched into its cushions, waiting for the afternoon to pass and the queen to summon him. He picked at a loose thread in the fabric and frowned.

Minutes later he stood and began to pace, his boot heels clicking across the stone floor. The fire crackled and spit in the hearth and faint voices from other parts of the castle drifted under the door. Zander shoved his hands deep into his pants pockets and hung his head as his stomach clenched into a nauseating knot. He did not relish the consequences he would undoubtably suffer when he told his mother he would not marry Princess Aerilla. But the time had come for him to stand up for what he wanted, even if it meant defying his mother. And he did not want to marry a woman he didn't love nor one he'd never met. He refused to be a pawn in his mother's quest for power any longer.

He found himself at the window once again staring at the vast city laid out in front of him. Like he, to it, the kingdom was a stranger. He hadn't lived in Ravenia since he was a young boy when his mother sent him to live with his Uncle Moricio in the Golden City. And as soon as he was old enough to venture out on his own, he'd left the empire and spent vast amounts of time sailing the seas in search of adventure. At least that was what he told himself. Deep down he knew he ran from his destiny and the woman who'd given birth to him. And since Cereli Damask of House Sand Serpent preferred to be queen of Ravenia rather than a mother, she'd let him roam.

Over the years he'd devised a new identity for himself: Zane the mercenary from the Gold Coast, an easier life than Prince Zander Damask, heir to the throne of Ravenia, son of the dark queen.

Thankfully, no one outside the castle recognized him anymore. He was another face in the crowd. When he was in the kingdom, those in his mother's employ were sworn to secrecy. It was a deal he'd made with her long ago, but if he was forced to marry Princess Aerilla, it would come to an end.

"One day you will have to accept your lot in life, Zander." His mother's words echoed in his mind. "And all that is expected of you."

Recently, Zander had been summoned back from the Gold Coast by the queen's royal guard commander, Tagar Garrate. His mother wished to speak to him about a matter of utmost importance was all he said.

He wiped the condensation from the windowpane. The kingdom bustled today because of the execution, which thankfully he did not have to attend. He had no doubt that whatever poor soul would be put to death today by the queen's decree was most likely innocent.

The knot in his stomach tightened as he left the window and poured himself a glass of port hoping it would calm his nerves. He'd been here almost a week and no summons appeared from his mother. Nor had he seen her yet, aside from a brief encounter when she passed him on the grounds as she walked with the chancellor. Her dark eyes had flicked briefly in his direction but not a word was spoken.

Typical.

He leaned against the wall and took a swig of the sweet port wine.

A week in Ravenia and he was already itching to leave. He felt trapped, unable to do as he pleased and desperate to find his way across the continent and back to the vast expanse of the Endless Sea.

Tomorrow.

Whatever the reason his mother wished to see him, Zander realized he could not put off telling her he did not want to sit on the throne of Ravenia or marry the princess of Kasmire.

It was finally time to stand up to his mother.

He drained the glass.

Today he would face her wrath, tomorrow he would leave Ravenia for good.

———

MOST OF THE ROYAL GUARDS KEPT THEIR EYES STRAIGHT AHEAD, INTENTLY focused on the emptiness in front of them as he passed. A slight nod was all he received as he walked down the dim hall toward the throne room.

"Prince Zander, it's nice to see you back in the kingdom."

He turned at the mention of his name. His mother's advisor, cloaked in the satin fabrics common in the Gold Coast, waved and hurried forward until he was walking in lockstep with him.

"I've been back for six days, as I'm sure you're aware."

His dark eyes scrutinized the court advisor, and he noticed the man's smile slip slightly. Yelin Barro was a small, curious man who flitted around his mother, whispering in her ear about the comings and goings of everyone in the kingdom. Nothing more than a glorified gossip, King Torrsen, his stepfather, used to say.

Yelin bowed. "Yes well, nonetheless, your mother will be pleased to see you."

Zander ignored the man's sarcastic tone and pulled open the throne room's heavy wooden doors.

When he entered, Yelin hurried past him and walked quickly to the queen, who sat on her throne at the far end.

After he whispered in her ear, Zander was met with dark eyes and a cold, penetrating stare.

His mother, Queen Cereli, shifted slightly on the throne as he walked toward her. Upon her head, a black and gold crown sat, crafted specifically for her. It was tall and thin with uneven spiked peaks. When his mother took the throne, she'd refused to wear the crown of Ravenia and instead had the artisans create one that represented both Ravenia and her Gold Coast heritage.

Zander hated it.

Or more so, the serpent head embellishing the front, its eyes bejeweled with rare black rubies from far-off lands. It represented House Sand Serpent, the ruling house of his family.

"Zander, come."

His mother swept her long fingers toward him, beckoning. The clipped tone in her voice made Zander feel even more apprehensive.

Besides the royal guards flanking the doors, the throne room was empty. Only his mother, Yelin, and Tagar, stood at the front.

Lightning flashed through the arched windows and the slow tap of raindrops on the window glass echoed through the vast space.

The dull day had turned dark.

As he neared, the commander's gray eyes assessed him. The man was freakishly tall with a crosshatch of scars on the right side of his face. His hands were the size of ham hocks, but it was his eyes that gave Zander a chill whenever he looked his way. There was no warmth in them—they were soulless pools.

Probably the reason his reputation as a cruel and heartless bastard was so well known across Exile.

Zander smiled coyly at the commander and then returned his attention to the queen. "You wish to see me, Mother?"

Queen Cereli forced a smile. "You look well, Zander. How was your trip?"

"As expected," he answered.

"Did you see Moricio after you arrived back in the Gold Coast?"

"Yes, he sends his regards."

His mother's older brother, Moricio Damask, was the empire's military general. He was battle-hardened and almost as ruthless as his sister. But Zander had a bond with him that he didn't with his mother.

Zander tugged at his sleeveless leather tunic, wishing his mother would avoid the small talk and get to the point. He hadn't seen her since her last summon, when she'd informed him he was to marry the princess of Kasmire. He suspected this summons would be of a similar nature—his mother wanted something from him.

"And all is well in the Golden City?"

Zander nodded. "The emperor has built a new arena. He intends to entertain his people with gladiator-style games."

Right on cue the fake smile disappeared, and his mother's beautiful face became a mask of disinterested boredom. Although proud of her heritage, Cereli Damask cared little for the childish frivolities of the emperor who, in his advanced age, was a mere shell of the once great leader and conqueror of the vast empire.

"And how is dear Silvalas? Yelin tells me he's unwell."

A sigh escaped his lips. There was nothing his mother did not know, especially when it might affect her directly. Emperor Silvalas was indeed unwell, on his death bed, in fact, which meant his eldest son Darrius was set to become the new emperor. "Yes, the magi have seen his ascent. His demise is imminent."

"How unfortunate," she said, glancing at Yelin. "So, it won't be long now before Darrius wears the crown?" It was a rhetorical question but one that had much meaning behind it.

His mother had planned for this day. The day when Darrius Mensah would become emperor and set his sights on Ravenia. Darrius had always disagreed with the leniency his father showed Cereli after the passing of King Torrsen. Since the Gold Coast did not allow women to rule, Ravenia as a kingdom within the empire should too have a king. Once Darrius ruled the Gold Coast Empire, it would not be long before Queen Cereli Damask was asked to marry and relinquish her rule to a man or be overthrown in defiance.

His mother's eyes darkened, and her fingernails tapped the arms of her throne. "Did you speak with Darrius when you were there?"

"Briefly," Zander said.

"What did you speak of?" she asked.

Zander frowned, uncertain as to why his mother would care. His gaze drifted toward Yelin Barro. The little man stood beside her, a smirk on his smug, round face.

"Nothing of importance," he responded. "Darrius always tries to get me to join the Gold Coast army when I am home. This time was no different."

"Wasn't it?"

"I am not sure what you are getting at, Mother." Zander's voice tightened. He was drowsy from the port and fed up with the interrogation. He wanted to go back to his quarters and take a nap.

The queen leaned back in her chair, her eyes narrowed. "You've been back in the empire for over two months, yet you stayed in the Gold Coast rather than coming here to ready yourself for marriage."

Zander's chest tightened and his breath caught in his throat. "About that—"

But the queen didn't let him finish, instead waving him off.

"I have a task for you, Zander. It has come to my attention recently that there is an object of great value hidden near the kingdom. An item that could change the fate of Ravenia."

And there it was. The reason for his summons. His mother indeed wanted something.

"And what object is this?" he asked, his tone biting.

The queen ignored his insolence, and with a sly smile said, "The Dagger of Crusade."

Zander almost choked on his breath. His dark mahogany eyes met his mother's. He was sure he would see humor twinkling in them, but there was nothing but a vast ocean of pitch black. "The Dagger of Crusade is nothing more than a myth."

Yelin chuckled beside her but quickly stifled it when the queen raised her hand.

"This is what I thought as well, but the myth's proven real, and I have discovered the dagger's location."

"How?"

His mother laid her hand on the staff that was always in reach. The highly polished wood gleamed, and as she touched it, the smoke in the glass ball at its top moved seductively, like a serpent in a glass cage.

Her patience had grown threadbare.

"Your place is not to question, my son. Trust that I have confirmed the item is real and its location is within a few day's ride of the kingdom." Lips of dark red pursed and eyes rimmed in black kohl dared him to question her again.

Zander felt the familiar resentment rear up as he studied his mother. Her jet-black hair was swept to one side and tied into a long loose braid. She wore a high-collared black gown embellished with black raven feathers and gold chain trim. Queen Cereli embraced her persona as the dark queen so completely that Zander barely recognized the mother who raised him. The loving, gentle soul who used to hold him in her arms when he cried, played with him in the surf along the beach, and bought him sweet bread and kites at the open market.

That mother was long gone.

With a biting tone he asked, "And where am I to go to retrieve the dagger, Your Highness?"

The queen straightened, taking note of Zander's shift to formality. Her dark eyes locked on his and a smirk formed on her blood-red lips.

"The Valley of Souls."

Zander's heart began to pound and a film of sweat beaded on his upper lip. The Valley of Souls was a place of dark magic and death. It was a barren land of fire and brimstone. Nothing lived there and none who entered ever returned. Next to the Isle of Haddes, the Valley of Souls was the last place any wanted to enter.

The prince's blood went cold, and he swallowed the angry lump that filled his throat. When he found his voice again it came with a surge of insolence, and he spat out, "There is nothing in that place worth risking my life for."

For a moment her porcelain expression cracked, and Zander saw the fury swirl in her eyes. Tagar reached over and gently squeezed her shoulder. Unfurling her fingers from the staff where they'd gone white knuckled, she quickly regained her composure. "The stories of the curse on those lands are highly exaggerated. Your stepfather shouldn't have filled your head with such tales. You are the prince of Ravenia, a warrior of the Gold Coast, a descendant of the greatest military empire in all the lands. There is nothing you should fear."

The queen stood, her long black gown pooling around her ankles. "We will speak of this no more. You shall do as your queen bids. Commander Tagar will accompany you, but the rest of your party you must solicit from the city. You will need men good with a sword, smart in mind, fearless, and not afraid to die. They must also be discreet. No one must know of the journey you are about to embark on. If successful, all will be handsomely rewarded."

She paid him no heed as she descended the stairs, walking past him toward the back of the throne room where a hidden door was located that led to her private chambers.

"Remember, Zander, you swore a covenant to your queen. Do not disappoint," she called as she disappeared through the door, followed by Tagar and Yelin.

Standing alone in the shadowy throne room, Zander fought the waves of nausea rolling through his abdomen. The pounding of his heart echoed in his ears.

He would not be leaving the Kingdom of Ravenia tomorrow, and if the Valley of Souls had its way, he'd never leave it again.

20
CERELI

Cereli swept from the throne room leaving Zander gaping after her. This was not what she'd planned for her son, but after Yelin's revelations, his quiet elimination seemed to be the only way. Unfortunately, the urgency of finding one of the Myths of Three was even more prevalent. If she didn't have an allegiance with the holy city through Zander's nuptials, then she *must* have the power of the old world's magic—mage magic. Once the emperor died it would not be long before Darrius came to claim what he thought was his.

No man can be trusted. The thought whispered through her mind.

Even though Zander had feigned disinterest, it turned out, like every other Gold Coast male, he wanted power. It was intoxicating, making it difficult to ignore.

All that time she'd allowed him to spend away from Ravenia—*from her*. Granting his whims, allowing him to adopt a new persona and become invisible instead of forcing him to accept his responsibilities as the future ruler. It had all led him straight into the clutches of Darrius Mensah. And now it was coming back to haunt her.

Because I didn't want to face the past, and the reminder of what and who Zander represents.

She cursed aloud, drawing the curious stare of the guard stationed outside the door that led to her private chambers.

She rushed past him without an acknowledgment. As she climbed the stairs she tapped the end of her staff on the stone steps, the sound a representation of her throbbing anger.

How could she be so stupid, so blind?

Zander had become the enemy within her walls, and she had no one to blame but herself.

She reached her chambers and slammed the heavy door behind her. Zander was no longer the man she'd raised to one day wear the crown. He was a usurper waiting in the shadows. And it was her duty as queen of Ravenia to dispel all threats to her kingdom.

Even if it was her own blood.

She leaned her staff against the wall. The dark smoke swirled lazily in the glass orb. The dark magic had grown stronger of late, but with the enhanced power had come the visions.

And those visions harkened back to a troubling fate.

Time was running out. Magic had a price, and hers was high. She needed to find the Dagger of Crusade and claim one of the Myths of Three for herself.

She sat on the edge of her bed, opened the black onyx jewelry box she kept on the side table, and stared at the only thing she had left that reminded her of Zander's father. He'd been the only man she truly loved. Yet that love had cost them both—everything.

The jade stones in the delicate necklace shone as she pulled it from the box. Their polished surfaces refracted the firelight. Small silver leaves hanging from the chain were connected to the stones by a smaller strand of clear crystals.

Zander's father had given it to her before he died, a token of his love and commitment to her. Little did they know at the time that mere days later their love would be laid to waste by an executioner's blade.

On that fateful day she'd been left alone and pregnant.

But through her sorrow, resilience had emerged. An individual power she swore no one would take from her. From that day Cereli realized she could no longer count on men. And they had become only a means to an end.

That way of thinking had given her the determination to outwit the most powerful of men. It had given her the throne of Ravenia.

A solitary tear slipped down her cheek as she placed the necklace back in the box and closed the lid. She couldn't dwell in the past when her future was at risk.

Fate, in an ironic twist, decided not to have a man instigate her downfall. No. Her crown wasn't to be excised by an emperor or a king, or even her treacherous son, but by a young woman.

A phantom no one knew existed.

The harbinger had appeared to her two years earlier and warned her of the day when a woman from her past would return to take what was hers—*Serifine Ravenia, the ghost princess*. The child who Tagar Garrate supposedly killed all those years ago when he'd slayed Queen Evinna.

At first, she hadn't believed it to be true. It was impossible. She herself had gone with Tagar to dispose of the bodies. They lay as rotting corpses at the bottom of the tarry swamps on the Isle of Haddes. But the legend of the harbinger was strong in these lands. Only a small few were ever visited by the old crone. She was both a revelation and a curse, for you were forever haunted by the destiny she revealed. And as time passed and the dark magic Cereli had acquired that day developed, she knew the harbinger spoke the truth —the dead never really stayed dead.

Cereli searched endlessly for any sign of the princess in the years that followed, but none could ever be found. And so she'd waited for fate to come forth. But then the darkness had reached out and provided her with a way to cheat fate and death—*the Myths of Three*. Powerful ancient artifacts imbued with mage magic and lost to time.

She'd spent countless years searching for their existence and it had eventually paid off. If the rumors were true, and Tagar was successful in his quest, the Dagger of Crusade would be in her possession within a fortnight.

An unbridled chill slivered over her skin as she reached for the leather-bound journal. Opening the book, she flipped through the parchment pages until she reached the ones detailing the old crone's words.

"Your greed and deceit have given you a throne you have no rightful claim to, and because of this, your hold on the crown is weak. Fate will find you on the first full moon of winter in the thirteenth year of your reign. Beware of the one who will rise from the shadows, a child of royal blood and the true heir to the kingdom. If fate sees its course, your blood will spill by her hand and the ravens of Ravenia will return once more, heralding in the new age."

That full moon of winter would rise tonight to shine like a beacon over the castle. An ominous reminder she could no longer outrun her fate. The ghost princess would seek her revenge and Cereli would defend her throne at all costs. Finding the Dagger of Crusade was imperative. It may be the only way to stop the prophecy and stop the ghost princess from rising.

She closed the journal and stood.

Her fingers slid over the dried blood crusted at the corner of her eye as she looked at her reflection in the mirror. Her face was gaunt, and under the caramel tone of her skin she could see dark circles emerging under her eyes.

She'd been sleeping less and less, causing her temper to increase while her patience dwindled. There were times when she found it difficult to think. And the headaches—

The dark magic was taking its toll.

A soft knock on her door indicated her escort was here.

With a last forlorn look at her appearance, she turned away from the mirror.

"Enter," she called.

The door creaked as it swung inward and Tagar entered.

"Are you ready, Your Highness?"

"Yes," she said pulling on a long leather cloak.

"Your citizens await." His sweeping arm indicated the open door.

"This will be the last execution in a while. Let's make it a good one."

The light outside had dimmed as another storm roiled in the distance. The castle was almost vacant aside from a few chambermaids and guards. Those under Tagar's command had been assigned posts outside of the castle, either at the gates or at the gallows to ensure the crowds of people watching the execution did not cause an unnecessary disturbance.

They rounded the final corner, and Cereli stopped and put a hand on her commander's arm. "Tomorrow you will gather a travel party and ready yourself to leave for the Valley of Souls. Like we discussed, my son is not to return. But I do not want you to kill him."

The commander's head cocked slightly. "Your Majesty?"

"Leave him wounded, maimed even but let whatever haunts that cursed place take care of him. A slow, painful death will be judgment for his betrayal."

"As you wish."

Cereli nodded and walked through the exterior door, following her commander through the castle grounds and down to the courtyard by the back entrance where her carriage awaited.

A cold drizzle began to fall as the noise of the crowds gathering in the town square reached her ears.

She smiled.

One more traitor. One more life to consume.

Death may be an end for some but for her it was a beginning.

21

FAELIN

Shouts and jeers drifted through the misty rain as Faelin and Vallaria neared the town square.

A lone bell knelled in the distance—a death toll for the traitorous royal guardsman who walked toward the gallows this day —a royal guardsmen who had been deemed a spy by the queen.

A spy whose real name was Alagarn.

Faelin's heart sunk. They'd gone to the meeting spot this morning and Alagarn had not shown. In his stead, a small, frightened stable boy had appeared.

In a meek voice, he'd whispered the answer to the question only Alagarn could have known. "I will live and die only for the true queen."

"What do you know, boy? Speak," she'd ordered.

"He's to die this afternoon at the gallows, ma'am. He told me to give you this."

She took the piece of paper from the boy and unfolded it as Vallaria stood wide-eyed but silent beside her.

After a few minutes she'd handed the stable boy a piece of silver and sent him away.

"What does it say?" Vallaria asked.

"Nothing that will help us now," Faelin answered crumpling up the piece of paper and shoving it into her pocket.

"What are we going to do?"

Faelin tipped her head back and closed her eyes. "We will have to think of another way to get you into that castle."

When they entered the foggy alley a few hours later, a chorus of voices drifted from the town square. They were no longer chanting "death to the traitor" but instead "hail to the queen."

Faelin turned to Vallaria. "Keep your head down, stay close, and do not bring attention to yourself. Understood?"

She nodded as she nudged Pax forward along the wet cobblestone. Vallaria's eyes narrowed. "What will you do, Faelin? Do you have a plan to save him?"

Faelin ignored Vallaria's question and quickened her pace.

A mob of people crowded the square, townsfolk with their children in tow, farmers still dirty from the morning chores, even the wealthy elite had donned their Sunday best to sit huddled under hastily hung canopies in the upper portion of the rickety bleachers. Royal guardsmen encircled the area, their eyes sweeping over the crowd looking for any indication of trouble.

Queen Cereli had turned the large square into an arena for a spectacle. Stands had been constructed around the perimeter. Royal banners hung from the shops and flapped sharply in the wind. At the square's center, a large gallows stood, an ominous spire underscored by the gray drizzly day. Only an execution block and a large wicker basket sat on its platform.

The gallows looked strangely out of place behind the low fountain that lay silent in the middle of the square, the water in its basin stagnant and green with algae.

Faelin's attention returned to the makeshift gallows. *So Alagarn would not hang from the end of a rope.*

A vision of Baladril's head being severed from his shoulders exploded in her mind. With disgust she pushed it back down into the recesses of her memory.

Anxious energy swirled through the crowd. Many looked uncomfortable yet oddly delighted in having something to distract them from their daily monotonous routines and pitiful lives.

A man will be executed, and these people will watch, content to give the queen her audience. Then they will return to their homes and farms and pretend it never happened. This is the compliant and numb society Cereli has created. People fear her and each other. Any anyone of them could be next to find a hangman's noose around their neck or an executioner's ax at their throat.

How many of them longed for the days of Ravenia's past? Where the town square was used for celebration instead of death and the people rejoiced and did not cower in fear at the mere mention of the queen.

Did any still remember the king and queen of old? Or the princess they bore? She glanced at Vallaria, who stood beside her clutching the small boy. The citizens of Ravenia stood in the presence of their true queen, but none were any wiser to her existence. A darkness had the kingdom in its clutches, and only Vallaria could bring the light before that darkness swallowed them whole.

A hush fell over the crowd, drawing Faelin's attention back to the makeshift gallows.

Queen Cereli swept up onto the platform. Clad head to toe in black leather, the serpent crown firmly on her head, she looked intimidating and every bit the dark queen.

Faelin's hand tightened on her sword as she fought the urge to run at the queen and drive the blade through her belly. Cereli Damask hadn't intervened to protest or stop the execution of Baladril at the hands of her emperor years before, and now she would watch as another elf was executed without a trial.

Power, control, and fear—the Gold Coast way.

Faelin's stony gaze drifted to the hulking man standing at the queen's side. Dressed in the black and gold of the royal guard, one side of his handsome face a cross work of scars, was Tagar Garrate, the royal guard commander. The queen lowered her arms, and the roar of the crowed swelled. Faelin saw his mouth twitch as the renewed chants intensified.

He's enjoying this.

As if hearing her thoughts, the commander's shoulders drew back, and his gray eyes swept over the raucous crowd. Faelin ducked and pulled her hood farther over her head, getting lost in its shadows. Even with the illusion masking her identity, a few were still able to see through the façade, and with the queen adept in the dark arts, Faelin did not want to take any chances.

She pulled Vallaria through the tightly packed throng, aiming for a position at the corner of the square, and out of the sightline of the commander. The rain ceased, and the observers' boisterous chants turned to a quiet mumble as the queen began to speak.

"Good people of Ravenia, your queen's been wronged. Someone from within my royal guard has been found guilty of treason. Someone I trusted has turned against me—become traitor instead of loyalist. We will not tolerate such treachery in our kingdom, because a betrayal to the Crown is a betrayal to all of Ravenia. And so, it falls on your queen to ensure a swift and decisive punishment is served. Today you, good citizens of Ravenia, will stand as witnesses to that justice."

With a sweeping gesture and a defiant tone, the queen said, "Bring out the prisoner."

The crowd burst into cheers.

Faelin glanced toward the steps at the back of the platform where two guards escorted the condemned man to the top. A black hood encased his head, but he still wore the uniform of the queen's royal guard. The two guards pushed the man to his knees behind the executioner's block and removed his hood.

Alagarn.

Although the crowd and Vallaria saw an older man with a craggy face and long gray tangled hair, Faelin saw through the illusion. A proud elf with pale unblemished skin, long silky white hair, his chin set firm and defiant in his last moment—that was who she observed on the platform.

Again, she grasped tight the hilt of her sword, trying desperately to control both her ire and her desire to use her shield magic to protect him from the inevitable.

The voice beside her was a mere whisper. "Is it him?"

Faelin nodded.

"You must do something. They are going to kill him," Vallaria said.

Her pleas did not fall on deaf ears but there was nothing Faelin could do.

This world will test you, daughter. Sometimes you must make an unjust sacrifice for the good of what is to come. Her father's words rang true today. A good man would die so a destiny could be fulfilled.

Gently, she sent out a small nudge of her shield magic, enough to get Alagarn's attention. At least he would know that he wasn't alone.

Almost immediately his steady gaze turned their way. His lips quirked and he nodded slightly, before turning back to stare blankly at the throng of people filling the town square.

"Faelin." Vallaria's voice was more urgent now.

"There is nothing I can do for him now," she hissed.

"What do you mean?"

Their raised voices were drawing the attention of the people around them, some of which frowned while others cast suspicious looks their way.

Turning to Vallaria, Faelin glared, silencing the princess.

"Come," she whispered pulling her away from the crowd and under the bleachers where the shadows gave them cover. From here she could still see the platform, but they were less conspicuous.

Pax huddled under Vallaria's arm, his wide eyes silently questioning—

accusing? Vallaria, her body tense, stared straight ahead and ignored Faelin.

Lowering her voice, Faelin explained, "Somehow the queen saw through his illusion and identified him as an elf. Until we understand how, we can't expose ourselves. If I shield him, I too will be discovered and then all of this will be for naught. Alagarn will gladly give his life if it means putting you on the throne of Ravenia. It's the only thing that matters now." She hesitated. "At any cost."

Faelin turned back to the platform, her eyes glued to Alagarn as the commander stepped forward and raised his ax.

Beside her Vallaria clutched her prayer beads and began praying to her gods, her mumbled words barely audible to anyone but Faelin.

Faelin's stomach clenched as the ax swung ruthlessly downward. She couldn't save everyone.

Alagarn's head, slid from his neck, lifeless eyes staring at the crowd, and toppled unceremoniously into the wicker basket. The commander smirked and casually wiped the blood off his blade with a gloved hand.

Sick bastard!

There was a crack overhead and as if Vallaria's gods themselves disapproved, the skies opened up. A heavy rain thundered to the ground washing away the stream of blood flowing from the corpse's exposed neck cavity and sending onlookers scurrying back to their homes.

The exhibition was over.

When Faelin turned to walk away, she saw the queen take a step toward the body. Her lips moved and she leaned the staff she carried toward the corpse. The glass ball at its top contained a dark mist, and it began to swirl as Cereli invoked an incantation. Alagarn's body jerked, and a white mist rose from the neck and glided into the staff.

Faelin joined the fleeing crowd that hurried from the town square. Queen Cereli was not just adept at the dark arts. Her magic was so much more. She was a *necromancer*. A sorceress of the dead, and she had taken Alagarn's life energy.

The fight for the throne had become much more difficult.

22

VALLARIA

"How could you let him die?" Water streamed down Vallaria's face as the rain continued to pour from the sky. Using the back of her gloved hand, she wiped the rainwater from her eyes.

"Look at me!" she said grasping Faelin's arm and forcing her to stop.

Jade eyes, their brilliance shadowed by her cape's hood, turned defiantly toward her, and with a calm but firm voice Faelin said. "Sometimes the decisions we must make are not easy, but they need to be made. They may not make sense to others, but being a queen is about more than ruling a kingdom. It's about sacrifice, ours and, too often, others. Instinct, not emotion. Since we left the kingdom, you have been reckless at times, and you need to learn to control your emotions and the actions that follow. You can't react without forethought. If you do, you will never regain the throne, let alone rule from it. I think it's high time you ask yourself what kind of queen you want to be, Vallaria."

Yanking her arm from Vallaria's grip, Faelin walked down the alley as the fog rolled in behind her, leaving Vallaria and Pax standing shivering in the icy rain.

The overhang of the building provided some relief from the weather and Vallaria hoped the storm would cease soon so they could run back to the inn without getting soaked to the bone.

A rumble and crack from above shook the structures.

The gods are angry.

Vallaria clutched her prayer beads and pulled Pax in tighter.

Townspeople ran in every direction, ducking under overhangs to escape the rain. Horse hooves splashed water upward from muddy puddles that had formed in the streets as their riders urged them onward.

Another crack of lightning lit up the street, and the image of Alagarn's head falling from his body reared in her memory. She had never seen anyone die before, nor witnessed a death so barbaric in its nature. But even more unsettling was how at ease the queen was with sentencing a man to death.

It falls on your queen to ensure a swift and decisive punishment is served.

Cereli's words echoed through her mind.

Pax shivered next to her, and she wrapped the end of her mother's wool travel cloak around him. In response he encircled her waist with his small arms. Her heart skipped a beat at his unexpected show of affection. The boy had been relatively passive and untalkative since the incident in the alley.

Rubbing his back, she said, "We'll be back to our room soon enough and you can sit next to the fire and warm yourself while I make us a nice warm cup of broth."

Vallaria realized she was stalling. It was not the rain that stopped her from returning to the inn—it was fear of facing Faelin. Outside of Mistenvale, in the darkness of this kingdom, the future queen of the elves showed a different side. The elf was more than stoic; she was cold and unsympathetic. The way she'd taunted those guards at the farm, the ease to which she'd slain the man in the alley. Was this the real Faelin? The warrior who'd become battle-hardened in a time before peace. Molded by a world Vallaria would never know.

Her mind drifted back to Queen Cereli. The power she commanded over people was undeniable. With a simple gesture she'd taken a life, without hesitation and with seemingly no remorse, completely unaffected by the horror of her actions.

And Faelin had done the same.

Vallaria stiffened. The realms of man were nothing like she'd imagined. Mistenvale had sheltered her from this dark world. From her perch in the ashen tree, she'd dreamed of what lay beyond King Elvander's kingdom, but she had neither the experience nor the imagination to create such a hostile and unfriendly world as this.

Maybe she didn't belong. Maybe she was too weak to exist in a harsh world.

Voices floated through the rain as it began to lessen. Small figures bent and broken hurried by. Like the kingdom they too were void of any life, any happiness, any good.

This was not her parents' kingdom. Not anymore.

"Let's go," she said to Pax, taking his hand.

They left the shelter of the overhang and hurried back to the inn.

The room was dark and cold when they entered.

Faelin had not come back.

Vallaria built a fire in the hearth and put what little vegetables they'd purchased into the pot with the broth. After feeding Pax, she tucked him into bed, hoping the nightmares that plagued his young mind and had him tossing and turning in his sleep were not worsened by what he'd witnessed this afternoon.

"Sleep well, little one," she said and kissed his forehead. It was nice having someone to focus on other than the overwhelming destiny that had been thrust upon her.

Sitting on the bed, she watched over him until his breathing calmed and the soft sound of snoring reached her ears. Then she crossed the room and picked up her mother's cape from the floor and laid it across the back of the chair by the hearth to dry. The fire crackled and spat, but it had filled the tiny room quickly with a cozy warmth and chased away some of the horrors of the day.

A tear slipped down her cheek as Vallaria watched the sleeping boy. Now that Alagarn was dead how would she ever hope to claim the throne? To honor her parents' memories or avenge their deaths? To give Pax and the rest of the citizens of Ravenia a kingdom they deserved?

She was up against a foe more powerful, and the odds were stacked against her. Was her destiny, like Faelin's current appearance, an illusion?

Pax made a small sigh in his sleep and turned over.

Surprisingly, the little boy had wormed his way into her heart, and Vallaria had no idea why. The little disfigured orphan was the last person she thought she'd care about when she entered the kingdom, but there was something that drew her to him. Something she couldn't quite put her finger on. Maybe it was his circumstance or his impressive resilience when faced with unsurmountable odds. Maybe it was the nightmares that plagued him in the wee hours of the morn and how she too related to those fears. Possibly, in the whirlwind of uncertainty that had claimed her life of late she needed an anchor. Whatever the reason, she found herself with an innate need to protect him and ensure no one would ever hurt him again.

But how could she do that when she couldn't even protect herself?

While she watched Pax sleep, a realization suddenly came to her.

Her upbringing with the elves had shaped her, but it did not define her. Only she could do that, and regrettably she had—poor little orphan to poor little princess. Always feeling sorry for herself, never accepting her circumstance and making the best of it or attempting to chance it. Always looking for someone else to blame by playing the victim and making everyone else the villain.

She stood and grabbed her cloak.

If fate called to her to claim her legacy and change the future of the dark kingdom, then she herself would need to change. No longer could she rely on Faelin, King Elvander, or others to guide her. The future queen needed to toughen up and start figuring things out for herself.

The hour was late, but she needed to find Faelin. She was not giving up. Tomorrow she would figure out another way to access the castle. Starting now, Vallaria Ravenia would learn how to become a true queen.

23
FAELIN

"Barkeep, another ale." Faelin waved her hand, indicating the empty tankard in front of her.

The burly tavern owner lumbered to her end and placed another stein on the bar top.

"Last call," he said, eyeing her with displeasure. He leaned down and lowered his gruff voice. "The lady may want to think about leaving before the lads."

Faelin lifted her gaze. "And why would the *lady* want to do that?"

The barkeep surveyed the crowd of patrons, most drunk and loud. "Wouldn't want the lady to get any unwanted attention."

"While I appreciate your concern, I can handle myself."

"I have no doubt, but the townspeople are on edge tonight what with the execution and all. They may not take kindly to strangers in their midst. Especially one as pretty as yourself."

Faelin cocked a brow. "I'll take my chances."

The barkeep shrugged and walked away.

Always the same, she thought. Nothing had changed in the years since Baladril died. Men still thought women weak and in need of their protection. Even in Ravenia with a queen on the throne, men treated women as inferior. Baladril had tried to change all that, and it had gotten him killed.

Faelin thought back to those days prior to his execution. Emperor Silvalas had become tense at their presence in his city. Although they had visited many times before, this time was different. Faelin had seen Baladril in a heated exchange with Silvalas only a day before his capture. She'd questioned him about the argument, but he refused to divulge any information, saying only that the emperor had a secret he didn't want to become public.

Faelin never spoke to Baladril again. The next day he was arrested and put to death without so much as a trail, and she was expelled from the city.

She slugged back the ale, threw a coin on the bar, then walked out.

The rain had stopped, and a fine mist hovered over the cobblestone streets. The night was dark, and a foggy halo encircled the lamplights. A chill bit into her skin as she left the warmth of the Boar's Tusk Tavern and stepped into the street. She pulled her cloak tighter and inhaled, filling her lungs, hoping the brisk night air would chase away the demons of the past.

Although the tavern was next door to the inn, she wasn't ready to go back yet. She felt numb from the ale, yet images of Baladril's and Alagarn's dead eyes still haunted her.

Cursing, she dug into her trousers pocket and removed the crumpled piece of parchment. Leaning against the lamppost, she read Alagarn's note for the umpteenth time.

The writing, written in perfect script, was old elven. Translated it said:

Faelin,
There is a conspiracy brewing in the castle. The queen may have found a way to interrupt the prophecy. Although I do not have any details to share, know this, Cereli is a worthy adversary. Do all you can to stop her, but do not underestimate her power.

*I'm afraid fate has come for me. I beg of you to not interfere. I will gladly
give my life to ensure the throne is returned to Ravenia's rightful heir. The
prophecy must come to pass. It is the only way peace will stay in these
lands and chaos will be kept at bay.*
*Stay hidden in the shadows and trust no one. The queen has eyes
everywhere.*
A.

Voices echoed down the dark streets toward Faelin as she walked
in the opposite direction to the inn, a lewd joke, a cackle, a variety of
night sounds. When she rounded the corner, she came face-to-face
with four men.

"Well, what do we have here?" one man asked, swaying on his
feet.

"You lost, sweetie?" another asked, hiccupping. "I can certainly
help you find your way home."

The other two laughed at their buddy's comments as they
advanced closer to where she'd stopped.

"I don't need your help." Faelin gripped her sword tighter.

The man hiccupped again, but his jeering smile faded, and a
mask of anger took its place. "I ain't askin', bitch."

Following their friends lead, the others advanced, each hooting
and grabbing at her with their hands.

She took a step back and pulled her knife.

"Easy darlin'," the man with the long gray beard said. "We're just
havin' a little fun. No need for anyone to get hurt."

"Then I suggest you take your fun elsewhere before one of you
does."

The hiccupping man hurled his mass at her, his face a ruddy
mask of drunken fury.

With a quick upward arc, she sliced the edge of her blade across
his midsection. His face crumpled into an expression of shock, and
he stumbled back, watching in horror as a blood stain appeared on
his torn shirt. "She's cut me. The bitch cut me!"

"There's more where that came from," Faelin said her voice calm and steady.

His blood dripped from her blade as she held it aloft.

Gray beard, his eyes red-rimmed and full of anger, reached into his jacket and pulled out a hunting knife. "You're gonna be sorry you did that when I carve up that pretty face of yours."

Faelin raised a brow, noting the faded scars on his. "I suppose I can't do much worse to yours."

"Bitch," he muttered coming at her with a swipe.

Ducking under the large knife, she elbowed him in the gut. The big man barely stopped before turning and lunging at her again.

She sidestepped another swipe but didn't see his empty hand coming up behind it. His fist connected with her jaw, sending her reeling back as pain exploded in her face. Cursing under her breath, she caught another man moving toward her from the left. With quick reflexes she kicked out, catching him in the groin and dropping him to his knees. Distracted by the other man's approach, she'd allowed gray beard the opportunity to get behind her, and before she could navigate away from his large hands, he'd hauled her into his body, an arm around her shoulders and his hunting knife at her cheek.

"Drop it," he said.

She allowed the knife to slip from her grasp, the metal clanging as it hit stone.

"Now where would you like the first cut?"

The tip of the knife dug into her skin as he pressed harder. The injured man, still sitting on the ground, began to taunt. "Do it, cut her up good. The bitch deserves it for what she did to me." His friend, holding his manhood and trying to catch his breath, nodded in agreement.

She could feel gray beard's stale, ale-drenched breath on her neck.

"Maybe we should have a little fun first," he whispered as his hand slid down to her breast.

Eyes searched for the fourth man, whom she found cowering in the shadows. The look on his face told her he didn't want any part of what his buddies were doing. Thankfully she wouldn't have to worry about him.

"I think I'd rather not."

The man chuckled. "You're not in a position to bargain, now are ya?"

"I'm not sure you really are either," she said closing her eyes as the elemental magic rose. In seconds, the man's hands loosened as she pushed her shield magic outward. A tingle of electricity rifled through the shield and the man yelped, releasing her as he staggered backward.

In an instant she was on him. A right hook found its mark, and the big man teetered. The left roundhouse knocked him on his ass.

"I think we've all had enough for tonight." Pointing at the man still holding his wounded gut, she said. "I suggest you get him home and put some ointment on his wound. When he sobers up that's really going to hurt."

The men, eyes glassy and filled with disbelief, grabbed their injured buddy and staggered away as fast as their drunken bodies would let them. Gray beard hurriedly picked himself from the ground, grabbed his hunting knife, and ran after them.

"Witch," he hissed as the shadows swallowed him.

"Damn it," she said to the night. Her anger flared at allowing herself to be caught in a situation where she'd needed her shield magic. Using her powers in the city of Ravenia was the last thing she wanted, but luckily the street was deathly quiet, and even if those men talked, hopefully others would consider it nothing more than a drunken yarn.

Although the night air and the adrenaline pumping through her veins had cleared her mind, she still felt the effects of the ale. She couldn't risk getting into another altercation with someone else. She needed to get back to the inn immediately.

Sheathing her knife, Faelin turned and came face-to-face with a dark silhouette. Before she had time to react, something hard hit the side of her head. Light exploded in her eyes and she felt herself begin to collapse. She fell to the cold, damp cobblestones. Just as dark waves of unconsciousness came to claim her, she saw Vallaria emerging from the shadows. Lit by the flickering light emanating from the streetlamp, she walked straight into the path of the dark stranger.

24
VALLARIA

The iron shackles dug into Vallaria's flesh as she twisted her wrists, trying to free herself from the binds.

"Fight all you want, lassie. It will do you no good," a gruff voice from the shadows said. A man stepped from the gloom, his gap-toothed grin recognizable. It was the tall slim man from the alley, the one whose buddy Faelin had shot in the eye.

"Surprised to see me, eh?" He wiped spittle off his wooly beard and squatted down in front of her. "I been watching you fer days. You and that bitch." He jabbed a dirty finger towards Faelin, who lay motionless beside Vallaria, with dried blood on her cheek. "You think no one cares about an outsider being murdered in the dark kingdom. Well maybe not, maybe people passing through don't mean much to the queen or her henchmen, but Jak was my older brother and he meant something to me. You shoulda minded your own business because now you gonna pay fer what you two did."

Vallaria looked into the man's bloodshot eyes. His breath was heavy with the scent of liquor and his teeth tarnished yellow by the stain of the cigarette he held in his hand.

"You accosted a young boy," she spat.

"That street urchin stole from us."

"He was hungry."

"I don't care what the reason was, you don't take what ain't yours."

Vallaria laughed. "You took us, and we're not yours."

"Payback is different." The stranger stood, his eyes narrowing. "When I'm done with you two, I'll find that little shit and give him the beating he deserves."

The man turned to walk away, and anger surged through Vallaria. "What do you intend to do with us?" she shouted.

Teeth bared behind a jeering smile as the man scoffed. "A slave trader works the ports outside the Golden City's borders. I sure he'll pay handsomely fer the likes of you two, and in turn he'll be sure to fetch double the price across the seas on the open market. Maybe you'll get lucky and a king will purchase you as a concubine, but if you're unlucky you could find yourself a drugged whore in a brothel where you'll live out your days on your back and knees."

Smoke filled the air as he took a long drag from his cigarette.

Chuckling to himself, he dropped the butt and crushed it beneath the toe of his boot. He sauntered back toward Vallaria, rubbing his crotch until the bulge grew. "Maybe I should try out the goods myself first. That way I can advise the trader what you may be best suited fer." His dirty fingers twisted themselves in her dark hair. "If you're nice to me maybe it won't be so bad fer you later."

Using her hair, he pulled her across the floor away from the still unconscious Faelin.

Vallaria yelled in pain and tried desperately to reach her head, but her hands, bound by a long chain and attached to her ankle shackles, would only reach to her chest. She was helpless to fend off his attack with her binds so tight.

He yanked her backward and pushed her flat to the floor, straddling her waist. Vallaria fought him the best she could, but he was strong, and she had limited range and no weapon. A biting sting inflamed her cheek as his hand slapped across her face. Tears filled her eyes as the pain shuddered through her.

"Keep still or you are going to feel the back of my hand again."

His bulk pressed on her as he leaned down. The pungent odor of his breath engulfed her, and she gasped. He bit the skin above her breasts as his hands clawed at her shirt, untying the laces. The flimsy cloth fell away, and she felt the dankness of the room caress her bare skin. She struggled more fervently, but it was useless. The heavy iron shackles resisted her every attempt at pushing him off, and with her hands pinned under his body weight she had no leverage.

Images flew through her mind: Pax, King Elvander, the parents she barely remembered. She'd let them all down. They put their trust in her and deemed her worthy of the destiny they'd so carefully protected. And she had failed them. Upon seeing Faelin fall she'd run from the shadows right into this man's trap. Once again she'd reacted without thinking through the consequences and, as such, had doomed them both.

A sudden fury exploded in her.

What kind of queen do you want to be, Vallaria? Faelin's taunting words rose in her mind.

Anger surged again, but this time something else rose with it.

While the man's hands groped at her naked breasts and his hot, stinky breath, covered her neck, a numbing cold flared against her leg. The sensation intensified the more she fought the unwanted advances of her captor.

The crystal.

It was in her pants pocket.

The man shifted his position on top of her and jammed his lips against hers driving his tongue into her mouth. One of his hands found its way between her legs.

She bit down and the man reared in pain. He raised his hand, ready to strike her again.

The cold flared, burning in intensity, and her vision wavered. She raised her shackled hands in defense as tentacles of ice coursed through her veins and under her skin, turning her fear and anger into a deep-seated chilling calm.

Above her, the man bucked and lifted his head, as a gurgle came from the back of his throat. A look of surprise filled his bloodshot eyes, and seconds later, blood began to drip from the corners of his mouth. Convulsions wracked his body as he struggled to separate himself from her palm, which was placed flat against the center of his chest.

Cold burned white hot and instinctively she pulled her hand away. A sucking slurping noise followed as the ice spear protruding from her palm slid out of the man's chest. Staring in horror, she watched blood pump from the gaping hole and the man go limp, falling sideways to the ground—*dead.*

Panic rose, and with it the cold sensation ravaging her body exploded. Crystals of ice appeared on the metal shackles and chains binding her. Tiny flakes of snow drifted through the air around her binds as the temperature plummeted. With a searing crack, the metal broke freeing her hands and feet. When the binds fell away, the cold dissipated as fast as it had come. The ice spear too had melted, the only proof of its existence the bloody water dripping from her hand.

"Vallaria." Through the dense fog that had wrapped itself around her head, she heard Faelin call her name.

"Vallaria, I need you to look at me." The calm in Faelin's voice soothed her raw nerves and calmed her spinning mind, but only for a moment. Her eyes darted to her shaking hands as she looked for any sign of the ice and cold, but her hands were normal, pink and warm.

The room began to spin as the pain in her head worsened. Warmth trickled down her lower lip, and she wiped at it with the back of her hand, which came away streaked with blood. And it began to tremble as fear and panic clutched at her chest.

What is happening to me?

"Vallaria, concentrate." Faelin's voice interrupted the rising panic. "You need to fight the weakness you are suffering right now."

Through blurry vision she found her friend still sitting on the cold stone floor in the corner. She, like the rest of the room, was covered in a fine mist of icy snow.

"You have to get off the floor, Vallaria."

With unsteady legs she managed to pull herself into a standing position. The room spun and a weary exhaustion encased her limbs. The pain in her head subsided, but the overwhelming fatigue did not.

"What is happening to me?" she asked again, her voice quaking as tears slipped from her blue eyes. Unfortunately, asking the question aloud did not make it any less terrifying.

"Unlock the shackles." Faelin raised her bound hands and pointed to the keychain clipped to the man's belt. "We have to get out of here. I promise once we're safe I will explain everything."

Weary and numb with confusion, Vallaria bent down and grabbed the iron key ring with shaking hands. She walked to her friend, fingers fumbling with the multitude of keys as she searched for the correct one that would unlock the iron shackles.

Freed, Faelin jumped to her feet and kicked open the door, pulling a stunned Vallaria out of the room and into a shabby kitchen. The hearth had gone cold and a dusting of snow covered most of the surfaces. Vallaria's breath puffed out small clouds of white as Faelin tugged her through the front door and into the dark street.

It had begun to rain again, but this time the rain was bitter cold. The chill sunk under her skin and deep into her bones. Icy drops stung as they hit her bare cheek. In her foggy mind, a jumbled thought came forward. It was inane but oddly comforting. This weather that blanketed the northern kingdoms and signaled the coming of winter, what had Faelin called it?

Oh yes—frost rain.

FAELIN PUSHED VALLARIA THROUGH THE DOOR AND THEN CLOSED AND bolted it. Vallaria could see the elf trying to regain her composure as she leaned against the door she'd shut and secured.

The fire in the hearth had burned down to embers, but the room was still a welcomed warmth from the bitter cold of the night's rain. Shivers prickled her skin, and she could still feel the sting of the searing cold as it tunneled through her veins.

"What were you doing out in the kingdom so late at night?" Faelin's question was more of an accusation than a concerned query.

"Searching for you?"

Faelin's brow dipped. "Whatever for?"

"I was worried. It was late."

"So you decided to creep around the enemy's turf in the wee hours of the night?"

"I wasn't creeping." Her voice had a harsh edge and she glared at her friend.

Faelin shook her head, choosing to ignore Vallaria's insolence. "This is what I mean when I say your impulsiveness will get you killed. You refuse to think before you act, unabashed and unaware of the consequences."

Slighted by Faelin's unfair judgment, Vallaria lashed out. "You were the one that took his brother's life. You set his revenge upon us."

The elf's eyes narrowed, and she flexed her right hand. Seconds passed without a word and then when Faelin did speak, her words dripped with venom. "I have lived a thousand mortal lifetimes, and I understand quite well the way of man and the rot that festers inside the belly of many. I killed him because he didn't deserve anything less. There's nothing good left in either of them, and my only regret is that I didn't kill them both."

Vallaria opened her mouth, but Faelin didn't give her the chance to speak instead raising her hand to indicate silence.

"This world is not Mistenvale. It is dark and unforgiving, and your naivety and misguided empathy will only make it more so. It is time you realize the world outside our borders is one that preys on the weak. Not the idyllic one you imagined as you sat perched in the ashen tree."

Faelin cast her gaze down to the floor. "That crook could have easily transported us both to the slaver, and then we would have been in a world of trouble. If your powers—"

She stopped abruptly, but it was too late.

Powers?

Vallaria's heart pounded in her chest and her hands shook. Immediately, Faelin's scolding did not feel so significant as the sight of the bloody hole in the man's chest resurfaced in her mind.

"Come," Faelin said. "There is more to your story and the time has long passed for you to know what that is."

They moved to the corner of the room beside the window. Through the frosted panes, Vallaria could hear the harmonic tapping of the icy rain as it hit the glass.

"There is much you don't know, Vallaria. Something far greater than the destiny of your family bloodline is afoot. You are linked to an ancient calling."

"What do you mean—ancient calling?"

Faelin leaned against the window frame and crossed her arms. "The ice crystal my father gave you as a gift is much more than a pretty bauble from a long forgotten past. It is a powerful stone capable of potent magic if wielded by one who has the power to call that magic forth—a frost mage."

Vallaria's brow furrowed as she listened. "I don't understand."

"There is a prophecy that's been whispered among the elves for centuries. The telling of the rise of one who wields the powers of old. A mortal born from the blood of the ancient frost mages who will harness those powers and bring magic back to this world. They would be known as the last mage and their rise would signal the dawning of a new age of magic."

A stilted laugh escaped Vallaria's lips. "And what does this have to do with me?"

"The baby the prophecy spoke of would be born under the glow of a blood red autumn moon to a family doomed to be betrayed," Faelin said.

Her heart wrenched as the pieces of the prophecy clicked into place. "You think my parents and I were that doomed family?"

"Your mother thought so. She had a vision long before you were born and your birth, on the eve of a blood red autumn moon, solidified her belief. It was the reason she went to so much trouble to keep you from harm. When she had a second vision of her own death, it validated her actions, and she became steadfast in her commitment to ensure you lived."

"That's preposterous. I'm no one special."

"Except you are." Faelin shifted her gaze and unfurled her arms. "Before we left the kingdom, my father told me of the signs that would indicate the coming of the last mage. The tells that would affirm the prophecy of old was coming to pass. Although vague, the prophecy relays a very stark warning of the future. A time when the kingdoms of man will set upon themselves and destroy all that is. That time is now, Vallaria. Conflicts are breaking out across this continent and beyond. Kingdoms once forged in peace are sparring. It's only a matter of time before war comes to these lands and everything we know is destroyed. Mankind has gotten too arrogant. They thrive on chaos and are doomed to be their own ruination."

Vallaria wrung her hands together and shook her head. "But kingdoms have always fought with one another, why is this time different? Why do you think the prophecy is coming to pass now and that I have any part in it?"

"Two reasons. The prophecy says, 'when winter winds scorch the lands, and the blackest of birds once again soar the dark skies, the time of the last mage will be nigh'."

"Black birds?" Vallaria said.

"Ravens."

Visions of the onyx-colored birds she'd encountered over the past few weeks rose in her mind and her stomach lurched.

"You've seen them, haven't you? The ravens of Ravenia."

Vallaria nodded.

"They haven't been seen since your parents perished. They took to the skies and have not returned since. Until now."

"Because of the prophecy?"

"That and they are bound to the blood of the Ravenia royal family."

"How?"

"That is a story for another time. But the birds have returned because the rightful queen has come of age. And another reason the last mage must be connected to a descendant of the Ravenia bloodline."

"It's why they are mentioned in the prophecy?"

"Yes. And secondly, the ice crystal. Where is it?" Faelin asked.

With shaking fingers, Vallaria dug into her tunic pocket and pulled out the stone. Its surface was cold to the touch and glowed a pale bluish white, and as she lifted it toward Faelin, a thin icy mist rose from it.

Faelin leaned in. "The magic in the ice crystal has been activated. Only the one who carries the blood of the frost mages can wield the magic as you did tonight. It was no accident you were able to manifest an ice spear in your time of need. The elemental stone only answers to a mage, and only the one prophesied could summon the ancient magic hidden within. There is no doubt in my mind your mother was correct. You are the last mage, Vallaria."

Faelin reached up, unhooked the window latch, and pushed the glass outward.

The clock hands had crept into the wee hours, but the darkness of the night seeping into the room seemed different, brighter.

Vallaria moved closer to the window.

The ice rain had ceased, and in its place, small white flakes drifted languidly toward the ground. A haunting silence, heavy in its presence, wrapped the city in its embrace.

Puffs of white escaped from her mouth as she stepped to the open window. The temperature had dropped considerably.

The elf pointed out the window to the left. Her gaze drifted to the spot Faelin indicated. She was shocked to see a full moon had broken through the dense cloud bank, and the turbulent sky had calmed.

In size, the moon was so large and hung so low in the sky Vallaria thought for sure it rested on the castle turrets. Never had she seen a moon of this magnitude or one so white.

"What is it?"

"An ice moon," Faelin said.

"Does it indicate the coming of winter?"

Her friend shook her head. "No, this is a prophetic moon, foretelling of what is to come."

Vallaria wrapped her arms around herself as a shiver slid over her skin. "The last mage prophecy."

Faelin looked back at the sky and recited. "A moon, white as snow and cold as winter will hang low in the sky, its light a sign of the coming. And under its ethereal glow the last mage will rise."

25

CERELI

The flicker of firelight emanating from the hearth cast long, wavering shadows across the stone floor. It was well past midnight, and the quiet in the castle was deafening. The distant peal of the church bells rang out the early-morning hours, the only other sound breaking the silence—the moan of the wind as it slipped through a crack in the windowpane.

Cereli shivered and pulled the wool shawl tighter around her shoulders as she looked out the frost-covered window on the sleeping kingdom below.

She hated this time of night, especially when she couldn't sleep. The quietness haunted her. It was too still, suffocating, but tonight the silence was the least of her worries. Tonight, a full moon hung low over the castle. Not just any full moon—an ice moon. It cast its foreboding glow across the city and signaled the beginning of a fate she'd hoped never to face.

Somewhere out there, the ghost princess drew near.

Flames flickered and danced in the hearth as a cold breeze caressed her skin. She shivered again, but this time not from the damp. An ominous energy had suddenly filled the room.

Turning from the window, she saw the obscure shape of a person hidden in the shadows. Alarm didn't engulf her, for she'd expected this moment may come with the arrival of the ice moon.

Cereli remained still, waiting.

Moments passed before the harbinger glided out of the gloom and moved toward her. Her black tattered cloak swished across the stone floor. Yellow sunken eyes peered from the shadow cast by the large hood, and as withered lips curled back to speak, the harbinger raised a gnarled finger in Cereli's direction.

"The time of reckoning has begun. The prophecy of old has come to pass and soon the battle for the crown will begin. The white moon has risen, and the icy tentacles of winter reach for your crown. Fate hangs in the balance, for what you think is real might prove not to be."

The harbinger's image shuddered, reminding Cereli of her place in the realm beyond. When the old crone came to a halt feet away, Cereli smelt a musty odor of damp earth wafting from the specter's garments and when she spoke, Cereli was overwhelmed by the stale odor of her breath.

Her stomach lurched, but she remained steadfast.

The crone's raspy voice cracked with age. "You have made many enemies and lived a life littered with broken promises and distrust. Tonight signals the beginning of your judgment. A haunted past searches for revenge."

She grasped Cereli's hand.

Her skin was paper thin, rough, and cold as a winter's freeze. The feel of bony fingers around her wrist made Cereli shudder.

"Are you worthy of that which you took?"

She answered defiantly. "I am."

"The prophecy has determined three destinies will intersect— death, love, and revenge will intertwine. Beware of that which the ghost princess desires, for all is never as it seems."

Cereli frowned as the harbinger glided backward. "Wait! You said three destinies. Who is the third?" But the old crone was already gone, swallowed by the darkness from which she came.

A tear slipped down Cereli's cheek and she angrily wiped it away.

The harbinger had first come to Cereli two years ago. Rumors of her existence had long plagued these lands, but she'd always shrugged it off as legend existing from days past. But then the old crone appeared, as she'd done tonight, to warn Cereli of the one foretold to take her kingdom. The last of the Ravenia bloodline and the rightful heir to the throne. The one the harbinger called the *ghost princess*.

She walked to the table and swiped at the metal cup on its edge, flinging it to the ground where it clanged against the stone.

Evinna had tricked her!

Her daughter had survived the overthrow and the bloodline Cereli thought she'd wiped clean from the earth all those years ago remained intact.

Since then, this prophecy had plagued her. How had she been so stupid? She and Tagar made sure King Ryguard, Queen Evinna, and Princess Serifine had been killed. *Or so you'd thought.* After that day no viable heir to the Ravenia throne was supposed to be left alive, except her husband Torrsen. But somehow Evinna had outsmarted them. She'd played a hand Cereli hadn't anticipated. The perfect and beloved queen was as cold and calculating as she. The elf had, without remorse, sacrificed another in her daughter's place.

But who? An orphan? Did it matter? Not really. All that mattered now was the heir to the throne of Ravenia was alive because of Evinna's cunning.

Cereli began to pace.

Since she was a young girl, she'd always had decisions made for her by men. First her father, then her brother Moricio, and lastly the emperor. When she'd finally broken free and tried to enforce her own independence, it had been met with cruelty and violence. She'd been promised to the son of a wealthy sea captain from House Sea Scorpion before her father's passing. But before the union happened, she'd fallen in love with another. Someone who brought shame to both the powerful Houses. But before they could escape the Gold Coast, the emperor had discovered their secret and had him killed.

In her debilitating grief, she hadn't argued when her brother, as head of the family, married her off to a man of means. Someone less interested in what others thought than in having a young pretty girl in his bed. He was even happy to raise Zander as his own and keep her bastard son a secret. For two years he'd beaten her and made her do unspeakable things, reminding her every day of the unwanted whore she was—until his untimely death. A few years later, in an agreement to join the Kingdom of Ravenia with the Gold Coast Empire, King Ryguard promised to marry her, the poor widowed mother. But like every other man in her life, he too had betrayed her by marrying another and leaving her to endure under the oppressive rule of the patriarchal Gold Coast Empire.

Her fingertips grazed the tips of the crown sitting on a crushed velvet cushion by her wardrobe.

But she'd shown them all. She'd clawed her way out of the empire's grasp by rising to power the way men did with cruelty, deception, and no regard to what was right or wrong. The men in her life taught her power was not earned, it was taken. And so she'd taken what should have been hers long ago—the throne of Ravenia.

But now it was all about to be challenged. And the irony was it wouldn't be a man fated to instigate her downfall but a young girl. One she thought dead long ago.

An image lost in her memories resurfaced. A young girl with raven hair and crystal blue eyes. A smattering of freckles across the bridge of her nose. Cereli had only met Princess Serifine once at her wedding to her Uncle Torrsen. The child had travelled to the Gold Coast with her parents for the festivities, but they were gone the following day. Cereli thought she would never see her again. But it seems fate had other plans. Sometimes fate was cruel.

Fingers clenched into a fist and nails dug deep into the flesh of her palm. The pain calmed her mind. She'd come so far since she was a young girl of the empire and had fought for everything she'd obtained. She would not give it up now, not without a fight. The prophecy had not been clear two years ago, and the harbinger had not made it any clearer this visit. There was still a chance for fate to look favorably upon her and reward her for all she'd sacrificed. And if not—then she would change fate as well.

A soft knock on her chamber doors startled her from her thoughts.

Only one person dared disturb her at this hour and in a strange way she was happy he'd chosen to on this night. A distraction was welcome.

Grasping the thick iron knob, she opened the heavy wooden door. As expected, Tagar stood on the other side. Dressed casually in a white cotton shirt that stretched comfortably over his muscular form and black britches tucked neatly into brown leather boots, he was an alluring sight.

"Your Highness," he said quietly, a mischievous look in his eyes. "Do you wish to see me?"

Cereli opened the door wider and motioned for him to enter. After the exhilaration of the execution this afternoon, she was sure he needed a release as much as she did. As a lover he was prolific, and she looked forward to his late-night visits to her chambers. Even tonight with her mind so preoccupied with the prophecy, she welcomed his presence, knowing she'd be thoroughly sated when he left.

When she closed the door, the commander didn't hesitate. He wrapped her in his strong arms, lifted her so she could straddle him, and pushed them both against the cool stone of the chamber wall. Hurriedly, he unlaced his pants and let them slip down his thighs as he hiked her nightdress up around her waist. No words were needed, only movement, and Cereli sighed at the comforting feel of his body against hers.

She relished the familiarity—after tonight nothing would be the same.

———

CERELI LAY DRAPED OVER TAGAR'S NAKED BODY, HER HEAD ON HIS CHEST listening to the cadence of his heart.

The howl of the winter wind subsided, and an eerie stillness surrounded the castle. The glow of the ice moon had intensified in the wee hours of the morn, fighting the oncoming dawn for dominance.

Her commander had mentioned the moon about an hour ago, worry apparent in his tone, but in a way she was relieved of its presence. It meant she didn't have to worry about the prophecy and whether or not the stories of a ghost princess were real. Instead, it justified all she'd done in the past to ensure she had a chance against destiny. Only a week longer and she would have what she needed to rule forever.

"Are you sure about your decision? With regards to Zander, I mean?" Tagar whispered, breaking through her thoughts.

She shifted her gaze to look into his concerned eyes. "Yes. My son must not return from the Valley of Souls."

"So you believe Yelin. That your son's been plotting behind your back with Darrius Mensah to steal your throne."

"Does it matter?"

"He is your son, Cereli."

It was not often the commander referred to her by her given name instead of her title, but when he did it was not out of disrespect.

"I thought you didn't like him. Do you now favor him, or do you no longer want to get your hands dirty in duty to the Crown?" she asked.

Tagar tensed. He hated when she questioned his loyalty to her.

"Neither. I don't want you to live with regret," he replied.

Sometimes it enraged Cereli to be questioned by him, but in this instance she understood why. She was the dark queen. A woman so revered and feared that no one dare cross her because of the swift and decisive consequences she imposed. So why then couldn't she bring herself to make an example of her son's betrayal and take his life in a public display of execution?

Because of him.

The voice in her head taunted her by invoking Zander's father's memory.

Coward.

Cereli shifted uncomfortably as the voice pointed out the weakness she so desperately tried to hide. Zander was the only thing left of his father, the only man she ever truly loved. She couldn't destroy her only son, but she couldn't allow him to live either. Maybe this was for the best. It would put both their lives in jeopardy if Zander ever found out who his father was. Other than Tagar, her brother Moricio was the only one who knew the truth, and Cereli would do anything to ensure that information never found its way to Darrius Mensah.

Returning her attention to her lover, she responded, "I will have no regrets. Just make sure it gets done?"

"As you wish, Your Highness." The terse tone and formality of Tagar's words indicated he was upset with her.

"I'm sorry Tagar. You are right to confirm my motives."

He softened. "I want to make sure this is truly what you desire and not a reaction to the forked tongue of Yelin Barro."

"I know you don't trust him, but please don't assume I do, or that I would ever act irrationally based off his words alone. Although he provides useful intel that keeps us one step ahead of our enemies, it is always received with wariness. Yelin Barro may serve me now, but I know who his true master is."

"Himself," the commander said his eyes narrowing as a sly smile shaped his mouth.

"Anyway, Zander has never really wanted to ascend to the throne, so the truth behind what Yelin says is of no importance. You have never trusted my son and if I can't count on my own blood then

. . ." She trailed off as she circled the tip of her forefinger through the hair on Tagar's chest.

Tagar shifted to face her. "It is true I've never thought Prince Zander worthy of the throne, but an alliance with the holy city would forgo you waging war. Although he does not exhibit the desire or the strength required to lead, he does make a fine pawn in your game. In that way he is much like his father."

Those words stung. Tagar had been a mere soldier in the Gold Coast army under her brother Moricio's command when Zander's father was murdered. To save face with the other houses, the emperor deemed Cereli innocent due to her being seduced and coerced by the outsider. Tagar was dispatched as her personal guard and to help her brother Moricio find her a suitable husband, *immediately*. What the future commander didn't know at the time was why it was imperative to marry her off so quickly. After Zander was born everyone assumed her child was her husband's. Only Moricio was aware of her pregnancy and who the child's father truly was.

That was until Tagar found out the truth about seven years ago. After a drunken night with her brother, Moricio let something slip and Tagar had confronted her about Zander's parentage. She'd stupidly confirmed his suspicions.

Although Tagar rarely mentioned it, it was why he disliked Zander so much and why on occasion his jealousy reared its head, making him react in kind. He'd been in love with her for a very long time, and he found it difficult to accept her heart would always belong to another—especially a dead man.

"Zander is not his father," she said, the tone of her voice a warning for Tagar to drop the subject. But Zander was very much like his father. It was the reason she'd pushed him away, let him explore the world and hide his identity instead of raising him to be a prince of Ravenia and a warrior of the empire. She'd allowed him too much leeway. "And he won't marry the princess of Kasmire."

Tagar's brow lifted. "What do you mean?"

"I know my son. He won't marry unless he's in love. In that way he *is* like his father."

Tagar fell silent.

The dig was unnecessary, but the part of her heart that died the day he was killed had hardened to a cold, black stone. It was that part that allowed her to do the indescribable things she'd done in the name of power, and it was also the part that prevented her from giving Tagar what he desired—*her love.*

Swallowing the lump forming in her throat, she softened her voice and said, "If the intel gathered with regards to the Dagger of Crusade turns out to be true, the only alliance I will need will be with you." She snuggled closer to her commander. "The kings of Exile will be begging for a coalition with Ravenia, for they will fear my godly wrath if they remain our enemy. Our power will be absolute, Tagar. Even the emperor will have no choice but to bend a knee."

Tagar kissed the top of her head. "Tomorrow I will gather men to accompany your son and me to the Valley of Souls. After I have the dagger in my possession, I promise you Zander will not see the consequences of his betrayal coming. He will suffer for his treason as will all who oppose your reign, and the throne of Ravenia will forevermore be yours."

Cereli laid her head on Tagar's chest once again and smiled, the curve of her lips making it much more wicked than joyous. Another thing that was absolute—Tagar's unwavering loyalty.

26
ZANDER

The rain continued as Zander and Tagar entered the city. The execution had brought people to the kingdom from near and far: commoners fearful of their queen, voyeurs and miscreants who revealed in the misery of others, and even the rich and powerful who deemed it their duty to support the death of those who threatened their lot in life. The entire thing was nothing more than a cruel spectacle, and Zander hated it.

He pulled the hood of his riding cloak farther over his head, shaking the rain from his shoulders as he did. The day was bleak, which was fitting since it matched Zander's mood. His stallion, Magnus, always proud no matter what the circumstance, trotted into the city with his head held high.

"Wouldn't you rather be in the royal stables with a nice bucket of oats?" he whispered in his horse's ear. In response Magnus bucked slightly and snorted.

"You won't be so happy when you see where we end up."

Following Tagar down the rain-soaked cobbled streets, Zander saw people huddled under awnings, shivering in the bone-chilling damp as they tried to go about their daily lives.

Just another day in the dark kingdom.

When he was home, he tried to make light of the kingdom's plight, but it became more difficult as the years passed. The entire city, the kingdom even, was constantly under a bleak cloud of darkness. When it wasn't raining, the sky was gray and gloomy. Soon winter would be upon them and the bitter rain would turn to icy snow. Zander couldn't remember the last time he'd seen the sun in the kingdom. It was one of the reasons he relished returning home to the Gold Coast and its warm, sunny seaport city.

He shook the water from his collar as he entered the tavern, the commander close behind. Zander was not happy to be ordered to the Valley of Souls, but he was less thrilled to have to make the journey with Tagar. There was nothing about the man he liked, and he certainly didn't trust him.

Tagar Garrate, royal guard commander, was only loyal to the queen and *himself.*

"Two ales please, barkeep," Zander said.

"Do you think it wise to drink?" Tagar's voice was steady, but Zander caught the reprimand in its inflection.

"Try fitting in, Tagar. The queen wishes for us to be discreet, and wearing street clothes is not the only way."

Zander scrutinized the commander's plain gray tunic and worn leather boots. The wool travel cloak he wore over his shoulders had patches where the fabric had frayed. Even out of uniform, the stalwart commander was a difficult man to ignore. Thankfully, Zander didn't have that problem. He'd made a habit of blending in. For years he'd rarely spent time in the kingdom, let alone in the city or the rural villages, so the people didn't recognize their prince. It was both a blessing and a curse to be invisible. "And remember to call me Zane," he said, lowering his voice. "We don't want anyone questioning my identity simply because I have the same name as the prince."

Tagar nodded, took the mug of ale Zander handed him, and raised it. "To the queen," he said, his gruff voice low.

Zander smiled, cocked his brow, and knocked mugs with Tagar. "To not dying."

———†———

BY MID-EVENING THEY'D EMPLOYED A SCOUT, A BLACKSMITH TO TEND TO their horses and weapons, and three mercenaries whom Tagar vouched for as men who'd been commissioned at one time or another by both Ravenia and the Gold Coast. In the morning Tagar would seek out the two best swords in the city to complete their band of fools.

They were a rough-looking lot, but at this point Zander didn't care who came along. If the stories about the Valley of Souls were true, there would be nothing but their bones and decaying flesh to greet the next group his mother ordered to do her bidding.

It was early evening, he was drunk, in a mood, and royally pissed at the queen who'd put him in his recent predicament. Besides being so cavalier about the dangers she was sending her only son into, she hadn't given any thought to the fact that two days ago was his twenty-fifth birthday. It was not like the queen to not acknowledge it. A passing well-wish or a simple gift was standard, but this year she seemed not to recall the significance of the day. Apparently, his mother had more important matters at hand, like getting her hands on a mythical dagger.

Zander hiccupped and took another swig, emptying the tankard. These days anything was more important than her son.

Pushing his mug away, he turned and leaned against the bar top. The tavern, like usual, was mostly filled with men, loudly proclaiming their prowess at boar hunting or brawling. The barmaids passed out tankards of ale and mead while nimbly maneuvering around the men's groping hands and ignoring their lewd comments.

"Come on, lassie, sit on my lap," one drunk yelled as he grabbed a barmaid by the hips. Without batting an eye, she hit him over the head with her tray and walked away, leaving him red-faced as his friends pointed and guffawed.

Zander's dark eyes tracked past the rowdy crowd to the back of the room where two women sat with a young boy. Although the city brimmed with strangers, these two looked completely out of place, especially in a tavern full of rowdy drunks. His interest peaked as he continued to study them, a pastime cultivated over years of traveling to foreign lands.

They didn't look the type to enjoy executions, and judging by the swords attached to both their hips, he assumed they weren't in the city looking for protection. The blonde's green eyes constantly moved, watching her surroundings. She certainly wasn't a stranger to a city such as this.

The young boy was another curiosity. He had the shy demeanor of a street urchin, yet he seemed oddly comfortable huddled up against the brunette.

Zander could only see her from the side as she sat facing away from him. Her ebony hair was neatly braided, its length hanging over one shoulder with soft tendrils framing her face. Pale skin, the color of a winter sky, offset the ruby red of her full lips, and when she finally turned his way, he found himself unable to pull his gaze from her piercing blue eyes.

He felt a pull and although he very much wanted to go over to the young woman and introduce himself, there was no point. She didn't look the type to fall into bed with a stranger, and he certainly wasn't looking to fall in love. Not even with a woman as stunningly beautiful as her.

Besides, he'd probably be dead soon.

Prying his eyes away, he turned his attention to the royal guard commander.

"Do you like my mother, Tagar? Be honest."

"I've been in your mother's employ for a very long time."

Zander hiccupped. "That is not an answer."

"I think you've had enough Zand—er, Zane."

The prince shrugged as Tagar pushed his mug of ale aside. "Well, I don't think she likes you much. Sending me to the Valley of Souls is understandable, but why send her most loyal soldier to certain death?"

"To keep an eye on you."

Zander's glossy eyes squinted at the commander. "I'm sure there must be a myriad of other tasks you would rather be undertaking than babysitting me."

The royal guard commander grunted.

Enjoying goading the man, Zander said, "Your reputation has become rather unpleasant of late, Tagar."

Tagar raised his head and frowned. "In what way?'

A cheeky grin formed on Zander's face. "Just the other day I heard rumor that you bathe in your victims' blood." Suddenly overwhelmed by the absurdity of his situation he began to laugh uncontrollably. Doubled over, he tried to catch his breath as tears streamed down his face.

After a few seconds he regained some semblance of control and glanced at the commander, who looked back stone-faced. "You don't, do you?" Zander asked, suppressing the laugh that threatened to erupt once more.

Unamused, Tagar said, "I think it's time for bed. I am meeting with the swords for hire in the morning at the blacksmith's."

Zander grinned and, slurring some of his words, said, "I don't think a sharp blade is going to save us from the horrors lurking within the Valley of Souls, Commander." He hiccupped and slapped Tagar on the shoulder. "Only the gods and a whole lot of luck can help us now."

27
VALLARIA

They sat in the corner of the tavern eating lukewarm boar stew and drinking bitter wine. Vallaria ripped off a hunk of bread from the stale loaf and handed it to Pax as they waited for Faelin to return to the table. Something had piqued the elf's interest amidst the numerous conversations in the establishment, and currently, she was engaged in a discussion with an unsavory looking gentleman at the back of the tavern.

They'd spent most of the day stocking up on supplies and roaming the city, familiarizing themselves with Ravenia. With Pax's help they'd searched for access points to the castle, but unfortunately, the wall and moat surrounding it were impenetrable. The only way in was through the heavily guarded front gates.

Faelin hurried back to their table and sank into her chair. "You see the man at the bar, the one in the leather tunic?"

Vallaria leaned forward and peered through the crowd, her eyes finding the individual in question. He was tall and muscular with a sculpted jaw and dark shoulder-length hair that curled gently at the ends. His bronzed skin seemed oddly out of place in a kingdom where the sun never shone. The black leather tunic he wore stretched snug across his broad chest and rippled with his every move. Although he seemingly had one too many ales, his mahogany eyes shone with the brilliance of a star-lit night. And when they locked on hers, she shivered.

"Yes," she said, her breathy voice barely a whisper. "Who is he?"

"Apparently he's a Gold Coast mercenary and he's looking for swordsmen to go on a dangerous mission."

"What kind of mission?"

"That was not clear. All the man said was it's by order of Queen Cereli."

Vallaria leaned forward. "You think we can gain access to the castle by helping complete the mission?'

The elf shrugged. "I think it's worth finding out more."

She glanced over at the mercenary who was now speaking to a burly man next to him. A man she recognized.

"Isn't that the royal guard commander?"

"It is."

"Then the queen must be involved."

"That would make sense," Faelin replied. "The commander is never far from her side unless he's off doing her bidding."

Vallaria watched the mercenary for a few more seconds. "Stay with Pax, I'll be back."

Faelin lifted a brow but remained silent.

Casually, Vallaria sauntered over to the bar. Standing only feet behind the mercenary, she ordered a drink and pretended to intently scrutinize a stain on the wood bar top while she eavesdropped on his conversation.

"I've been her errand boy for years, Tagar and have never needed an escort. Why now? If the rumors about the Valley of Souls are as greatly exaggerated as the queen suggests, then why do I need an entourage of unsavory individuals to retrieve a dagger?"

"Keep your voice down," the commander replied. "The queen does not want its whereabouts known."

"Well, we know."

"Yes, and I suggest you keep that information to yourself if you wish to see riches instead of the queen's gallows."

Vallaria lifted her gaze in time to catch the silencing look the commander gave the mercenary. In response the mercenary lifted his hands in feign surrender and took a step back, directly into her.

"Hey," she yelped as his boot heel caught the toe of her foot.

He whirled at the sound of her voice, and when she looked up, she was met with a pair of dark, brooding eyes highlighted with flecks of gold that simmered in the low light of the bar.

"My apologies, my lady. Are you hurt?" His words were slightly slurred.

"I'm fine," she said, the throb in her toe fading. "Thank you."

The mercenary cocked his head and smiled. His white teeth shone bright against the burnished brown of his skin. "The name's Zane. May I buy you a drink to apologize?" He leaned in closer, and Vallaria could smell the faint scent of the sea. Like the breeze that drifted across the meadow in Mistenvale, he smelled of salt water and fresh air. It was both strange and delightful in a place so dark and miserable.

Before she could respond, the bartender placed the goblet of wine down in front of her. "That will be half a silver coin, miss."

She fished in her pocket for the payment, barely able to look away from the man who stood uncomfortably close to her. "Your offer is kind, but I already have a drink." Lifting the goblet in acknowledgment, she broke his gaze and hurried away without looking back.

Crossing the crowded tavern gave Vallaria time to regain her composure. Zane was even more handsome up close, and she could not deny the appeal of his boyish grin.

Refocusing, she sat at the table and looked at Faelin.

"Anything?" the elf asked.

"It seems they are being sent by the queen to retrieve a dagger."

"Sent where?"

"The Valley of Souls."

Faelin's expression darkened.

"What is it?" Vallaria asked, concern marring her face.

"The Valley of Souls has been shrouded in mystery and myth for centuries. It is a place of death where lost spirits roam and any who enter rarely leave. For the queen to send anyone into the valley, especially her royal guard commander, it must be imperative."

"Do you know of any daggers of this magnitude? Something worth risking everything for?" Vallaria asked, watching as a shadow crossed Faelin's features.

The elf shook her head. "Not for a very long time," she replied.

Vallaria sighed. "They also mentioned receiving riches from the queen. This may be our only viable plan to gain entry into the castle."

The elf turned her head slightly. "How so?"

"If we joined the mercenary's hunting party and retrieve this dagger the queen desires, we would have to enter the castle in order to get paid."

"You can't be certain of that."

"No, but what else do we have?"

Faelin's gloved fingers drummed the surface of the table. "It's too risky."

"In what way?"

She lowered her voice. "Besides traveling with the likes of Tagar Garrate, you are unable to control your powers. There is much we need to understand about your capabilities before we set you out into the world."

"You mean the world that is currently under the largest prophetic ice moon imaginable?" Vallaria's curt tone sliced through the air.

Pax huddled deeper into the corner, focusing his attention on the remaining stew in his bowl while Faelin glared.

"An ancient prophecy is not something to make light of. Neither is the magic you have been gifted. Both can be extremely volatile if misunderstood. And the Valley of Souls is not a place you wish to enter unprepared."

Leaning in, Vallaria said, "Your father discerned the prophecy to be about me. My mother gave up everything to ensure I lived to see it pass. If it is my destiny to save the world from chaos, then I must face whatever obstacle is in my way without fear of consequence, including that which contains the darkness infecting these lands."

After a long minute of contemplation Faelin replied, "You must heed my instructions: we cannot trust this mercenary nor the royal guard commander. I have no doubt neither will hesitate to slit our throats if they have any inclination of who we truly are. Further, this valley is a dark place, and one wrong move could end in your death or mine. And lastly, do not show the elemental stone or your magic to anyone. I am quite confident that if you do, very bad things will happen. Agreed?"

"Agreed."

The elf sat back, her pretty face a mask of quiet calm. "This is the time to find out who you are, who you are meant to be. This world will mold you or break you. Either you rise or you fall. Make your choices carefully, trust your instincts, and most of all, know you are not alone."

It was time for her to become a queen, a leader. To say goodbye to the little orphan girl who carried a chip on her shoulder and blamed others for all that was wrong in the world. It was time to let go of the past and forge her own future.

Vallaria grasped Faelin's gloved hand. "I know I can do this."

"Then I suggest you figure out a way to convince the handsome mercenary and his brutal bodyguard to take on two women as their accomplices."

28
VALLARIA

Without the perpetual rain falling from the sky, the day seemed warmer. Vallaria tucked her father's prayer beads into her pocket and pulled her mother's red wool travel cloak over her shoulders as she exited the inn. It was a blessing not to be constantly chilled by the dampness penetrating one's skin.

Last night she'd prayed again for guidance, and yet this morning she felt the familiar aching emptiness that had followed her prayers for weeks. Her gods had gone quiet and she didn't know why. It was not like they spoke to her; it was that for her entire life when she held her father's beads and prayed, she'd always come away with a sense of peace. That she wasn't truly alone in this world. But since King Elvander had revealed her true heritage, the loneliness had become prevalent as the peace her prayers always invoked disappeared.

Waiting outside the Rosewater Inn for Zane and the commander to emerge, she thought about the other conversation she and Faelin had last night after returning to their room at the inn.

"You're not thinking of taking the boy with us?" Faelin had said.

"We can't leave him here."

"Why not? He fended quite well for himself long before we came to the city."

"Did he?" Vallaria said, motioning to her ear.

"The Valley of Souls is no place for a child, regardless of his current circumstances or his unfortunate past."

Faelin spoke truth. To even think of taking the boy with them was selfish but the thought of leaving him to fend for himself was too much to bear.

"What is it about this boy that endears you so?" Faelin had asked.

Vallaria didn't have an answer then, and as she stood in the street watching Pax kick stones down the road, she still didn't.

Over the few days since they'd met, she'd learned little about the boy but enough to know why he distrusted everyone. A few years back Pax and his family had lived in a small farmstead to the west. One day a patrol of royal guards had come, killed his father for lack of payment to the queen, set fire to their house, raped his mother, who a day later killed herself after drowning his baby sister in the well. He'd survived, but only because he hid in the cellar in the barn. He'd been too afraid to move for days and was only discovered when a passing merchant saw the smoldering ruins of his house and investigated. The merchant buried the bodies of his kin and took him to the city of Ravenia's workhouse, but before he could release him to the master Pax had run away and hid in the alleys until the merchant had moved on. From that point he'd become a part of the underbelly of the city—surviving in the shadows.

When Pax opened up to her, it meant in a small way he trusted her, and because of that, even though she faced an unpredictable future, she couldn't bring herself to abandon him, not after everything he'd been through. No matter how much Faelin protested.

Soon, Zane emerged. He looked rather unsteady as he shielded his eyes from the dull light that escaped through the gray clouds. The ale he consumed last night had taken a toll.

She stifled a giggle as he stumbled slightly, catching himself on the hitching post. He ran his hands through his dark curls and glanced up, his dark eyes full of interest as he noticed her watching him.

He grinned and shrugged and then turned away as the royal guard commander appeared.

"I asked around," Faelin said, coming to stand beside her. "The queen's commander is definitely going on this mission, but no one seems to know exactly where or what it entails. Which is not surprising. When it comes to the queen most in the city mind their own business."

"Maybe she doesn't trust the Gold Coast mercenary," Vallaria, said watching as Zane filled his horse's saddle bags with supplies.

"I'm not sure the queen trusts anyone really, but the commander has her ear and has been in her employ longer than any. I've no doubt there's a specific reason she's sent him along."

Vallaria nodded. "Wish me luck."

The elf crossed her arms. "It's not luck you will need to get the commander to agree to your terms."

"I guess we will see." Vallaria strode across the street and planted herself in front of Zane, who stood rubbing his temples, eyes closed.

The royal guard commander intervened quickly. "May I help you, miss?"

Hearing Tagar's voice, Zane opened his eyes.

"I hear you're looking for a sword," Vallaria said, not taking her eyes from the mercenary.

Zane cast a look of confusion at the commander.

Vallaria continued, "For your mission to the Valley of Souls. I'm here to offer you my blade."

"How do you know about that?" The commander stepped forward, gripping the hilt of his sword. Zane raised a hand stopping him.

"Alcohol and secrets rarely mix," Vallaria said. "Many in the tavern last night, including you two, were talking about it."

The commander stiffened and cast Zane a disdainful look.

"Those we hired don't know the destination but half the drunks in the kingdom do."

Zane rolled his eyes.

"Well since I do know and still wish to go considering the valley's malevolent reputation you should be happy to hire me." Vallaria shifted her stance to stare straight at the commander.

"Or I could kill you," he said without pause.

"That won't be necessary, Tagar." Zane stepped between them, his bloodshot eyes questioning. "You think we should hire you?"

"And her." Vallaria pointed across the cobblestone street to where Faelin stood, crossbow casually slung over her shoulder.

Zane began to laugh and then immediately seemed to regret it as he cringed and went back to rubbing his temples. "Whatever for? I'm in need of seasoned adventurers and skilled warriors hardened by battle and void of fear. You are none of those."

"We're both extremely capable and skilled."

"I am sure you are, miss, but no woman has any business being in the place we're going." His tone changed as he glanced at the commander. "Especially considering there is a high probability none of us will return."

The commander's expression darkened.

"A demonstration then?"

Zane frowned as Vallaria ignored his warning.

She turned to Faelin and signaled. The elf raised her crossbow and fired. The bolt sliced neatly through the air, flew inches passed the commander's head, and embedded its tip into the center of the O of the Boar's Tusk sign next door.

Tagar's jaw clenched, but he remained silent.

"I'm sure we can find a bowman with equal skill," Zane said, although the quirk at the edge of his mouth told Vallaria she had his attention.

Vallaria pulled her sword and pointed the tip at the mercenary. "A duel then? And a wager. If I win, we come with you to the Valley of Souls. If I lose, we walk away, and you never see us again."

"While the offer of an early-morning duel is tempting, both my head and my hand are in an unacceptable state."

Vallaria noticed a small blood-stained bandage on his right hand.

"I'm sorry, miss," he said, mounting his horse. "Trust me when I say the gold is not worth the trouble. Good day ladies," he called over his shoulder.

When they rode away, Vallaria heard Zane say, "We meet the others at the bluff north of the city wall after dawn tomorrow."

And the commander replied. "Yes, but the two swords I hired this morning found themselves a bit of trouble last night. They will need to help the blacksmith for the day, but they've assured me they'll be at the rendezvous point in the morning."

Vallaria's heart dropped. Without Alagarn helping her enter the castle, this seemed to be the only other way and now it too appeared to be a dead end.

Faelin came to stand beside her, Pax in tow.

"It was stupid. Why did I think they would even consider us?"

"Maybe that is the problem. You left the decision up to them."

"What do you mean?"

The elf's green eyes flickered as Zane's horse rounded the corner and disappeared. "To be a queen you must stand up for those who are weak and put down those who aren't. To be a great queen you must know when to enforce your will on others and not let others enforce their will on you."

Vallaria's brow furrowed and she remained silent for a moment before asking. "Do you know where the blacksmith is?"

"I do. Why?"

She gave Faelin a sly grin. "If their swords don't show up at the bluff at dawn tomorrow but we do, they will have no choice but to allow us to go."

"Or the commander could make good on his promise to kill us."

"I would like to think he would see the value in keeping us alive."

"So your plan is to incapacitate two of the best swords in the city and take their spots?"

A mischievous glint flickered in Vallaria's blue eyes. "A queen knows when to impose her will on others, but she should also know when to use her womanly wiles to get what she wants."

It didn't take long for Vallaria to identify the men Tagar Garrate hired to be their swords on the mission. Apparently, the trouble they'd found had landed them in the jail for the evening. When Tagar found this morning, they were released with strict instructions to help the blacksmith clean the livery stable for the day.

With their focus on detaining the men and taking their place, Faelin concocted a light sedative with herbs and other ingredients she'd procured from different shops and places around the city.

For her part Vallaria bought rope.

"Seduce them, drug them, and tie them up. That's your plan," Faelin said after Vallaria had explained her scheme.

"It's probably the only good thing I learned from Riva."

Faelin's brow lifted. "Do tell."

"She was speaking of her journey with her father to a small kingdom in the south. Aside from all the boring details, she mentioned that mortal men's biggest weakness is the flesh of a beautiful woman."

"You were eavesdropping."

"I was already sitting in the loft of the stables when she came in with Darnica. What was I to do?"

Faelin shook her head but motioned for Vallaria to continue.

"Apparently, a man falls under some kind of spell when they see a woman's breasts and become easily coerced into saying or doing pretty much anything. It's also the reason Jale follows her around hanging on every word."

Her brow raised slightly as Faelin rolled her eyes. "Riva has been known to enjoy the company of mortal men from time to time, but I will not show any man from this city my naked breasts," she said, placing her hands on her hips and lifting her chin.

"You won't have to. We get them back to the inn under a false pretense, then drug them, and once they lose consciousness we gag and bind them. They won't make the dawn rendezvous, but we will, and by the time a chambermaid finds them we will be halfway to the Valley of Souls. Since Tagar said none of the hires knows where they are going, they won't be able to follow."

Since Faelin couldn't see any gaping holes in her plan, she decided it might work.

From across the street, Vallaria watched the swordsmen muck out the final stall and empty the manure buckets into the well out back. Night fell, and the temperature plummeted as a light snow began to fall from the sky.

Winter was creeping closer.

Her eyes tracked skyward. The ice moon hung in its place over the castle, a hazy halo circling its outer edge. Its haunting beauty both mesmerized and terrified Vallaria, for something about the moon had triggered the magic inside the mage crystal.

Earlier, after Faelin and Pax left to purchase ingredients for the sedative, the magic had surfaced as she gazed at the moon. Without warning the elemental crystal began to glow and its surface chilled to a stinging cold. The icy blur of the ancient magic followed, plummeting through her veins. Small crystals of ice formed on her palms, creeping up her hands, wrists, and arms until a thin layer of frost covered her skin up to the elbow; panic rose, her chest constricted, and the room spun. Within seconds she was on the floor in a ball, cold tears falling from her eyes and freezing on her cheeks. She lay there for what seemed like hours, unable to move even after the magic had dissipated and the stone went warm. Her head throbbed and waves of nausea wafted through her. She'd been too weak to stand, so she lay and thought about the magic she couldn't control.

It's controlling you.

When she finally regained enough strength to pull herself off the floor, she realized why it had surfaced in the first place: fear, uncertainty, distress. Feelings and emotions that were raw and deep and *make me weak.*

The magic's protecting me. I can't control it because those emotions are too overwhelming and chaotic.

She'd gotten into her own head after Faelin and Pax had left. Her mind wandered to her mother, Queen Cereli, the Valley of Souls, and the nightmare—

the young girl in the mirror, the raven, the dark place beyond. And the magic had surged. It reacted to all the things that made her fearful, made her doubt herself, and caused pain. It fed off her deepest darkest wounds, and then it spun out of control, consuming her and rendering her helpless. To control the magic, she needed to understand the ice crystal, but most of all she needed to understand herself.

Embrace it or it will consume you.

"Here they come," Faelin said, bringing Vallaria back to the moment.

She adjusted her leather vest so the top buttons were undone, and the swell of her breasts were visible. "Ready."

The elf nodded. She'd styled her blonde hair into a high flowing mane down the middle of her head. Small braids at the temples pulled it back from her face. Her green eyes were rimmed in dark kohl that flared out at the corners into sharp peaks. Regardless, if Faelin was under an illusion or not, she was stunningly beautiful.

Vallaria tugged on the end of her dark braid and, as the men drew closer, wondered if they'd even give her a second glance.

"What have we here?" one of the men asked as he stopped in front of them. "Are you ladies lost?" His eyes immediately dropped to Vallaria's chest.

"No," she said. "We were looking for a warm place to enjoy a drink."

The man smiled. "Well, you are more than welcome to join us at the tavern. We were heading that way."

His friend moved closer to Faelin. "You look like you could use a little warming up," he said.

"And I suppose you're the man to do it?" she responded.

Vallaria immediately recognized the tone in Faelin's voice. It was subtle and by the look on the man's face, he hadn't caught it. The undertone in her question was a challenge, a dare, a warning that you had no idea what you were getting yourself into.

It was the future elf queen finding it difficult to play a role.

Quickly, Vallaria redirected the men's attention, pulling a bottle of whisky from beneath her cloak.

"We already have the drink."

Remembering the way Riva acted with Jale when she wanted something from him, she leaned in, smiled, and batted her lashes. "Do you have somewhere to go?"

They already knew the men had a room at the Rosewater Inn. Both men, born in Ravenia, moved around a lot due to their chosen profession—highly regarded swords for hire. When they were in the city they stayed at the inn or at a farmstead on the outskirts of the kingdom. Faelin's reconnaissance had also provided them with names—Wes and Bram. They also had a reputation as womanizers who loved the drink. It was those vices that landed them in hot water last night. They'd gotten drunk in the tavern and chosen to bed the young daughters of the magistrate. A night in jail and a day of mucking stalls was their sentence after the queen's royal guard commander had stepped in and *suggested* the magistrate lessen their punishment.

The man already taken with Faelin asked, "Are you from Ravenia?'

She shook her head. "Just passing through."

"So no relatives that will be looking for you tonight?"

A quirk lifted the corner of her mouth. "Not a soul."

The man cocked his arm and offered it to Faelin. "Then a warm place and a good drink it is."

Vallaria followed, holding onto the other man's arm, her free arm gripping the neck of the whisky bottle.

The trap had been laid and the bait taken. After a drink or two of Faelin's tainted whisky, the men wouldn't be any wiser to their predicament until they woke up late in the day tomorrow.

Her plan was back on track—*for now*.

29

ZANDER

The demon was as black as night. Its body nothing more than a shimmer of smoke and ash and glowing red eyes. Body parts littered the valley and the sounds of agonizing wails drifted on the stale wind. His heart thudded wildly as he ran for his life. He felt the hot, rancid touch of its breath on the back of his neck and the sting of sharp claws as they raked his skin. Panic rose. There was no escape from the dark evil; he would die in this place—*tonight*. As the demon's claws began eviscerating him, he opened his mouth to scream, but there was nothing but silence. Hot blood sprayed across his face and an aching terror rattled through his bones. Darkness surrounded him and when he begged for death, he saw *her* standing atop a pile of skulls, *his mother*.

Sweat drenched the sheets as Zander woke from the nightmare.

Breath labored in his lungs as he tried desperately to shake off the lingering wisps of dread clinging to his skin. He inhaled and flexed his shaking hands, blinking as his eyes adjusted to the din.

He was in his room at the inn and the hour was late.

Laying back on his pillow, he thought about the nightmare.

He'd been in the Valley of Souls of that, he was sure. Memories from his childhood shaped the world in the dream, and his subconscious had taken him there, just like in the past. Only this time he wasn't alone.

Mother.

"It was only a dream Zander, born from the tales your stepfather told," he said aloud to the dark. "Your mind manifested it from memory just as it did the image of your mother. It means nothing."

But what if it did? The curse on those lands was legendary.

The Valley of Souls was a burial ground for the mages of old. Betrayed by the kings of man who feared the magic they wielded, they were mercilessly slaughtered, their bodies burned and buried, and their heads encased in stone so the elemental magic would remain forever silent.

But the magic wouldn't die. And the valley, soaked with their blood and saturated with their power, remains to this day a cursed graveyard enshrouded in darkness. Some believe the mage's vengeful spirits are trapped in the valley waiting until the dawn of a new age of magic.

A slithering chill ran up his spine. The Valley of Souls was aptly named.

Zander rubbed his eyes as the first rays of dawn peeked over the distant horizon. *Just a story, Zander, nothing more.*

A bang on the door startled him from his thoughts.

"Curses," he said, rolling out of bed. Pulling on trousers, he opened the door.

"I'm surprised you're awake."

Zander didn't miss the sarcasm that dripped from Tagar's words. "I'm sure most of what I do surprises you."

The royal guard commander's eye twitched, the way it always did when he thought better of engaging. "I'll meet you at the stables in twenty."

Zander leaned against the doorframe and watched his mother's faithful servant disappear down the hallway.

A click behind him drew his attention, and when he turned, he saw *her*. The young woman from the tavern, from the street, whose pale blue eyes drew him in and wouldn't let him go.

What was her name? Yes, *Vallaria*.

She crept from the room next to his and softly closed the door. Her skin looked radiant under the dawn's gray light filtering through the hallway window. A smattering of freckles cascaded across the bridge of her nose and a dimple appeared in her right cheek as she turned and noticed him standing there.

Those eyes drifted over his bare chest and her lips quirked. He found himself involuntarily reacting to her gaze but was relieved to find her eyes had already returned to lock on his before his body had betrayed him.

"Good morning," she said as she turned to walk away.

"Vallaria, wait."

She stopped.

"I'm sorry about yesterday, but I meant what I said. The Valley of Souls is not a place anyone should be, especially someone like you."

The words were out of his mouth before he could take them back. *Someone like you.* Internally he groaned.

Vallaria raised an eyebrow and shrugged, ignoring his unintentional slight. "Fate has a way of putting people where they need to be, don't you think?" A curl turned up the corner of her pale pink lips and without another word, she escaped down the stairs, leaving him to ponder her statement.

Returning to his room, he smiled as he closed the door. That girl was mysterious, bold, and nothing like any woman he'd met before. Zander guessed there was much more to Vallaria than what one saw on the surface.

And he found that very intriguing indeed.

THE HORSES WERE WATERED AND FED AND THE SUPPLY MULES LOADED. WITH the commander in the lead, and the scout and blacksmith in tow, they exited the city gates and headed north up toward the bluff, where they would meet the other five: three mercenaries and two Ravenia swordsmen.

Arriving at the bluff just after daybreak, Zander saw the mercenaries but no one else.

"Your blades have not yet arrived," Zander said.

The commander turned his gray eyes to him. "They will be here."

Dismounting, Zander studied the three mercenaries as Tagar handed them each a small bag of gold, a down payment on services rendered and a way to ensure they didn't run once they were told where the mission would take them.

Zander chortled to himself as he eyed the largest of the three, wondering if any would throw the money back. Probably not, he thought, looking from the man's neck tattoo to his black eye patch. These types of men cared little for fables and lived only for lining their pockets with gold.

The gray sky lightened as the hour wore on, yet the Ravenia swordsmen had still not shown. Tagar had begun to pace and curse under his breath.

"Where are they?" he snarled.

Before any could respond, two horsemen appeared at the top of the ridge.

"There," said the scout, pointing at the dark figures riding toward them.

"Finally," growled the commander. He was not a man who liked to be kept waiting, especially by those who the queen paid handsomely for their services.

When the riders drew closer, the muted gray light hit their faces and Zander swore under his breath. The riders weren't the swordsmen Tagar had hire—it was Vallaria, the woman with the crossbow, and the young boy.

"What are they doing here?" Tagar's voice rose as he too saw who rode toward them. The sound of steel being released from a sheath had Zander turning toward the commander.

"I don't think that will be necessary," he said, pointing to the sword.

"They have no business being here. Get rid of them at once."

Zander nodded, and with a quick press of his boot heel, he and Magnus galloped off to intercept.

He came within shouting distance and was struck again by a breathlessness when he gazed into Vallaria's bright blue eyes. Dressed in black leather with a red wool shawl across her shoulders and her dark hair pulled back in a long loose side braid, she gave him a sly smile as she stopped her horse beside his.

"What are you doing here?" he asked.

"You need swords, and we have them."

"We already hired the best."

Vallaria scanned the bluff where the others waited. "Clearly not the best if they aren't here."

Zander leaned back in the saddle as something dawned on him. "They're not coming, are they?" His eyes flitted to the blonde who sat emotionless on her horse, her green gaze steadily staring back.

"They may be a little tied up at the moment," she said.

Inhaling deeply, he turned his horse away. "I'll let the commander know we will be shorthanded."

"We will go in their stead."

"The commander is very particular about who he works with," he said, glancing back.

Blue eyes scanned the men in the distance. "I can see that by the distinguished group he's assembled."

Zander stifled a grin. "He doesn't know you; therefore he doesn't trust you."

"But something tells me the royal guard commander does believe in honor."

"That he does."

"Then I refer back to my original proposition. A duel. I win, we go with you and get a cut of the reward. I lose, and we turn around and you never see us again."

"Why is this so important to you?" he asked, miffed.

"That is my business."

Zander squared his shoulders. "I'm not fighting a woman."

"Are you afraid?"

He raised a brow. "Afraid I might hurt you."

"I can take care of myself."

"Of that I have no doubt." His smile widened as he watched her pretty face crumple into a frown as she slipped off the saddle and onto the ground. Unsheathing her sword, she held it aloft. "Duel."

He sighed, but before he could say a word, she lunged at him and hit him in the abdomen with the butt of her sword. The breath escaped from his lungs and he teetered backward, flailing for a hand-hold as he gasped for air, only to miss the horn of the saddle and land heavily on the ground. Laying on his back, a small groan escaped his lips. "What did you do that for?"

"Get up," she said, standing over him, her face flushed.

Zander rolled over onto his knees then slowly rose to his feet. He turned to face her. "Are you serious about this?"

"Arm yourself," she said, indicating the sword that hung from his hip.

He cursed as she kicked dirt toward his face. "I'm not going to take it easy on you," he said as he pulled his sword.

"I'd expect nothing less." Vallaria raised hers.

Zander swung the blade up, wincing as a stitch of pain rippled through his abdomen. Vallaria blocked his sword, the edges of their blades singing as they slid against one another. She whirled, slicing her sword through the air, the tip just missing his chin as he leaned back out of its path.

She's quick.

He ignored the pain in his abdomen and lunged at her, clipping her arm with the flat side of his blade. Her face darkened as she stumbled backward.

"Had enough?"

"I'm just getting started," she said as she placed two hands on the sword and came at him in a flurry of uppercuts and cross swings. It took all he had to deflect and evade her onslaught. Wherever she came from, someone had taught her well. Timing her swings, he waited for his opening, which came as she heaved the sword over her head for a downward cut. He kicked out, catching her in the gut. She doubled over the tip of the sword, digging into the ground. But she didn't stay down long.

Zander took a step back, impressed at her toughness and determination.

His eyes looked over at the commander who, along with two of the mercenaries, had rode over to watch.

Raising his sword, he flicked his fingers at her, indicating his readiness. Vallaria spun and lunged. He met her steel and twisted his sword. The movement bent back her wrist, and she involuntarily released her sword, watching in disbelief as it sailed through the air.

"And now?" he said, sure that she would realize her defeat. Instead, she turned her ice blue eyes on him, and her pale pink lips arched into a mischievous grin.

"Are *you* ready to give up?" she asked, walking slowly toward him.

He wiggled his sword at her. "I'm not the one without a weapon." He smiled, enjoying the game.

With a speed he didn't expect, she whirled to his left, twisted, and pulled a dagger from her hip pocket. Zander only saw a glint of the blade before its sharp edge lay tight against his jugular. Her eyes flicked with amusement. "Should I slit your throat now and save the queen some coin?"

Zander smiled meekly, dropped his sword, and lifted his hands. "And miss seeing me eviscerated by the creatures of the Valley of Souls?"

"So we can come along then?"

"You won fair and square, and although I did not agree to the wager, I will honor it. If you and your friend are determined to put your lives at risk for some gold coin, then yes. And since you seemingly derailed our other two swordsman, what choice do I have?"

He glanced at Tagar, who nodded, then rode off.

"And the boy comes as well."

"I'm not sure that's wise. I can't guarantee his safety."

"I can."

"No doubt," he answered, as she withdrew her weapon from his throat and extended her hand.

He clasped it tightly. For a woman who'd clearly held a sword for many years, the skin of her palm was oddly smooth and void of any calluses. But as she tightened her grip and shook his hand, he felt the strength her fingers possessed.

Vallaria sheathed her knife and picked up her sword from the ground as he glanced at the blonde who sat atop her horse with the crossbow casually resting on her shoulder. Her green eyes studied him, and something about the passive look on her face filled him with unease.

"Where did you say you were from?"

"We didn't," she said, digging her heels into the horse's flank and following the commander and Vallaria toward where the others waited.

He watched the two women ride off before he mounted Magnus and followed. While he rode behind the others, his eyes traveled over each of them. They were a band of ten individuals with nothing in common but the desire to either please the queen or gain some riches. Except for Zander—he neither wished to please his mother or take her gold.

I wish to leave this accursed place never to return.

After he was called back to Ravenia he'd made the decision to tell his mother he didn't want to marry the princess of Kasmire *or* sit on a throne. He was prepared for her wrath, but in the end he was confident she would release him from his responsibilities and let him live the life of his choosing. But he'd been terribly wrong and what he hadn't expected was instead, she would send him to his possible demise.

A surge of anger rose inside him.

His mother suspected what might lurk in the mist-shrouded valley. Even if the rumors surrounding the Valley of Souls were only tall tales, something ominous infected those lands. Many men had gone looking for the riches rumored to be hidden in the valley's caves, but none had ever returned. At this point he figured his chances of survival were minimal at best.

Brushing away his miserable thoughts, he galloped up to the others. "The Valley of Souls is less than a two-day journey north. We will ride to the other side of the forest and make camp at the river's edge tonight. In the morn, we will trek to the valley and seek the whereabouts of the lost artifact the queen desires."

He looked from one person to the next until his eyes landed on Vallaria. "Understand, this is a dangerous journey we undertake. Many of you know the legend of the Valley of Souls and the curse that was put upon it. Truth or myth, some of us may not survive. If any man or woman wishes to vacate, now is the time. Just return your gold and be on your way."

Grumbling could be heard among the mercenaries, men who were either too proud or too stupid to understand the danger. Tagar's gray eyes quieted them with one look.

The blacksmith shifted uncomfortably in the saddle, but both he and the scout stayed quiet.

"Looks like no one here is afraid of ghostly tales, Zane. Are you?" the commander asked, a small smirk forming on his lips as he turned his horse toward the north and galloped off. Slowly the others followed, leaving Zander alone and irked that his plans for a new life evaporated in one command from his mother.

He clicked his tongue, signaling for Magnus to move. His mind drifted to thoughts of the cerulean blue sea and the soft sandy beaches of the Gold Coast. He missed the vibrant atmosphere of his homeland: The hustle of the market at mid-day as citizens and foreigners alike mingled in the narrow streets. The scent of exotic spices shipped in from all over the world as it merged with the fresh salty breeze rolling in off the sea. And the sound of the surf as it washed against the shore lulling him to sleep at night. At this moment, as he rode toward his impending doom in the Valley of Souls, he wished he'd never come back to this forsaken kingdom.

30
FAELIN

Faelin assessed every individual in their party as they rode through the northern part of Ravenia. The elderly blacksmith and young scout were inconsequential. The mercenaries were an unruly bunch, as expected. The short, stocky one with missing teeth liked to belch. The muscular man with a bald head, tattoos, and eye patch seemed to be the leader and the closest to Tagar. The third mercenary, tall and lean with long, tangled hair, kept looking back and winking at her. But it was Zane who occupied her mind.

Watching him fight had brought up a strange sense of déjà vu, as if she'd seen it before. The way he flicked his wrist before swinging the sword and how his eyes narrowed before stepping up for a jab. It was oddly familiar and uncanny considering she'd never crossed paths with him before. It also seemed clear that Zane and the commander disliked each other immensely. Although there was a distinct familiarity within their exchanges, their subtle passive-aggressive tones hinted toward a history between the men that wasn't favorable. Her instincts had always served her well, and in this moment they were telling her to keep an eye on Zane. Especially since it seemed that there was something between him and Vallaria.

She'd caught the way he looked at her and the way Vallaria subconsciously reacted to his gaze. It seemed like a good idea at the time, but now she questioned their decision to join this quest. Not because of what they may encounter in the Valley of Souls but because of the distrust she sensed simmering around the men.

While she wasn't surprised the three mercenaries were wary of the others, there was something strange about the interaction between them and the royal guard commander. It seemed too intimate, too familiar. Like they shared a secret the rest of them weren't privy to. They also seemed oddly subordinate to the commander, as if they were taking their cues from him.

Faelin recalled the conversation she'd had with her father days before.

Vallaria needs you. Not your sword, your bow, or your magic, she needs you to balance her fury. To watch over her in a land she knows nothing about. If it's proven she is the last mage she must learn to control the ancient magic. In the interim, you must do your best to keep her from releasing the very worst of herself on mankind. Vallaria's destiny must play out as it's meant too. While you may guide her, only she can decide who she's to become.

Looking back at the men, she surmised that some of them were undoubtably the worst of mankind. And if Zane proved to be one of them, she'd put him down before letting him tempt Vallaria with his charm and good looks.

A yell brought her attention back to the present. Up ahead she saw the scout fall from his saddle, an arrow protruding from his shoulder.

With cat-like reflexes the crossbow was off her back and aimed toward the tree line.

They were at the edge of a thick, dark forest, and as Faelin's eyes scanned the shadows, she saw no visible proof of an enemy's presence, but she could sense them. The way they moved in harmony with the rustle of the leaves and the faint whispers that floated on the wind.

Wilders.

Her mind reeled and she suddenly felt warm with animosity.

The Wilders were a band of nomads who lived off the land. Hunters and gatherers who normally stayed far away from any civilized group.

They were also the ones who'd killed her mother.

While she scanned the trees, the others in the party scurried from their horses, weapons drawn. They were in the open and easy targets for those hidden in the forest.

Shouts and questions met her ears as the others tried to figure out who was attacking them. The commander dragged the scout behind his horse and tugged the arrow from his shoulder.

The man wailed in pain.

The grip on her crossbow tightened as she sensed movement in the trees. What were they doing this far north, especially with winter fast approaching? They should have migrated south months ago.

While pondering their motives, her ears heard the unmistakable sound of a bowstring and the hiss of an arrow flying through the air. Seconds later, she returned fired. Her bolt carved a path directly toward the oncoming arrow. The sound of metal hitting wood reverberated back to her as the bolt tip cut the arrow precisely in half down the middle.

Quickly she cast a glance at the others. Thankfully none had seen the shot. It was an impossible shot for any human to make and now was not the time to draw any unwanted attention or cast suspicion on who she and Vallaria really were.

You are travelers passing through the kingdom, looking for a quick windfall of gold to enable you to buy passage on a ship across the sea to the land of Brulle.

That was the story they agreed to tell if anyone asked. Strangers were not foreign in Ravenia, people passed through the city for many reasons, but the unexpected execution had been a good cover as most assumed strangers were in the city for the spectacle.

Suddenly whoops and yelps exploded in the air as a few dozen crazed men ran from the forest, weapons raised.

She placed another bolt in the channel as a bitter rage welled up inside her.

This was not going to end well—*for them*.

In front of her, Vallaria was off her horse, sword drawn. Pax was hidden behind the only rock near where they stood. The mercenaries had run forward and were already engaging the Wilders, cutting them down with their long blades before they could pull back a bowstring or jab a small hunting knife into their guts.

One, wild-eyed and screaming, swung a club lit with fire at the royal commander. But like those who fought the mercenaries, he didn't stand a chance. The commander easily outmaneuvered the Wilder and with one uppercut of his sword, sliced the man from his pelvis to sternum. Innards spewed from the wound and the man dropped to his knees, his face a brief mask of fear and surprise.

The Wilders were no match for the skills her group possessed, and within minutes, at least a half-dozen bodies lay in the field while the others turned tail and retreated into the forest.

Faelin stood in front of the final Wilder, still willing to engage, and raised an eyebrow as the crazed man leered at her. His face was streaked intentionally with mud, his hair matted and gnarled into knots. He wore simple three-quarter length trousers and a tunic, both dirty and discolored. The toes on his bare feet dug into the dirt as he circled her. The long unkempt beard was full of twigs and spittle, which crystalized in the cold air.

The sight of him disgusted her. Why her mother ever trusted them—

In his hand, he held a piece of flint chiseled to a point and tied with twine to a spindly wooden handle.

A homemade dagger.

He waved it menacingly at Faelin.

It didn't seem fair, she thought, looking down at her heavy steel sword, its thick blade razor-sharp on the edges.

She smiled and stuck the tip into the ground.

The man grunted.

At this point, she could feel the eyes of the others upon her, but she didn't care. The Wilder wanted a fight, and she would give him one, but she'd allow him an advantage. No weapon.

Faelin wagged her fingers at him, and the Wilder charged. His weapon pointed straight out. With quickness and skill, she grabbed the man's outstretched arm and, at the same time, lifted her knee kicking him in the groin.

He buckled and dropped the knife.

Before his knees hit the ground, she was behind him. Her arm tightened around his throat, slowly squeezing the air from his lungs. He clawed at her arm, but his attempts were weak as the last of his consciousness slowly left him. Right before he passed into the darkness, she twisted his head so quickly and violently part of his spine punctured through the skin. Releasing him, she watched the body crumple to the ground, her face a mask of indifference.

Wilders were nothing. As a people, they lived a life of simplicity. They were uneducated and uncivilized and had no tactical fighting skills, so killing them was easy.

Faelin eyes lifted to the far tree line. She could feel eyes upon her, and she searched the shadows until she saw him—the Wilder chief.

He stood to the left of a large tree. The white cross painted on his bare chest indicated his position within the tribe. His dark eyes penetrated her, and for a brief moment, a chill of recognition ran through her.

Does he know what I am, who I am?

Since the others were far enough away, she dropped the illusion around her eyes only. Her vision, no longer clouded by magic, intensified and she saw every inch of his weathered face.

Although he stood still, his jaw clenched as he stared into her lilac eyes.

He knew exactly who she was now.

Her mind raced, and it took everything she had to not sprint across the distance and stab him through his eye.

Instead, she said a silent warning.

My mother tried to help you, and instead of gratitude, you killed her, mutilated her body, and buried her under leaves and vines. It's been a long while, but someday I will have my revenge and you will pay for the life you took.

As if he heard the words inside her head, the chief's lips moved briefly, then he turned and walked back into the woods until the shadows swallowed him, along with the memory of her mother.

31
CERELI

Dark eyes followed the small annoying man as he entered the throne room and scurried forward to bend a knee at her feet. His blue brocade tunic glittered in the candlelight, and she wondered for the hundredth time why he insisted on dressing so elaborate, so Gold Coast.

Yelin Barro had been her adviser since the day she'd married King Torrsen. A gift from the emperor himself. Someone to help her succeed in a foreign land, he said, but Cereli knew better. Yelin was the emperor's eyes and ears. After Torrsen's passing, the emperor insisted Yelin become senior advisor to the Crown. As the first ruling queen in Exile, she would need a man at her side to ensure the other kingdoms respected her as a leader. And if she refused to marry, then a male diplomatic advisor would have to suffice.

To appease the kings.

Her dark eyes narrowed as she looked down at the greasy-haired man kneeling at her feet. When Silvalas Mensah was dead and his son Darrius rose to power, who would dear Yelin serve then? Yelin Barro was the type of man who continuously schemed to find the best way to enrich himself. He had a forked tongue and a legion of people that passed him information, but Darrius Mensah was smart, ruthless, powerful, and well connected. It was a gamesmanship Yelin may find himself unworthy of playing.

"Get off your knees, Yelin," she said.

Her advisor jumped to his feet, fidgeting restlessly as he always did when delivering news—good or bad.

"Well?"

"News from Tagar, Your Majesty. He has commissioned the help you asked for and they've begun their journey to the Valley of Souls this very morn."

"Good."

Yelin grinned, his obscenely white teeth flashing under his bushy black mustache. "There is something else, my queen."

"What is it, Yelin? I have other matters to attend." Cereli was already irritated by his presence.

"I have received word from your brother, Moricio."

Cereli stiffened.

"He will be arriving in the kingdom in a few days."

She sat up and glared at her advisor. "Why is he coming?"

"He did not say."

Queen Cereli's already dark eyes blackened as the corner of her mouth twitched. "I'm sure he didn't."

"If there is nothing else, my queen. I too have matters that need my attention." Yelin bent into a sweeping bow and hurried from the throne room.

Long fingernails tapped the arm of her throne as her eyes followed him out. Lucky for him, she still found him useful, she thought as she seethed at his veiled jab.

After she claimed the dagger for herself, she would not only rid the kingdom of that disgusting parasite but every man who'd looked down on her rule.

Cereli Damask had worked hard to set herself and her kingdom apart from the wealth and dominance of the Gold Coast. While proud of her roots, she'd grown up under the shadow of powerful men, oppressed by their ignorance and greed. Beautiful and cunning, she'd found a way to charm men into getting what she pleased, and unfortunately for them, they usually paid a heavy price for her ambitions.

Before brothers Ryguard and Torrsen there'd been other victims. Boys and men who'd treated her poorly. She'd watched and learned from the men around her and eventually she began to outwit them. And because she was a woman, no one thought her capable of such calculated and cruel behavior until it was too late.

One thing she'd learned was all men had a weakness. Yelin's was self-preservation, Tagar needed to be in control, and Zander craved anonymity from the Crown. And over the years she learned how to manipulate those weaknesses to her advantage. And then she discovered a different kind of power, a dark magic that allowed her to keep kings from both ally and enemy kingdoms at bay. It had elicited fear from those around her and rendered any challenge to her throne mute—until the prophecy.

Her hands began to shake, and a wave of exhaustion rippled through her. It had been days since the execution and the darkness needed feeding. If she didn't give it life, it drained hers. Since the ice moon had risen it had gotten worse. But it was a small price to pay for the magic she wielded.

Standing on wobbling legs, she steadied herself before stepping off the dais. She needed to get to the dungeons and replenish so she could seek the answers she desired.

Today she would look to the past to find the missing link by revisiting the time it all began.

———————

UNBEARABLE FATIGUE SATURATED HER BONES AND MUSCLES BY THE TIME SHE made it to the dungeons. Dismissing the guards, she searched the cells hoping she would find exactly what she needed. The life force of the executed royal guard had not been nourishing enough—she required youth, strength, and vitality.

In the cell farthest from the stairs she found him. A handsome young man crouched in the shadows, his feet bare and his hands bloody. Bright green eyes stared sadly from a dirt-streaked face as she approached. Inhaling deeply and summoning the last of her waning strength, she called him over.

"Queen Cereli? Have you come to free me?" His voice was barely a whisper, hoarse and parched from lack of water. She filled a tin mug from a bucket beside his cell and handed it to him.

"What is your name?"

"Haspian," he said between long gulps of water.

"And what is your crime?"

"My father died, and our cows produce less and less milk each passing year. My little brother needed medicine for his leg. He was born lame and I couldn't afford it."

"You stole it?"

"I'm sorry, Your Highness. I'm not a bad person. I didn't know what else to do."

'The queen set her staff to the side and lifted a hand through the bars, touching the young man's face. "I will free you."

"Bless you. My brother is alone, and I don't know what will become of him without me."

"Come closer." Cereli reached into her pocket and withdrew a slim, silver dagger. When the young man came forward, she thrust the knife through the bars and stabbed him in the neck.

Blood squirted from the wound and Haspian's eyes widened in fear and surprise. The cup dropped with a clang to the floor as he clawed at the protruding object embedded in his throat. Stumbling back, he dropped to his knees, gasping as his limbs went limp. With a final jerk his lifeless body collapsed into a pool of his own blood.

For a moment the queen's heart clenched and her eyes dropped to the floor. A weariness rose inside her and she clutched the bars, trying to stop the dizziness that accompanied it. Her breath came in gasps, and as she tried to insert the key into the cell's lock, her hand began to shake. Finally, the key found the hole and with a thunderous click the cell door swung inward. Without the barrier to hold her weight Cereli fell forward into the cell and tripped over the body of the young man.

Sprawled on the floor, she labored to catch her breath. Her head pounded with a searing hot pain that sent small white dots of light dancing across her vision. Too weak to stand, she forced herself to crawl toward the young man. Every fiber in her body screamed. The sinister cold of the darkness slid through her veins, draining her.

She'd waited too long!

With a pounding heart, she clawed desperately at the dead man, pulling his face toward her. Glassy eyes void of life stared back. Whispering the incantation, she lifted her eyes toward the cell door, relieved to see the smoke in the glass ball atop her staff begin to swirl.

The dark magic answered her call.

She repeated the incantation, watching as the young man's face turned ashen and the hollow eyes sunk deeper into the skull. His lips grayed and cracked, and his skin under her fingertips turned ice cold. Slowly a white haze began to escape from his open mouth. Fighting the urge to succumb to the overwhelming fatigue that battered her body, she inhaled deeply, pulling the young man's life force toward her. The smoke in the staff swirled faster and the white haze drifted with more ease toward her.

The energy of the young man flowed through her, strengthening every muscle, energizing her blood and fibers, and giving the darkness inside the sustenance it desired.

Seconds later the fatigue dissipated, and the headache lessened.

Standing, she brushed the dust from her gown and stepped over the corpse. Cereli walked from the cell, closed the door behind her, then grabbed her staff from where it leaned against the cell. Turning, she eyed the young man and again her heart clenched.

"You have been freed from this world of misery," she whispered, making a mental note to have a royal guard member go retrieve his brother. She would put him to work in the kitchens or the stables and provide him with the medicine he required. It was the least she could do for his brother's sacrifice.

Cereli swept her black gown up into her hands and hurried from the cells, following the damp and dimly lit hallway to the far end, where a thick metal door led to the wine cellar and food storage.

She couldn't waste any time. Her brother was arriving soon, and she had no doubt bad news would accompany him.

Cereli needed answers to the prophecy, and she needed the dagger.

Beyond the storage rooms a small hallway led to another door that opened into the sewage ducts. Passing the locked door, she hurried to the end of the hallway—a dead end if you didn't know what to look for.

Her nimble fingers found the crevice in the stone and she pulled at the lever lodged within. The stone wall rumbled and an opening appeared as the hidden door swung in.

After entering the passage beyond, she hurried to her secret room.

The small space was chilled with the damp air trapped between its walls. Rubbing her arms for warmth, she quickly lit the wall lanterns and ignited a fire in a small pit in the corner.

This room had provided her with solace for many years. A safe place to understand and harness the dark magic that had latched itself to her on that fateful day in the Isle of Haddes. While she still didn't understand exactly *what* it was, she'd learned over the years its basic chemistry and how it reacted with her own.

At first the magic had been a parasite, something that drained her life force and reacted in chaotic ways to her emotions and fear. After a while she understood that magic of this magnitude was only controlled by a mortal if it was contained within a magical item. It took her two trips abroad to find the mage's ball that now sat atop her staff and contained the dark elemental smoke.

Magic had become scarce in the world since the mages disappeared. Besides the elves of Mistenvale, she'd discovered a small coven of witches in the cold lands across the Endless Sea on the continent of Brulle and a tribe of shamans in the south. During an ancient ritual, the shaman elder had been able to extract a part of the invading magic within her and trap it into the mage's ball. The pain had been excruciating, and for a moment, Cereli had thought her life would end, but the experience had only proven to make her stronger.

Upon her return, hours were spent in this very room cultivating the magic, learning how to use it, and understanding what it needed. Wherever it had come from, Cereli finally understood the magic she now brandished was born from necromancy and it gave her the power over life and death connecting her to a place beyond the veil where the two briefly existed as one.

The room warmed, and she prepared for her journey into the past. Bottles of elixirs and potions sat on thick wooden shelves that lined the wall over a table strewn with dusty tomes, scrolls, and crinkled sheets of parchment. She chose the items carefully and mixed up a gooey paste in a small wooden bowl, then poured a blood-red liquid into a silver chalice.

She opened a large tome and flipped through the thick pages until she found the incantation she desired. Carefully she dipped the tip of her forefinger into the paste and drew a cross on her forehead.

She walked to the far wall, took a black velvet cloak from a hook, and wrapped it around her shoulders, pulling the large hood over her head. With a shaking hand she took a pinch of black powder from a jar and dropped it in the chalice. The liquid bubbled in response and a dark burgundy haze of smoke rose from its surface.

Cereli carried the chalice into the center of a white chalk pentacle drawn on the stone floor. Sitting, she lit the tall white taper candles that protruded from the black iron stands at each of its points. They flickered to life, burning a bright blue, the flames dancing and spitting on their wicks.

It was time to seek the answers buried in the past. If Serifine

Ravenia had not died on Tagar's sword that day, then who did? Cereli, certain it was connected to the prophecy and the ghost princess, needed to know. And with knowledge came power. A power she desperately needed if Tagar failed her and didn't retrieve the Dagger of Crusade. The crown of Ravenia was hers. She'd schemed and killed for it, and she wasn't about to let it slip through her fingers without a fight. She would remain queen of Ravenia, whatever it took.

She began to chant the words from the tome. As she repeated the incantation for a second time, the flame of the wall lanterns flickered and died. Darkness covered the room, the only light a faint glow from the burning candles.

Lifting the chalice to her mouth, she parted her lips and the elixir slid down her throat. Within seconds she felt the fingers of time wrap around her, pulling her toward the past. White smoke swirled at her feet and snaked around her body, and the room began to fade as her conscious mind succumbed to the magic she'd cast. Slowly she slipped into the past, her own voice reverberating through her mind.

Whatever it takes.

32

CERELI

Cereli heard the slurping sound before she saw what made it. Although her sight was still obscured by darkness, her other senses alerted her to the familiar surroundings of the Isle of Haddes. The noise reaching her ears was that of the tar pits as large bubbles rose to the surface and burst. A dry, cold breeze blew across her skin like gnarled fingers caressing, searching.

She shivered.

The creak of the deadwood trees mixed with the other unharmonious sounds of this place: a clattering din of unpleasantness.

As her vision adjusted and the darkness evaporated, she found herself high above the ground, perched in the branches of a tree. Her eyes searched the area, which was set alight by the eerie white glow of the ice moon that had appeared unexpectedly only a few days before. This part of the memory was jarring, as Cereli had forgotten that an ice moon hung over Ravenia during this time as well.

Two prophetic moons signaling the beginning and the end of my reign. How ironic.

The air was ripe with the scent of decay. Rot and dampness permeated every corner of this place. Nothing grew and little thrived. The Isle of Haddes was nothing more than a tomb littered with remnants of death.

Cereli recognized the small knoll rising from the middle of a large tar pool and the gnarled trunk of a deadwood tree on its east bank, roots exposed as it tipped precariously toward the swamp.

I've been here before. A long time ago.

Gripping the deadwood, her head turned as voices carried toward her on the breeze. Coming through the swampy landscape was Tagar pulling a small wagon. He spoke to someone cloaked in black who followed slowly behind. A crawling tingle flitted over her skin as she watched the scene below.

"It's up here." He was breathless from heaving the wooden cart through the muddy swamp.

In it she saw two bundles wrapped in dirty gray oil cloths bound with thick twine. One much smaller than the other. Cereli knew who was in those wrappings. As Tagar came closer, the face under the cloak of the one who followed came into view.

It was a face she knew well because it was hers.

She was watching the past, but the dark magic had brought her back only as an observer.

While she watched herself come to the edge of the pool, she felt a strange sense that she wasn't the only one watching. Her eyes flicked around, but no one else was visible.

"Are you sure this is the right place, Tagar?" she heard herself say.

"You asked for a burial place that would not only be permanent but ensure Evinna's life essence would not find the afterworld of her people. The tar pits hold death—nothing will escape."

Sitting in the tree watching the familiar scene replay, Cereli realized how vindictive and emotional she'd been back then. Refusing to return Evinna's body to her people for a proper burial and then dumping her out here where she would never be found was spiteful. Jealousy had guided her decisions back then. *Probably the reason the prophecy is upon you now.*

"Do it," the queen, said taking a step toward the edge of the swamp.

A gray mist hovered inches above its surface, and when Tagar pushed Evinna's enshrouded corpse into its depths, it parted, making a path.

Cereli watched from the deadwood as the body sunk beneath the tarry waters.

When Tagar went to retrieve the second bundle from the cart, movement in the mist caught her eye. Cereli's gaze was drawn to the knoll, and she shivered. An apparition now stood there motionless, her feet bare and bloody, watching the scene unfold before her. It was the woman from her visions.

Cereli shuddered and her heart began to thud. Turning back to where she and Tagar were busy unloading the corpses, she saw no indication that either of them even saw the apparition.

A cold film of sweat appeared on her skin at the realization. The woman was not from the past; rather she was like Cereli, here in this moment observing. As if in confirmation, the apparition's gaze left Tagar and moved directly up to her.

The black orbs in the sockets were as obscure as the tar pits. The pale of her skin ghostly. Long white hair swept down her back like tentacles spreading out across the knoll behind her. Black lips pulled back into a frightful grin, showing pointed teeth dripping with black liquid. Lace accents, torn and tattered, hung in ribbons from the sleeves and collar of her white dress.

A funeral gown.

Tagar pushed the second body, the small one, into the tarry swamp and as it began to sink, the apparition let out a bloodcurdling wail, a howl full of pain and despair. When the body disappeared under the thick black surface of the pool, the apparition flickered as if she were caught between two worlds. Black eyes filled with hate turned back to Cereli, and the wail morphed into a violent scream. Unexpectedly, she flew directly at the tree.

Cereli's scream matched the apparitions as the specter tore

through her as if she wasn't even there. Her breath collapsed in her lungs, and she gasped as an icy chill shuddered through her, following the woman's path. For a moment she felt the apparition's hatred and vengeance. Losing her grip on the branch, she began to fall, and as the dark magic pulled her through time, she realized she'd felt something else as the apparition passed through her, something Cereli recognized.

It can't be!

With a jolt she returned from the vision collapsing in a heap on the cold stone floor. The warmth of the black tears that fell from her eyes did nothing to dispel the sickening chill that churned in her stomach.

There was another.

As the waves of pain wracking her body subsided, she felt a presence enter the room. Slowly she turned her head toward the shadowy corner and there stood the harbinger.

"The ghost princess is not the one you thought."

"How could I not know?" she said.

The crone shuffled closer to where Cereli sat on the floor. "Because you didn't want to. Revenge takes many forms. You were blinded for so long by hate and greed that you missed that which was right in front of you."

With shaking hands, she rose from the ground and faced the harbinger. "Is my destiny already written. Is it too late?"

Yellow watery eyes shifted behind the shadow of the hood as the crone slid back into the shadows. Seconds later the room grew silent and Cereli was once again alone.

"Damn," she screamed as she turned and swiped the vials and parchment off the table with her hand. Glass crashed on the stone floor, followed by the pieces of parchment that floated lazily after it.

Bent over the table, breath heaving in her chest, Cereli fumed. How could she be so stupid? How did Ryguard and Evinna keep such a secret?

She paced the floor of the dungeon room. It all made sense now.

The ghost princess the harbinger had warned her of had finally risen, but she was not the one to take the throne, her desires were much more personal—she desired only revenge. But the threshold between this world and the next had not yet broken, so currently she had only the one in this world to worry about.

Extinguishing the lanterns and candles, she hurried from the room. She climbed the steps to her bedchamber as the bells in the church steeple rung out the early-morning hour. Three shuddering bongs. The castle was deathly quiet, and the deep throaty peal echoed off the cold stone and filled the halls with an ominous sound.

Cereli wrung her hands together as beads of sweat formed on her upper lip. Her fate now lay solely with her royal guard commander. If he retrieved the Dagger of Crusade from the Valley of Souls, then he would have a place by her side for as long as he lived. If he didn't, she would cut his throat before fate came to cut hers.

33

VALLARIA

"Will it rain again?" Pax asked as he clung to Siron's mane.

Vallaria encircled his frail waist with her arm and pulled him back into her as she shifted her weight in the saddle. His skin was cold, and his little body shivered with the chill the rain left behind. She took the end of her wool travel cloak and wrapped it around him as best she could.

"I don't think so. The sky is just talkative today."

"Are we almost to where we are going? I'm weary."

"It won't be long now," she said, wondering for the second time today if bringing Pax along was really the right thing to do. *What was the other option? Leave him at the mercy of the streets?* Again, she justified her decision by reminding herself of how the man who'd threatened Pax had also kidnapped her and Faelin. Even though he and his brother were dead, there would always be others like him. No matter where this journey took them or what dangers they faced, she'd convinced herself the boy was safer with her and Faelin.

The morning rain had ceased, but it left behind a bite that still stung her cheeks. Winter was upon them, and soon the rain would turn to ice and snow. The sky overhead had gotten darker. Ravenia's atmosphere was so uninviting it was no wonder the citizens were constantly angry and miserable. Whatever darkness the queen harnessed had blotted out the sun and blue skies for years, making it a depressing, unwelcoming place.

After leaving the city and tangling with the Wilders, the group entered the surrounding forest, heading north through a bramble path toward a bridge at the far end. Water rumbled in the distance. The waterfall Tagar spoke of wasn't far.

Gray clouds churned overhead as another rumble echoed through the air. They'd been riding most of the day and no matter how far they traveled nothing above them changed.

She cast a look at Faelin, who rode beside them. While it was odd to see her friend with an altered appearance, she still had the same mannerisms that Vallaria had grown accustomed to. Faelin still sat perfectly upright in her saddle and held the reins in her right hand. Her face was both a mask of perfection and one of disinterested boredom. Whatever the circumstances she always managed to remain calm and regal. Vallaria, on the other hand, had a constant knot of doubt in her stomach. She only hoped this unexpected detour would progress the way she intended and end with admission to the castle and the queen.

And if not, what then?

Vallaria had no other plan. If she couldn't gain access to the castle after this, what else was there? She had no army, no inside man, even her powers were useless if she didn't know how to control them. This had to work. She couldn't fail. Too much was at stake.

Stop dwelling on that which you can't control, she scolded herself silently. "Do you know anyone whose been to the Valley of Souls before, Faelin?" she asked, redirecting her thoughts. They were far enough away from the others, but Faelin still lowered her voice.

"Yes, my father's friend and leader of the Elvish army. His name was Baladril and he acted as an emissary for our race when my father could not."

Vallaria had not heard this name before. "What happened to him?"

"He was killed."

Vallaria caught the pinched tone in Faelin's voice when she said those words.

"By something in the Valley of Souls?"

"No, his excursion to the valley was, as I've been told, uneventful. His death came at the hands of the Gold Coast Empire."

"What happened?"

Faelin's hand tensed on the reins and her eyes flicked quickly to the others who rode farther ahead. "An indiscretion put him in the direct sights of their brutal ruler, Emperor Silvalas Mensah of House Blood Viper. He was unjustly sentenced to death by beheading. After that, peace between our kingdoms was fractured. My father pulled back from any diplomacy with them and that, coupled with the violent overthrow of Ravenia, pushed our kingdom into a tense co-existence with the kingdoms of man."

Vallaria had often wondered why there was so much pause with the elves anytime she'd asked questions about the world beyond their borders—clearly wounds ran deep within the elvish race, even if they didn't show their emotions outwardly. Not wishing to dig up the past any further, she asked, "Do you think the myth surrounding the Valley of Souls is true? Do dark creatures dwell there?"

Faelin's eyes drifted to Pax who had fallen asleep wrapped in Vallaria's arm. "There is darkness everywhere, not only in Ravenia. If the legends are true it won't be long before we know what horrors walk the cursed lands of the valley. Nothing will stay hidden in the shadows once our presence is known." She glanced down at Pax again. "I hope for your sake, and his, the stories are only myth."

She kicked Krest's flanks, sending her into a quick gait. "We are almost at the bridge. I will scout up ahead," she called over her shoulder.

Vallaria sighed as Faelin galloped off.

She hadn't hidden her displeasure with Vallaria for bringing the boy with them. The elf was against it and thought the risk too great. But Vallaria had insisted, and yet the closer they came to the valley, the tighter the knot of uncertainty grew in her stomach. What if Faelin was right and she was being selfish? What if she was callously putting Pax's life in danger?

And for what?

Revenge answered the dark voice within.

THEY FOUND A SMALL DELL AT THE BASE OF THE RAVINE ON THE OTHER SIDE of the bridge. It was the perfect spot to camp for the night. The grass was lush, making for a comfortable sleep. A small stream with clear drinking water ran through its center, and tall walls of rock bordered three sides, giving them protection and peace of mind.

Vallaria tied Siron to a tree and helped Pax from the saddle, while Zane gave orders to the blacksmith.

"Tend to the horses. Check their hooves and feed and water them. They will have a difficult trek tomorrow." He then turned to the scout and two of the mercenaries and tasked them with gathering firewood and buckets of water. The mercenaries looked at Tagar, who nodded before they complied. Zane cast the commander a look that reflected the dislike that seemed to simmer between the two men.

Vallaria thought it odd that the queen would have two individuals so at odds with one another on a mission that she deemed so important.

"I've found the perfect spot for Pax."

Vallaria jumped at the sound of Faelin's voice. "Why would you sneak up on me like that?"

The elf raised a perfectly sculptured brow. "I did not sneak." Her gaze shifted to Zane and then back to Vallaria. "Maybe you should stay focused on the task at hand and not get distracted by the help."

The statement was jarring, and Vallaria immediately whirled on her friend, but Faelin had already grabbed Pax's hand and walked away. Without a target for her anger, it subsided quickly, and with a quick look at Zane she followed her friend to the far end of the dell.

A small crevice in the rock wall was the perfect spot for Pax to curl up in and sleep soundly, away from the ruckus that was sure to ensue when the ale began to flow around the campfire later. She'd finished making his bed when Zane sidled up beside her.

"Take a walk with me," he said, his dark brown eyes shimmering as a lopsided grin appeared on his face.

Her heart skipped a beat. "Where?"

Zane motioned to a small thicket across the stream. "Berry picking."

She glanced back toward the main camp. Faelin had taken Pax down to the stream to catch minnows and the others were busy scurrying around while Tagar barked orders. Frowning, she paused before responding, unsure if she wanted to be alone with the mercenary.

"Shall we go?" he prodded.

She nodded, grabbed a pouch, and followed him toward the other side of the stream.

"Where do you think you're going?" Tagar asked as they passed by.

"I saw a berry thicket over here. Thought I might grab something to sweeten your salty demeanor," Zane said.

The commander's eyes narrowed. "Don't be long."

After they crossed the stream and where out of earshot of the others, Vallaria said, "You and the commander seem not to like each other much."

The corner of his mouth lifted, and he scoffed. "Tagar and I have known each other for a very long time. He doesn't like anyone."

"He seems a bit gruff," she said, trying to act like someone who knew nothing about the man before meeting him the other day.

"That's putting it mildly." He pushed past a low-hanging branch and into the shadowy darkness beyond.

Vallaria followed.

They emerged into an opening. Shadows stretched from one end to the other, being chased by the dull gray light that filtered through the treetops above. Vallaria looked around the area. It was a grove. A few dozen berry bushes were scattered over the dark lush soil.

The grove was quiet, peaceful, a sanctuary of beauty in a stark land.

Small yellow finches darted back and forth, their melodious chirps drifting airily through the grove. The fragrant scent of fruit assaulted her nostrils, mixing with the pungent odor of damp earth and the crispness of the rain.

"It's beautiful," she whispered, not wanting to disturb the serenity with her presence. "How did you know this was here? You couldn't see it from the trail."

Zane shook his head. "I've traveled all over the kingdom. I know of many things and many places." His smile widened and Vallaria noticed how white his teeth were against the coppery gold of his skin. He grasped her hand and pulled her between the bushes. "Close your eyes."

"Why?"

"Trust me."

"I barely know you."

"We know each other well enough. You saw me half naked." His face lightened with a mischievous grin.

She opened her mouth to respond, but he pulled her closer.

"Close your eyes," he said, his voice low and soft.

A warm ripple cascaded over her skin and her arm tingled where his hand held it. Her breath hitched, but she did what he asked.

"Now open your mouth."

A shiver ran through her. Slowly, she parted her lips. Vallaria knew she shouldn't trust Zane, but there was something exhilarating about being alone with a stranger, dangerous even.

With her sight negated, all her other senses intensified. She smelt the tangy-sweet aroma of the berry before he put it in her mouth and felt the roughness of its skin. Her heart skipped a beat at the tingling feeling his fingers created as they lingered a second too long on her lips, and from the warmth of his breath on her cheek as he leaned in and whispered in her ear.

"Savor it."

Closing her mouth, she allowed the berry to marinate against her palette. At first, the flavor was slightly bitter and salty, but then the berry began to melt and abruptly a surge of sweetness flooded her mouth. After it mixed with the tangy briny exterior, the flavor profile became both exotic and comforting.

Swallowing, she opened her eyes. "I've never had anything that tasted like that."

Zane smiled. "This is a very old grove. Most likely a product of the elves."

Taken aback, she hesitated. It was the first time since arriving in Ravenia she'd heard reference to the race who'd raised her.

"Did you enjoy it?"

She nodded. "What is the fruit called?"

"I have no idea. I found this thicket a few years back and was pleasantly surprised to find this grove in its midst. Because of the overgrowth, these bushes hardly see any light, yet they always provide a bountiful harvest."

"Like magic."

'Yes," he said with a grin. "Like magic."

"You come here often?"

"Not as much as I'd like. I try and come here whenever I'm in the kingdom. It's peaceful." A shadow darkened his eyes and for a moment he seemed wistful.

He moved in closer, his dark curls fluttering in the breeze. "What is your story, Vallaria?" he asked as his dark eyes penetrated hers.

She swallowed. Her mouth had suddenly become dry.

"Why do you think I have a story?"

"Everyone does."

"Mine is of no interest."

"I'm sure that's not true."

His fingers grazed her cheek as he brushed back a stray hair from her face. He had a small scar on his upper lip and another intersecting his brow. The dark lashes framing his eyes were long and thick, and when he spoke his voice became husky.

"You are a very interesting woman."

He leaned in, his lips hovering above hers.

Vallaria!

Faelin's voice echoed through the grove, interrupting the intimate moment.

She stepped back. "I have to go." Her voice was breathy, and her heart raced. Breaking from his intoxicating gaze, she turned and ran back through the thicket, not daring to look back.

What are you doing, Vallaria? she asked herself. Since the moment Faelin had pointed Zane out in the tavern, she'd been intrigued by the handsome mercenary. Besides his tantalizing good looks, he had a mystery about him that lured her in. He was evasive yet still had a way of making one feel like he was telling you something of importance. His casual demeanor and impish attitude were hard not to like as it made her feel comfortable in his presence.

And that was part of the problem. Besides being an unwanted distraction, Zane had a way of disarming people, which could be detrimental to her goals.

She was in the kingdom for one thing, and she couldn't let anyone get in her way no matter how charming they were. Her head must remain clear and focused.

No distractions!

Whatever was happening between her and Zane, nothing could come of it. They were from different worlds: he a mercenary from the Gold Coast and she a princess of Ravenia determined to take back her throne. And when she did, war would certainly come to her door and she and Zane would find themselves on opposite sides.

At first the whispers were nothing more than hisses on the wind. But as Vallaria walked farther into the dense mist, the voices became clearer, more persistent. A chorus of words surrounded her, but she couldn't make out what they were saying. Icy fingers stroked her skin as the fog twisted around her.

As the voices rose, so too did the pulse of the mage crystal, its cold surface bleeding through her pocket lining and freezing the skin beneath.

Her hands grew cold and she held them aloft, watching as blue light ebbed under the skin.

The whispers grew louder.

Directionless in the thick haze, Vallaria's heart thumped wildly in her chest. Lost in an endless fog she turned, and the toe of her boot clipped something wedged into the ground. Tripping, she landed face down on the cold earth.

Suddenly, the mist thinned and swirled away from the ground, revealing the object she'd stumbled over.

Staring at her with lifeless eyes and withered lips, open as if in a silent scream, was a severed head. Worms crawled from the eye sockets and the tongue, swollen and purple, protruded slightly from the mouth.

Her breath quickened and her hands clawed at the ground as she pushed herself away.

The whispers surrounding her reached an eerie crescendo. In a moment of lucidity, as a screamed bubbled up in her throat, she realized the voices were coming from the head.

Vallaria woke with a start, her blouse saturated in sweat and her skin clammy.

Just a dream.

But her instincts told her it wasn't. Whatever had been calling to her in the mist was real, and it was calling for her to come home.

34

ZANDER

Zander couldn't sleep, his mind was cluttered with thoughts of Vallaria. Somehow she'd gotten under his skin. Although beautiful with striking pale blue eyes a man could get lost in, he was sure there was much more to the complicated and mysterious stranger than her looks. Never had he met a woman like her, and it intrigued him in a way something or someone hadn't in a very long time. She was defiant, determined, and at times infuriating, but those traits made her even more attractive.

His relationship with women had always been simple. Don't get too close. Bed them, make no promises, and disappear before they start talking of a future together. He also had a strict rule: never engage with a woman he might see again. But for Vallaria he may have to amend his way of thinking.

Scoffing, he reminded himself that if he lived through this nightmare quest, he was leaving Ravenia and never coming back.

He would get as far away from his mother and her insatiable appetite for power as he could. A mercenary on a merchant ship, or a woodsman in the large forests of Brulle, he could even sail to the far side of the world and find work as a laborer or sword for hire.

Anything would be better than being a pawn in his mother's power grab.

He'd only been nine when his stepfather Torrsen had become king and it was shortly after that his mother had insisted he go live with his Uncle Moricio in the Gold Coast. That was where he grew up, only returning to the Kingdom of Ravenia when his mother beckoned him. Over the years those visits became less and less and his mother more distant and colder.

Turning over onto his back, he placed his forearm under his head and thought about the day he realized the mother he knew as a young child had disappeared. He and Moricio returned to the kingdom for King Torrsen's funeral. Strangely, the funeral was small and certainly not worthy of a ruler. His mother had been, for a widow, oddly cheerful. Although dressed in black, she smiled and laughed with those in attendance. Zander had found it all unsettling, but what was even more so was not once did his mother comfort him. Not even when she found him sobbing in the corner of the royal crypt by himself.

"Zander, you are a young man not a small child. Dry your tears and do not embarrass me again."

Straightening her crown, she'd glared at him and stalked from the room. She hadn't spoken to him, nor did she check on him for the remaining days he and Moricio were at the castle. When they left a few days later, Zander could remember turning around as they rode off. His mother stood on the upper balcony, staff in hand, *smiling*.

A tear escaped from the corner of his eye, and he wiped it away as rowdy voices drifted toward him from the main camp.

Unable to sleep, he got up and walked toward the fire, where the blacksmith and the mercenary with long hair were drunkenly singing ballads. Moving in the shadows his eyes searched for Tagar.

His bedroll was empty, but low whispers from the tree line caught his attention. The commander was in deep conversation with the two remaining mercenaries. When Zander walked out of the shadows, their conversation immediately ended.

"Can't sleep?" Tagar asked.

Zander shook his head as he eyed the mercenary with the eye patch.

"Well, why don't you join us at the fire for a drink?"

"You're not at the fire." His eyes dropped to the men's hands. "Nor do I see ale."

Tagar's eye twitched and his mouth drew tight into a thin line. "Then I suggest we go get us a mug."

It was not a statement but a command. The mercenaries gazed at Zander with contempt in their eyes. He'd interrupted something—of that he was sure. Something Tagar did not want him to know about. Turning he walked to the fire and sat down. Moments later, Tagar handed him a flagon of ale.

"Best enjoy this tonight, boys. You never know what the Valley of Souls holds for us tomorrow."

The glint in his eye told Zander that he was correct. The commander was hiding something, and his gut told him it most likely had to do with him."

Hours later, Zander stumbled back to his bed. When he lay down he caught sight of a sleeping Vallaria, and his heart skipped a beat. He'd so badly wanted to kiss her earlier.

You don't need this and neither does she.

Even in his drunken stupor he was right. He was a loner, a wanderer, and maybe even a little damaged. Not to mention she had no idea who he truly was. Maybe Prince Zander Damask wouldn't appeal to a woman like her the way a Gold Coast mercenary might.

BLEARY-EYED, ZANDER FOUND HIS WAY DOWN TO THE STREAM AND SPLASHED ice-cold water on his face. One jug of ale had turned into two and then three and soon he was drunk and listening to Tagar drone on about all the men he'd bested in his past. The commander was an insufferable braggart who regaled in horrifying his audience with vividly descriptive retellings.

"I gutted a man while he screwed a whore. The bastard didn't even see it coming. Opened him up from shoulder blade to ass cheek and pulled out his innards from the back. He was still inside the crying bitch when I left."

The blacksmith had thrown his supper up on his shoes, prompting Tagar to go at the man for ten minutes, insulting him and calling him sissy boy.

Zander had stayed quiet and drank more ale.

"You look terrible."

His head lolled as Vallaria interrupted his recollection.

"Thank you. I feel even worse."

He stood and turned to look at her. Unsurprisingly, she looked refreshed and as beautiful as always. Her black leather pants were offset by a gray wool tunic and the red travel shawl she always wore. She'd swept her ebony hair off her face and gathered it into a ponytail that sat low at the nape of her neck. Small tendrils of hair blew across her face, and Zander fought the impulse to push them off her cheeks.

Her blues eyes narrowed as she tilted her head. "It might do you good not to stay up half the night drinking."

He nodded in agreement. "Did we keep you up?"

"Only for a bit." She hesitated before saying, "I heard you speaking with the commander last night about the elves. Do you really not like them?"

"Not particularly," he responded, rubbing his temples.

"Why not?"

Zander shrugged. "I suppose it's because they deem us the inferior race. Or maybe because after King Torrsen took the throne, they abandoned the kingdoms of man."

Vallaria stiffened and her tone tightened. "You seem to know a lot about the elves."

"I know they are spiteful, vindictive, and can't be trusted."

"But you mentioned to the commander that you'd never met one."

"I haven't, not to my knowledge anyway. The elves of Mistenvale rarely leave their kingdom anymore, but their past actions have left a stain on their reputation. For too long the kingdoms of man have resented the way the elves have treated them. You will be hard-pressed to find any who would welcome them."

"And if you did meet one, what would you do?"

Zander's bloodshot gaze lifted. "Why do you ask such questions?"

"It's interesting to me that you can so profoundly dislike someone you've never met."

He groaned and rubbed at his forehead. He wasn't in the mood for this.

"Maybe one day you will meet one and you will change your mind." Vallaria smiled as Faelin came down the hill.

"I doubt that will ever happen," he grunted. "While magic can still be found in this world, it's been relegated to the shadows. I suspect the elves may not be as powerful as they once were or maybe by now they too have disappeared entirely."

Faelin stepped beside him. "I wouldn't be so sure. The elves have been here long before man, and I suspect they'll be here long after mankind has found a way to destroy itself."

The calm yet searing way Faelin delivered that statement did not escape Zander, not even in his current state. "Well, I guess only time will tell." Quickly changing the subject, he said, "Are you ready for the day's adventures?"

"We are, but I'm not sure you are up for the task?" Faelin answered. "I suggest you get some coffee first. You don't want to enter the Valley of Souls without a sharp mind. There's a fresh pot on the fire."

"Thanks. Coffee," he said, pointing toward the camp.

Nodding, Vallaria stepped to the side and let him pass. He hesitated as his heart reacted to her proximity. "Are you afraid?" he asked her, his eyes locking on hers.

"Of the valley?"

"Of what may lurk there."

Her brow furrowed and her nose crinkled slightly. "Is it worse than what lurks out here?"

He smiled at her evasion. "Probably not."

Walking away, he turned to look back, watching as Vallaria knelt and filled a canteen while she spoke with Faelin. He had no idea where they'd come from, but one thing was apparent: Vallaria was either extremely brave or extremely naïve. Either way they were all about to find out if the myths surrounding the Valley of Souls were true.

While he walked back to camp, Zander's addled mind reflected on the stories he'd heard on his numerous journeys across the continent. Stories morphed and changed over time, but one thing stayed constant: the Valley of Souls was cursed, saturated with the blood of the old mages whose tortured spirits roamed the lands. Dark magic poisoned the air, drenched the earth, and corrupted all who entered. And any who did were never heard from again.

Ghost stories. Tales of the unnatural and the unholy. Stories like these were commonplace all over Exile, Brulle, and beyond. Many cultures had their own demons and horrors woven into their past. Even the Gold Coast. But nothing compared to the Valley of Souls. If the Dagger of Crusade was real, this would be the best place for it to be hidden.

"We leave now," Tagar yelled as Zander gathered Magnus from the makeshift stable. Waving in acknowledgement, his head pounding he thought again about the warm sea winds that blew into the market back home.

"We'll see the Gold Coast again, my friend," he whispered as he patted Magnus's neck. But the words were hollow as nothing about his future was certain anymore.

An hour later they were looking down at the Valley of Souls from a ridge. The atmosphere had already changed. Gone was the invigorating chill of the rain and in its place a stale, heavy air hovered over the valley. *Stagnant,* as if no breeze ever blew across its surface, no rain fell on its soil, and no warmth ever wrapped it in its embrace. The air seeping from the valley made one feel as if death itself reached out and grasped you in its bony fingers, sending an otherworldly chill into your very soul.

Zander shuddered.

A thick mist swirled at the bottom, obscuring their view to the very bottom. *Better to hide the things lurking there.*

No sooner had the thought crossed his mind then a hollow moan rose from its depths.

"What was that?" Pax said, his eyes wide.

"There is nothing to worry about—sounds can't hurt you." Zander smiled at the boy. He too had surprisingly grown fond of the young fellow. Pax was a calm and innocent soul in a tortured and ugly world.

"Unless that sound comes from something that can." Tagar's gray eyes shifted from the boy to Zander and a menacing grin curled his lips.

Smug shit. The man couldn't pass up an opportunity to terrorize someone.

Zander leaned forward in the saddle and gripped Magnus's reins as he glared at Tagar. "Maybe if we're lucky it will see your ugly mug first."

The commander sneered. "For your sake, you'd better hope it does." The mercenaries laughed as Tagar turned his horse and started down the gravel trail into the valley.

The knot that had buried itself deep in Zander's stomach tightened as a little voice in his head screamed out a warning. He needed to watch his back. Tagar Garrate was up to something, and it wasn't just retrieving a dagger for his queen.

He followed the others into the valley while he whispered a prayer to his gods. He didn't know why. He couldn't remember the last time he'd done so. Maybe it was because he'd seen Vallaria's prayer beads wrapped in her fist as she slept last night, or maybe it was because it might ease the helplessness gouging at his insides. Whatever the reason, it probably wouldn't help. The gods had been silent for years, and he had little faith they would come to his aid now.

The scout's mare reared as they rode lower into the valley and the fog thickened. Cursing as the horse stumbled, the man dismounted and walked her the rest of the way down the incline.

Windless air surrounded them, thick and heavy against their skin. When they reached the basin, they heard a whispering wail far off in the distance. Although muffled by the thick fog, it still managed to burrow under Zander's skin and cover it with goosebumps.

Zander grasped Magnus's reins tighter. "Everyone stay close. We don't want anyone getting lost in this dismal place."

He did not miss the smirk that formed on the commander's lips at his statement, nor did Faelin, who cast him a suspicious look. There had been a few times in the past days that he'd caught the blonde watching him. Her calm green eyes never wavered, even when he stared back. He tried to ignore her, but something about the young woman that made him feel self-conscious.

Soon they came to a small wooden gate attached to two adjacent trees. It hung crooked from rusted hinges and creaked as it swayed in the nonexistent breeze. The twisted trees were the skeletal remains of what Zander assumed used to be majestic hardwoods. The base circumference was as wide as a doorway and the tops of the trees disappeared into the mist above. The trunks were stripped of bark and weathered to a grayish white. Their branches were bare of vegetation and stretched out awkwardly, deformed limbs with no purpose.

Zander shuddered, chilled by the damp mist and the otherworldly atmosphere of the valley.

"I don't want to go in there."

The voice was small and wavered with fear. Zander looked over at Pax, who was huddled into Vallaria, his eyes wide as he stared up at the dead trees.

"There is nothing to fear, Pax. I won't let anything hurt you."

The angst in Vallaria's tone tugged at Zander's heart. Both she and the boy were afraid. He glanced at the others, a group of pale, worried faces. Damn, they all were.

"Get the gate," the commander grumbled, pointing to one of the mercenaries.

While Zander waited for the man to unblock their path, he thought about Vallaria and Pax. He hadn't bothered to ask Vallaria what the connection was between her and the boy when she'd approached him in the city. At the time he'd been hungover and cared only about the incessant pounding in his skull. When he'd mentioned it yesterday, she shrugged and changed the subject. He assumed they weren't related as there was no resemblance in their appearance, and although Vallaria looked fondly on the young boy, it didn't seem like their relationship was intimately personal like that between siblings would be.

He tilted his head and frowned as he watched her try and comfort the fearful boy. It seemed more likely she'd met Pax in one of the villages in the kingdom or on the streets of the city, but if that were the case, why bring him on such a strenuous and most likely dangerous trek?

"After you, Zane." Tagar's voice broke through his thoughts.

Nodding, he pushed his heel into Magnus's side. "Easy boy," he whispered as the horse moved forward.

As they traveled father down into the valley, the gravel trail turned muddy and damp from the cold mist that hovered above it. A few times, one of the horses slid as the thick muck acted like ice under their hooves. The dense fog restricted their field of vision to only a few yards. It was disorienting, and with blunted senses, a cold creeping panic slide up Zander's spine.

Something waited in the mist.

Before he could scold himself for his overactive imagination, a menacing snarl echoed through the gray wall of fog.

Pulling back on the reins, he held up a hand, indicating to the others to be silent.

The gray light of the day made it difficult to distinguish what the fog hid.

Another growl echoed.

He squinted, seeing dark shadows move in the haze.

Zander whispered, "Be on the lookout. Something moves up ahead."

"There?" Vallaria cried as three creatures covered in thick black fur emerged from the fog. Their stance was predatory and their growls a distinct indication of their displeasure at finding intruders on their turf.

Zander sized them up as the mercenaries and commander drew their weapons.

They were dark beasts, large in stature with massive paws and gleaming orange eyes. Long pointed fangs dripped with dewy saliva and as they crouched, pawing at the ground, their growls turned from a warning to something more threatening.

A wave of cold dread gripped Zander as he recognized the fabled creatures before them. *Hellhounds!*

"Nobody move," he hissed.

His mouth had become parched, and he found it difficult to swallow. The stories of old were true. Dark and malevolent creatures did reside in the valley. He searched his memory for the story King Torrsen told him about hellhounds on one of his few trips back to the Kingdom of Ravenia.

"Guarding entry to the valley are hellhounds, demon dogs cursed to walk the earth and protect all that reside within the dark basin. They are fierce and difficult to kill; although they seem to be of this world, they are not. It is said one bite can render a man fraught with hallucinations, their blood becoming infected with its toxic saliva."

That story had kept Zander up most of the night, afraid to close his eyes in fear the demon dogs may find a way into his dreams.

As he watched the hellhounds pace menacingly in front of him, he could only imagine what waited for them farther into the valley.

"Wolves?" Vallaria whispered, moving slowly in beside him.

In response to the movement, the dogs gnashed their teeth and snapped at each other. Thankfully they'd stopped their approach, content to guard their territory from a distance. They were much like dogs in that way, choosing to show a display of dominance rather than attack.

Keeping his eyes on the threat, Zander shook his head and answered, "I believe these are hellhounds."

She frowned. "I don't know what that is."

"Beasts from the underworld."

Her pale blue eyes turned his way, and she raised her brows. "I'm sure they're just very large wolves."

Zander didn't know if she was trying to convince him or herself, but the way she furled and unfurled her prayer beads told him that a part of her believed the creatures standing in front of them may be otherworldly.

"Watch the outline of the body," he whispered back. "If you look closely, you will see it flicker. They are still attached to the other-world, which leaves their form not fully realized in this one."

Vallaria nodded as she took notice of what he said.

"We need to get by," Tagar said. He lifted his sword and motioned to the three mercenaries. "Kill them."

Under the penetrating gaze of the commander, the men slid from their mounts and advanced forward, swords raised. Uncertainty masked their faces, and Zander noticed the small, stocky merce-nary's hand tremble so violently he almost dropped his sword.

The hellhounds snarled as they deemed the men a threat. The largest beast shook its fur in a show of dominance and pawed at the ground, scraping up dust and clumps of dirt with its thick pads and long claws. Another threw its head back and let out a long, mournful howl.

The unholy bay cut through Zander like a freshly honed blade.

Even though he dreaded engaging with something not of this world, and therefore completely unknown, they weren't going to get by these creatures without a fight.

He dismounted from Magnus and drew his sword, wincing at the hollow ting it made as it slid from the sheath.

Orange eyes turned his way, and the smaller hellhound took a step forward, curled back it lips, and bared its fangs. At the same time another charged the mercenaries.

He glanced at Vallaria. "Be careful," he mouthed as he moved forward in what he hoped was an unthreatening manner.

Without warning the beast pounced. It bared its teeth as it sprung, traveling ten feet through the air before it landed heavily on him. Surprised by the hurried attack, Zander didn't have time to plant his feet, and as the demon dog's massive paws impacted with his shoulders, he toppled to the ground. Seconds before the razor-sharp fangs bit him, he slammed the flat side of his sword into the hellhound's throat, using it as a barrier between his face and those teeth.

The beast thrashed on top of him, trying desperately to breach the obstacle. Zander's muscles burned as he struggled to maintain the distance and not inhale the pungent stench of rotten meat emanating from the creature's mouth. He turned his face to the side, struggling to catch a breath of clean air and avoid the hot saliva spraying from its jaws.

After a few more seconds of aggression, the demon dog pulled back and licked his lips, staring Zander down with defiant red eyes. Warmth blossomed on his leg, as something wet soaked through his trousers. For an instant Zander's mind refused to comprehend what he was feeling but then—

Did the goddamn hound just urinate on me?

Fury rolled through him, and he pushed the sword harder into the hound. The edges of the blade cut into his palms and fingers. Blood trickled down his hands and wrists from the wounds as he fought the thrashing beast on top of him.

As he struggled, he could see Vallaria in his peripheral vison running toward him, sword raised. With one swing, the blade cut through the hellhound's neck, severing part of its head from its body. Hot blood spurted outward, coating Zander's face in the sticky, dark red fluid. He gasped as the animal fell on top of him, its weight crushing the breath from his lungs.

With hands burning from the cuts, he desperately tried to push the hellhound from his chest. After sheathing her sword, Vallaria pulled at the creature's fur, helping to yank the body off Zander.

"Thanks," he said moments before a swooshing sound echoed through the air, followed by a yelp. The beast attacking the mercenaries teetered and fell to the ground in a heap, the bolt from Faelin's crossbow wedged in the front of its skull.

The mercenaries, one with claw marks gouged into his arm, looked at Faelin in silence and then begrudgingly nodded their thanks.

The largest of the three was the only one left, and as Zander stood, he noticed it stood motionless, watching.

"That must be the alpha," Tagar said, coming to stand beside them.

The alpha's burnt orange eyes travelled back and forth over the group. His lips curled away from his pointed teeth, and a slow rumble escaped his lips as he pawed the ground.

"What's he doing?" Vallaria said.

Tagar chuckled. "He's warning us by showing his dominance in a passive-aggressive way."

"Like someone else I know," Zander said, sarcasm dripping from the words.

He could feel Tagar's gray eyes bore into him, but instead of taking Zander's bait he said, "The beast is sizing us up. Be ready for anything."

The hellhound growled a throaty howl that raised the hair on Zander's arms. Unlike the other two, this one seemed in no rush to tear their throats out. It shook its black fur and clawed at the ground, stretched, and flicked its long bushy tail, and even yawned, but it didn't move from the spot where it stood.

"What is it waiting for?" Vallaria asked.

Zander shrugged.

"It's not waiting for anything," the commander responded. "It's toying with us."

Saliva dripped from his mouth as, slowly, eyes never leaving its prey, the demon dog began to walk forward. As it moved, the outline of its body swayed like smoke drifting lazily from a campfire, the edges ebbing in and out of this world and the next. The black fur shimmered as it moved, and its eyes deepened from a blazing orange to a sickly red.

Tagar stepped forward and raised his sword.

Zander lay a hand on Vallaria's arm and hissed at the commander, "What are you doing?"

"There can only be one alpha today."

Cursing, Zander pulled his sword as the beast reared and pounced. Tagar swung as the hound sailed past him, but the blade missed completely instead nicking Zander's right bicep. Blood seeped down his arm, and he eyed the commander with mistrust and anger. Tagar stared back, his eyes full of hate as a smirk curled on his lips.

That was no accident. And by the look on his face, he was only sorry he missed.

A snarl tore through the air as the hellhound turned toward them and charged again. It lunged, and Zander ducked underneath, lifting his sword up quickly. His sharp blade punctured the skin, cutting a path through the belly. A hellish howl split the misty air, and the beast landed in a pile of blood, whimpering and panting. Zander walked to the defeated creature as the last of the demon glow left the hound's eyes. A small mewl escaped its lips and it shuddered out its final breath, its body going limp.

While Zander watched, the bodies of all three hellhounds began to change. Their physical forms shifted, melting into black smoky shadows that swirled together, hovered over the dirt momentarily, and then disappeared into the ground.

The cut in his arm ached and he clasped his hand around it, trying to stop the blood flow as he glanced at Tagar. The commander had rejoined the mercenaries, and as he looked back at Zander with those dead gray eyes, his lips quirked and the tic below his left eye twitched.

A twinge pulled at his stomach.

Zander would need to watch his back. He was certain the commander had an ulterior motive, a motive that Zander knew would turn out to be detrimental to his welfare.

35
CERELI

"Your Majesty, where on Exile have you been? I've been looking for you everywhere." Yelin's scarlet cheeks indicated how flustered he was as he bustled into the throne room.

"What is it?" she asked, ignoring his attempt at gaining information. No one realized a secret room existed in the dungeons. She'd had it designed and built before many of the current staff were employed.

"Your brother has arrived," he said, pausing for effect as he came to a stop before her. His small hands flitted around as he waited for her reaction.

With a steady voice, she said, "He's a day early."

Yelin flipped his hand in a casual way as if the premature arrival of her brother was no big deal. "He's waiting in the kitchens, Your Majesty."

"Whatever is he doing in the kitchens?"

"He said he was hungry from his journey."

"So you allowed him to prepare a meal himself?" Cereli's ire grew as she watched the twitching little man in front of her. Her brother

Moricio was like all military men, domineering and intimidating, but powerful men never seemed to bother Yelin, nor did he make a habit of cowering to any. Therefore, there must be a reason he thought allowing her brother to roam freely through her castle was a good idea.

"He insisted."

Insisted indeed. Moricio Damask had a way of doing things that made it clear to everyone around him that he was in charge, and that no matter where he was he would not obey any rules he deemed beneath him. Including staying out of specific rooms in *her* castle.

"I'm surprised he didn't ask to wait in my bedchamber," she spat.

Yelin cringed at her tone, and his face flushed. "My queen, he wouldn't."

"Get out," she said, waving him off. "I will find my brother and welcome him to the kingdom."

"Are you sure you wouldn't like me to accompany you?"

Raising a perfectly sculpted brow, she glared at her advisor. He wanted to know what news Moricio brought and how it would affect the kingdom. Yelin Barro made himself indispensable by knowing everything about everybody and every situation and using it effectively to advance an objective. But this time, he would not be at her side when she greeted her brother.

"I haven't seen my brother in years, Yelin. I would like time alone to catch up. I will call for you if any matters regarding the kingdom arise."

His brown eyes narrowed. "Very well." With a short bow, he turned on his satin slippers and hurried from the room.

Cereli walked to the window and stared out across her kingdom in the direction of the Gold Coast. Her brother's arrival could only mean one thing: Emperor Silvalas had passed.

Her eyes scanned the horizon as she thought of her homeland.

Darrius Mensah in charge would mean changes coming to the empire, and in turn, to her kingdom. Silvalas had allowed her to rule

Ravenia in peace, and in return, she agreed to acknowledge the kingdom as part of the Gold Coast Empire. It was a small price to pay to be left alone. But Darrius didn't agree with his father's leniency toward a female ruler, specifically one not of royal blood. He'd pushed the emperor and the council to have her marry so that a king could once again sit on Ravenia's throne, but he'd always met resistance from the emperor.

Cereli slammed her fist on the windowsill and cursed. She'd be damned if Darrius would take the throne from her. With the power of the Gold Coast Empire and the Ravenia army behind him, Emperor Darrius would sack every kingdom on the continent until there was nothing left not under his rule or laid to waste under a pile of rubble. He was power hungry, unrelenting, and had no problem spilling blood to get what he wanted. His father had always kept Darrius's worse tendencies at bay, but with the emperor no longer in this world, Cereli had no doubt sooner or later he would come for her throne.

With a deep cleansing breath, she left the throne room and headed in the direction of the kitchens to find her brother. No use putting off the inevitable, better to know what was coming than to be blindsided by fate.

"Moricio!" she said, flinging open the kitchen door and rushing into the kitchens. "What a lovely surprise."

Her older brother, twelve years her senior, tall, handsome, his eyes dark pits of intelligence, smiled as she entered. He'd finished devouring the remainder of last night's leg of lamb and the bone lay neatly hidden under a perfectly folded napkin.

Never anything out of order with the general.

"It's nice to see you again, sister." He took her gently by the shoulders and kissed both cheeks. "You look well."

His smoldering gaze told a different story as he scrutinized her from top to bottom. Moricio had never approved of her "dark queen" alter ego. He thought it vulgar and, frankly, egregious considering the Gold Coast was known for its opulence.

They were complete opposites. She dressed in black and he in red and gold. Her brother, even out of uniform, never diverted from the bright and lavish colors and fabrics the empire was known for. Although not a garish dresser like Yelin, her brother took pride in his appearance. He looked the exact same as when she'd seen him last, only now a hint of gray flecked his ebony hair at the temples.

"How is everyone back home?" she asked, making small talk.

"Marta is pregnant."

Marta was the youngest of his three wives and with this birth she would give him his eighth child. She was also younger than two of his children. "Do you hope for another boy?"

"Boys are easier."

Cereli's lip curled. What Moricio meant was boys were more accepted in the Gold Coast and less of a burden. They had direction, while females were good for only one thing: bringing more males into the world. Thankfully, of his seven children, Moricio only had two daughters. At nine and thirteen, they'd already been promised to two of the sons of House Desert Vulture, both already in their early twenties.

"I suppose they are." *Until they stab you in the back.*

"And where is your son, Cereli? After you summoned him back to Ravenia, I expected he'd be here to greet me, but Yelin says you have him out on some errand." His dark eyes flashed. "I hope he will be back soon."

Cereli cocked her head. Was there a hint of warning in Moricio's voice? She smiled, and in a syrupy tone said, "Tagar needed help with palace business and Zander was tired of being cooped up—you know how he hates it here—so I allowed him to go. I'm not sure they will be back before you must return to the Gold Coast, unfortunately. And when is that precisely?"

Moricio clenched his right hand and stared at her with a stern expression. "As soon as my business here is attended to."

Cereli's expression darkened. "And what exactly is your business, Moricio?"

Her brother glanced at the kitchen staff. "I think we should find somewhere more private."

She nodded. "The library," she said, indicating for him to follow.

"Thank you for a wonderful meal," he said to the cook as he passed. Taking the older lady's hand in his own he smiled. "The lamb was divine."

The cook blushed and thanked him.

Cereli rolled her eyes. Moricio Damask excelled at two things: warring and charming people, and often he did them both at the same time. Her brother's reputation as a tough general in the empire's vast military was strewn with rumors of his enigmatic charisma. General Damask was known to charm enemies into submission as often as he brutalized them. Cereli, amused by the stories, believed something closer to the truth was that her brother charmed the women of his enemies into his bed. The Damask men were known for their infidelity. Just like their father, after their mother's death, Moricio cared little for discretion, and he'd unfortunately passed that unabashed way of thinking on to her son, Zander.

Opening the sturdy door of the library, Cereli stepped aside, allowing her brother to pass across the threshold first. The long and narrow room's walls were lined with leather-bound tomes, journals, scrolls, and codex. At the middle, a wood table sat covered in maps and surrounded by tall leather chairs.

"What was so important that you made the journey to my kingdom yourself instead of sending a messenger?" Cereli asked.

"Emperor Silvalas is dead."

Even though she'd expected those words from her brother, now that they were unceremoniously out in the world Cereli found it hard to breathe. She stared blankly at her brother as he continued.

"There will be the standard one month of mourning then Darrius will ascend as the empire's new ruler. When he does, he will expect Ravenia to come fully into the empire."

"The emperor had my kingdom's allegiance and Darrius will as well."

Moricio raised a brow at her response. "You know he won't accept the way things are. Darrius Mensah is not his father, Cereli. He doesn't see things as Silvalas did. He never agreed or understood why his father showed you such leniency. Why he let you rule free of male governance."

Cereli's brow furrowed as she glared at Moricio. Leniency, she thought. It was not like the emperor handed her the crown. In fact, it was quite the opposite. If it hadn't been for her, Ravenia would still be a sovereign nation under King Ryguard's rule instead of an independent faction of the Gold Coast Empire. Instead of admonishing her brother's triteness she said, "Emperor Silvalas was gracious, but he understood I could rule as well as any man."

Moricio's eyes darkened and he absently stroked his goatee. "I'm not sure his motives were that simple."

There it was. Her brother's evasive response every time she brought up Emperor Silvalas's reasoning for allowing her to be a ruling queen. "Then what do you think the emperor's motives were? Since you were his general, you must be privy to such information." The clipped words amplified the defiance in her tone as heat rose to her cheeks.

Moricio ignored the query and her change in attitude, instead choosing to focus on the reason he was here. "Darrius wants a king on the throne. You best prepare for an arranged marriage or to be unceremoniously dethroned. If you wish to stay a queen, I suggest the former."

"And you, Moricio, what do you want?" she asked, running a long nail down the smooth edge of the finished wood tabletop.

"I serve at the pleasure of the emperor no matter who wears the crown. My opinion matters little."

"But you are also my brother. That must count for something."

Moricio stiffened, and his dark eyes locked on hers. "Darrius Mensah is a cruel and vindictive man. He will not hesitate to cut down any who stand in his way. He plans to rule the empire with an iron fist the way his father used to in his younger years. You do not want to cross him. Even I won't be able to protect you then." He leaned in closer and lowered his voice. "I know of the darkness that obeys your every whim, but trust me when I say your magic is no match for Darrius Mensah's sorceress."

Taken aback by his revelation, Cereli's pulse quickened. "Sorceress?"

"From the Dark Isles of Atune," he said, his tone sharp and impactful.

She shuddered. *Impossible!*

Legend claimed the Dark Isles of Atune were once home to an immortal race of sorceresses. Their magic was said to be unmatched by any other, even the mages. But as time does, it turned their existence into nothing more than a myth and the stories faded into the past.

To her knowledge no one had been to Atune for centuries. The waters surrounding the isles were treacherous. Coral reefs sliced ships to ribbons miles off its shores. The seabed was strewn with the wreckage of the doomed ships, and any sailor who did survive lived only for a moment before being pulled under the waves where they drowned, or worse, became food for the sea creatures inhabiting the Dark Isle's murky waters.

Her mouth gaped. "The Atune sorceresses are myth."

Moricio's face fell, and his eyes filled with pity. "There is much you don't know, hiding here in your dark kingdom. Darrius has been preparing for his father's demise for years. He plans to take the Holy City of Kasmire and only you and Ravenia stand in his way."

"Kasmire is an impenetrable fortress that has stood against enemies for centuries. It will never fall. Darrius is a fool to think it will."

He lowered his voice and his eyes bore deep into her own. "Do not underestimate his determination or that which he has under his control. With the sorceress by his side, Darrius will get everything he desires."

"And you've seen this sorceress?" Her tone challenged Moricio, even though the tightness in her stomach confirmed he wasn't lying.

With a stoic expression he nodded. "She's as powerful as the stories say, exotically beautiful, and as venomous as Darrius. Whatever your plans, going against him will be a fatal mistake. It is best to accept your fate."

"And if I do, who does Darrius plan for me to marry? Who does he want to be the King of Ravenia?"

"Jerome."

The name floated effortlessly from his mouth, and Cereli almost choked on it. *Jerome,* Darrius's younger brother. Moricio couldn't be serious. For everything Darrius was, Jerome was the opposite. He was quiet, weak, and fearful of the world outside the gates of the Golden City.

"He's no ruler," she spat.

"He's Darrius's blood, and he will never go against his brother. Jerome is loyal to a fault, which is all Darrius cares about. He requires a king on the throne of Ravenia who will rule as proxy and not think for himself."

Cereli's mind began to whirl. For years her focus had been the prophecy and cultivating an allegiance with the holy city, and of late finding the dagger. Her attention hadn't been on Darrius and thus she'd ignored a very real threat. And now her lack of judgment might cost her everything.

She began to pace. Moricio's dark gaze followed her. Zander was part of this coup—she was sure of it, but Yelin had it wrong. Her son would not be king of Ravenia—he never wanted to be. Betraying her was designed to ensure that would never happen. Darrius Mensah had offered Zander the one thing he desired over anything else and the one thing she never gave him—*freedom.*

And now her freedom was at stake.

Whatever it takes, Cereli, she thought to herself.

"I have a lot to consider, brother," she said, eyeing Moricio. "If you will excuse me there is much I need to attend too. Please make yourself at home."

Without a backward glance, she exited the library and hurried to the stables. There was a matter she needed to deal with, and it could wait no longer.

36

CERELI

She rode her steed steadfast through the lands, passing rivers, dells, and farmsteads until she reached the dark forest in the north of her kingdom. Her scouts had reported seeing him here days before, and she hoped, knowing his insufferable ego, that he was still lingering in her domain.

A whiff of campfire smoke confirmed he was.

Pulling on the reins, she directed her horse off the main road and into a beaten trail that led straight into the heart of the thick forest. It took her only minutes to see the glow of the campfire and hear the crackle of the burning wood.

Dismounting she tied the reins to a tree and proceeded to walk carefully toward the encampment. The last thing she needed was to startle one of the most infamous assassins on the continent. If her death was to come soon, it would not be at the hand of this man and his unsavory lot.

While mulling over her potential demise, movement to her left caught her eye.

From the shadows of the trees stepped a hulking figure. He wore a black leather jacket tight over his large frame with matching pants tucked into brown leather boots. The sleeves were pushed high up his muscular tattooed forearms and the jacket was open, revealing a dark hairy chest. Multiple small silver rings pierced his nostrils, and a solitary silver key hung from a thick black cord around his neck.

It was rumored that key opened a vault hidden somewhere in the Kingdom of Zion that was full of riches. Cereli surmised it was all a ploy, a rumor started by the big man in front of her to enhance his already ominous reputation.

"Fancy seeing the queen herself in this forest." His voice was deep and bellowed through the stillness of the night. The gold tooth at the front of his mouth glinted as he spoke.

"It is my land," she pointed out.

"It is that, but so far away from the comfort of the castle." He looked around. "No royal guard commander?"

"I've come alone."

A wry smile slid over his face. "Do you think that wise, Your Majesty?"

"I think it smart."

"How so?"

"I like to keep my business private."

"Ah, so you've come to hire, then?"

"Yes."

"And what could the powerful queen of Ravenia possibly need a treacherous fiend like me for? Doesn't the commander do all your dirty work?"

Cereli remained passively disinterested. "The commander is otherwise engaged."

"So you've come to ask Dagget Ra to fill in?" He chuckled and gestured for her to follow him to the fire.

Dagget Ra was a for-hire type mercenary. If the price was right, he didn't care much for the details of the job. He'd steal, kill, maim, kidnap, mutilate, or rape if someone lined his pockets with gold. His only redeeming quality, and it was a stretch, was that he did none of those things for fun.

After pouring her a goblet of sour wine, he sat across from her and asked, "What is it Her Majesty wishes done?"

"I want Jerome Mensah dead."

Dagget Ra raised a brow. "That is a big ask."

"I am willing to pay your price."

The leader of Zion raised his large hand with the missing finger and pushed it through his tangled mess of dark hair. Moments passed without a word while he stared, frowning at the ground.

"Lots of gold, of course, and a place in your kingdom."

Cereli was taken aback. Not by the request for gold but by the desire to work in her kingdom. The Kingdom of Zion, regardless of its name, was not a true kingdom at all. There was no monarchy or king, no royal bloodlines, only a small sentry of murderers and thieves living in an abandoned fortress in the northeast corner of the continent. The kingdom and its leader Dagget Ra were well known near and far, for many a king had used their services at one time or another. She had never had the need since Tagar fulfilled her every whim. But these were extenuating circumstances, plus Darrius Mensah hated Dagget Ra, which was precisely why Cereli wanted him for this task.

"What place in my kingdom could possibly appeal to a man of your means?"

Dagget Ra grinned, showing a mouthful of stained and chipped teeth. "I think I'd be best suited for a leading place in your army or a personal bodyguard for Your Highness."

Cereli eyed the big man in front of her. "As much gold as you can carry, and my word that if the Gold Coast Empire ever threatens your sovereignty, the Ravenia army will be at your disposal."

The man scoffed. "The Kingdom of Zion has stood for decades precisely because we do not need the help of any of the dominant kingdoms. We are never threatened—we are the threat." He grinned again, but this time his dark eyes held a murderous gaze.

"Once Darrius is emperor that may change."

"Let him come."

"Gold is the bounty," Cereli said, her tone firm and final.

Dagget Ra frowned, tilting his head as he studied her. "You are a fine queen, and the dark magic you wield, I admit makes even me slightly uncomfortable, but this is not why I will accept your offer. No, I will kill Jerome Mensah because he is a sniveling, timid coward who hides behind the power of his birthright. And men like that make me sick."

He spat on his hand and extended it toward Cereli. "We have a deal."

Cereli took his hand and shook it. "Sooner rather than later, yes?"

"Understood," he responded as he pulled his massive frame up onto his horse. "I'll be in touch, but keep in mind there may come a time in the future when I ask a favor of you." Before she could respond, he rode off into the woods, quickly disappearing behind the thick foliage.

Cereli suddenly felt very exposed standing alone in the clearing. Gathering her skirts in her hands, she hurried back to her horse and rode through the dense forest back toward the main road.

With Jerome dead, it would give her more time. Darrius would be preoccupied with finding his killer, and he wouldn't give a second thought to Ravenia or finding a suitable suitor for Cereli.

She may have made a deal with the devil, but it was necessary. Dagget Ra would surely change the terms of their agreement after he'd killed Jerome, but she would deal with those consequences when they arose. For now, she had a kingdom to run and a plan to devise for how to deal with a very much alive Serifine Ravenia.

37

FAELIN

Something had been nagging at her for the past few hours. Like a thread being tugged at the edge of a sweater, she expected it to unravel at any moment, but it never did, and she was left with the same puzzling uncertainties that had bothered her since she first laid eyes on Zane.

Faelin glanced toward the mercenary again and frowned.

What was it about him that left her filled with an unwanted sense of familiarity?

She'd never met him before, of that she was sure. Could she possibly have seen him in passing during her last trip to the Gold Coast? Impossible, she thought. After Baladril's death she'd only returned to the seaside city once, and he would have been a mere child at the time.

Pulling Krest up beside Zane's horse, she pointed to the strips of fabric wrapped around his palms and asked, "Are you all right?"

He lifted a blood-soaked hand and nodded. "The cuts aren't deep."

"You should cleanse the wounds with whatever alcohol your

friends have with them and then wrap them with gill-weed leaves. You don't want infection to set in."

"They're not my friends."

Her green gaze stayed steady. "But they have alcohol."

"You seem to know a lot about herbal remedies."

Faelin deadpanned. "Any adventurer should know simple remedies for wounds and injuries."

A boyish grin formed on Zane's face. "True, which is why I already have gill-weed leaves under the bandages."

"Good. Then we won't have to worry about your hands needing to be chopped off."

"Not today."

Changing the subject, Faelin asked, "Where did you say you were from?"

"Originally from the Gold Coast, but I've traveled all over this continent and the next. Why do you ask?"

His dark stare was full of interest, but the look, as simple and normal as it appeared, gave her an instant sense of recognition.

"Just making small talk." She smiled, hoping the mercenary wouldn't become wise to her prying. There was something about Zane that didn't sit right, and she intended to find out what. "And the commander. You two know each other well?"

He shrugged. "The commander has been at the queen's side for many a long year. Working for the kingdom means working for him."

"He doesn't seem to like you much," she said, indicating his bandaged hand.

Zane chuckled and small crinkles appeared at the corners of his dark eyes. "The commander doesn't like many people." His gaze shifted to Vallaria, who rode in front of them, and he lowered his voice. "What is her relationship with Pax?"

"That is something only Vallaria can answer in truth, but Ravenia is a dark place and sometimes the vulnerable need a helping hand."

"Let's go, girl," she said to Krest.

The horse promptly moved into a trot and strode away. She had no desire to have a meaningful conversation with the mercenary or give him too much information about their situation. There was too much at stake.

When they rode farther down the path into the valley, the mist thinned, and a haunting rustle filled the dead air.

"What is that?" one of the mercenaries asked as his horse stopped and backed up a few feet in distress.

Ahead was a line of grave markers, approximately a dozen or so. Stone crosses placed in the ground that time and the elements had pushed askew. They now leaned in awkward directions, their stone surfaces chipped or cracked. A wet moss clung to some, vines to others but each had one thing in common: their facings were blank, no writing or indication for whom they were laid.

"This is cursed land," the blacksmith stuttered. "We have to get out of here." His pale face, eyes wide, turned to the commander. "The legends are true. These gravestones mark the place where the bodies of the mages lay. Quiet graves with no epitaphs. It's a sign of disrespect and a slight to those who lay beneath this earth." He yanked on the reins, turning his horse the other way.

Faelin could see the fear in his eyes and the tremble in his hands that shook the reins.

The commander unsheathed his sword and pointed it at the blacksmith. "That's enough. I didn't hire you to provide historical context. We are here for one reason. Find the artifact the queen desire—and no one is leaving until it is found. Is that understood?"

The blacksmith swallowed but nodded in compliance.

"We do not fear the dead," Tagar said, putting his sword back into its sheath on his hip and guiding his horse around the markers.

Faelin followed, her gaze drawn to the gravestones. Along with the worn and overgrown stones, nature had also disturbed the earth. As she passed, she could see fragments of bones protruding from the muddy ground. Her mouth pulled into a grim line. There was nothing more sacrilege than a poorly buried body. The kings who'd massacred the mages had made desecration the point.

Maybe we should fear the dead—those with tortured souls.

"Faelin, are you okay?" Vallaria asked.

She nodded, noticing the concern on her friend's face. "I'm fine, but I think there is something else going on with this quest. I suspect those mercenaries and the commander are not only here for the Dagger of Crusade."

"What do you mean?"

"I'm not quite sure yet, but we should be vigilant and not trust any of them until we retrieve the artifact and get back to the kingdom."

Vallaria's eyes narrowed, but she didn't ask any more questions, and Faelin was thankful for that. She and Vallaria had been in each other's lives long enough for her to know that an elf's intuition was rarely wrong.

They followed the others toward a stone archway in the distance. When they neared the structure the temperature began to drop, and a cold mist rolled across the ground toward them.

"It's suddenly turned cold," Vallaria whispered, pulling Pax closer to her.

Coming to the edge, Faelin looked down into a massive pit. She couldn't see far as a thick mist swirled approximately twenty feet below, obscuring her view to the bottom. Her eyes scanned the rock walls surrounding the hole. Most of the stone was covered with sheets of ice, wet moss, and overgrowth.

That would explain the drop in temperature—and the smell.

The stink emanating from the walls was tangy, earthy, and scented with the foul odor of rot that made her nose twitch in disgust.

"What do you think's down there?" Vallaria asked, coming to stand beside her.

"Nothing good, I suspect."

"Can you sense something?"

Faelin shook her head. "Nothing but dead, stagnant air."

"That's good, right?"

"No. It just means that whatever might lurk below that mist doesn't want us to know it's there."

Vallaria moved in closer and lowered her voice. "But how can it hide from you?"

Her friend appreciated how acute and precise an elf's senses were, but even Faelin had limits. "When a land is cursed by ancient magic and twisted and corrupted by violence, like the slaughter of the mages, it taints the earth and everything it touches and draws to it all the negative energy it can reach. A place like this can hide from anyone—even me."

Their quiet conversation was interrupted by the commander.

"Now that we are here, I can reveal why you've been paid so handsomely for your attendance and inform you that all who make it back will be given an additional bonus of one bag of gold, presented to them by Her Majesty the queen herself, along with the other half of the agreed upon bounty."

A murmur rippled through the group as they glanced at one another and then back to the commander.

"Down there at the bottom of the pit, there is an altar. Atop that altar is the artifact the queen desires—the Dagger of Crusade."

Silence ignited the air momentarily until the mercenary with the neck tattoo snorted. "You've brought us out to this cursed place and risked all our lives for a myth." The others nodded and began questioning Tagar's words.

"What would you have us do, Tagar? the short, stocky mercenary asked. "Go down to the bottom and roam around all day hoping to find it? What the queen seeks is not real. Nothing more than a far-fetched yarn passed down through the ages."

Tagar Garrate held up his gloved hand, silencing them. "I would not have brought any of you out here, including a small boy, if I believed the dagger was not here." The commander glanced at Pax and smiled as if to ensure the boy there was nothing to fear, but

Faelin felt it came across as though the commander instead used him as a prop to manipulate the others.

When the mercenaries continued to grumble, the commander's face darkened. "I will also remind you that you greedy bastards took the queen's money, so if you attempt to back out now or flee I will put the blade of my sword so far up your arse you will taste your own shit."

Faelin's gaze returned to the three mercenaries, who paled and quickly shut up. Her eyes then fell upon the blacksmith and the scout as Tagar continued.

"It is said the altar is guarded by a monster fiercer than any we have seen before. Finding the altar will be difficult, but getting the dagger even more so. Move cautiously, stay upwind, and do not make any sudden movements no matter what you see— understood?"

The blacksmith and scout gaped at the commander and looked like they were about to pass out. Faelin assumed the information provided to them about the journey left out the horrors haunting the Valley of Souls. Since the blacksmith wasn't deft at handling a weapon, she feared sooner or later his lack of skills outside of his trade would get him killed. At least the scout could wield a sword.

"Let us proceed," Tagar said as he pulled the reins toward the only path leading into the pit.

Reluctantly the others followed, with her and Zane bringing up the rear.

Their progress was slow and uneasy as the thick mist obscured their vision and sent an unearthly chill into their bones.

Vallaria shivered beside her. "I'm beginning to think this wasn't the great idea I thought it was two days ago."

Faelin raised a brow. "Let's focus on the here and now. Stay alert and stay close."

When they reached the bottom, Faelin noticed it was much colder. But the mist had thinned, and they could now see farther and make out shapes in the distance. Nightfall was still a few hours away, but the pit's atmosphere was gray and dull, the same as the rest of Ravenia.

A scraping noise in the distance caught their attention.

"There is a sound coming from that direction," the scout said, pointing toward his left.

Tagar nodded. "From here we go on foot," he whispered. "Eyes open, we don't know what else is in here with us."

They tied the horses to a couple of tall tree stumps, then gathered their swords and provisions. The commander motioned for the mercenaries to go first. With swords at the ready, they crept forward toward the sound.

As they walked deeper into the pit, Faelin noticed Pax was dropping tiny pebbles he'd picked up from the stream by the bridge. *Smart kid. He's marking a trail.* She caught his eye and winked, and he gave her a small grin acknowledging they had a secret from the others. When she looked back toward the others, Vallaria smiled— she too had noticed the young boy's pebble trail.

A few hundred feet more and the scraping noise seemed to be all around them now. It echoed through the mist, which in turn amplified it and made it impossible to pinpoint.

"Eyes open," said Tagar as he unsheathed his sword.

Moments later a large, scaled tail swiped at them from the fog, catapulting one of the mercenaries into the air. His shrill scream was quickly matched by a bone-chilling hiss as a large snake head reared up above them, green gooey saliva dripping from its enormous fangs.

38

ZANDER

As the mercenary with the long hair ran by him, Zander ducked as the second swipe of the tail missed him by inches. Zander turned his head in time to see the man land on the ground about one hundred feet away, unconscious. He turned his attention back the other way. A pair of beady eyes appeared in the mist as a snake the size of ten horses slithered toward them.

"What type of demon from hell is that?" screamed the short, stocky mercenary as he slashed his sword at the snake and backed away when it lunged. Again, it swung its massive tail toward them, this time missing the mercenary, who tripped over a rock and fell to the ground. The snake reared, its mouth opening wide to reveal its deadly fangs.

Without thinking Zander ran forward and grabbed the man by the shirt collar, yanking him back as the snake attacked, its fangs sinking into the ground where seconds before the mercenary had lay as helpless prey.

"Get off me," the smaller man yelled as he struggled to his feet. "I don't need your help." His eyes were venomous, and a cold anger rose in Zander.

"I saved your life," he spat. "You might show a little gratitude."

The mercenary ignored Zander, raised his sword, and ran to help the scout, who barely dodged the strike of the snake's massive head.

"Ungrateful, aren't they?" said Tagar.

Zander shrugged and eyed the commander. "I expect working for you means they only care about themselves and the gold."

"Harsh," said Tagar, eyeing the two mercenaries and the scout, who were slashing large cuts into the giant snake's body. "I only do as the queen commands."

"You keep repeating that as if it absolves you from all the atrocities *you've* committed."

"In the name of the Crown," Tagar sneered, his eyes flashing with that particular brand of disdain he saved just for Zander.

"You enjoy the freedom that gives you, don't you, Tagar?"

The commander leaned in closer and said, "Freedom makes men do funny things, doesn't it, my prince? Even betray those we love." Tagar lifted his sword and ran toward the giant snake, who was bleeding profusely at the neck and teetering as it continued to try and pierce the skin of the men with its deadly fangs. It had been weakened considerably by the others, and now the commander would go in for the death blow.

Zander stared after him as a sinking feeling filled in his belly. His last statement sounded like a warning, and with the suspicious and hateful way the three mercenaries looked at him and the flagrant way the commander had missed the hellhound and cut Zander, he was now even more positive the reason for his being here was not to help retrieve the dagger for his mother, but something much more ominous.

"HELP!" a bloodcurdling scream came from his left and he turned to see the unconscious mercenary very much awake and buried chest deep in the ground. The commander, the scout, and the other two mercenaries were still trying to fell the monstrous snake. Faelin and Vallaria were attacking small baby snakes that had slithered out from the pile of bones and skulls their mother had swept into a nest. And Pax and the blacksmith huddled in fear behind a large rock.

He was the only one able to provide aid.

"Please help me!" the mercenary screamed, his voice ladened with panic.

"Damn," Zander said under his breath as he sheathed his sword and ran toward the man. As he got closer, he saw the man had landed in what looked like some type of wet sand. The more he struggled the more he sank.

"Don't move," yelled Zander as he searched for something the man could grab onto. His eyes fell on a large piece of wood, flat and wide. He grabbed it and ran back to the edge of the sinking mud hole. Cursing under his breath, he placed the piece of wood across the shortest expanse of mud and lay across it, clutching the man's extended arms before his shoulders disappeared below the surface.

"Pull," the man demanded, his eyes full of fear.

Zander leaned in closer. "Not until you tell me what Tagar is up to."

The mercenary squirmed and sank another inch into the mud. "What the hell do you mean?" Anger edged his voice where moments before fear had.

"What I mean is why did Tagar miss the hellhound and cut me? He never misses his target."

"Maybe he still hasn't." The man spat. "Get me the hell out of this mud."

Zander loosened his grip. "If you don't want this to be your final resting place, I suggest you tell me what you know."

The man's mouth was barely above the surface now, and his long hair was caked with the mud. His eyes widened in fear. "He wants you dead."

"Why?"

"Because the queen commanded it. It's why you were sent here," the man gasped.

Just as the words left the mercenary's mouth, Zander felt a tug.

"Something has my leg," he screamed. "Pull me out."

But it was too late. By the time Zander tightened his grip and began to pull another snake emerged from the muck, with the man deep in its throat. Zander let go and stumbled backward, the snake's beady eyes trained on him as he swallowed the terrified mercenary whole.

On solid ground, Zander stood and drew his sword waiting for the snake to strike, but instead it hovered over him and then silently receded back into the muddy hole.

"Zane, are you all right?" Vallaria asked, suddenly at his side.

"Yes," he croaked.

He wasn't, of course, but he didn't know if that was because of the abominations they'd battled or the fact his mother had ordered Tagar Garrate to kill him and leave his body to rot in this cursed place.

39
VALLARIA

Vallaria watched in horror as the massive snake swallowed one of Tagar's men whole, then trained its eyes on Zane. Muffled screams from the men still battling the female snake reached her ears, but she didn't care—she ran, ran toward Zane. Her heart pounded in her chest as the snake pulled itself up to its full height.

It's going to kill him.

She ran harder.

Zane's blade glinted as he raised it toward the snake.

He looked so small compared to his foe. It was a match he would never win.

Her leg ached where the razor edge of a baby snake's tail had sliced through her pants and cut her skin. It wasn't deep, but it stung.

She ignored the pain and kept running.

Just as she reached him, the snake disappeared under the mud.

Relief flooded through her until she saw the look on his face. "Zane, are you all right?"

"Yes," he responded, but the tortured look that marred his handsome face said otherwise. Her heart clenched as she watched him struggle with whatever it was that had him rattled.

"Are you sure?" Vallaria placed a hand on his arm.

Zane's dark eyes turned her way and he said, "I'm sure." His gaze flicked to Tagar who, covered in blood, walked toward them. A darkness filled his eyes and he stiffened as the commander said, "Well that was fun."

"A man was eaten alive by a gigantic snake," Zane fumed. "Fun is not what this is."

"He understood the risk."

Tagar turned to the others, most splattered with blood, and said, "Let's move out. We need to find the altar and retrieve the dagger before any more of you die. You can split his share of the gold amongst yourselves." He pointed at the dead man's sword. "And pick that up, we may need it."

The scout ran over and retrieved the weapon before following Tagar and the others out of the snake's nesting area.

"We are all going to die, aren't we?" said the blacksmith his voice cracking as he spoke.

Vallaria took the older man's hand, hoping he wouldn't notice that hers shook. "Not if I can help it." It was all the comfort she could muster. She wasn't sure how many of them would make it out alive.

The mist had lightened as they slogged across the pit's ever-changing landscape. From the snake's nest they'd gone north through a bog that stunk like sour cow's milk. On the other side was a small forest of trees that wept black oil. The scout made the mistake of touching the slimy substance, and it quickly ate away the skin and flesh on two fingertips down to the bone. Faelin had bandaged up his hand using a bit of gill weed and a salve she'd created before they'd left the city.

Currently, they were on what could be a hunting ground. Scattered across the earth were hundreds of bones, skeletal remains of animals who'd become prey for one predator or another. Tall snags, their trunks stripped of bark and full of holes, reached out gnarled and bent limbs as they passed. The wind whistled through this landscape, catching in the dead trees and creating an aching haunting cry.

"Be careful," Faelin said, pulling Vallaria away from the others. "There's something sinister here. An energy I can't identify, but it senses us and is not trying to hide its presence."

Vallaria nodded and held tighter to Pax's hand. "Stay close," she whispered to the young boy.

A few minutes later a subtle breeze slipped past Vallaria's ear, followed by a faint whisper. A shiver crept up her spine. The whisper was intended for her. Her feet slowed and she released Pax's hand.

"Run and catch up with Faelin. I'll be right behind you."

Pax studied her intently for a few seconds before he nodded and ran up ahead.

Her feet slowed even more, and the distance between her and the group widened.

Another breeze, another whisper.

She glanced around but saw nothing and no one.

The snags creaked and shuddered around her, not as if moved by the same wind, but individually as if an unseen hand pushed one and then another.

As the distance between her and the others increased, so did the whispers, until a soft chorus rang in her ears. With a final glance at Pax, she ducked behind a thick trunk. The ancient mage magic began to sizzle in her veins as the whispers ebbed and flowed around her. She didn't know how, but the voices belonged to the mages of old, the ones slaughtered by the kings of the past on this very ground, of that she was sure. But why only she could hear their murmurs was not clear.

Leaning against the tree, she closed her eyes and allowed the whispers of the past to engulf her completely. Soon her mind was

filled with chants, voices that became clearer the more she relin-
quished herself to their will.

Help us.

Bring us peace.

Revenge for our deaths.

Suffer those who spilled our blood.

So many voices. Echoes of the past. All connected by pain,
betrayal, and death—and *now* to her.

Within seconds, Vallaria understood their desires—*vengeance*
against those who'd betrayed them. Not the kings of old, for they
were long gone. No, they thirsted for the blood of man, all man. They
wished for magic to return to the lands and for man to kneel at the
feet of those who could wield it. The ancient mages desired the
power they'd lost.

"Vallaria." A familiar voice brought her out of the trance, and she
turned to see Faelin, arched brows knitted together, staring at her.
"What are you doing?"

She caught the scolding tone in Faelin's voice. "Nothing."

The elf's green eyes flashed, and momentarily, the purple glow of
the elven race showed through. Grabbing Vallaria's hands, she
shoved them upward until they were level with her face. "This is not
nothing," she hissed.

Vallaria felt the cold before she looked down. Both her hands
were covered in ice crystals as a blue glow pulsed under her skin.

"I—"

"You must try and control your magic, Vallaria. If the royal
commander or any of his henchmen discover you have ancient
powers, we are as good as dead. Or worse, you become a trophy for
the dark queen."

When Faelin walked away, Vallaria felt the familiar breeze in her
ear. But this time, the whispers remained silent.

With reluctance, she followed Faelin and caught up to the others.
When they left the strange terrain, Vallaria felt the sensation that

accompanied the spirits dissipate and the magic in her veins calm. But the tickle at the base of her neck told her the mages were watching—*waiting*.

And when the time was right, they would reveal themselves again.

40
VALLARIA

Their journey through the Valley of Souls to find the Dagger of Crusade now led them straight through a vast plain of huge boulders covered in sheets of ice. While the temperature was cold, the air was oddly arid. Dust clouds were kicked up by their movement and small lizard-like creatures leapt out from the rocks, clinging to their clothes and squealing. They seemed harmless, but Vallaria didn't enjoy being covered with a dozen little creatures all looking up at her with bulging lidless eyes.

"We are almost there," Tagar said, pushing the blacksmith down as he stumbled again on the uneven terrain. "If I'd known you would be such a burden, I would have brought a whore instead. At least then I could have gotten some pleasure out of it."

"Easy," Zane said, helping the man to his feet.

The commander scowled at him. "You are too soft, Zane. Always helping those weaker than yourself. Probably why the queen—" Tagar stopped as a chilling roar ripped through the air in the distance. He pulled his mouth into a twisted grin. "We're close."

Hurrying his pace, he and the two remaining mercenaries headed toward the sound. A few minutes later a dark shape loomed before them.

"There," said Tagar, pointing at the shadowy figure. "The protector of the dagger."

Another roar erupted that shook the ground under their feet. As they moved closer, the mist thinned, revealing a terrifying sight. Quickly, the mercenaries retreated and found refuge behind a group of massive ice-covered boulders.

Vallaria stood motionless, staring in disbelief at the creature before her.

Faelin grabbed her and Pax and pushed them behind another group of boulders.

Vallaria's heart pounded as she pressed her back into the icy stone and closed her eyes. Subconsciously she'd pulled out her father's prayer beads and now gripped them tight to her chest, silently praying to her gods. Something she hadn't done in days.

She pushed the beads back into her pocket and whispered to Faelin, "What in the gods is that?"

"Something that should not be in this world. A remnant from a long-lost past and one I never expected to see again."

Vallaria peered out from the rock at the creature that was making the earth-shattering sound. Atop a spire constructed behind a stone altar was a dragon. The razor-sharp claws at the end of its front legs clung to the stone while its long serpent tail coiled around the bottom of the spire.

Its eyes were a blistering ice blue.

When it roared it spat out a bitterly cold chill and flakes of snow drifted downward, covering the ground in its icy dust.

"I didn't know any still existed," Faelin whispered as she too peeked out from their hiding spot.

Vallaria slowly pulled her sword as the beast stretched its massive wings. "What is it? A dragon?"

"Yes, but not your typical fire-breathing kind. The ancients called them *dal braga* or the cold monster. They are serpent dragons, known to my people as the ice dragons of old."

"And what is it doing here in the Valley of Souls?"

"I would assume it's protecting the Dagger of Crusade from people like us," she answered, indicating the graveyard of bones, shields, and swords scattered across the ground.

"So we are not the first to know of its location," Vallaria said, her eyes roaming over the fallen remains of knights, warriors, and treasure seekers.

"It looks like many before us have also tracked the legend of the Myths of Three, leading them here to their deaths."

"How do we get past it?"

"There is no way to defeat an ice dragon. They are too powerful."

"Then how do we retrieve the dagger?"

"We will have to get it to move."

Vallaria frowned at Faelin, her mouth pulling into a tense line. "Get it to move? How? By asking it nicely?"

The elf chose to ignore Vallaria's sarcasm.

The royal guard commander's raspy voice interrupted them. "We need bait," he said from behind a boulder to their left.

Vallaria frowned. "What do you mean bait?"

"To distract the monster. Something it will chase so it will leave the altar thus leaving the dagger unattended."

His voice reverberated through the air, attracting the serpent dragon, who quickly dispelled an icy blast in their direction. Vallaria could instantly feel the temperature drop to a frigid cold as the boulder they hid behind was covered in another layer of ice.

"That was close," Faelin said. "We are not safe here."

Tagar turned to the man standing behind him and hissed, "YOU, blacksmith, go distract the beast before we all die."

Vallaria glanced at the older man, whose face paled as he began to tremble. He shook his head no and ignored the glare of the royal guard commander. Instead, he watched with terror as the creature crawled even lower on the spire.

"It knows we are here," Faelin said.

"Shit." Tagar stood and pointed his sword at the blacksmith. "You will distract that damn abomination so I can retrieve that dagger, or I will gut you where you stand. And if that is not motivation enough, you can be certain when I get back to the kingdom I will go to your house, behead your vile children, screw your ugly wife, and slit her throat. Now go!"

Another icy blast tore through the air toward them. The royal guard commander ducked but not soon enough. Luckily, the boulder and his sword took the brunt of the blast, and he was left only with a cold burn on his palm as the ice spread through the metal. He dropped the sword and cursed again.

"Get going," he growled, giving the blacksmith a murderous stare as he held his injured hand.

The blacksmith looked like he was about to vomit, or worse, faint. Vallaria felt for the man. *He's going to die.* She glanced at Zane, who stood to the left of the blacksmith, but there was nothing he could do either. If any of them tried to stop this insanity, it would be their lives as well as the blacksmith's. She only hoped that death would find him swiftly and painlessly.

The dragon changed its position as the blacksmith crept closer. Its serpent tail swept back and forth, shifting stones, dirt, and frosty snowflakes across the ground as it descended lower on the spire. Its blue eyes never left the man as he moved nearer.

The older man looked back, his eyes wide and his body trembling. "I can't," he stammered.

The dragon stretched out its massive head at the sound of the blacksmith's voice and sniffed the air, inhaling deeply the threatening scent of man.

Vallaria waited, her body tense as she gripped the hilt of her sword and watched the beast rear up.

The poor man is going to die.

"Now run!" the commander yelled, but it was too late.

The blacksmith paralyzed by fear, lifted his hands in front of his face as the serpent dragon unleashed a torrent of icy breath. It encapsulated the man in a wall of ice and snow, freezing him solid instantly. With a thrash of its mighty tail, the beast shattered the frozen blacksmith into hundreds of shards of ice.

Red flakes drifted softly to the ground as the shards flew in multiple directions, landing in a sickening harmonic crash on the ground.

"You." The royal guard commander's gloved hand indicated Vallaria. "Go retrieve the box and try not to get yourself killed. I did not come all this way to go back to the queen empty-handed."

Before she could object Zane intervened. "I'll go."

Tagar picked up his sword and pointed the tip at Zane's neck. "You will back off and let the lady do my bidding, or I will kill her, right now, in front of you."

The two mercenaries stepped forward and pulled Zane back.

He struggled against them. "Get your hands off me."

"Be a good boy and do as the commander says," the short stocky one with the missing teeth said.

Zane snarled at him and yanked his arm from his grasp, turning and slugging him in the mouth.

Might be another tooth or two missing now, Vallaria thought as the man struggled to his feet and wiped the blood from his chin.

"You bastard, I should—"

"ENOUGH!" Tagar Garrate yelled, the look on his face conveying his annoyance.

"I'm going to kill you, you murderous swine," Zane spat.

The commander grinned. "Probably be the only smart thing you'd do in your life, boy, but I doubt you have the balls to even try."

Zane lunged at Tagar but was stopped by the stocky mercenary who still had him in his grasp.

"Shhh," Faelin whispered, pointing to the serpent dragon who had climbed back to the top of the spire and was watching them intently.

The commander turned back to Vallaria and lowered his voice. "I will not say it again. Go get my fucking dagger, or I will slit that little imp's throat."

The fury in Tagar's eyes was unmistakable. He was everything his reputation touted. A sadist that took pleasure in people's pain and even more so in inflicting it. He was cruel and heartless, a real bastard.

A perfect match for the dark queen.

Vallaria pushed Pax behind her and glared at the man. "You lay a hand on him and I will kill you myself."

The commander laughed, as did the two mercenaries. "The girl may be stupid, but at least she has guts. Why does that little street rat mean so much to you anyway?"

"None of your business," she said. The truth was she didn't really know herself. Maybe it was because she had grown up an orphan or because when she looked at the small, helpless boy she felt a sense of knowing. Like something in the past now stood right in front of her.

"I'll go," she said.

"Vallaria, no." Faelin grabbed her wrist.

She turned her blue eyes to her friend and smiled. "I'll be fine," she said attempting to reassure her.

The commander would kill Pax without hesitation if she didn't do as he asked. She had no choice.

"Stay with Faelin," she said to the young boy.

To Faelin, she said. "Look after him."

She began to walk toward the beast, then heard a soft "no." Looking back, she saw Pax run toward her. When he reached her, he wrapped his small arms around her waist and looked up at her with dark eyes full of tears. Her heart ached, and for a moment, a memory surfaced in her mind. Another small child clung to her, but the face was a blur and Vallaria didn't know if it was real or a remanent of an old dream.

"Go back, Pax," she said, pulling his arms from around her.

The commander's steely gaze stared at her from behind the safety of the boulder. Slowly, he slid a finger across his throat.

Vallaria pushed Pax away as she glared at Tagar and his silent threat. "Go to Faelin, now!"

She turned, took a few slow steps, and felt the familiar cold of the mage crystal flare in her pocket. *Please, not now!* She looked down at her hands, expecting to see the frost magic forming. But thankfully her hands were nothing but pink skin.

When she neared the serpent dragon, it lowered its head and sniffed. But it made no moves that Vallaria deemed aggressive. Instead, it watched her, its ice blue eyes locked on hers. She took another few steps. Its nostrils flared, and an ethereal blue glowed in the nasal cavities. The beast's claws scraped the concrete spire as it slid its body downward.

It's getting agitated.

As if it could hear her thoughts, it unwound its thick tail, climbed down the spire, and stood on the dusty ground.

Vallaria eyed the altar. *How far is it? Ten, twenty feet?* Her eyes tracked across to where a gilded chest sat. *The Dagger of Crusade must be inside.*

Without warning the ice crystal flared to a searing cold and an icy blast ricocheted through her temples. She stumbled backward and grabbed her head in agony. Through the visceral pain she thought she heard someone calling her name, but the searing cold inside her head was all she could focus on. Her knees hit the ground, and she bent over as another blast of ice ripped through her head. Tears streamed down her face as she writhed in pain.

Somewhere behind the sting of the burning cold, she sensed a presence—a voice. Not the mages of old. This voice was different—it felt familiar.

It should have been you!

The words screamed through her mind, angry, accusatory. And then as quickly as it came it was all gone.

"Vallaria, get up," Faelin's panic-stricken voice called to her.

Vallaria lifted her head and looked straight into the eyes of the beast. It glared at her from the other side of the altar, talons clicking on the stone.

Swallowing her fear, she rose unsteadily to her feet.

The ice crystal still throbbed in her pocket, and as the dragon slipped across the altar, she was oddly glad for its presence and the ancient powers she possessed. It may be the only thing that could save her.

She prayed silently to the gods, asking for protection and hoping the mages and their magic would answer.

The serpent dragon pulled itself up to its full height.

Vallaria froze, daring not to even breathe.

Before she could react, the end of its tail arched toward her and knocked her backward into a large boulder where she crumpled, winded at its base. She lay on her back, trying desperately to regain her breath, but pain exploded in her side with every inhale.

She heard Zane yell, but it was all so hazy. When she turned her head, she saw him running toward her, but one of the mercenaries tackled him to the ground. He thrashed against his captor and called out her name.

The commotion agitated the serpent dragon even more, and it leapt over the altar and flew toward her. Its feet dragged across the skeleton-strewn earth. Bones clacked together and the grating sound of metal filled the air, as its claws dragged along the surfaces of the shields strewn across the ground.

This is how I will die. Not by the blade of an adversary or the dark magic of Queen Cereli, but by the cold kiss of death given by a beast relegated to myth centuries ago.

The irony was not lost on her.

The ice dragon swayed above her, its nostrils flaring with bright blue light. Frantic, her hand clawed at the ground, searching for the sword she'd dropped. Not that it would protect her, but it may give her comfort in her final moments.

When the creature lowered its head and opened its frightful

jaws, Vallaria's heart began to race and she closed her eyes, waiting to feel the cold sting of the dragon's breath.

But nothing happened.

Opening her eyes, she looked up. The dragon remained above her, its wings flapping, its mouth wide, but the icy breath seemed stuck in the back of its throat.

Through prickling tears, Vallaria looked over her shoulder. Where was Faelin? She scanned the darkness and discovered her hidden behind a boulder away from the others. Her hands were raised, and her lips moved ever so slightly. Vallaria had witnessed her use her magic enough to know she was using it to shield the dragon from expelling its cold breath instead of shielding Vallaria from the danger. But the elf would weaken quickly as shield magic was not meant to be used on others. It was only a matter of time before she would no longer be able to contain the beast or its magic.

"Get up and get my dagger," Tagar yelled. "He was too distracted to notice Faelin was missing, and for this Vallaria was thankful.

She shifted and tried to stand. Pain exploded in her side, and she fell again to the ground. At the same time, she saw Faelin's hands collapse to her sides. Her gaze flew back to the serpent dragon, who seemed slightly disoriented but completely in control once again.

Within seconds its blue eyes locked onto Vallaria and its jaws began to expand. Simultaneously the ice crystal in her pocket exploded with cold and she trembled as the mage magic raced through her veins, covering her skin with a thin veil of frost.

No! Not now.

The scorching ice breath flared in the back of the dragon's throat, and as it rolled outward, Vallaria instinctively threw up her hands. A pale blue light coursed from her palms and as it widened in front of her, it turned to a thin sheet of ice.

The dragon's cold fire hit the protective shield and bounced back, striking it in the torso and creating a nasty wound on its chest. The beast roared in agony and staggered backward, front limbs flailing. It expanded its wings and with one shuddering flap took flight.

Holding her side, Vallaria scrambled to her feet and dragged herself to the altar. The wounded dragon careened in the air, swiped the side of the spire, and fell to the ground in a thicket of dead brambles near the mouth of a cave.

It roared again as it dragged itself into the dark hole, its bellowing cry echoing back from the cavern's depths.

Standing on unsteady legs she heard voices and commotion behind her.

Faelin was the first to reach her.

"Just so you know everyone saw your magic," she hissed, grasping Vallaria's trembling hands seconds before she collapsed.

A headache ripped through her skull and small pins of light fractured her vision. She could hear Faelin call her name, but the echo was too painful to acknowledge. The magic still ebbed in her blood, but the cold was no longer one of power; it was debilitating, as if a hundred thorns pricked her skin.

Strong arms lifted her from the ground, and she leaned into a warm, muscular body. "Vallaria, are you unharmed?" It was Zane's concerned voice.

The world had stopped spinning and the headache was lessening, but she felt tired, so very tired. She allowed Zane to hold her for a few minutes longer, and then she pulled away, confident she could stand on her own, rather wobbly legs.

"My, my," exclaimed Tagar Garrate as he strode up with the other two mercenaries and the scout. He held Pax tightly by his collar, a small blade at his throat. A look of repulsive smugness darkened his features. "You've been keeping something from us."

"Let him go," Vallaria said, cringing as a twinge of pain erupted in her side. She wiped at her upper lip with the back of her hand. *Blood.* Her nose was bleeding same as the last time she'd used her mage magic.

"Not until you tell me who, or better yet, what you are."

"I am nobody, nothing."

The royal guard commander chuckled. "I think we both know that isn't true."

The mercenaries moved forward, weapons drawn with a look in their eyes that dared her to lie again.

Tagar moved the small blade from Pax's neck and placed it on top of his uninjured ear. "Maybe making this little street orphan completely deaf will get you talking." He pushed down on the blade and blood began to trickle down Pax's face. The boy squeezed his eyes shut.

Vallaria took an unsteady step forward, still weak from the magic, but Faelin placed a hand on her forearm and stopped her. She glanced at the elf, who shook her head in warning. Looking into her green eyes, Vallaria recalled a memory. Tales Faelin used to tell her when she felt alone and lost. Stories of witches from across the waters.

"Talk," Tagar commanded, "or the boy will lose his ear and then his tongue." Scowling at the man, Vallaria tried to recall the details or the stories. Truth or fiction, it was the only way to explain her magical abilities without getting herself or the others killed. Or so she hoped.

"I'll tell you," she said with venom in her voice. "I'm from a land far across the seas. Where my kind remains one of the last vestiges of magic. I am one of the witches of Brulle, and I have come to the continent of Exile looking for more of my kind. Those who are born from magic."

Tagar leaned forward and stared directly into her eyes. "The witches of Brulle are extinct. Gone the way of the mages and sorceresses. There hasn't been a witch seen on Brulle in a hundred years or more."

"We've not been seen because we make it so. To keep us safe. The kings of old wanted magic to exist only for themselves and when it threatened them, they destroyed it. Many of us went into hiding, and we have lived that way for generations. There are few of us left and my only desire is to discover if any more of my kind exist anywhere else in this world."

"I can assure you there are none with magic on Exile other than the elves, and if I had my way, that high-brow lot would meet an untimely demise as well," the commander said, glancing over his shoulder. The smug comment elicited a laugh from the mercenaries. Even the scout chuckled, but Vallaria noticed Zane did not.

Faelin's hand, still on her forearm, tensed but she remained silent.

"I hear the elven kingdom is still powerful in these parts. Is that true?"

Tagar lowered the blade from Pax's ear. "The elves exiled themselves years ago and do not interact with the kingdoms of man. While their magic is still strong and their army an impressive force, the time of man and elves co-existing will soon be over."

He spat on the ground as if to make his point.

Vallaria eyed the commander. He'd sounded assured in his assessment that the elves, a race older than that of man, would soon be gone. Was that the dark queen's plan? To use the Dagger of Crusade to build an army big enough and powerful enough to destroy the race of elves?

Angered by her silence, Tagar continued, "The time of magic is fading. Soon all your type will be gone, and man will once again rightfully rule."

Faelin tensed beside her, and Vallaria sensed the rage roiling below the surface. Although she remained stoic on the outside, there was no doubt the elf wanted to slice the man's gullet out.

41
VALLARIA

"**K**eep your eye on her and the other one," Tagar Garrate said to his men.

The mercenaries circled Faelin and Vallaria with blades raised and lascivious grins contorting their dirt-stained faces. One clutched her arm, and the other grabbed Faelin by the waist and pulled her back, grinding his crotch into her as he held a small blade to her neck.

Faelin's hands clenched but she held her temper in check. She had hidden her powers for this long—she was not about to reveal them now and give herself away as elf kind.

That would most certainly mean death.

Tagar pushed Pax to the ground, sheathed his blade, and strode to the altar.

Without the ice dragon protecting the chest, it was easy to break the lock with the hilt of his knife and take the Dagger of Crusade from its resting place. Tagar held it aloft with both hands, turning it over to admire the craftsmanship. After a few moments, he pushed the dagger into his waistband and walked back to where they stood.

The mercenaries released Vallaria and Faelin. The tattooed bald one pushed Vallaria and chuckled as she stumbled.

Zane glared at the man and then looked at the commander. "We got what we came for. We should leave the valley before nightfall."

Vallaria noticed the slight bitterness in Zane's tone and the way his eyes narrowed when he looked at the commander. There was definitely no love lost between the two men before, but something had changed since they entered the Valley of Souls: the acrimony between them had increased.

The mercenaries guffawed at Zane's comment while glancing at the commander.

"We?" Tagar unsheathed his sword and swung it in a circle. "Did you think you, or the others, would be leaving this valley?" He took a step forward. "You can't be that naïve. The queen will not want so many pockets returning looking to be filled with gold."

The royal guard commander nodded at one of his men. The one with the eye patch acknowledged Tagar and in one arc of his sword, the mercenary cut the head from the scout's body. Blood splattered across Pax's face as the decapitated body crumbled to the ground, the head rolling, eyes wide, to his feet.

The young boy screamed.

Vallaria ran to his side and scooped him up. Cradling the terrified boy, she backed away from the scene that was unfolding.

Chaos.

"Get the boy out of here, Vallaria," screamed Faelin as one of the mercenaries stalked toward her, malice contorting his face.

Vallaria stumbled on a rock. How in the gods did this happen?

Setting Pax down she looked around for Zane, finding him near the back of the altar, his sword slicing through the air as Tagar fought back. The mist had begun to roll back in as the light faded.

Where was the other mercenary? The shorter one with the gap-toothed grin. As she turned, she saw him running directly at her from behind a snag. He held two knives, one in each hand, and the look on his face indicated he meant to use them.

Vallaria pulled her sword as he charged toward them and pushed Pax out of the way. Gripping the hilt, she carved an arc forward. The tip of the blade ripped the man's shirt. Blood saturated the shredded material, but it didn't slow him down; in fact, he didn't even seem to notice the small gash in his chest.

He lunged at Vallaria, striking her across the cheek with the butt of his knife.

Pain exploded in Vallaria's face as she stumbled back, tears blurring her vision. Instinct made her raise her sword in defense as he stabbed the knife forward for another blow.

Metal clashed with metal.

Through watery eyes, she saw the murderous look he gave her.

With a surge of strength, Vallaria pushed him back.

The mercenary lunged again, but this time she was ready. A quick move to the side and his blade missed. She felt the breeze by her ear as it swiped the air beside her head. The momentum from his attack carried him forward a step or two, and Vallaria took advantage of the seconds he was off-balance.

She pulled the sword back and rammed the hilt into his ribs. The mercenary screamed in pain and dropped one knife. He fell to his knees holding his ribs and slashed at Vallaria with the one he still held.

"I'll cut ya to ribbons you wretched slag," he huffed, gasping for breath.

His face was dark purple, and spittle ran down his chin. He winced as he spoke, and she wondered if she'd broken a rib or two.

Out of the corner of her eye, she saw Pax crouched behind a large boulder, eyes wide, watching.

The mercenary glanced over at him and laughed. Spitting blood, he got to his feet. The blade of his knife shone in the light of the torches as he wagged it at her. "After you, I will gut the street filth. Or better yet, maybe I'll have my way with the laddie first."

The mercenary's chubby face shone with sweat, his eyes leering as he looked from her to Pax. A shudder ran through Vallaria, and she lifted her sword.

"You won't touch him, you filthy pig," she growled through clenched teeth. Her blade clashed against his as she blocked his stab. She pushed him back with a foot to his groin and thrust her blade forward, knocking him off-balance. The blade sliced through the flesh of his upper arm and he howled, his cheeks burned crimson as he dropped his knife and grabbed the wound. "Wench," he screamed.

Blood dripped through his fingers as he charged toward her. His eyes, small holes of black tar, were bloodshot and wide with pain and fury.

Vallaria spun, placing her back to him and drove the sword backward at the precise moment he reached her. She felt the blade puncture his flesh, the razor-sharp edge opening his innards. She pushed the blade farther into his belly and with a twist of her wrist, she wrenched the blade to the right, carving him up from the inside.

A gurgling sound drifted by her ears as the last of his breath escaped his body. A second later, she felt his full weight fall on her sword. Without looking back, she yanked out the blade and walked forward.

His body fell with a thud to the ground behind her.

Vallaria sheathed her sword without cleaning the blade and ran to where Pax huddled.

Scooping him up into her arms, she ran.

She didn't stop until they'd reached the high cliff. From here it was a direct route out through the valley, to the forest and bridge, and back into the kingdom.

"Run Pax, as fast as you can. Go back to the dell and hide there for the night. Hide well and in the morn, run as fast as you can back to the city of Ravenia."

Squatting down, she handed him a small leather pouch. It was all the money she had.

"Do not come back, do you understand? There is nothing here but death."

The little boy's face, still marred with the blood of the scout, was full of fear and confusion, but he nodded anyway.

She drew him in and hugged him tightly. *He shouldn't be here. This is my fault!* Vallaria tried to let Pax go, but she couldn't, so she held him tighter, comforted by the rhythm of his small heartbeat against her own. It had been a long time since she cared about someone this much. When she first saw Pax, all she wanted to do was save a young boy from two thugs. It wasn't about anything else but doing what was right. And now—

She closed her eyes and squeezed a little tighter. Her life had been one of uncertainty, about who she was and her purpose in life. Living with the elves had been, at times, unbearable, but freedom had only brought a life of more uncertainty. Whatever her future held, all she cared about was that Pax would be okay. She thought keeping him safe meant keeping him by her side, but she'd only put him in more danger. Letting him go was the right thing to do—for him.

The sounds of the fight below intensified as the clash of metal echoed off the ice-covered canyon walls. She must get back. Faelin and Zane needed her help. Who knew what unearthly creatures still lurked in the Valley of Souls waiting for prey?

She released Pax and pushed him back to arm's length. His big dark eyes were full of tears as they looked at her, scared and unsure. She stifled the urge to run with him, and instead took a deep breath, wiped his tears, and said, "Go Pax. Run as fast as you can and don't look back. I promise everything will be fine. I'll find you."

Vallaria prayed the gods would keep him safe. She pushed him away and as his small legs picked up speed and he ran toward the opening in the trees. While she watched him disappear into the mist, her eyes began to prickle, and a single tear ran down her cheek.

Lifting a hand, she wiped it away.

She couldn't remember the last time she'd shed a tear for someone else.

42

ZANDER

From the corner of his eye, he saw Vallaria pick up Pax and run.

His heart soared. *At least the two of them would escape.*

As he ducked under Tagar's swipe, he heard Faelin behind him. Her blade sang as it arced through the air clashing against the metal of her opponent. It was only the two of them now.

"Do you think you can beat me?" the commander taunted Zander as he circled him. "You, who has never seen battle or used a sword against a real enemy?"

It was true that Zander had grown up in a peaceful world. Other than a few rebellious conflicts arising in the kingdom after his step-father ascended to the throne, there had been no war. Along with her dark powers, the alliance with the Gold Coast Empire ensured no one challenged his mother's rule. But Tagar was wrong in assuming Zander had never touched blade to flesh with intent to harm or kill. That was the beauty of leading a life away from the kingdom and the watchful eye of his mother's henchmen. They never truly knew you, what you'd done, or who you'd become. Hubris had driven him to train relentlessly with a sword and he possessed exceptional fighting skills, but the commander had no idea how lethal he'd become.

"I guess we'll find out, Tagar."

Zander had killed his fair share of people, mostly swindlers, thieves, and murderers. Those considered the dregs of society, who lingered in the shadows preying on the weak and innocent or committed atrocities in the name of the Crown.

And now it's your turn, Tagar. You who have done my mother's dirty work for years.

The blood trail leading from his mother's throne to Tagar's sword had ceased to surprise Zander over the past few years—it was immeasurable.

Zander smirked as he and the commander circled each other.

Tagar and his mother were made for each other but what the commander failed to realize was if the opportunity presented itself, Queen Cereli Damask Ravenia would slit his throat rather than relinquish power. Tagar's love for the queen had blinded him, and now here he was willing to kill the prince of Ravenia and firstborn son of House Sand Serpent.

It was an act of treason against the empire.

If Mother wants a war with the Gold Coast Empire this is a good way to instigate one. And so be it. Both had betrayed him. *If I ever get out of this godforsaken place alive, I'll sail across the Endless Sea and never look back.*

The commander advanced, a wicked grin forming on his face. "Show me what you've got, then."

Their swords met.

Steel on steel.

Zander pushed Tagar back and then swung his sword up, but the royal guard commander was no fool; he blocked the swing and retaliated with a downward arc. Zander whirled away, but the edge caught his arm, tearing through his tunic sleeve and opening the skin underneath.

A stinging heat flared in his bicep as blood seeped from the wound. It throbbed, but the pain only made him more furious about Tagar's deception.

"You are nothing but a bully, Tagar. Always hiding behind the power of the Crown and trying to erase your past."

Tagar Garrate was also from the Gold Coast, and Zander knew of his upbringing. The one he so desperately wanted to forget. "Your mother worked in the royal kitchens and your father was a fish merchant. You were nothing more than a commoner whose rise in affluence was thanks to your skill with a sword and your unwavering devotion to clean up Darrius Mensah's messes. The same traits my mother appreciates in you."

Zander knew he'd hit a nerve.

Tagar's eyes flashed, and his knuckles went white where he gripped his sword. "I see your Uncle Moricio has been telling tales. Well at least I don't run from my responsibilities. You are nothing but a weak coward. No wonder your mother wants you gone."

Rage burned like a hot fire in Zander's stomach as he lunged at the man striking him with a vicious blow to the ribs.

Tagar staggered backward, clutching his ribs and with a surprised look said, "Maybe I misjudged you."

"Maybe you have." Zander replied, his focus only on the burning hatred he felt for the royal guard commander.

Smirking, Tagar raised his sword. "I doubt it," he said. "If there is one thing about you that is consistent, it's how easily distracted you are. First, with whining about how mommy didn't love you enough and now by this witch who clearly has you under her spell." The commander looked around. "Where did she go, anyhow? I would have liked to have a go at her myself."

Zander's hot rage turned into a white-searing loathing. This man did not deserve to live. He clenched his teeth and readied his sword for another blow, but before he could strike, excruciating pain exploded in the back of his head and the world began to turn black.

Distracted.

He'd been so focused on the commander and consumed by his emotions, he hadn't noticed the singing of Faelin's sword had stopped nor the crunch of gravel under the mercenary's boots as he crept up behind him.

———

THE PAIN IN HIS HEAD RICOCHETED THROUGH HIS SKULL, HAMMERING HIM into an unwelcome consciousness. With trepidation Zander opened his eyes.

He was on his knees being held by Tagar's man. The royal guard commander stood in front of him, leaning victoriously on Zander's sword.

Tagar Garrate bent down and lifted his face. "Your mother will be pleased."

"Will she now?" Zander spat blood. His eyes narrowed as his face grew hot.

"It's an unfortunate situation, but your mother has no intention of giving up the throne, not now or ever."

"I never wanted the throne," he said through clenched teeth.

"You say that now, but the lure of power is one of man's greatest weaknesses. Sooner or later, you would have fallen victim to it."

"And what of the princess of Kasmire?"

"Ah yes Aerilla, the beautiful bride to be. With the dagger in hand your mother will no longer need that alliance. Her army will rival any on this continent and the next."

"So I have become expendable then."

Commander Garrate squatted down and looked Zander directly in the eye. "You always have been."

The hot raging fire in Zander's gut erupted, and he fought against the mercenary who restrained him trying to get to the commander.

Through gritted teeth, he said, "You better kill me, Tagar because

I will hunt you and your idiot henchmen down, slit you from gut to sternum, pull out your innards, and let the vultures feast on your carcasses."

The mercenary laughed and then kicked him hard in the stomach.

He buckled as pain shot through his abdomen, taking his breath with it. He could feel the tears well in his eyes as he gagged down the vomit that threatened to spill from his gullet.

"I look forward to that day, Your Highness," the commander said with a laugh. "Not that it will ever come."

"May the gods burn you alive, you traitorous swine," Zander croaked.

"Such a foul mouth for a prince. Your mother will be glad to be rid of you." Tagar absently rubbed the scars marring one side of his face. "Unfortunately, she asked me not to kill you. Thinks you don't deserve a quick death. She instead wants you to suffer." He motioned to his man. "Put him with the others and then go find that little street urchin."

"You and the queen can rot in the afterworld together," Zander snarled, his eyes pits of black fury.

The royal guard commander sneered and stepped forward. Leaning in, he lowered his voice until his tone was a quiet fury. "You have been a burden since the day you were born. Why your mother didn't drown you at birth is beyond me. You are an abomination, and the world is a better place without you."

Abomination. It was a gut punch. Over the years Tagar had made veiled comments to Zander, insinuating he was something different, something unworthy or tainted. Pay him no mind, Zander always told himself. Tagar was a bully trying to get a reaction. He had ignored him, but a part of him always wondered what Tagar meant.

"You don't know anything about me," Zander spat.

The commander grabbed Zander by the chin. "I know more than you."

A red haze crossed Zander's sight as the commander's mocking face hovered near his. Blood raced through his veins, and his heart thumped wildly in his chest. Without forethought he spit in the commander's face.

Tagar pulled back and dragged his sleeve across his cheek. "When night falls and the mist thickens, pray those who hide among it give you a quick death, half-breed."

43

ZANDER

Vallaria and Faelin had already been tied to thick wooden posts buried in the ground. He caught Vallaria's eye as the men dragged him into the pit and toward the third post. Contempt filled her gaze.

He turned away, his gut wrenching.

His mother had betrayed him and he, in turn, had doomed the others. He should have known when she insisted Tagar accompany them there was something up. And if he hadn't been so drunk in the tavern that night, maybe he would've paid more attention to the men Tagar hired for the job. The mercenaries were obviously not just randomly picked by the commander.

Half-breed.

Tagar's words. Why would he say something so untrue? *He's trying to get under your skin.*

Tagar's man pushed his back against the empty post and bound his hands behind it. For the first time, Zander really looked at the tattoo covering one side of the man's neck. It was a dagger clenched in the jaws of a wolf head but the lettering inside is what caught his eye. *Zion.*

He was one of Dagget Ra's men.

As if the mercenary knew what he was thinking, he grinned, winked with his good eye, and tapped Zander's cheek with his large hand. "I should gut you here and leave you to die. The commander may be too afraid of the queen to go against her command, but I ain't. Fortunately, I prefer a challenge when I kill and your pathetic arse ain't worth the effort." He tucked a small silver medallion inside Zander's tunic pocket and leaned close, whispering in his ear. "Goodnight, sweet prince. Enjoy purgatory."

Zander glanced over at Vallaria as the mercenary walked in her direction. She stared straight ahead, her beautiful face a mask of defiance.

Why did you come back? He questioned silently.

From the moment he'd seen Vallaria in the tavern he'd been inexplicitly drawn to her. *I should never have agreed to let her come. But you couldn't walk away. You are selfish, Zander Damask. When it comes to women, you always have been.*

Chastising himself was not going to help them get out of this situation. He strained against his binds, trying desperately to break free.

The mercenary sauntered back over and threw Vallaria's sword on the pile with the others and Faelin's crossbow. "Those ropes are from the Gold Coast," he said, pointing at Zander's bound feet and hands. "Use 'em on boats, I hear. Strong. Won't break even on the unruliest of seas. I doubt a weakling like yourself will break them."

He punched Zander in the stomach again.

"Enough!" Tagar strode in front of him and pushed the mercenary aside.

He swung the Dagger of Crusade around in his hand as he strolled back and forth. "First, it would be highly ungracious of me not to thank you for your assistance with this matter." He held up the dagger in victory. "I'm sure the queen will also be grateful, but sadly you won't be around to receive her appreciation."

He stopped pacing and stood in between Faelin and Vallaria.

"Second, it is unfortunate that it has come to this, but you two can thank Zane for your untimely deaths. I suspect you'll now rue the day you decided to come on this little adventure." He chuckled.

Faelin remained resigned, green eyes staring straight ahead, shoulders back, but Vallaria struggled against her binds, cursing.

Tagar smiled and stood before her, waiting until she'd settled. "And lastly. You, my dear, intrigue me greatly." He lifted his hand and with his index finger wiped the blood from her cheek and tasted it.

Vallaria pulled back in disgust.

"Your beauty is unmatched, but your powers—" Tagar shook his head. "Such a waste to have to destroy something so unique. You could have been an asset to the kingdom. Know that it will be my burden to have your blood on my hands."

Without warning, he lifted the Dagger of Crusade and plunged it down. The blade sliced through the air and embedded itself into the wood post, scarcely missing her cheek.

Zander gasped, but Vallaria didn't flinch.

Tagar's lips curled into a crooked smile. "Intriguing indeed."

He yanked the dagger from the wood and stepped back.

"As pleasing as it would be to slit all your throats myself, the thought of the valley taking three more victims is too tempting to ignore. Whatever your fate, it will be much more painful and torturous than anything I could dream up."

Stepping forward, Tagar grabbed Vallaria's braid and yanked her head toward him, mashing his lips against hers.

Rage ripped through Zander as he watched her struggle against the kiss. "Tagar," he yelled. "Leave her be!"

The royal commander pulled away from Vallaria and glanced back over his shoulder, grinning at Zander. Slowly he wiped his mouth with the back of his gloved hand. "Enjoy the last few moments of your life," he said, looking from one to the other. "The night is upon us and soon the mist will roll back into the basin and there will be no one to hear you scream except the ones eating you alive."

"I'm going to kill you," Zander hissed.

The royal commander smiled and walked back over to him. He leaned in and whispered in Zander's ear, "I would like nothing more than to slit your throat and pull out your blasphemous words, but alas I promised your mother I would not kill you."

The commander pulled back. His gray eyes, void of any emotion, stared directly into Zander's as he lifted a small hunting knife in front of his face and twisted it menacingly. "But she didn't say anything about me taking a piece of you as a trophy."

Tagar ran the blade across Zander's midsection. "What should I take? A part of your liver? Maybe a chunk of flesh? Or carve out a nice hole for the maggots to nest in once you're dead?"

The commander's smile turned wicked, and he pushed the tip of the blade against Zander's stomach.

Zander winced and inhaled as the sharp knife punctured his abdomen. A searing pain exploded from the wound as a warm flow of blood trickled down his skin.

"What was that?" the mercenary asked as he searched the darkness.

The commander withdrew the knife and stepped back.

Zander exhaled, his breath coming in gasps.

"Something is out there," the man said as a swooshing noise echoed from the advancing fog.

"Let us leave, Kagge," Tagar said to the mercenary.

He cast Zander a sly smile. "It seems I will have to remember you in other ways."

Tagar pocketed his knife and turned to Vallaria and Faelin. "I do hope you understand this is nothing personal. I did try and warn you off this journey, but you were just so persistent."

The commander shrugged and followed the mercenary from the pit.

Zander watched him go. His temple throbbed and his gut seared with pain from the knife wound. In an explosion of fury, he screamed. "I will find you, Tagar Garrate, you bastard. In life or death, I'll find you, and when I do, I will gut you until nothing remains but a hollow carcass of bones and skin."

Vallaria glanced over. Her eyes conveyed the same sentiment. He did not doubt that she too would like to rip the commander's head from his neck.

"Do you feel better?" Faelin asked, her green eyes steady and her voice calm.

"No," Zander snapped. He glanced down at the red stain blooming on his shirt. Beads of sweat slipped down his face as the pain from the knife wound raced through every fiber of his body. It hurt like a son-of-a-bitch, but it wasn't deep. It wouldn't kill him.

He cursed and strained at his binds.

Because of him, the scout and blacksmith were dead. Men whose names he hadn't bothered to remember. And now Faelin and Vallaria would perish, fated to die as food for whatever else lived in this cursed place.

How had he been so blind to his mother's treachery?

"I should have never agreed to let you come. I'm sorry," he said. He grimaced as another burning wave of pain rolled from the gash.

"Don't be," Vallaria said. "We came of our own volition. Besides you had no idea your friend would turn against you."

"He's no friend of mine. He works for my—" Zander stopped short. "The queen, and so do I. That is the extent of our relationship. The man is a vile piece of cow dung and always has been. The kingdom would be better off if it were rid of him."

Zander thought about how often Tagar Garrate had tormented him after King Torrsen died and he became Queen Cereli's second in command. Always at her side and in her ear, even more so than Yelin Barro.

Another pompous ass.

Why was it his mother filled her court with idiots?

So she wouldn't have to get her hands dirty.

Queen Cereli was nothing if not deceptive and cunning.

Her court, her guards, the kingdom, they were all either part of her deception or blissfully unaware they were being duped. The dark queen did not always need dark magic to pull the strings of her puppets.

Zander mused about his mother as the last of the light left the valley, and the chill of the oncoming fog wound its way across the ground. The cold felt good against his burning skin and the throbbing ache in his gut.

The thick ghostly mist rolled toward them. It ebbed and flowed as if dancing to an unheard tune. It snaked around their feet and curled languidly up their legs.

Another noise came from the fog.

Ignoring the pain in his belly, Zander strained against the restraints. The thick rope burned and chafed his wrists as he tried desperately to free himself. He had no intention of dying like this, torn to pieces by demons or the other horrid creatures trapped in this cursed place.

The stories his stepfather had told him were coming true—tortured spirits, demons, broken bodies, and things that nature never intended walked this earth. The Valley of Souls was supposed to be myth. His mother had scoffed at the king's stories, but she knew better than any what dwelled in this place. She was the dark queen after all. And yet she sent her only son to die here without even a hint of remorse. In this moment Zander wanted nothing more than to kill Tagar Garrate and then look his mother in the eye one more time before he left Ravenia forever.

Fog swirled around him, and the noise that had sent Tagar running echoed again toward them. Zander refocused his attention and struggled against his binds, but it was hopeless. His wrists were raw, and blood dripped down his hands. He turned his head and looked at Vallaria and his heart clenched. He ached to touch her again, to feel his hand on her skin. Inhaling sharply, he silently chided himself for not kissing her when he'd had the chance.

Cursing under his breath, he leaned his head back on the post and closed his eyes. *How could I have been so stupid?* He'd led them all to their deaths, and now the one woman he truly wanted was the one woman he would never have.

He shivered as the fog rose in icy coils. It reeked of death. Its wisps heavy with despair. He turned again in Vallaria's direction, but the fog had swallowed her in its thickness.

Off in the distance a scraping noise echoed toward him. His muscles tensed and he squinted, searching the fog for any sign of its source.

Suddenly, a creeping shadow appeared and then a whisper.

Zander held his breath.

Something was out there moving through the mist.

44
VALLARIA

Vallaria had run straight into trouble.

Upset about Pax she hadn't assessed the situation before showing herself.

Zane was unconscious on the ground and Faelin was sitting at knife point on a rock. The look she gave Vallaria when she'd run into the area was one of surprise and then disappointment.

Once again she'd acted before thinking, and now she was tied to a post waiting to die.

Faelin had every right to be angry. She'd fought so hard for Vallaria to be free and Vallaria had screwed up. If she'd run away with Pax, she'd have made it back to the kingdom before Tagar.

But then what would you have done?

She twisted her arms, hoping to move the ropes to another place on her wrists. Her skin was raw and burning and the cold fog swirling around her made the open wounds sting.

Her entire life had been about nothingness. No family, no home, no idea who she was—*nothing*. Although King Elvander, Faelin, and Kelena had shown her compassion, she still created a wall between her heart and kept everyone at a distance. The ashen tree had become her place of solace. Somewhere to reflect, to dream, but mostly it was a place to hide. Hide from the elves, from the unknown, and from herself.

But you can't hide anymore, Vallaria Ravenia. You know who you are and what's expected of you. Except she didn't know how to actually *be* that person.

She sighed and flexed her hands—again nothing.

Like everything and everyone, her magic had abandoned her when she needed it the most.

The mage crystal in her pocket remained silent. No matter how hard she willed it to grow cold, it remained unresponsive.

Vallaria gave up. She looked toward Faelin and Zane, but there was nothing to see but a thick wall of white fog. Their voices echoed through the night air, but she couldn't make out a word they were saying. It felt like they were miles away instead of a few steps. The mist had taken on a strange glow as it nipped at her skin with a cold clammy bite.

The thumping in her chest reverberated in her ears as she fought against her binds. A thin layer of sweat covered her clammy skin and as she struggled against the rope it stung at her raw skin.

A scraping noise reached her ears, followed by a whispering swoosh.

Something moved in the mist.

A shadow.

It weaved its way toward her from Faelin's and Zane's direction.

The fog swirled.

Her heart quickened as she pulled her wrists apart, moving them in circles to try and loosen the rope. She bit her bottom lip as warm blood dripped down her hands and the ropes to cut into her flesh. She winced but kept trying to free herself.

Her attempts were futile—whatever was in the mist now stood only feet away.

The scraping sound echoed around her as the shadow got closer, breaking through the wall of fog and into her field of vision.

She cringed, waiting for the end, but then a sense of relief flooded through her.

"Pax!" she said, both thrilled to see him and angry that he didn't leave the valley as he was told.

"Shhh," he hissed and then pointed to the mist. His brown eyes were round and troubled, his small jaw clenched tight. And without any more words she understood that something else lurked out there.

Quietly he circled her and used a small knife to cut her bindings.

The flesh on her wrists was raw and bleeding. Tearing at the bottom of her undergarment, she gingerly wrapped strips of material around the wounds. The material touched the open flesh, and she flinched, cursing under her breath at the sting.

"We must free the others," she whispered, grabbing her sword from the pile of weapons the commander had left behind.

He nodded and headed in the direction of the post that held Faelin captive.

Vallaria ran through the mist to where she thought Zane was, but within minutes she was lost in the soupy fog.

She called out softly, but the thick mist swallowed her voice, and the only reply was the swooshing sound that had now seemed to be all around them.

A chill snuck down her spine as the temperature dropped abruptly, and a deep despair overwhelmed her. The sensation ignited a memory and Vallaria suspected she knew what was out there.

Wraiths!

King Elvander had told her stories of wraiths, mortal spell-casters who used their magic for a dark purpose, *immortality*. While their desire was achieved, they became a shadow of their former selves, a soulless creature stuck between the world of the living and the dead, forever searching for a way out. Whenever one was near, anyone in the vicinity was encompassed in its misery. This overwhelming emotional void made one vulnerable to the wraith and its touch, which could steal your soul and leave you an empty corpse.

The hilt of her sword felt slick as she pulled it from its sheath. Panic rose, and her eyes darted back and forth, searching the stagnant fog for any sign of them.

How many wraiths are in the mist? Is this why my mage magic is absent?

A rumble shook the ground beneath her feet and the pounding of hooves sliced through the silence of the dark night. She raised her sword, and the mist before her swirled chaotically as a wraith on an emaciated horse, part of its skeleton visible through rotting wounds in its hide, rode from it. An unholy scream exploded in the air as the wraith swung the glowing black blade of a sword toward her. When it passed, the sharp edge barely missed her shoulder as she leapt aside. The wraith's face, nothing more than a dark hole in the hood of its tattered, flowing black cape, screeched again. The horse's eyes flamed hell red and its hooves beat like a death drum on the dry ground as it slid to a stop and turned around.

Another wraith emerged from the mist and a similar blast of heavy despair followed. Her stomach lurched as the forlorn emotions overwhelmed her. She fought the urge to give up, to cry, to die as the second beastly horse bore down on her. As she staggered out of its path, she felt its hot, stale breath on her cheek as it thundered.

Vallaria struggled under the misery that wrapped its tendrils around her, attempting to draw the life from her. While the two wraiths circled her, their horses snorted and stamped the ground with their hooves.

She wiped her brow and prayed to her gods.

She could feel the small indents of her father's prayer beads in her pocket. If her gods truly were benevolent beings, surely they would answer in her time of need.

One wraith pointed a bony finger at her, its tattered cloak flapping in a non-existent breeze. The other raised its sword as its horse reared up on its hind legs, a hazy breath streaming from its nostrils.

The night became deathly still, all sounds filtered out by the thick despair.

Cold wrapped itself around her, chilling her to the bone.

Only the eerie glow of the fog gave the pitch of the night any definition.

When the other horse flared its nostrils and pawed the ground with an infected hoof full of maggots, Vallaria raised her sword. How did one kill that which had already given its life to the darkness?

Her chest tightened and she found it difficult to breath as another wave of despair wrapped itself around her. Her sword shook in her hands as the first rider galloped past, swinging his blade in her direction. Instinctively she met his sword with her own. Metal clashed. The force spun her sideways, directly into the path of the second rider. A second sword swung, the blade catching her across her dominant arm before she had time to react.

Vallaria unwillingly dropped her sword, clutching at the wound as blood seeped from the gash and through her fingers. Her head spun as she looked for the wraiths in the fog. Before she could set her feet, one came charging from the left, its sword stabbing. With an awkward jerk she managed to sidestep its attack.

A soft whisper slipped by her ear. Where the mages here?

The rider turned its horse around and galloped back toward her. Vallaria pulled the dagger Faelin had gifted her from it sheath, and as the horse passed again, she ducked under the downward swing of the sword and jabbed the tip of her blade into the horse's flank, tearing it open slightly.

It jerked and neighed, pulling the dagger from her hand.

Fire sprang from its mouth and black mist leached from the new wound.

Hooves pounded the ground behind her, and she turned as the second rider sprinted by her. The wraith clipped her shoulder with the flat edge of its sword, and she sprawled to the ground, breathless.

The wraith returned to where she lay. Its bony finger pointed toward her once again. Instinctively she searched for her sword, but it lay in the dirt, out of reach, and her only other weapon was embedded in the thigh of the other wraith's horse.

She had no way of defending herself.

The black blade glowed a pale, sickly green as the phantom raised its sword high above its hooded head. A hollow laugh filled the air.

Death had come for her. In a futile attempt to protect herself, Vallaria raised her wounded arm.

Suddenly, from the curling fog, Zane appeared. He lunged at the wraith as the black blade fell toward her. With one swing he met the ominous sword mid-air, blocking it from reaching its target.

The phantom screeched and turned his hooded head toward Zane.

The distraction gave Vallaria time to get to her feet and scramble to where her sword lay. Faelin and Pax also emerged from the fog, and Vallaria's stomach lurched as she saw the young boy. So innocent yet surrounded by horrific things he should never have to see.

She had to get Pax out of this dreadful place, and since she had no idea how to defeat a wraith, there was only one plausible thing to do.

We need to run!

"Watch out!" she heard Faelin yell as she raised her crossbow.

Gripping her injured arm, Vallaria turned in time to see a wraith drive his black blade into Zane's shoulder. The tip sliced through the skin and muscle and exited through his back. He cried out in agony and fell to his knees as the wraith turned his horse back around.

The bolt from Faelin's crossbow narrowly missed its target as it sailed by the wraith's shrouded face. It let out a bone-chilling wail and lifted its sword. Streams of fiery breath flashed from its horse's nostrils as the steed snorted. Its teeth bared as the rider pushed its knees deep into the beast's flanks, sending it galloping toward where Zane knelt, wounded and spent.

He's going to run him over.

In desperation, she sheathed her sword and tried to drag her weary body over.

"Shield him," she yelled at Faelin, not caring if she outed her friend as elf kind. Zane was about to die. But the elf was preoccupied, and in danger herself, as the second wraith circled around her,

Vallaria's stomach twisted in knots as she willed Zane to get up.

Before she could do anything more Pax ran toward Zane and placed himself between him and the oncoming threat. A furrowed brow and pursed lips contoured his small face, and he raised a thin blade.

"NO!" Vallaria yelled as the beast galloped past him.

Pax rotated on his small feet, and his expression changed to one of disbelief. His arms dropped limp to his sides and the knife slipped from his hand as a thin line of red appeared across his throat.

Vallaria stared in horror, her insides cramping in fear.

The boy swayed and then as if his brain recognized what happened his fingers groped at his neck. Blood sprayed outward with every breath he attempted to take.

Vallaria tried to run, but her legs felt heavy. With every ounce of strength left in her muscles, she forced herself to move forward until she reached Pax, catching his small body in her arms before he hit the dry earth. His eyes found hers and they widened in fear, then just as quickly glassed over in acceptance.

"Don't try and speak," she whispered, cradling his head in her arms as blood oozed over his neck and chest. "You'll be fine. Faelin can fix—"

But before she'd finished her sentence, she felt his small body go limp.

Her heart exploded in grief. He was gone. The gods had taken him.

Sorrow and anger flared deep inside her and she began to wail, as she clung to Pax's lifeless body.

This wasn't supposed to happen! He's too young to die!

She stared into his vacant eyes as Zane and Faelin continued to clash with the wraiths. Neighs and the tinny clang of metal filled the air, but Vallaria didn't care. Pax was dead and she had killed him.

Whispers filtered through the fog, muted at first and then rising like a chorus around her. Her head began to throb, and she felt the familiar deep chill radiate from her pocket. The mage stone was reacting, not to her needs but to the desires of those long dead.

A bone-shattering cold seeped from the crystal, weaving its icy tendrils under her skin, through her blood, and into her bones. She didn't fight it. She was no longer afraid. Instead, she closed her eyes and let it flow undeterred through her. The powerful fury of the ancient mages surged, and the desire for bloodlust washed through her as the whispers now chanted clearly inside her head.

Death to them all.

Gently, she laid Pax's still body on the ground. His lips had turned blue, and a light layer of frost covered his clothes where she'd held him.

The sword came easily from its sheath as she stood.

The ghostly voices reached a crescendo as the chill running through her fingers extended to the metal of her sword.

Ice crackled down the blade.

Suddenly, the dark of night lessened, as if her eyes pushed past the swirling gray fog.

Something was happening, and as if they felt it too, the wraiths, Faelin, and Zane, turned to face her. The wraiths, their glowing black swords slashing the air, galloped toward her, their interest no longer on Faelin and Zane.

Ear-splitting screeches filled the air.

The closer they got, the colder the crystal in her pocket became.

For Pax.

The cold power flowed through her, but it was no longer unbearable, nor did she fear it. It felt comfortable, familiar, like it belonged to her and her to it.

She widened her stance and glared at the oncoming wraith. No longer was she weary. The tired ache in her muscles had disappeared, and she no longer felt pain in her shoulder.

A wash of cold swept through her veins as she swung the sword.

The first rider fell to the arc of her frost-covered sword, and the ancient magic surged. The fallen wraith wailed as a black mist escaped from the open wound in its chest. Vallaria whirled and slashed its legs just above the knee. The wraith crumpled as thick ice clung to the edges of the gash.

Another pitiful wail escaped from the shadows of the cloak.

Vallaria straddled the fallen wraith, and another layer of ice appeared on her blade. Her lips twitched into a wicked smile as she drove the tip into the hood where the wraith's face would be. A shriek filled the night sky, its pitch so high and shattering that Faelin and Zane dropped their weapons and put their hands over their ears.

Throwing her head back, she closed her eyes and felt the dark magic that created this abomination shrivel under her cold power. She opened her mouth and exhaled in pleasure as her sword vibrated and the frost magic filled every fiber of her being.

Without opening her eyes, she sensed the second wraith as it whirled around and galloped away. The deep despair saturating the area dissipated as the wraith vanished back into the void between this world and the next.

Vallaria yanked her sword from the shriveled corpse. Sheathing it, she ran back to where the small body of Pax lay. Scooping him into her arms, she rocked back and forth, cursing the gods for taking the life of an innocent and herself for selfishly putting him in harm's way.

A single drop of blood dripped from her nose.

She wiped at it and looked down at Pax. But this time she didn't shed a tear. This time all she felt was the thumping of her cold heart, and the vengeful whispers of those long dead.

45

FAELIN

Faelin watched Vallaria from afar as she sat with the young boy, before her gaze drifted across the dry gully.

The fog had lifted, and the ice-covered walls of the valley could be seen. They were not far from the sloping incline and the trail that would take them back up to where they'd entered.

They didn't have the dagger, but at least Vallaria was alive and that gave Faelin hope they could still somehow regain the throne of Ravenia.

Zane limped toward Vallaria. He held his injured shoulder and winced as he moved. The blood on his shirt where Tagar knifed him had dried a dark reddish-brown. The wrap she'd hastily put on the wound after untying him from the post must have stopped the bleeding. Faelin made a mental note to clean and patch his wounds once they were free from this accursed place.

She watched as he knelt by Vallaria's side and whispered something in her ear. Faelin cocked her head and listened.

"We will take the boy back with us, Vallaria. He won't be left here alone."

Turning her pale face toward him, she nodded and allowed him to take Pax's body. Gingerly Zane lifted the boy up with his good arm, wincing as he had to use his injured one to secure the boy's lower half.

"I'm fine," he said when Vallaria offered her help.

The three of them walked across the dry and dusty pit until they reached a small patch of brown grass where Zane gingerly laid Pax down. Faelin could tell he was in agony, but he refused to ask for help and out of respect for his male pride she did not offer.

Vallaria stared at the small boy as she stood over him.

Faelin studied her. Vallaria stood stiff and unmoving. There were no tears, no outward expressions of emotion, just a stoic, apathetic attitude toward the body before her. Something had changed. In that moment when the ancient magic had surged within her, the defeated and broken part of her had disappeared.

"Vallaria," Faelin said, her voice soft and low.

"You were right. I should have never brought him," she said. Her blue eyes were flat as she turned Faelin's way.

"We had no way of knowing what would dwell in the valley or the treachery that the commander would bestow on us."

"Didn't we? The Valley of Souls is legendary, or so you and Zane said. A place where the slaughter of hundreds of mages tainted the soil with their spilt blood. Zane's stepfather told him of the things that lurked here, hidden by the thick mist. How could we not at least suspect that some of it were true?"

Her voice faltered slightly as she continued. "Pax had no business being in such a place, but I was selfish and foolish thinking the kingdom would be worse for him than this nightmare. I wasn't keeping him safe. I lured him to a horrific end."

Anger rose in Vallaria, and once again Faelin saw flashes of the defiant, spiteful, and rebellious young woman who only a few weeks ago found out she was a princess from a stolen kingdom. A throne she must take back if the kingdoms of Exile were ever to find a lasting peace again. And if that wasn't burden enough—

Vallaria whirled on Zane. "This is your queen's fault. She sent you here to die and treats her subjects like they're chattel. Only worthy if they can provide her with a service or payment in kind. Her royal guardsmen rape, pillage, and assault, and she looks the other way. There is nothing good about Ravenia anymore, but that is going to change."

Before Vallaria could slip up and reveal who she really was, Faelin put a hand on her arm to quiet her. For a second, before Vallaria jerked her arm away, Faelin felt the cold of the ancient magic simmering under her skin. Her eyes were full of tears—not tears of sadness but of anger. As they spilled over onto her cheeks, they froze. Perfect lines of ice trailed down Vallaria's pale skin, her blue eyes glistening like melting dewdrops on a sunny winter day.

Faelin's heart thumped. Her father had been right—the last frost mage had risen. Now they must hope the king was wrong and Vallaria would learn to control the powerful magic. For Faelin was unsure if she could really kill Vallaria if that time ever came.

Vallaria turned back to stare at Pax's body and again went quiet.

"Can you explain to me what happened with her magic?" asked Zane as he stood beside Faelin. "You did see what I saw, right?"

Faelin nodded. The memory flashed in front of her eyes. When the magic had surged it had not just been visible in her hands. It was like a bolt of lightning crackling inside her body. The blue light had been everywhere.

Before Faelin had a chance to answer, a bloodcurdling roar filled the pit. It echoed from the back where the dragon's lair was.

Zane drew his sword and took a step forward.

Vallaria turned toward him and held up her hand. "It's in pain."

Faelin strode to where Pax's body lay and grasped Vallaria's arm. "We must leave this place."

Vallaria glanced at Zane who stood a few yards away. Lowering her voice, she whispered to Faelin. "Can you heal it?"

The elf's eyebrow raised. "You want me to lay hands on a serpent dragon."

Vallaria nodded. "I injured it and the beast is suffering. I must try and help."

Faelin heard the desperation in her friend's voice. This wasn't about the serpent dragon; it was about her gaining back some sense of control. She couldn't save Pax, so maybe she could save the beast.

A memory surfaced of a small girl sitting lodged in an ashen tree. A place where she felt safe and although always alone, more herself than when she was among the elves. Vallaria had sat in its branches hundreds of times over the years and eventually Faelin had begun to understand the significance of that tree. It was the one place Vallaria felt in control. In a strange way, Faelin supposed the serpent dragon was Vallaria's tree.

The pit was hauntingly quiet. There was no breeze, no sound but their voices and the mournful roar of the beast. Faelin looked at Vallaria. Dark circles framed her eyes and bloody dirt soiled her clothes. She looked a mess: tired and injured, but the vacant look deep in her eyes, the part only an elf could see was what concerned Faelin the most. *What happened to you when the ancient magic surged inside of you. Did it give you power, or did it take something from you?*

Faelin was afraid it may have been a little of both.

Another pain-filled roar reverberated around them.

"Let me go finish it off," Zane said, taking a few more steps toward the cave.

"No. We will go," Vallaria answered, looking at Faelin.

"That's not a good idea," he replied. "You saw what happened to the blacksmith. And it almost happened to you."

The pain on Zane's face showed his conflicting emotions. Faelin understood his struggle. Vallaria was at times impulsive, stubborn, and exasperating, but she needed to stand on her own two feet and learn to lead, even if mistakes were made.

Vallaria shrugged. "It was protecting the dagger, nothing more."

Zane opened his mouth, but Faelin interjected, "Are you sure about this, Vallaria? Serpent dragons are dangerous and unpredictable. One that is injured, even more so. I doubt it is going to let us get anywhere near it. We will be lucky to even get through the mouth of its lair before we are blasted with its icy breath."

"We must try."

"We may die."

"I thought you said I was the last mage?" she hissed, lowering her voice so Zane couldn't hear and leaning toward the elf.

"But that doesn't mean you're invincible. You are still a human made of blood, flesh, and bone."

The deepening of Vallaria's frown told Faelin she wasn't going to change her mind. "Fine, but don't say I didn't warn you."

Vallaria looked toward Zane. "Stay with Pax."

"You are not going in there," he said, lowering his sword and sticking an arm out to stop her as she strode by.

"I am."

"Then I'm coming with you."

"That's an even worse idea." Faelin pointed to the fresh blood staining his shirt. "You're injured. If we have any chance at all of surviving, we cannot enter its lair covered in the scent of blood."

"Why must you go at all?" he asked. "Let the beast die of its wounds."

"It's suffering. At the very least we shall end its torment and give it a quick, painless death," Faelin said, her green eyes moving quickly to Vallaria.

As Vallaria moved closer to Zane, her tone changed, and she pulled back her shoulders and lifted her chin. "There's been enough death and suffering on this journey. I need to do this. But if we don't return, you must promise you will get Pax to a peaceful resting place."

The mercenary shook his head and grasped her hands. "Please don't. It's too dangerous."

Without a word she yanked her hands from his and looked at Faelin. "Let's go."

They walked toward the cave. Faelin could feel the serpent dragon's pain and anguish. Although she didn't have the sensory abilities of her mother, as a healer her intuition was strong. *The beast is dying.*

Reaching the mouth of the cave, Faelin could hear the beast's labored breath and the ensuing shuddering moan.

They entered the damp and cold cavern. A rancid odor wafted from its depths and beside her, Vallaria gagged. The musty air within was ripe with death. Not the pungent and malodorous odor of one who was dying but the stale, heavy, rotting scent that clung to one long after death had found them. Faelin had no doubt the cave would be littered with the bones and corpses of those who'd attempted to defeat the serpent dragon in the past and claim the Dagger of Crusade for themselves.

Signaling for Vallaria to follow, she crept along the far wall, tiptoeing deeper into the beast's lair. The deeper into the cave they walked the more overwhelming the smell became. Vallaria gagged again, her eyes wide as the sound reverberated through the dark cave.

Another roar came from the darkness. It vibrated all around, them shaking dust and debris from the cave's ceiling.

They were close.

A blue glow caught Faelin's eye, and she peered around the corner to find the serpent dragon huddled in a dark corner. Its breath came out in quick icy spurts and brilliant blue eyes blinked rapidly as it flapped a massive wing.

The creature was dying, and in that moment Faelin felt a deep sorrow for the past and the magic that had been disappearing from the world for centuries. While she pondered on the situation, a wave of cold air passed by. Vallaria, her hand wrapped around the throbbing blue frost crystal, walked toward the serpent dragon.

"Vallaria, what are you doing?" Faelin asked, but Vallaria ignored her and continued to walk to where the beast lay.

Faelin drew her sword and quickly followed. *Her impulsiveness is going to get us both killed!*

By the time Faelin caught up, Vallaria stood in front of the serpent dragon, her hand laying on its snout. The beast looked at her, its gaze forlorn. The small puffs of cold air coming from its mouth did not have the cold power it did when it was whole. It was weakening and with it so did its magic.

"Go ahead. It knows why we are here. It will not hurt us," Vallaria said, her hand still touching the dragon.

"How do you know?" Faelin asked.

"I just do. The ancient mage magic is a thrum in my ears instead of the burning cold in my blood. It's a sound of comfort telling me this beast is of no threat to us."

The dragon made a strange noise, almost like a husky whimper as Faelin laid trembling hands around its raw, festering wound. Muttering under her breath, Faelin closed her eyes. Speaking in the tongue of her people, she pushed her magic forward and out through her hands. She opened her eyes and glanced down to see the familiar green glow flow from her palms and move into the serpent dragon, weaving its way under the beast's thick hide.

Minutes later the wound stitched itself back together, and the beast, with a mighty roar, clamored to its feet, lifted it massive wings, and flew from the cave.

"You're welcome," Faelin said.

"It's grateful, in its own way."

"I'm sure."

Faelin took a small leather pouch from her pocket and removed two small polished white stones. Squatting, she carved a circle in the sand with her finger she placed the stones inches apart, and then muttering, she pushed each into the ground.

"What are you doing? asked Vallaria.

"Giving back to the elements for the magic I have dispersed. Between protecting you from the dragon and then healing it, I have used a lot of magic. These stones have been consecrated by the elders. An easier way to ensure that balance is reached."

Vallaria crossed her arms. "I get nosebleeds and excruciating headaches when I use the mage magic, but you push some pebbles into the ground and your magic remains balanced and you unaffected by it. Seems fair."

Faelin smiled. "Mortals are not meant to wield magic. Be thankful headaches and a little blood from your nostril is all you experience."

"As I learn to control it, will the consequences of its use diminish?"

Faelin shrugged. "I don't know how the ancient magic will affect you. Many mortals through history have found a way to take magic and use it for themselves, but there have always been consequences —most dire."

"Like?"

"Magic tends to end up controlling a mortal and inevitably leads to one of two things: death or the individual is driven mad and then dies.

"So death then?" Vallaria said, looking down at the silent ice crystal in her palm.

"I'm afraid so," Faelin said.

Flipping the crystal over in her hand, Vallaria frowned. "Ravenia needs its rightful queen. It needs to rise from the dark magic of Queen Cereli and give light to a new way, a new future, and a new era of magic."

The ice crystal began to glow again, and frost appeared on Vallaria's fingertips. Faelin watched as her friend unknowingly willed the magic forth.

She's getting better already.

When they walked from the cave a rippling darkness crossed Vallaria's bright blue eyes. "I will be that future."

46
ZANDER

Zander finally began to breathe easy again as Vallaria exited the dragon's lair. He hadn't realized he'd been holding his breath intermittently and pacing. Twice he had to stop himself from running headlong into the cave, especially after the serpent dragon flew out of the opening and up into the thinning mist still hanging over the highest edges of the valley.

When she and Faelin reached where he stood, he asked, "How? Are you all right? I saw the beast fly away."

Faelin tugged on her long blonde hair and glanced at Vallaria. "We're fine. Thankfully, the witches across the sea are blessed with many gifts."

Zander wasn't sure what Faelin's evasive answer meant. Besides his mother's dark and unholy magic, Zander had not seen much magic in the world. He'd come across a small group of tree dwellers in the far reaches of Brulle who mixed magical tonics and elixirs and performed blood rituals for their tree god. And there was, of course, the magi of the Gold Coast, but never had he seen magic so visual or met anyone who had active powers.

During his many travels, Zander had heard whispers of a group of witches who resided in the cold lands of Brulle. Although, truth be told, he'd always thought the tales were nonsense. Stories made up by sailors and mercenaries who regaled patrons in brothels and taverns with their outlandish fables. To his knowledge the elves were the only magical race in existence with powerful magic like the type Vallaria had displayed.

His Uncle Moricio had spoken about the elven kingdom a few times during his younger years before he and his mother moved to Ravenia. While his uncle didn't have much good to say about the elves, his mother refused to even let anyone speak of their kind in her presence. Zander assumed it was because it was an elf who'd stolen, King Ryguard from her. Even though Ravenia bordered Mistenvale, he never paid the elven kingdom much mind growing up. There was no reason too, for elves and man no longer intermingled. In all his travels throughout the continents he'd never seen an elf in person, and he was thankful for that.

But a witch.

A part of him wanted to recoil from Vallaria, but surprisingly a larger part was even more intrigued by her because of it.

"Did you heal the beast?" Zander asked. He'd been shocked when the dragon flew from its lair because he'd seen the significant wound on its chest. The flesh had been burnt, not by fire but by extreme cold, which left the edges seared but the inside flesh raw and festering. It was a wound the serpent dragon would have died from eventually.

"The serpent dragon was not as wounded as we initially thought," Vallaria said. "It only needs rest and time to heal."

The two women were not telling him the truth, but he was too exhausted and too in pain to push for more clarity. He wanted to leave this cursed land and clear his head so he could figure out what to do from here. Going back to the kingdom was not an option as Tagar and his mother would surely find another way to dispose of him and he wasn't sure making his way to the Gold Coast was any better. Was Moricio in on the plans? Was Darrius Mensah? Zander didn't know who he could trust anymore.

It had been a long time since Zander felt this alone. Although he never really felt like he had a true home, always shuffling between Ravenia and the Gold Coast or escaping for a few months on merchant ships, he'd never experienced the bewilderment of not belonging, somewhere—not until now. In a matter of a few days, he suddenly felt like he didn't know where he fit into this world.

Sighing, he picked up Pax's small body, turned to Vallaria, and said, "Where will you go from here?"

Although he didn't know where he would end up, he wasn't sure he wanted to be somewhere she wasn't. He wanted to know more about Vallaria, to spend time with her that wasn't fraught with danger and treachery.

"Back to the city of Ravenia to find a way to enter the castle."

Her answer was completely unexpected. He assumed she would journey to the western coast of Exile or back home to the cold lands of Brulle but never to the heart of the dark kingdom.

"Why the city?" he questioned. "After everything that's happened. Why would you want to go back to that dreadful place?"

"I have my reasons."

"Are you planning on stealing the gold you were cheated out of?"

She shook her head. "I have no need for gold."

Zander's forehead wrinkled and his eyes narrowed. "Is it revenge? Do you wish to kill Tagar?"

"Only if he gets in my way."

Her evasive answers told Zander one thing: Vallaria wasn't going to trust him with whatever she had planned. And who could blame her? They met in a tavern when he was quite drunk. He allowed her to goad him into going on this quest even though he knew it was a bad idea. He'd been completely blindsided by his mother's betrayal, and it had almost gotten them all killed. Why would Vallaria want to confide in him?

Don't forget you've been lying to her about who you truly are as well, Your Highness.

Zander's mind whirled with all the issues his being alive could bring.

What about his upcoming marriage to the princess Aerilla? Had his mother, the grieving queen, sorrowfully called it off yet? Would he still have to honor the agreement if the king of Kasmire knew he was alive? His mother had already accepted the dowery. *Which if I died, she'd be able to keep with no repercussions.* Could he tell King Tirus he didn't want to marry his daughter? *Sure, and then the Knights of the Divine Pyre would be after me as well.*

He groaned inwardly and pushed the thoughts out of his mind. *Another day.*

Shifting Pax's lifeless body around in his arms he addressed the women: "We have a long way back, and it will take us twice as long without the horses."

Vallaria nodded.

Before Zander could take a step toward the incline that would lead them from the pit, the altar began to shake. Subtle at first, but within minutes the stone began to crack, and the spire swayed as the ground beneath it shook. Pieces of rock tumbled down in clouds of dust and debris.

Faelin scanned the area. "We need to get out of here. The altar seems to be reacting to the missing dagger *or* the missing guardian."

As soon as the words left her mouth, the altar and spire disappeared into a large chasm that continued to spread outward, devouring everything in its path.

They tried to run, but the earth crumbled beneath their feet as more cracks appeared.

"Give me Pax," Faelin yelled. "I can make the incline quicker than you."

Zander did not argue. In order for all of them to get out alive he would need both his hands free. As soon as he passed the young boy to Faelin, he turned and ran to Vallaria, who was now on the opposite side of a widening crack.

"Jump," he shouted over the rumble of falling earth. "I'll catch you."

Vallaria didn't hesitate, launching herself over the void and into his waiting arms as the crack yawned open. Wincing in pain, he managed to pull her away from the edge, and together, hand in hand, ran toward where Faelin stood with Pax's body.

"Hurry," she yelled as more cracks formed in the ground and chunks of it beneath their feet disappeared into the black void.

In his urgency Zander stumbled and his hand slipped from hers. He tried to regain his footing but soon realized there was nothing beneath his boots but air. He flailed, desperate to regain his balance and a foothold, but it was futile. He began to fall into the chasm beneath him. As he slipped over the edge and into the darkness, he heard Vallaria's voice and then a hand grabbed his wrist.

"Hang on," she screamed over the rumbling as the earth broke into pieces around them.

He stared up at her. Her blazing blue eyes were filled with determination, but he could feel gravity working against them as it pulled his weight away from her. He struggled to find footing on the sides of the chasm, but the edges were slick with water and mud, and he couldn't find a toehold.

He watched in fear as she strained to hold him but instead found herself slipping over the edge with him.

"Let go," he said.

She shook her head furiously in response and set her mouth in a taut line. Her nails dug deeper into his flesh as she pulled with all her strength, refusing to let go.

Another rumble from the earth and the chasm cracked again. Debris and dust filled his mouth and nose as it rained down on him. He coughed and sputtered as he dangled helplessly by her hand.

"Please, Vallaria, let me go or we're both going to die." He looked into her eyes, silently pleading with her to save herself. But she refused to release his wrist, and the last thing he remembered as a falling rock hit him on the head and blackness pulled him into its quiet oblivion was her slipping over the edge toward him.

THE LUMP ON HIS HEAD THROBBED AND HE FELT A WARMTH TRICKLE DOWN his temple.

"Zane." A voice in the distance.

"Are you okay?"

The voice reverberated through his skull, and he winced. *Quiet.*

"Can you open your eyes?"

No! But they fluttered open anyway. Bright light blinded him as the blackness he so badly wanted to remain wrapped in slipped away.

"Zane. Can you hear me?"

He groaned. "Vallaria?" he croaked. His throat was dry and sore.

"Drink this."

Cool water flowed over his lips and he swallowed as much as she would allow.

"Easy," she murmured.

Her long fingers were cool as she brushed back the hair from his forehead.

"What happened?" he asked, his voice barely a whisper. "I saw you fall."

"Shhh. You're safe. We all are."

His eyes adjusted to the light, and he scanned his surroundings. He recognized this place. It was the dell. They were no longer in the Valley of Souls. But how?

Faelin stood behind Vallaria. Her face a mask of calm, which considering everything that happened was a tad unsettling.

"How did we get here?" His memory was cloudy, and he struggled to sit up.

A shadow passed over Vallaria's features, but she quickly replaced it with a smile. "You need to rest."

Zander let her guide his head back down. Exhausted, he closed his eyes.

Vallaria had saved his life. He'd no idea how, but they were all safe, and he was grateful. His mind drifted to the happenings of the last day, the betrayal of Tagar, of his mother. His stomach clenched as much of it replayed behind his closed lids. In that moment he made his decision. He would help Vallaria, no questions asked, even if it meant disclosing to her who he truly was. He would get her into the castle at Ravenia. And he would face his mother. If it ended with his head being severed in the town square, then so be it.

He owed Vallaria his life.

But he owed his mother so much more. He would not let her treachery go unpunished this time.

47
VALLARIA

They laid Pax to rest on a hill in the dell overlooking the river. It was a peaceful place away from the ravages of the world he'd been born into. Vallaria found wildflowers to scatter on his grave, and Faelin spoke an elven blessing for his soul to join the gods the mortals served.

It was all so surreal, the three of them placing the body of a young boy into the earth to rot.

Vallaria inhaled sharply. It was her fault he'd died.

She'd taken him from the kingdom thinking it was the only way to keep him safe and instead she'd gotten him killed. A young boy, trying desperately to survive in a dark world. It wasn't enough to save him from those men in the alley, no, Vallaria had to drag him to a place even worse so she could tell herself she was saving him, when in reality her actions were only furthering her self-interests.

That's the way it's always been. Ever since you were old enough to understand your parents were gone and that the elves took pity on you, you've walked around with a chip on your shoulder. Making decisions and judgments without any forethought to the consequences—many of which were dealt out to those around you.

She'd grown angry and pushed those who truly cared away, instead finding a cruel comfort in sparring with Rian and the others. *And when you went too far, who was there for you? Who took the brunt of the consequences? Faelin.*

She glanced at her friend, and a wave of remorse swept over her. *You were selfish then and you're selfish now. Only this time someone you cared about died.*

Pax had been collateral damage. And she would never forgive herself.

Pulling her shoulders back, she pushed the guilt and grief down, somewhere in the darkest regions of her heart. She'd gotten good at guarding her emotions over the years, but to be a queen she would need to learn to control them.

A wind lifted the tendrils of hair that hung around her face. The air smelt like rain and the gray sky overhead rumbled. It would be a long and arduous walk back to the kingdom in the morning. Tagar and his men had taken all the horses and supplies. It was the three of them, weary and injured, but resilient, nonetheless.

A fire burned in each of their bellies, born of betrayal and revenge. Soon enough the dark queen would find them on her doorstep and the battle for the throne would begin.

Vallaria felt a cold rush of water chill her veins and smiled. A battle she had no intention of losing.

As they walked back to their encampment, she lagged, replaying her earlier conversation with Faelin when the elf had expressed her concerns about Zane.

"I know we've never met but I feel like I know him," she said.

"In what way?"

Faelin had shaken her head. "It's a feeling? Intuition. It's the little things, how he moves and holds his sword; there's a sense of familiarity."

"Could you have come across him in one of your ventures to the Gold Coast?" It only required an elf a brief meeting with someone for that person to be permanently ingrained in their mind.

"He would have been only a boy last I was there."

"Maybe he reminds you of someone else then," Vallaria offered.

"Maybe."

Now, watching her casually talk to Zane, Vallaria knew Faelin would be digging for information. It wasn't like her friend to let such curiosities go.

Vallaria shifted her attention to the problem at hand. The deal struck with Tagar and Queen Cereli had been broken and she would not have access to the castle to claim her gold. Tears pricked her eyes as her fists rolled up into tight balls and her nails dug into the flesh of her palms. She was no further along than when she and Faelin first entered Ravenia, so how then was she to go against someone so powerful and take back her throne?

The tumultuous gray sky turned into a black void as night fell, but thankfully they'd been spared any rain. A heavy exhaustion pulled at her muscles and her mind. Her stomach rumbled with hunger, but she was too tired to care. The fire crackled and sent small sparks floating upward. Small pinpoints of light fracturing the heavy darkness. Zane and Faelin were both asleep, and Vallaria huddled deeper under her cloak, thankful for the soothing warmth cast out by the flames.

While she listened to Zane's even breathing, she thought about that moment in the pit when he'd begged her to let him go. But she couldn't. Even when she felt his arm slipping through her grasp, all she could see were the depths of his dark eyes. She couldn't let him fall, not even if it meant she died too. But what happened next surprised her more than the rush of emotions she'd had for him at that moment.

Thankfully he seemed not to recall the incident. At least not yet.

She lay her head close to his. A good night's sleep, Faelin's healing magic, and a little luck and he would be strong enough to travel in the morning. It might take a few days, but they would make their way back to Ravenia.

Yawning, she closed her eyes, which had grown heavy with sleep.

As she drifted off, an image appeared in her mind. She stood over the corpse of Queen Cereli. Her body, blue from the cold, lay sprawled, broken on the stone floor. Her dead eyes stared unblinking. In her hand she gripped her staff, but the smoke in the glass ball was gone and from her throat a long blade of ice protruded.

FAELIN STOOD OVER HER WHEN VALLARIA WOKE THE NEXT MORNING.

"We need to discuss what happened yesterday," she said.

Wiping the sleep from her eyes, Vallaria nodded. She knew this conversation would happen. The elf would not pretend and let such powerful magic go unnoticed. It was somewhat of a relief because of all the eerie things the magic inside her had done, this was by far the most disturbing.

Zane still slept soundly beside her.

"Let's take a walk," she whispered to Faelin.

They strolled into the grove, far enough out of earshot in case he woke.

"Your powers are growing," Faelin said. "How do you feel?"

Vallaria's brows knitted together. Odd question. How was she supposed to feel? Confused? Terrified? All powerful? "I don't understand what you're asking."

"I mean physically. Do you feel like there are any side effects from the magic?"

The memory of her and Zane falling into the abyss flashed through her mind, and Vallaria shuddered. In the memory she could feel his hand slipping through hers and the pain in her arm as she pulled against his weight with every ounce of her strength. He was so heavy, and her body was being pulled into the abyss. He'd wanted her to let go, but she didn't, couldn't, wouldn't. Instead, she slipped over the edge and together they fell to what should have been certain death.

"Vallaria, you conjured a portal and transported both yourself and Zane out of the Valley of Souls. Portal magic died with the mages. It was a pillar of their powers and why their magic was so valuable to the kings of old. But it also drained any mages who used it."

Shrugging, she frowned at the elf. "I feel nothing other than the headache and nosebleed, which have become commonplace with the mage magic."

Wary of her recall, she thought back to that moment in time. She closed her eyes taking her mind back. Darkness surrounded them as they plunged downward. Her hand clutched Zane's and she could feel the familiar cold rush through her blood. *But then.* Her nose scrunched as she remembered how the cold pushed outside her body as if seeping through her pores. *And the voices.* Yes, the whispers had returned. Voices of the past. *Let go.* They'd wanted her to drop Zane, but she wouldn't. The chorus grew. A fevered pitch of anger. The cold exploded from inside her and suddenly the pitch black broke and a swirling blue circle appeared. They passed through it, and she'd found herself, still clutching an unconscious Zane, at the entrance to the Valley of Souls.

A heavy silence surrounded her. The voices had gone quiet once more.

On impulse Vallaria gazed at her hands, flipping them back and forth as if she expected to find the answers there. Her voice became breathy. "I don't know how it happened and I don't know what it took out of me."

Green eyes narrowed as the elf pondered her friend. "You will let me know if anything changes? If the mage magic starts to affect you in ways we did not anticipate?"

"I'm fine."

"That may be, Vallaria, but your destiny is much more than being a lost princess of Ravenia or a future queen. You are the prothesized last mage. You have the power to change the future and to bring stability to the kingdoms of Exile, but you also have the power to bring darkness and chaos. Your powers are untested and unknown when wielded by a mortal, and as they grow, the magic could become too much. Do you understand?"

Vallaria understood all too well. The power flowing inside her was not to be ignored or taken for granted. But it was there to be used, and Queen Cereli would be the first to feel her frost-covered wrath, for taking the life of her parents, for taking her childhood, for taking her home. And once she'd regained the throne of Ravenia, she would look south to the Gold Coast. They too must pay for the atrocities brought to her kingdom, her people, and her parents.

Cold ignited in her veins and the voices rose in her mind.

Make them pay, they whispered in unison. *Blood, frost, fire, and shadow.*

48
CERELI

Four days had passed since Tagar and the others set off to retrieve the Dagger of Crusade from the Valley of Souls.

"He should be back by now," she said aloud to the empty room.

Cereli had grown anxious since her brother's arrival and the appearance of the ice moon. If her royal guard commander could not find the dagger in the Valley of Souls, she was afraid, one way or another, her fate would be sealed.

Either the ghost princess will come for my crown or Darrius will.

The harbinger had shown herself again last night and the old crone's warning still rang in her ears.

No man nor woman can cheat fate. Once it has been set in motion it will find a way to pass regardless. Your enemy nears. Will your destiny be one of unbridled power or one of death? Only you can determine which path fate will follow. Choose wisely.

She paced in her bedchamber as she mulled over the harbinger's warning. *I can't cheat fate, but I can determine its direction. I can mold destiny in my favor, and possessing the Dagger of Crusade will do that.*

Once she had one of the Myths of Three the others would be easy to detect. And with all three, there would be no one alive or dead who would again threaten her rule. Darrius Mensah would bend a knee at her throne and the ghost princess would forever be trapped in the place that made her.

And what of Princess Serifine Ravenia? You stole her legacy.

In days past Cereli had sent guardsman and members of her army out into the kingdom to look for her. Every village, farmstead, and home were to be searched. The city had guardsman posted on every corner; anyone who didn't belong in the kingdom was suspect.

Your enemy nears.

Tagar must return with that dagger.

A knock on her door reminded her the day was still only half done.

"Enter."

Yelin Barro scurried in, bowing as he entered. "Your Highness, Jerome Mensah is in the throne room."

A knot churned in the pit of her stomach as she felt the rage burrow into her brain. Dark eyes turned toward the little man, and she hissed, "What did you say?"

The tremble in his hands and the way he cowered told her he was as surprised as she at the arrival of such a visitor.

"Your brother is with him."

"OUT," she yelled, the fury of the moment erupting.

Yelin moved as fast as his little gold slippers would let him.

Obviously Dagget Ra has yet to fulfill his contract. Cereli clenched her fist and cursed the leader of Zion. *This is Darrius's doing. Moving the pieces on the board before I've had a chance to assess the game. He's reminding me of my place in the empire, my place in the Gold Coast.*

Cereli had been born into wealth and privilege. The only daughter of House Sand Serpent. With her golden-hued skin, dark almond-shaped eyes, and silky black hair, she was desired by all men. Many tried to possess her, others fell so deeply in love they lost their way, but all had one thing in common: they were easily manipulated. Even Darrius Mensah.

In her early twenties she'd attended a dinner hosted by the emperor for the heads of the seven houses of the Gold Coast Empire and their families. Later that evening she'd caught the young royal gazing at her from across the room. Even then Darrius had a reputation, a reputation his father tried desperately to assuage. Darrius, in his late teens, enjoyed the company of both women and young men. Unfortunately for the emperor, most of the young men worked in the palace, and it cost a lot of gold for their silence.

Yet that night, it was she who caught Darrius's eye.

Smiling coyly, she'd quickly looked away and waited. Cereli had played this game before—the prince would be at her side in moments. He hadn't disappointed, and from that night on, they snuck away often to see one another. One night, after the palace had gone dark, Darrius had snuck out to meet her at the fountain in the courtyard. Mere minutes before he kissed her, the emperor and his guards came out and rushed the prince off. The panic in the emperor's eyes at finding his son with her quickly turned to a confusing sadness when he told her to go home and never return.

Weeks went by without seeing Darrius. Her father had scolded her and told her to stay away from him, but she was young and impulsive, and she wanted what she could no longer have. Soon after she'd been in the market with Moricio, and the prince and his guards walked through. Her heart lurched when she saw him but crumbled just as fast when she met his cold and hateful stare.

"Moricio," he said, nodding at her brother as he passed but ignoring her completely. She'd been crushed and for days had stayed in her room and cried. But it had been a lesson that steered her toward a different path and eventually to the one true love of her life.

Cereli inhaled deeply, clutching at the bodice of her gown.

The ache in her heart was small, but it had carved out a place and buried itself there as a reminder of him, Zander's father, the man who Darrius and Emperor Silvalas had taken from her.

After Darrius she ran wild, bedding merchants and noblemen to obtain silks, jewels, and money, but that all ended when she'd met

Zander's father. He was kind, gentle, a powerful man in his own right but fair and someone who treated her with dignity, unlike the men of the Gold Coast.

His face drifted through her memory and his name formed on her lips, but she shoved both away quickly. She had not spoken his name since his death.

Within a few months she'd discovered she was pregnant with Zander, and to ensure she brought no shame to her father's great house, Moricio had found her a nobleman to marry. And from that moment nothing mattered but getting out from under the patriarchal hold of the Gold Coast. She wanted a chance to be equal in a world dominated by men, and to do that she needed power, real power, not just sexual prowess. She wanted men to fall at her feet because of her status—not because they wished to be in her bed.

That chance finally came years later in the form of King Ryguard of Ravenia. As the eldest daughter of the second most powerful house in the Gold Coast, and a tragic widow, she was promised to him in a bid for peace and prosperity. A joining of two kingdoms through marriage, but like most men, he too had betrayed her, choosing to break the pact and marry Evinna, the elven whore.

Never had Cereli been so humiliated, and in that moment, she'd vowed revenge.

Marrying his brother King Torrsen had been the easy part. Convincing a man who'd never desired the throne to overthrow and murder his brother had taken patience, but in the end, his desire for her had made him weak, and weak men were easy to control. After that, it was a matter of time before the throne, the kingdom, and the power she'd desired were hers.

Cereli gazed at herself in the mirror and brushed down the wrinkles of her silk skirt. She'd chosen the slim gown that showed her curves and her cleavage. The thick black collar around her neck accentuated her collar bone. She'd let down most of her hair, leaving the parts around her face pinned to the top of her head. The black crown finished the look.

Powerful and sexy. Jerome Mensah had no idea what he was getting into.

With a last look at her reflection, she swept from the room and went to meet her honored guest.

The throne room doors opened wide, and she strode in staff in hand. Moricio stood to the side of her throne, speaking in a low voice to a small man who stood on the dais steps. When she entered, they both looked in her direction.

Jerome Mensah looked the exact same as the last time she'd seen him at Torrsen's funeral. He had a baby face of bronzed hairless skin surrounded by long dark hair he pulled back into a perfect braid. He wore travel clothes of pale brown trousers and a brown tunic trimmed in gold. His dark eyes flitted back and forth as she walked toward them, and same as when he was a young boy, the nail of his forefinger picked at an imaginary thread in the seam of his pants.

"Your Highness," she said, bowing slightly as she reached him.

With a shaking hand he reached for hers, kissing the top of it with dry, cracked lips. "It's a pleasure to see you again, Cereli. You look stunning."

She could feel Moricio's disapproving gaze. He knew what she was up to, he'd seen it before. Lure them in with her womanly wiles and then bleed them dry.

"Men are prey," she'd blurted out one night when an angry Moricio returned from having to appease the enraged wife of a local merchant she'd been sleeping with. That outburst had cost her three nights of cleaning the house top to bottom and another week of not being able to leave it.

"Stay away from the married ones, Cereli. Please, for the sake of our good name."

That was all that was important to her father and Moricio. The power that House Sand Serpent carried and the respect the Damask name garnered. A great house where generations of Damask males became military leaders. Proud generals serving in the emperor's vast army.

Prominence. That's all the men in her family cared about, and it angered them at how easily she tarnished the Damask name.

A sly smile curved her lips as Jerome dropped her hand and looked up at her. "Please, tell me what has brought you all the way from the Gold Coast."

He fidgeted a bit more as she walked up the final step and sat on her throne.

Her eyes looked her brother up and down. "I see you changed, Moricio. I had no idea you'd brought your military uniform. I thought you'd come on an unofficial visit to see your beloved sister." Cereli spoke in short stinging words to ensure Moricio understood her displeasure at his deception. It was clear he knew Darrius was sending Jerome, a fact he'd failed to mention as he made himself comfortable in her castle.

He stiffened but didn't respond.

Jerome came and stood in front of her. "Queen Cereli, as you know, my father has passed."

Leaning forward so her cleavage swelled, she said, "It was a great sadness when my brother told me the news. Please accept my deepest sympathies. Your father was a great man."

Watery eyes flitted back and forth, and he brushed his hand across the back of his neck before pulling a small gold box from his tunic pocket.

"I request your hand in marriage," he blurted out, dropping the gold box from his trembling hands. It opened as it hit the steps and a gold ring with a huge diamond rolled out.

From the corner of her eye, she saw Moricio roll his eyes as Jerome squatted to pick up the box and ring.

"I'm sorry, Cereli, please—" he said, holding the ring out toward her as he bent to one knee. "Please, would you do me the honor of becoming my queen?"

A roar ignited in her ears as she looked at the meek man in front of her. *My queen.* The way he said it was meant to ensure she understood her place. Not at his side as an equal but as the woman who stood behind him.

"No." The word came out of her mouth with ease.

"Cereli," her brother said, a subtle warning in his tone.

"No," she repeated, this time with more conviction, the word now sounding clear as it fell from her lips. She stood and grabbed her staff, sweeping down the dais steps and passing the stunned Jerome, who still knelt in front of the throne holding the ring.

"Cereli Damask!" her brother roared.

The blood thundering in her ears reached a fevered pitch, and the dark magic began to rise. The smoke in her staff swirled, and with a renewed conviction, she turned, focusing her dark flashing eyes first on Moricio and then on Jerome.

"It's Cereli Damask *Ravenia*, brother," she hissed. "Both of you can leave my kingdom immediately, and when you arrive back in the Gold Coast, tell Darrius I will not give my kingdom to you or any other man."

What she did was equal to a declaration of war, but the silence following her out of the throne room was so very satisfying.

Hours later, as the castle slept, there was a soft knock on her door. Only one person would dare to disturb her this late at night.

Her heart pounded as she ran to the door, not even stopping to pull on a covering over her night gown. She didn't care. She knew who was on the other side, and he'd seen much more than what one could view through the thin fabric.

"Tagar," she said breathless as she flung open the door.

"The Dagger of Crusade, my love." Tagar's gray eyes shone in the torchlight as he held aloft the sacred dagger of myth. "The power to raise an unbeatable army."

Her hand wrapped around the curved hilt, taking it from him. The black steel dagger was heavy, weighted at one end. The blade was long and thin, its edges lethally sharp. A delicately curved line wound its way along the blade. A detail representing the endless power of the dagger. The overall craftsmanship was breathtaking, but it was the pommel topping the handle which drew her attention.

Her fingers caressed the circular cage. The latticework, designed to look like metal thorns, looked delicate, but like the rest of the dagger its strength was immeasurable. Inside, a small vial containing a deep red liquid glistened.

Whatever could it be?

Squinting, she raised the dagger to her sight line and tipped it slowly. The red liquid moved to the other end, slowly, for its density was thick like honey rather than water.

Interesting.

There was nothing in the legend that spoke of the artistry of the three ancient artifacts or if the mage who designed them did so with any specific purpose. But this dagger was no ordinary dagger, not in its detailing nor in its power.

Quickly, she hurried to the other side of her bedchamber where a fire blazed in the hearth. On a small table sat a black lacquered box. Lifting the lid, she placed the Dagger of Crusade carefully inside and covered it with a deep red piece of silk.

Her dark gaze returned to the royal guard commander, who'd left his position by the door and now stood feet from her.

"And my son?"

"He's been taken care of, Your Majesty."

Her lips twitched and her hand caressed his scarred face. "You've done well."

Lifting herself onto her toes she pressed her lips to his and as his strong arms encircled her waist, she felt the familiar heat rise in her loins.

Like always, he took her with a commanding force, whispering her name as he pleasured her. As a lover, Tagar was attentive, skilled, and unselfish, never thinking of himself until she was completely sated. Even when Torrsen was alive, it was always Tagar who'd given her what she needed. Stolen moments in the maid's quarters or the stables became long leisurely lovemaking in her bedchamber when the king was away on diplomatic missions. At times they'd been stupidly careless and apparently lucky for if her husband had found out, she was sure he would have had them both beheaded in the town square.

Fortunately, he met his untimely death completely unaware of her infidelity with his royal guard commander. And now she was free to bed whomever she pleased, and she did. Tagar had not been her only lover. If she desired a man, she used her exotic beauty and stature, to seduce, manipulate, and conquer.

Her power over men was intoxicating, especially when they bent to her will in other ways. Over the years men had become a means to an end, and although she cared for deeply for some, like Tagar, they were all pawns in her elaborate game.

Hours later they lay in her bed, her head and upper body draped across his torso. She liked the way her dark skin contrasted with his pale flesh. It reminded her of another time, another man. Her heart clenched at his memory, and she quickly moved past it.

"My brother and Jerome Mensah were here."

She held her breath and waited.

It took a moment, but the muscles underneath her tensed. "What did they want?" His voice was husky as he held back his temper.

Like most Tagar thought Jerome a pathetic and useless fool. A plaything for Darrius to wield at a whim. The Gold Coast prince idolized his older brother, even though they were so different, which made it easy for Darrius to control him.

"Moricio came to deliver the news of Emperor Silvalas's passing. Jerome came to marry me, under Darrius's order, of course."

The words hung heavy in the air, and she closed her eyes and waited for Tagar to explode. But he didn't.

"So now Darrius has finally gotten the power he's craved, he's after your throne and wants things back in order—kings rule kingdoms, queens produce more kings."

The words of every emperor who had ever sat in the Gold Coast palace. Even Emperor Silvalas, Jerome and Darrius's father.

Yet he made an exception, for you.

And she never did understand why.

"I assume you said yes." Tagar's gruff voice had a hint of mischief now.

"I did, the wedding will be over my dead body."

Tagar chuckled. "What did you really say?"

"I kicked them both out of the castle and told them to give a message to Darrius for me."

"You threatened the new emperor?"

"Maybe."

He wrapped his strong arms around her shoulders. "He will come for your throne with the most powerful of armies. The Gold Coast and all its allies will rise against you."

"Let them come." He couldn't see the defiance in her eyes, but the royal guard commander was no fool. He and the other men of the Gold Coast had taught her an invaluable lesson—take what you want and show no mercy.

She intended to do both.

49

FAELIN

Within hours of leaving the dell, Faelin felt eyes watching them. Miles passed underfoot without any visual confirmation of their whereabouts, but Faelin sensed their presence hidden somewhere in the shadows of the trees, following, observing.

Like she'd done twice in the past hour, she stopped as her gaze moved from the forest's edge to the dark storm clouds churning overhead. The first days of winter were upon them. The clouds were no longer heavy with rain but laden with the first snowfall of the season. The temperature had dropped considerably since daybreak, an indication snow would soon blanket the lands.

Her eyes drifted back to the forest and another chill crept across the back of her neck.

You're being paranoid, she scolded. But seconds later, a warning sensation tingled across her skin as her shield magic alerted her to danger. Instinctively her gloved hand lifted to the hilt of her sword and her eyes scanned their surroundings. Up ahead the trail ran parallel to the edge of the forest and was flanked on either side by a hill of large boulders. If someone lay in wait, there would be the perfect ambush spot.

Abruptly the wind shifted its direction, and Faelin bristled as a familiar scent reached her nose, but before she could call out a warning to Vallaria and Zane, who were a few hundred paces ahead, Wilders sprang from the trees, lobbing arrows in their direction.

"Take cover," she yelled, knocking an arrow from the sky with her sword.

Ahead of her, Vallaria ducked behind the nearest boulder, dragging Zane to the ground with her.

Faelin dropped to the ground, released her sword, and snatched the crossbow from her back. From the cover of the long grass, she fired. One bolt after another flew with perfect precision, each hitting its mark as the tribe broke cover and emerged from the forest. Behind her, a noise rose in volume, the pounding of feet on dirt and the yelp of a battle cry. Still engaged with the bowmen, she heard the unmistakable ting of steel meeting steel. A quick glance over her shoulder confirmed there were more, as another group of Wilders appeared from a trench on the far side of the trail. Vallaria and Zane fought them, but it was futile as the two of them were severely outnumbered. It took only seconds for the Wilders to surround them, disarm them, and bind both their hands behind their backs.

A yelp came from a young tribesman near the tree line, and the others bellowed in response. Faelin pushed the grass aside and looked in the direction he pointed, watching in disgust as the chief emerged. His dark eyes flashed with determination as he called out to his people. After reloading, she aimed, and fired a bolt directly at him. It flew straight and true toward his head, but at the last minute, another man intercepted it with his body, taking the bolt meant for the chief.

Seconds later, surrounded with spear tips pointed at her throat, Faelin dropped the crossbow and raised her hands. A tribesman pulled her from the ground and bound her wrists behind her. Dragging her to where Vallaria and Zane knelt, he pushed her to the ground next to them.

"What do they want?" whispered Vallaria.

Faelin shook her head as she watched the chief walk slowly to where they knelt. "Wilders are a primitive race. Their customs are unique, and it would be unwise for me to speculate if we were to be a sacrifice to their god or not."

"Human sacrifice?" Vallaria paled and her blue eyes shifted back and forth between Faelin and the tribe.

Her friend's knowledge of Exile's populous was limited since she'd only had her focus on the text and scrolls that pertained to the main kingdoms on the continent. The Wilders were a sect who lived on the fringe, never interacting with the kingdoms or their people. Nomads who preferred to be alone. They moved continuously, never staying in one spot for any extended period, which was why Faelin found it curious they had yet to move south this close to winter.

The chief, his dark eyes circled in black kohl, spoke with one of his tribesmen. His robes were dirty and tattered and he wore a beaded collar around his thick neck. Dangling from it were small white teeth. Human? Faelin couldn't be sure, but it wouldn't surprise her.

Faelin's anger simmered as the chief cast her a long, steady gaze. *Why did my mother want to help these people?*

Some tribe members began to grunt and chant. Others spoke softly in their dialect, casting curious glances at the three of them. A few came close and poked Faelin with dirty fingers but scurried back when their chief snarled. Walking over, their leader grabbed her arm and pulled her roughly to her feet. His dark eyes flashed with anger, and he slapped her with the back of his hand directly across her cheek. Her shield magic surged, but she quickly got control before it could be detected. Since she had no idea what her mother shared with these people about their magic, she would rather feel the pain than have the Wilders suspect she was an elf.

Bright pins of light floated before Faelin's eyes, and she shook her head, hoping they would dissipate. Zane cursed and struggled to get up, but a Wilder kicked him in the stomach.

The acidic flavor of blood filled her mouth and she defiantly spat it on the ground at the chief's bare feet. Her ears rang with the tinny sound of the slap, but she refused to show any weakness, and instead glared at him. Faelin straightened, waiting for another blow, but the chief nodded his head and walked away.

He whispered something to a younger tribesman, then cast Faelin a backward glance.

"What the hell was that?" Vallaria hissed in her ear.

"I don't know. Retribution for trying to put a bolt in his forehead. Is Zane all right?" She wanted to focus on anything other than herself and her unbecoming desire to murder as many of these Wilders as she could.

A week before her mother's departure, Faelin had tried to talk her out of going.

"The Wilders are unpredictable, dangerous."

"They're misunderstood, Faelin. They serve a different god and therefore, have different beliefs."

"Then take an entourage like Father suggested."

"You and your father worry too much. I'm a healer, not a warrior. I am no threat to anyone."

She'd never seen her mother again . . . until they'd carried her body back to Mistenvale and buried her in the sacred tombs. On that day Faelin swore revenge, but her father wouldn't hear of it.

"Let your mother's spirit rest in peace. She would not want blood on your hands in her name."

The chief whistled, bringing Faelin back from the past. Several tribe members rushed over and dragged her and Vallaria to their feet. Zane struggled, but he too was forced into a standing position. They tied long ropes to their bound hands and placed them in a line.

Vallaria leaned toward Faelin and lowered her voice. "Where is my magic when I need it," she complained.

Faelin could sense the mage stone as it lay cold in Vallaria's pocket. Since the onset she'd been trying to figure out how the ancient power manifested. While they waited for the Wilders to lead them somewhere, it finally came to her.

She'd wrongly assumed Vallaria's magic emerged when she was in danger, like when the man from the alley or the serpent dragon attacked her. But Faelin could never equate it with why her magic remained silent when they'd been tied to the posts in the Valley of Souls. Did the act of danger need to be imminent? *No,* because Vallaria was no different than the mages of old, the witches of Brulle, or the sorceresses from the Dark Isles of Atune. They were all conjurers and thus used their hands to wield their power.

Faelin watched as Vallaria tugged on the rope binding her wrists. *Without the use of her hands, her powers were useless.*

But it wasn't enough to bind them. Her hands had been bound when she'd slayed the man from the alley, but they'd been bound in front. Binding them in the back broke the visual and mental connection so the conjurer's magic remained inactive. It was how kings of old punished the mages who served them; severing their hands effectively made them undesirable goods and unable to retaliate with magic.

Now all Faelin needed to figure out was how to get Vallaria's hands untied before they reached their destination.

IT HAD BEEN HOURS SINCE THEIR CAPTURE AND THEY HAD YET TO STOP. THE Wilders moved deftly through the trees, instinctively knowing the easiest path and therefore covering acres of ground quickly and efficiently. Thirst parched her throat, but although Faelin tried to communicate their need for water, the tribe ignored her.

A yank on her rope pulled her sideways and she stumbled.

"That's enough," Zane yelled as Vallaria too was yanked in a different direction and fell to her knees in frustration. For his troubles he received a backhand to the mouth.

The chief stomped back to where she'd fallen and hauled Vallaria back to her feet, and then turned to Faelin. Her green eyes shot daggers as he closed the gap, and she stiffened, ready for another confrontation. But instead, he took the end of the rope from the Wilder who held it and dragged her to the front of the group.

Faelin looked back to see Vallaria kick the Wilder who held her in the shin, only to have a spear tip pressed against her throat. *She will never learn.* Vallaria had spent her entire life provoking the elves, and she now thought it commonplace to lash out. But out here that type of attitude could mean death. *I won't be able to keep her safe long enough to challenge Cereli for the throne if she gets herself killed out of stupidity.*

As she was dragged up front, she caught Zane's eye and gave him a stern look. He nodded as his tongue darted out to lick the blood from his split lip. She hoped he understood that he now needed to ensure Vallaria didn't do anything rash. If that was even possible.

Ever since they left Mistenvale, Vallaria had found trouble, the guards at the farmstead, the man from the alley, Zane. All because she didn't think before she acted.

Zane. He might be the worst trouble of all. Not because he'd led them into a trap. She couldn't fully blame him for Tagar and the queen. He hadn't wanted to bring them in the first place. And he obviously had no idea what the queen's plan truly was. No, it was because of the way he looked at Vallaria and she at him. A chemistry simmered between them, but Vallaria was naïve and inexperienced, and Zane was not. Faelin had seen his type, many times through the decades, the good looks, charm, and ability to say the right thing. But it always ended the same way, with a trail of broken hearts. Vallaria didn't need the distraction nor the pain. If they could find their way out of this ordeal, they needed to part ways with the mercenary before things became even more complicated.

Another hour passed before they finally emerged from the shadowy forest. Two of the Wilders hurried toward some brush to the right of a tall stone and moved it aside to reveal the entrance to a tunnel.

Faelin was pulled into the dark by the chief. Moments later she heard Vallaria call her name. The darkness blinded her, and she stumbled along in the pitch black. A cold born of lightlessness saturated the tunnel, permeating from its stone walls.

She missed her home. The way the sun rose bright in the morning and the warm wind blew in from the sea. How the grass whispered as it swayed in the breeze. The comforting glow of the lantern lights in the eve.

You will see Mistenvale again.

A faint noise up ahead drifted to her ears, and she tilted her head. The tunnel walls were weeping. Faelin could hear the unmistakable sound of running water. There must be cracks in the walls to which rainwater seeped through or there was an underground vein or spring somewhere.

She ran her tongue over her dry lips.

Another yank on the rope spun her sideways. She cursed as the twine dug into her wrists. Why would they attach the lead ropes to their bound hands, especially when they were tied behind their backs? There was no way they could know what Vallaria was or what she could do.

Unless they were watching us in the Valley of Souls.

Before she could ponder more on that thought, a faint light appeared and they exited the tunnel into a large underground cave. Water cascaded down the walls and dripped from huge stalactites hanging from the high ceiling. A large crack at the cave's pinnacle was open to the outside and let in light and air. Faelin looked around as the Wilders spoke to one another.

At the center of the cave was a small pool of clear water. Steam rose from its depths and bubbles broke its otherwise glass-like surface.

It's a hot spring.

One Wilder pushed her to the ground beside Zane and Vallaria and handed her a wooden cup. Walking to a small natural basin near the entrance, he dipped a bowl into the water it contained and came back with the cool liquid for her to drink.

She guzzled it down, and then passed the refilled cup to Zane and Vallaria to drink.

When they'd finished, the Wilder nodded and then followed the others to the hot spring where they stripped and jumped in. The chief was already being bathed by three of the female Wilders. Faelin only counted about half a dozen among the thirty or so males. *And no children.* Was this a scouting party? If so, why was the chief with them? *Or is this all that was left of the once populous nomadic tribe?*

"If we ever get out of this, I hope I never see another Wilder again," Zane said, interrupting her thoughts. His tongue flicked out to slide over the cut on his lip. "Twice was enough."

"Twice?" Faelin said.

"Yes, once on the way to the Valley of Souls and then again on the way out. That place is bad luck." His eyes narrowed and he leaned in closer. "Or you two are."

She stared at him, her eyes full of indignation, and ignored his slight or attempt at humor. Whatever it was. "How have you traveled the entire continent of Exile and never come across an elf *or* a Wilder?" she hissed.

He shrugged. "I stick to the well-traveled roads between kingdoms."

She raised a brow but remained silent. There was still something about the mercenary she didn't trust.

"What do you think they want from us?" he asked.

"I'm not sure, but they want us alive for it."

"That's good right?"

"Not necessarily. If you'd paid more attention to *all* the peoples of Exile you would know the Wilders practice human sacrifice. They believe bathing in the blood of their victims appeases their god."

Before Zane could respond, the Wilder who'd given them water returned and indicated they should get on their feet. He frowned as he looked at Zane. Raising his finger, he rubbed it over the cut on the mercenary's lip and then put it in his mouth and licked off the blood.

Zane recoiled looking as if he was about to faint.

When they left the humid warmth of the underground cave and headed back into another dark, damp tunnel, Faelin's mouth formed into a self-satisfying smile.

The mercenary is not so tough after all.

50

ZANDER

"Salt air," Zander whispered.

"What?" Vallaria's voice floated toward him in the dark.

"I can smell the sea."

They were close. There was no mistaking that smell. He knew it better than any other. The pungent tang. The crisp briny scent that made your nostrils flare and gave you a slight jolt of arousal. Although Zander belonged to a Gold Coast land House, the sea had his heart and soul.

It was home to him.

Many times during his youth he would go out on the fishing boats or travel the near isles with the merchants. Over the past few years his travels had taken him farther, across the Endless Sea, on the merchant ships of House Storm Eel and the gold and gem trader ships of House Dragon Legion. He'd even spent a year patrolling the waters on a military ship commanded by House Sea Scorpion.

Zander understood the sea, its soothing motion, its briny salty tang, the crisp scent as it filled your nostrils. It was in his blood, much more than the hot sands of the great desert stretching across the empire between the Golden City and the kingdoms to the west.

Maybe it was why he never felt at home in the city or why his Uncle Moricio often expressed disappointment every time he boarded a ship. House Sand Serpent was the house of great military leaders. For generations they'd served in the emperor's land army, fighting wars and ensuring the Gold Coast remained a dominant force on the continent of Exile.

His heart sank as he thought of his last conversation with Moricio.

"Once you marry Princess Aerilla, the king of Kasmire will expect you to hold a military rank before you take the throne. You will join the Gold Coast army and give up your wandering ways across the seas. It is time you became a true son of House Sand Serpent, Zander. I expect it."

Against his uncle's wishes, his mother had allowed him freedom to do as he pleased, but even she expected him to adhere to his House's legacy after his union.

If I go back, nothing will change. My mother will either attempt to murder me again or expect me to marry the princess of Kasmire. If I go to the Gold Coast, Uncle Moricio may spare my life, but he will expect the marriage doctrine to be upheld, and for me to give allegiance to the emperor as my house dictates.

"It's good for the House, Zander. And it's good for diplomatic relations," Moricio had said when Zander spoke to him about not wanting to marry the princess. "The Holy City of Kasmire has been a solitary entity for centuries. The fact that the king is even entertaining a union between two kingdoms is a miracle. Your mother has done well."

And now a year had passed, and the spring nuptials were not far off.

"Zane." Vallaria's voice echoed in the dark.

A Wilder grunted and feet scuffled. "Stop pushing," she said.

And then silence again.

Zander's heart clenched. He was a prince promised to another but inexplicably drawn to the feisty, mysterious, and beautiful Vallaria.

A witch from Brulle whose last name he did not even know.

And who doesn't know you are the son of the queen who tried to have her killed.

He sighed and focused his attention back to their current situation.

He'd become disoriented in the dark tunnels. The black void had interfered with his keen sense of direction. So had the exhaustion. His legs burned as he trudged behind the Wilder who held his lead rope. His wrists, raw from the constant friction, throbbed and the damp chill of the tunnels had seeped into every muscle and bone in his body.

He wanted to lay down, to sleep, to go completely numb.

A sharp sting in his shoulder reminded him of the ointment-laden wound under the bandages. Faelin had managed to close the gash on his abdomen and packed his shoulder wound with gill weed to speed up the healing, but both were still raw and tender.

Having his arms bound behind his back did not help either.

Think, Zander. He shook his head trying to rid himself of the heavy fatigue that lingered around his brain. Where on the coast could they be?

Crossing to the northeast shores of Ravenia in less than a day was a remarkable feat. By horse, the trek from where they'd been kidnapped would take at least a half day, and that was if you pushed the animal and the path through the mountains was clear. *These tunnels must go directly under the mountain range. If you didn't need to follow roads and trails—*

The dim light of day appeared farther up the tunnel, and as the group walked toward it, anticipation mingled with his mind-numbing fatigue.

Squinting as he emerged from the inky black of the tunnel, Zander found himself on a bluff overlooking a tumultuous sea. The waves crashed on the jagged, black rocks about thirty feet below. The roaring gales battered his ears as he followed the others along a narrow path on the cliff's edge.

Zander knew precisely where they were. This was the farthest northeast quadrant of the continent bordering Ravenia. Regrettably, they were miles from any village, kingdom, or port. The Kingdom of Zion was to the south through an unused and dangerous mountain pass. But here at the continent's edge, the lands were treacherous, the sea even more so. Cliffs fell straight down into enraged waters, and for miles dangerous reefs lay hidden below the sea's surface, ready to tear unsuspecting ships to pieces.

For sailors, this was no man's land.

Splashes of icy water stung Zander's face as the surf pounded into the bluff with a volatile fury. This was no ordinary sea—this was a winter sea, the most dangerous of all. For two months at the beginning of the season, the sea rolled with massive waves, and tumultuous high tides battered the coastline as she unleashed a fury on any sailor brave enough to face her.

He'd spent enough time on the sea to know the horrors of her wrath.

The path narrowed, and Zander became concerned about the softness of the soil they walked upon. The winter sea had battered this path for days now and the unstable ground was ripe for tragedy.

No sooner had the thought crossed his mind than he saw Vallaria's boot slip toward the edge. Desperate to rebalance she flailed but with her hands bound tightly behind her it was impossible. He watched in terror as the side of the bluff, drenched from the sea's lashings, began to slide away under her feet. Before he could call out a warning the cliff disintegrated, and she disappeared over the edge.

Her shriek carried toward him on the winter wind. An echo of her peril. The others turned and the one holding the rope, realizing what was happening, dug his heels in and braced for the full impact of her weight.

It came seconds later, jerking him forward.

Zander's stomach lurched as bile filled his throat. He struggled against his binds, racing forward in panic. He wasn't sure what he would find when he looked over the edge, but he was sure both Vallaria's arms would be broken from the impact or at the very least dislocated from her shoulders.

The Wilder holding her struggled to stay upright on the collapsing ridge. He gritted his teeth as he grappled to hold Vallaria's weight. He was young and strong, but gravity and nature worked against him.

Zander had come to the end of his rope and now stood in front of the Wilder who led him through the dark tunnels. From here he could see her twirling below like a rag doll. The red wool shawl around her shoulders flapped in the wind and her frightened pale face a stark contrast against the glistening jagged black rocks below.

For a moment a sense of relief saturated his insides. The rope was looped around her waist, not attached to her bound hands anymore. The Wilder must have made the adjustment at some time after they left the hot spring.

But his relief was short lived as the grunting man began to slide toward the edge.

"Cut me loose," he screamed at the Wilder who held his rope. "I need to help him, or he'll go over the edge too."

The man stared at him wide-eyed.

Frustrated, he turned and searched out Faelin, who was yelling at the chief. Although animated, he couldn't hear what she was saying over the bitter howl of the wind.

"Hold on," he yelled, hoping Vallaria could hear him. She swayed back and forth like a pendulum, her head coming precariously close to the cliff side.

With determination and sheer blind panic, Zander twisted in a circle so the rope tied to his hand was now wrapped one turn around his waist. Facing the Wilder who held him, with muscles tight from the bitter cold and feet numb from his wet leather boots, he stepped backward, one foot at a time, pulling the man with him. His boot heels dug into the wet mud, and he continued to strain against the weight until he finally stood beside the Wilder who held Vallaria's life in his bare hands.

One more step, Zander.

With a strength he didn't know his weary body possessed, he pulled against the tribesman one last time. He took another step back and placed himself between the other Wilder and the edge of the bluff. He leaned back into the young man, pushing as hard as he could.

He felt his rope go slack, and he glanced over. The man had let go, finally understanding what Zander was trying to do.

"PULL!" he shouted, using his weight to anchor the man.

Through his wet shirt he could feel the Wilder's heart pounding, the rhythm getting quicker as he began to panic.

If he lets go of the rope—

Zander's mind whirled. Vallaria would fall to her death, broken by the rocks below.

Somewhere to his right, he heard Faelin screaming, her voice getting louder. No, not louder, she was getting closer.

He glanced sideways.

The chief approached, followed by another Wilder with Faelin in tow at the end of her lead rope. She stumbled on the slick ledge and cursed the chief.

As they neared, Zander could hear what she shouted.

"You can't! You must help her. Just lift her up. Please don't do this!"

For the first time since meeting Faelin, he heard an unfamiliar panic in her voice.

That's when Zander saw it—the huge hunting knife in the chief's hand.

He's going to cut the rope!

Why were the others not helping?

The chief was getting closer. The blade of his knife glinted.

"Pull her up!" he yelled over his shoulder, not knowing if the young Wilder behind him understood what he was saying.

Zander's heart pounded and his legs cramped from the exertion, but he felt the rope move, sliding past his thigh as the man reeled Vallaria in.

From the corner of his eye, he saw the chief come toward him, knife raised.

"NO!" he screamed.

Almost simultaneously he heard Faelin yell, "NO, she's a witch of Brulle."

The chief hesitated and cast a confused look at the Wilder who'd come with him. The man whispered in his ear and the chief nodded.

To Zander's relief he sheathed the knife and took a step forward.

His dark eyes studied Zander, then without a word he grabbed the rope and helped pull Vallaria to safety.

Relief washed over Zander as Vallaria lay panting on the ground. The chief grunted and pointed at the group of Wilder's who'd gathered around. They all scurried away. He then grabbed Faelin by the arm and pushed her back to the front of the line.

With Vallaria no longer in peril, and the Wilders seemingly in no hurry to get them moving, Zander collapsed onto the muddy path beside her. Trying to slow his thumping heart he gulped in the cold wintery air. Wet icy water splashed on him from the powerful surf, and he closed his eyes. His strength was sapped, and his muscles burned as if a molten fire ran through them, but he didn't care, because Vallaria was alive.

Wet and shivering, she lay in the mud beside him. He moved closer so his head was next to hers. He so badly wanted to take her in his arms and hold her, but he couldn't, so he lay beside her and remained silent.

A few moments later, a Wilder kicked Zander gently and pointed toward the others. They were leaving and he was happy to go with them. Whatever fate they walked toward, he would deal with when the time came. Right now, he wanted to get Vallaria off this treacherous bluff alive.

51
VALLARIA

Cold wracked her body and she shivered uncontrollably as they walked away from the bluff. Vallaria's mind still couldn't comprehend all that had happened, so instead she decided to thank the gods she was still alive.

The mage crystal had lay dormant during her ordeal, but her father's prayer beads had been a comforting presence in her trousers pocket as she hung helpless above certain death.

Maybe her gods hadn't abandoned her.

Or maybe the only thing keeping them alive is your misguided faith.

Vallaria shook away her doubts.

She was alive.

Thanks to Zane.

Another step; another spasm wracked her body. While she'd anticipated the end of her fall and tried to minimize its impact, her back had been badly bruised by the rope and her muscles strained to their breaking point as she fought the violent wind and the awkward position.

At least she was no longer being led around on a rope like a dog.

After their ordeal the Wilder's had decided not to tether them, instead allowing them to walk on their own and at their own pace.

Zane walked beside her and occasionally his shoulder brushed hers. It was comforting. She wasn't exactly sure what happened before the chief and the other Wilder pulled her up, but she assumed Zane was involved. And she was thankful.

The group seemed in less of a hurry now, and Vallaria wondered if it was the accident or if many were as bone weary as she. Her eyes felt heavy as she slogged down the path from the bluff, weaving in and around rain-slicked boulders.

A light drizzle had begun, and as it hit her cheeks, she felt the sharp sting of ice. She'd begun to welcome the cold, which accompanied her powers, but right now all she wanted was a warm bath and a hot cup of cider.

Vallaria's tired mind drifted to Kelena's kitchen. The blazing fire in the hearth, the steaming bowl of stew, the bread fresh from the oven.

Her stomach growled. How long since they'd eaten?

She'd lost track. She'd lost track of a lot of things, the number of days since they'd entered Ravenia, the time of day, why she ever wanted to leave the comforts and security of Mistenvale and her tree.

Vallaria had sat in that ashen tree dreaming about what lay over the horizon and thinking it had to be better than where she was. How wrong she'd been. The images she'd created in her mind of glittering kingdoms, lively city markets, and rolling pastures were fantasy. The real world was dark, angry, and unforgiving.

Her destiny, her legacy, her throne had given her nothing but grief from the moment it was revealed. Every step forward resulted in three back. How could she ever hope to dethrone Queen Cereli when she couldn't even control her own destiny? Her powers were sporadic, her luck atrocious, and she had absolutely no idea what she was doing.

Was she ready to be a queen?

Another step; another blistering pain shot through her hip and back.

How she longed to be back in that tree, warm, safe, and nobody special.

Finally, the path from the bluff evened out and she found herself at the mouth of a cave. The side facing the sea had an opening carved by years of exposure and pounding surf. When the angry waves crashed against it a gushing spray entered the cave.

The chief nudged Faelin and pointed to a small ledge leading into the cave's interior just above the waterline. Handholds were anchored into the rock above. He pulled his knife from his waistband and cut her binds, freeing her hands, then turned and cut Vallaria's and Zane's.

Vallaria thought she saw Faelin nod as if trying to indicate something to her, but she was too overcome with pain and weariness to care.

A dozen or so of the tribe had already shimmied across and were waiting on a ledge at the other side.

The chief grunted, pointing again at the ledge.

"You go next, Vallaria," Faelin said. "I'll be right behind you."

She shuffled to the opening and reached up to the first handhold. A twinge of pain ignited in her ribs and she sucked in her breath.

You can do this.

Grasping the handhold, she stepped out onto the ledge. After a few feet, Faelin moved in beside her.

"You are a conjuror," the elf whispered. "Your hands are the conduit for the ancient magic. If they are bound behind you, it breaks the connection and renders you powerless."

Vallaria's head pounded as the surf crashed in behind her. She could only make out a few words of what Faelin was saying and strung together it made no sense. Conduit, bound behind, the connection.

Her mind swam as her numb fingers grabbed for the final handhold, but it was slick with sea water, and she had no strength left.

Just as she felt her fingertips slip, a hand grasped her arm and pulled her to the other side. A young Wilder, no more than a teenager, his eyes full of wonder, helped her across and then to a rock as she tried unsuccessfully to stand on shaking legs.

So tired, she thought, as the young Wilder retied her hands behind her back.

Faelin looked dejected as she stared at Vallaria before a tribesman led her away.

Closing her eyes, Vallaria listened to the pounding surf and waited for Zane and the others to finish crossing.

Her head lolled.

"Vallaria."

That voice. She recognized it. It had a slight accent and was husky and musical all at the same time. *Zane.* She opened her eyes and found herself staring into two pools of molasses-colored irises.

"There she is," he said. "Come, we have to go."

The chief had already disappeared, Faelin was nowhere in sight, and only a few Wilders were left waiting for them.

I must have dozed off.

"I think we're almost there."

"Where?"

Zane shrugged. "Wherever they're taking us."

Vallaria honestly didn't care at this point. She was exhausted, the flesh on her wrists were raw, her boots soaked through, as were her clothes, and she felt physically ill from hunger.

"Hopefully they will kill us quickly."

The mercenary pulled her to her feet. "Don't talk like that. We are getting out of here. We are making it back to Ravenia, and we are getting the gold you are owed so you can continue your travels in search of your people."

My people, she thought, as she allowed the young Wilder to lead her from the cave. If he only knew who "her people" actually were.

Zane had been right. It didn't take long for them to reach their destination.

A short walk through a maze of sea tunnels, where the wind passed by like a ghostly bard howling the praises of the sea, and they emerged onto a precipice.

Vallaria gasped as she looked over the edge.

A hundred feet below a landscape of ecru sand, its grains glistening, covered the floor of a narrow gorge. Sheer rock walls rose skyward. The stone, a kaleidoscope of ochers and chiseled by time and the elements, had natural grooves worn into its surface. Ivy and moss, oddly lush and green for this late in the season, crawled up the walls as if reaching for the boisterous gray clouds churning overhead.

Her eyes scanned the sand where the other Wilders were already busy preparing camp.

Palm trees swayed in the breeze that blew in from a grotto at the far end. Like the sea herself, the waters of the grotto surged frothing into a salty pool as it washed up onto the sand. Fiery red bushes peppered with large sea green flowers added a splash of color to the serene terrain.

Astonished by the beauty and magnitude of this place, Vallaria almost failed to notice the primitive structures scattered around the gorge floor. Hastily constructed wood dwellings were tucked back in the shadows of the rock walls.

The Wilder behind her poked a stick into her ribs, indicating his desire for her to move down the rock steps to her left.

She winced. "Okay."

It was another precarious trek, but thankfully, she and Zane made it to the bottom without incident. As she stood on the sand, her gaze drifted to the top, and the narrow staircase she'd descended.

She inhaled sharply.

With no guardrail, one wrong step would've meant another long fall to certain death.

This had been a really bad day.

The Wilders accompanying her and Zane pushed them forward in the direction of a large wooden pen built at the side of the gorge. Inside was Faelin.

They turned them around and went through their pockets. The young tribesman who'd led Vallaria pulled out her father's prayer beads and held them up, tilting his head to one side as he studied them.

"Give those back," Vallaria snapped as he put them into a pouch slung on his hip. Snorting, he opened her tunic and found the inside pocket.

No, not the ice crystal!

She willed the cold magic to come forward, but the crystal lay dormant. Her blood didn't run cold with the frosty touch of the mages of old, nor did she hear the whispering voices. Just silence.

A dirty hand reached in and removed the crystal.

"Ooooh," said the other who had taken Zane's pocketknife.

The Wilder flipped the crystal back and forth before putting it in his mouth and biting it. Nodding and grinning, he put that in his satchel as well.

Vallaria grunted as they pushed her face first into the poles of the wooden pen. A knife blade slipped through the binds around her wrists and cut the restraints. Seconds later they freed Zane and left.

After the Wilders locked the pen, Vallaria collapsed in the corner, pulling her knees to her chest and rested her head on them. Her entire body ached with exhaustion; every muscle burned in protest. And her wrists were raw and bloody, much like her pride.

This was not how it was supposed to be.

She was the rightful heir to a powerful kingdom, prophesied last mage, and savior of mankind, and here she sat locked in a cage, with no powers, and no plan.

A failure.

She felt a familiar hand on her arm, and she looked up.

"There is only so much I can do. They took my ointments and gill weed, and I don't want to draw too much attention using my powers." Faelin's head jerked to the left, indicating Zane, who was busy limping around the pen rattling the poles looking for any weak spots. "But I can give you a little relief."

Vallaria nodded, thankful for whatever Faelin could do.

The elf took off her gloves and laid her bare hand on Vallaria's arm. Closing her eyes, she began to recite an elven torv or healing spell.

Vallaria had never quite understood Faelin's gifts of healing—she'd never really understood the powers of the elves in general. Well, not the true breadth of them anyway. After the incident on the cliff, when Faelin had saved her with her shield magic, King Elvander had sat her down and told her of their race's gifts, of which there were many: mystics, shields, nurturers, healers, sentients, lightwielders, and elementals. And of course, the elder sect of enchantment elves. Although the idea of magic had piqued her interest, it remained intimidating to someone who possessed none.

But now I do.

"How does it work?" Vallaria asked.

"What?" Faelin said.

"Magic in the world."

The elf raised a brow. "That is a very broad question."

"I mean how can someone like me be more powerful than someone like you?"

Faelin tilted her head and smiled. "I suppose it depends on what one deems power with respect to magic."

Vallaria frowned.

"While my powers may be limited in scope compared to yours, they are not restricted by outside interference. As a conjurer and a mortal, you require the use of your hands and the ice crystal to channel the ancient magic, otherwise you are a mere mortal touched by the magic of the mages with no way to use it."

"But you use your hands?" Vallaria looked down at the elf's fingers, which remained on her arm.

"Only to feel the person I am healing or, in rare cases, shielding, but I can do both without touching if necessary. My magic is a part of me; all I need is my mind and the natural world."

"You didn't shield me when I fell off the bluff."

"No," Faelin said, removing her hand and standing up. "You should feel a little better in an hour or so."

"Why?"

The elf turned, green eyes glittering in the firelight of the torches that had been lit after dusk. "I didn't see you fall until it was too late."

Vallaria saw a brief shadow of anguish darken Faelin's features. She knew the elf was pained by Vallaria's near-death experience and the fact she couldn't do anything to change what had happened. They'd been lucky, this time.

"The chief was going to cut the rope, wasn't he?" Vallaria asked.

Her friend inhaled deeply. "He was."

"What did you say to stop him?"

"The truth, or a version of it."

"Which is?"

"She told him you were a witch of Brulle."

Vallaria had not seen Zane come up behind Faelin, but the lack of reaction from the elf indicated she was aware of his presence.

"Why would that matter?" Vallaria asked, looking back to Faelin.

The elf shifted. "The Wilders are a people deeply rooted in the land and nature. Their god, the great mother of life, or earth mother is a sacred being, and any who possess the ways of the earth are therefore her children. Elves, Wilders, witches, any who draw their powers or beliefs from the natural elements are, therefore, sacred."

Her eyes darkened momentarily before she continued, "They would never harm a child of the mother of life."

Vallaria could feel the pain and anger her friend tried to suppress. Many years ago, Faelin had confided in her the story of her mother's death. It was these people who killed her, so Vallaria understood how much the elf despised them and how difficult it must be to not want to exact revenge.

"So what do we do now?" Zane asked rattling the pen's poles again.

"We wait," Faelin answered. "There is a reason they are still up north this late into the season. And that something must have to do with us."

"Why would you say that?" he asked.

"Because a nomadic tribe tends not to interact with people unless they have to. They certainly don't make a habit of kidnapping them. They want something."

"To bathe in our blood?" Zane said.

Faelin's eyes narrowed, and her lips quirked. "I may have told an untruth."

The mercenary rubbed the back of his neck. "So, pulling my leg, then?"

"Maybe a little."

"No human sacrifices or cannibalism either?"

"While they have been known to perform rituals using human sacrifice, its rare. But they definitely do not eat human flesh."

"Well, that's comforting," he said, casting a sidelong glance at the tribesmen. "You know a lot about the Wilders."

"You're not the only one who's traveled the world, mercenary. The only difference is I actually look at it."

"Touché," he said.

"What are they building?" Vallaria asked, rising and hobbling over to the door of the pen.

Faelin followed. "It seems as if they are preparing for something."

"That rare human sacrifice you mentioned?" Zane asked, watching as they constructed what looked like a tall tower in the water off the beaches edge.

The elf shook her head, acknowledging his jest. "No. And it's not the harvest season so it would be odd for them to complete a ritual that wouldn't be rewarded.

"Harvest season?" Vallaria asked.

"Their aforementioned god, the mother of life, is the giver of life and *death*. The Wilders revere her and the power she has over the land and all its creatures. They believe she can enrich the soil and provide a healthy bounty or inject it with poison and cause a famine, which could kill thousands. Harvest season takes place right before they migrate south. Without a plentiful bounty, many would starve on the long trek."

"Then what are they doing?"

"I'm not sure. The Wilders have never been a people who are easily understood. And, therefore, should never be trusted."

There was an acidic edge to Faelin's tone as she said the last words.

Vallaria's mind drifted to Queen Cereli.

To be so close to the one who killed your loved ones must be torture. If they ever got out of here and back to Ravenia, she supposed she would find out how unbearable that must be.

52

FAELIN

After the fires died down and most of the Wilders retreated to the huts for the night, two came to the pen.

Their unexpected presence roused Vallaria from an uneasy sleep. "What's going on?" she mumbled.

"Nothing," Faelin said walking to the open door. "Go back to sleep."

"Where are you taking her?" Vallaria said as the men grabbed Faelin's arm, pulling her from the enclosure and locking the door. Vallaria jumped up, shook the pen and called out, "Faelin."

"I'll be fine," the elf said, looking over her shoulder and seeing both Vallaria and Zane staring through the bars, their faces shadowed in worry. Although as the words left her mouth, Faelin wasn't sure that sentiment would be true.

The men pushed her along the sand to a corner near the grotto where the largest of the huts stood. There the chief sat in a tall-backed wood chair. A young woman knelt, washing his feet, and the same man who'd been at his side all day stood to his left.

Grim-faced, she stared at the chief, waiting.

The man stepped forward and shooed away the woman, then glanced at the chief, who nodded.

Turning back to Faelin, he said, *"Fer ley ah bre-siha mel."*

Faelin was taken aback by the young man's words. "You speak elvish?"

"I speak many languages. I am not Wilder born, but I've lived among the tribe for many years."

Enraged by this sudden revelation, Faelin clenched her fists and spat. "What do you want?"

Speaking in his native tongue, the chief babbled to the man who nodded, held up a hand, and returned his gaze to Faelin.

"The chief knows who you are."

"And I him," Faelin said, her eyes hardening as she glanced at the Wilder leader.

"He says you can help his tribe."

Faelin scoffed bitterly. "I will not help any who murder in cold blood."

The young man turned to the chief and spoke in the Wilder tongue for a moment before addressing her again.

"He's not asking."

"Is that why you kidnapped us? Treated us like the enemy and were willing to kill my friend? You expect me to help you after all that?" Faelin's normally stoic demeanor began to crack. A sheen of sweat covered her upper lip and a flush brightened her cheeks.

"You are elf kind. You showed yourself when we first encountered you at the edge of the forest—"

"You mean when you attacked us."

"Defending—the queen's men have assailed us before. The royal guard commander is not a good man."

Faelin scoffed. At least they agreed on something. But she didn't want to hear their excuses; she wanted to know the chief's motives."

"Yes, I'm elf kind. Why does that matter?"

"There was another. Here. Before you."

"My mother." Faelin's green gaze looked to the chief, and for a moment his face softened as if he understood her words.

The younger wilder gaped and quickly turned to the chief and whispered in his ear.

The chief stiffened and in a deep voice said, *"Gro' da mul ta,"*

Faelin shook her head, not understanding the chief's words.

"The chief apologizes for the way you have been treated, but the news is one that is hopeful to his ears. Your mother was a wonderful healer and was helping to stop a disease that taints the blood of these people.

A rush of blood exploded in Faelin's ears. "Then why did you kill her?"

"We did not. But we suspected your people thought as much. There is something you must see."

The chief reached under his chair and pulled out a box. Lifting the lid, he pulled out a silver amulet and handed it to Faelin.

The metal was iron, and it was hammered in a rough and unappealing way. Nothing like the craftsmanship of her people.

Turning it over, she gasped.

Carved crudely into the center was the insignia of the Kingdom of Zion. The mark of Dagget Ra.

"Why are you showing me this? This is a death amulet." Her tone was forceful as she shook the piece at the chief. "What does this have to do with the murder of my mother?"

"You recognize it, then, and know who it belongs too?"

Faelin's eyes blazed as she challenged the young man. "Of course I do. It's Dagget Ra's."

He nodded and turned to the chief, speaking once again in the Wilder tongue. After a lengthy back and forth, he turned to Faelin and spoke. "Your mother had almost found the cure for the ailment that is killing these people. She only needed one more ingredient to finish the elixir. But to get that ingredient, she required a rare plant that grows only at the sea's edge. When five moons had passed, and she had yet to return, the chief sent out a search party." The Wilder hesitated and pointed to the amulet in her grasp. "We found your mother's body with this left on her."

"Are you saying my mother was killed by Dagget Ra? For what purpose?" Faelin was stunned by the admission but still suspicious of the tale. It didn't make any sense.

"Your mother was a kind woman who cared very deeply about all the people in these lands. But she also cared about peace among the kingdoms, which is not the desire of all. We believe your mother's death was an attempt to start a war. A way to pull the elves from their self-imposed exile."

"My people have not interfered in the interests of man for many years. Why would anyone want to provoke us to do so?"

"Someone who is determined to rule all the kingdoms. If the elves attacked a nomadic people unprovoked, it would be much easier to turn allies against the race. The last race of magic."

Do not tarnish your mother's memory by seeking revenge, Faelin. Her father had repeated this over and over in the first year of her death. She'd been angry, resentful. "And who would that be?"

The chief grunted and pointed to the amulet. The young man nodded.

"Dagget Ra does not kill senselessly. Only for money. Someone hired him to kill your mother and we believe that person is Darrius Mensah."

There it was. *Like father like son.* "But Darrius was not emperor when my mother died."

"No, but his father was ailing so it was only a matter of time. Darrius has been preparing for his ascension for years. We have been watching from afar. The kingdoms of Exile scheme and plot against one another. Exile is nothing more than a large board where the pieces are moved continuously so one kingdom or another gains an advantage."

Faelin suspected what the young Wilder said was true. Peace had been nothing more than a facade for decades. Even though no wars had been fought since Ravenia had been sacked, it didn't mean peace had come to these lands; it only meant the kingdoms of man had used tactics that were less overt.

She turned the amulet over in her hand and then looked at the chief. "Why should I believe you? My mother had been with your tribe for months and then she ended up dead. You could have found this amulet anywhere in your travels. If you didn't kill her, then why not return her to us so we could bury her properly?"

The young Wilder spoke softly to the chief and then said, "His people are a simple tribe; they live off the land and give back to the great mother of life who bore us all. They believe death is not the end but the beginning of another journey in the beyond. Where a life ends is where another begins. Moving your mother's body would have separated her cha or spirit from the physical vessel, and therefore, it would not have been able to traverse to the great realm beyond. Upon finding the body the scouts took the amulet and covered her with the death blanket of our people."

He paused composing himself. When he looked back at Faelin his dark eyes shimmered with tears. "Your mother was kind to us, and we would never treat her with anything but respect, even in death."

Faelin's heart clenched. Through her anger and grief, she recognized the young man spoke the truth. For all these years she'd let a lie eat away at her heart. Hated the people her mother had tried to save. She, her father, the entire elven kingdom had been deceived by the Gold Coast Empire.

Again.

Baladril's face floated through her mind. A diplomatic mission, an indication of peace, so they could publicly kill an elf and show the rest of Exile they were not afraid of any race who existed in these lands.

Emperor Silvalas, Darrius Mensah, Queen Cereli, and Dagget Ra, they were all the same, ruthless and cut from the same undesirable cloth. She flipped the death amulet over in her fingers and her mind churned. They want the Elven race back on the game board then they would get their wish, but this time it would be in allegiance with the rightful queen of Ravenia. Once Vallaria took back her stolen throne, the Gold Coast would have their war.

Green eyes flashed and Faelin looked from the chief to the young man. "Tell me about my mother's work and the final ingredient needed."

53
VALLARIA

Anger bore a hole inside her gut after the Wilders took Faelin away.

The last mage, Vallaria scoffed. What good was a destiny for the ages and unbridled power if you couldn't wield it in your time of despair? Or if wasn't born of you but channeled through you?

You're just a mortal, touched by the magic of old, nothing more.

She thought about the shield that burst from her hands when the ice dragon was about to kill her. And the cold energy rifling through her veins, down her sword, and into the wraith. What of those powers? Where had they gone?

With the ice crystal.

She pressed her head into the bars of the pen and closed her eyes. How could her gods be so cruel? To give her a powerful destiny, yet limit it to possessing an ancient stone. How could she hope to overthrow Cereli with magic so unworthy?

Opening her eyes, she shivered. The night was cold and the sound of the angry sea crashing against the rocks echoed through the grotto.

Faelin had been gone for hours.

Most of the Wilders had retreated into huts long ago and only the blaze of a small torch wandering around the encampment signified any were still awake.

Yawning, she cast a sidelong glance at Zane, who lay asleep in the corner. He looked so at peace. Vallaria wished she could feel that way. Her dreams, like her waking hours, had been haunted of late. The dream of her reflection and the raven were never far from her subconscious, but as the days wore on and the ancient magic flowed through her blood, the dream had shifted. It was the same but different; something lurked around the edges, something out of sight, out of reach. Every time she woke, she felt trepidation as if at any moment whatever was there in her dream would reveal itself, but it would be too late.

Stretching, she realized that her muscles were less sore, her back no longer flaring with sharp pains. Faelin's healing magic had indeed helped.

Vallaria yawned again and then curled up next to Zane. She would do no one any good if exhausted to the point of collapse.

Casting another glance at the lone torch in the distance, her heart clenched.

Faelin would come back—she had to.

———

HOURS LATER, VALLARIA WAS ROUSED BY ZANE.

"Faelin's back," he whispered.

Her gut twisted as she searched the gloom for her whereabouts. Relief flooded through her as her eyes made contact and she saw for herself her friend was unharmed.

Vallaria ran to the gate as the Wilder who'd escorted Faelin opened it. She threw her arms around the elf and hugged her. "I was so worried."

"I'm fine, Vallaria. Truly."

"Where did they take you?"

"The chief requested my company."

"Why?

"Well, that is a very long and interesting story."

A shuffling outside the pen drew Vallaria's attention. Two female Wilder and one young male stood outside. Each had their arms full.

"The chief sends his apologies. There are no more huts, but these provisions should make our stay more comfortable."

Zane moved closer as the gate opened again and the three Wilder entered. "Our stay?"

"That is part of the very long and interesting story, but first—" She pointed at the trays of dried meats and fresh fruit and the bundle of animal skins the young man laid out for their beds.

"I don't understand," Vallaria said as she accepted the jug of water handed to her.

"Thank you," Faelin said as the Wilders left and locked the gate behind them.

Zane shook the pen. "So we are still their prisoners, just well-fed ones?"

"Eat and I will explain."

Wrapping themselves in the warm furs, they sat around the trays of food. For the first few minutes no one said anything. Vallaria couldn't remember the last time she'd eaten, and she devoured everything without pause. Even the small crispy burnt bits, which she feared may be bugs.

Between mouthfuls she inquired as to what had conspired between the chief and Faelin.

"He needs our help."

Zane swore. "Why should we help them?"

"Because otherwise they will die out. There is a disease that's infected their blood and is killing them off by making their women infertile. It is the reason there's no children. It's been years since any Wilder has given birth."

"How can we help?" asked Vallaria, wondering if this had anything to do with Faelin's mother.

"Many years ago, an elf healer from Mistenvale came here to help the tribe. For months she took samples, made elixirs, and after much trial and error found a cure."

It did have something to do with Faelin's mother, Vallaria thought as she caught the elf's eye.

"Figures an elf would be involved with this lot," Zane said disdain dripping from his words.

Faelin cast him a look but ignored the slight.

Playing along, Vallaria asked, "What happened? Did the cure not work?'

Shifting uncomfortably and taking a long swig of water before she spoke, Faelin looked at Vallaria, her eyes tinged with tears. "The elf was murdered before she could harvest the final ingredient. The elixir was never completed, and the Wilders numbers have been depleting ever since.

"And why does the chief assume we can do anything to help? They obviously need an elf healer," Zane asked.

Vallaria glanced at Faelin, her mouth a tight line.

"What are you not telling me?" he asked, acknowledging the strange look that passed between them.

"I am a healer. I can finish the potion well enough," Faelin said.

"But don't you need elven powers or their incantations or something?"

Clearly Zane understood more about the race of elves than he liked to admit, Vallaria thought, as she waited for Faelin to respond.

"There are many ways to heal that don't require magic." The elf's voice had a slight edge as she gazed at Zane. "From what I understand, the elixir is a simple concoction, but it's the ingredients that makes it unique. Well, one in particular," Faelin said.

"Which is?" he asked.

The mercenary had grown impatient. Vallaria could feel the

tension swirling around him. "Zane," she said, touching his shoulder. "Let Faelin explain."

He shrugged off her hand and said, "I don't understand why we need to help these people. They took us forcefully, treated us like combatants, and were going to let you drop to your death from the cliff."

Throwing off his pelt, he stood and stomped to the cage door, yanking on it with all his might. "You want our help? Let us out of here!" he yelled to the dark encampment.

Nothing answered except the hollow sound of the wind as it wound its way through the cavern and the thundering crash of the sea as it pummeled the rocks.

Faelin stood and walked to where he stood fuming. "This was on the elf's body when they found her."

He took the amulet and flipped it back and forth between his fingers. "Dagget Ra."

She nodded. "The Wilders believe he killed the elf healer on the order of Darrius Mensah, who hoped the setup would lure the elves into a revenge war."

"Why would the elves retaliate against the kingdoms of man for one elf?"

Faelin leaned against the bars. "You don't know who the elf healer was, do you?'"

He shook his head. "I was a boy when the elves retreated into Mistenvale and turned their backs on the kingdoms of men. While I have traveled across this continent and the next, I have never encountered one, so I know nothing about the healer who died with this tribe."

"Yet, you have such malice for them."

"I've heard the stories."

"The stories?"

"How the great elven king looked down on the other kings. How he sent out his finest warriors to pillage the lands for treasure and the cities for their gold. He ended trade with the Gold Coast on a whim and punished King Torrsen for his brother going mad and killing his wife and the princess."

"Is that what you think?" Faelin hissed. "That King Ryguard went mad and killed Queen Evinna and Serifine?"

Vallaria rose as the tension spiked between them.

"It's what happened."

"If you were a mere boy at the time, how would you know what the truth is?"

Vallaria stepped in between them and raised her palms in both their directions. "Fighting amongst ourselves is not helping our current situation."

Zane took a step back. "It seems your friend has an affinity for the elven race."

"There is more to this world than the Gold Coast Empire, mercenary," Faelin shot back.

"Stop it!" Vallaria spat. "I for one would like to help the Wilders if possible so we can get the hell out of here. Like it or not, the three of us have the same enemies, and it now seems the Wilders may not be one of them. We must put our differences aside and make the most of a bad situation to further our own end."

She glanced at Zane, his handsome face sullen. "Do you not wish revenge on Tagar and the queen?"

Zane nodded and handed the amulet back to Faelin. "Who was she?"

The elf tilted her head. "Who?"

"The healer who Ra killed."

Inhaling deeply, Faelin pocketed the amulet. "Her name was Gisele, from the Loriad royal bloodline. She was the wife of King Elvander, and queen of Mistenvale."

Raising a brow, he let out a low whistle. "And the king did not exact revenge."

"Maybe he is not the high-brow invader you think he is. Maybe those stories are not based in truth but created from contempt."

Zane shrugged. "What is the ingredient needed to make this concoction?"

"That's where it gets tricky. It's in the sea. Well, it's in a sea creature. It's a fluid found in a sac in their neck."

"And what sea creature is this?" The mercenary's interest peaked as he leaned in, waiting for Faelin's answer.

"The chief doesn't know. He said the elven healer told him only that it was large and dangerous."

Frowning, Zane said, "That could be one of many creatures that dwell under the waves. How are we supposed to prepare for a creature we can't identify?"

"The answer to that question will gain us our freedom."

Vallaria looked at her friend. "If we capture this creature and drain the fluid required, the chief will free us?"

"*And* make the elixir, but yes."

"How does the chief expect us to do that?" Zane asked.

"He told me you would understand once the creature shows itself."

Zane pointed at himself. "Me? How would I know?"

"He says you are from the sea."

The mercenary tilted his head. "Why would he say that?"

"He said you smell like sand and saltwater. He also saw the way you looked at the sea as we exited the hot springs tunnels—longingly"

Zane shook his head. "Well, I've traveled on it plenty but I'm not born from it like others from the Gold Coast. I'm not a fisherman or a treasure hunter. I know how to get from one place to another, to throw lines and hoist sails. I understand the direction of the winds, how the stars line up at night, and the way the waves move with the tide. And although I do know of some of the creatures that live in the deepest parts of the sea, I have only ever encountered a few. I am no expert."

"Well, let's hope that whatever this creature is you have some basic knowledge. But it is you Vallaria that will have to capture this creature."

"Me? How?"

"Your powers."

"But I don't know how to control them," Vallaria blurted out.

"What do you mean you don't know how to control them?" Zane looked confused as he pointed at her. "Aren't you a witch of Brulle?"

The heat in Vallaria's cheeks spread as she scrambled for a response. Thankfully Faelin intervened.

"Vallaria's powers are new. Some witches are born magical, and others gain their magic through a twist of destiny."

The mercenary's dark eyes narrowed. "While I may not have encountered an elf in my lifetime, I have traveled to far-off lands and met some individuals practiced in the magical arts. But I've never heard of any gaining powers through destiny." He motioned towards Vallaria's pocket. "I'd keep those prayer beads close and pray to the gods your destiny sees fit to bless you with magic in our time of need."

The ball in Vallaria's throat felt huge as a panic grew inside her. Was this the time when her secrets would all come out? The lies kept amassing, and it was getting increasingly more difficult to keep them all straight. She wanted to tell Zane the truth, but Faelin would not approve, nor was Vallaria completely sure he was on their side.

Best to keep lying.

As she opened her mouth to speak, the first light of day crept over the top of the rock walls. The grotto was awash with the pale gray dim of the dawn.

Faelin glanced at the sky. "The Wilders will soon wake, and some will attempt to lure the sea creature from the deep. We must be ready."

"How can we be ready for something we know nothing about," Zane asked, yawning. "We are tired, injured, and completely unprepared. Without a plan there is no being ready. Considering what's on the line for his tribe, the chief has a lot of misguided faith in a bunch of strangers."

Faelin glanced at Vallaria. "Sometimes faith is the only thing one has, misguided or not."

Vallaria's gaze dropped to the prayer beads in her hand. She hadn't realized she'd taken them from her pocket and was absently rolling them through her fingers.

Where is my faith?

The gods she'd spoken to for so many years were silent. Their comforting presence had been absent for so long she assumed they were either angry with her or had abandoned her altogether. She'd tried to remember when she'd stopped experiencing the calm euphoria that accompanied her prayer. But it escaped her. She'd felt alone in the world for so long, and although the gods never actually spoke to her, the understanding of their presence had made her feel a little less so.

Faith.

A surge of anger rose in her gut, and she shoved the prayer beads back into her tunic pocket. Anger turned to guilt. Maybe she had done something to offend them. But without knowing what she'd done she couldn't offer atonement.

But the gods are supposed to be with you in your time of need, are they not? the voice of doubt whispered.

"Vallaria." Zane's voice cut through her thoughts.

Her head jerked in his direction.

Faelin stood at the gate watching as a Wilder unlocked it from the other side. The chief, in all his ceremonial glory, stood a few feet back, plumed headdress, beaded collar, long leather sarong-style skirt. In his hand he held a long handled knife. Vallaria's eyes scanned it from tip to hilt. The metal was light gray and gleamed too much under a dull gray morning. The handle was pure white. *Bone?* Tied to its hilt, a dark red leather string weaved its way up and down the handle approximately an inch in each direction. From its ends were tied with what Vallaria thought were a dried bunch of weeds.

The gate opened and Faelin passed through; as she did she bowed to the chief and then stepped aside. Zane followed and he too bowed in the leader's direction.

The chief spoke in tongue, his hand animatedly waving. A young Wilder stepped forward and in perfect English said, "The chief hopes the renowned power of your house guides you this morn."

Zane shifted uncomfortably and then shook his head. "I do not know of what the chief speaks."

The young man turned to the chief, the exchange brief before he turned back to Zane. "Are you not from the Gold Coast Empire?"

"I am."

"And do you not sail across the seas on the merchant ships?"

"I have, yes."

Zane seemed bewildered by the line of questioning.

"Do the houses of the Gold Coast not dictate that to which a born son's path must take?"

"Yes, but I am not from a house. I am nothing more than a lowborn mercenary."

The young man cast his eyes on Vallaria and then to Faelin. He smiled and nodded. "My apologies, the chief must have mistaken you for another." Turning, he lowered his voice and spoke briefly to the chief. The leader's eyes bore into Zane, and he grunted and then spit at his feet.

Quickly Zane moved on, leaving the chief glowering directly at Vallaria.

She could feel his penetrating stare and once again she felt that need to disappear, to hide in her ashen tree and pretend the world didn't exist. Her stomach clenched as the Wilder motioned for her to come forward.

On shaking legs, she approached the chief—bow, nod. Her eyes flicked back and forth, and she fidgeted. *Stop Vallaria,* she scolded herself.

"Our chief would like to apologize to you for the incident on the cliff. He hopes you are well and that your injuries will not interfere with the task at hand."

"Which is?" she asked.

"The slaying of the sea beast. The chief surmises that as a witch of Brulle you have the best chance at using your powers to subdue the creature."

An involuntary laugh escaped her lips. Heat rose in her cheeks, and she dug her nails into the palms of her hands. "I am unsure as to what I can do that will enable us to extract the fluid your chief desires."

The chief held out the knife.

"This is a ceremonial knife, imbued with the innards of fish, the blood of the sail whale, and tied with the dried root of the rare herb the sea creature is known to desire."

Vallaria accepted the knife the chief presented. It was surprisingly light, and carved into the handle were three symbols, none of which she recognized.

"Use this knife on the left upper side of the creature's neck below its gill. Once the fluid flows you will need to capture as much as you can in this vessel." He handed Vallaria a wood flask.

"How do you know where the fluid is if you don't know what type of sea creature you are luring?"

"All the information we have from the elf healer is that which we pass on to you. She did not tell us the name of the creature, only the location of the fluid. We hope that one of you may complete what she could not. She was to train us in how to subdue the creature when it was time, but sadly, that time never came."

A crack in the young man's voice told Vallaria that Faelin's mother was very much loved by this tribe of Wilders. Vallaria did not remember much of the elven queen, for she was only in the kingdom for a few weeks before Queen Gisele left Mistenvale never to return. But she recalled her beauty, her regal presence, her kindness, and her penchant for peace in the world. Much of those qualities were a part of Faelin even though she had her father's stoic demeanor and military prowess.

A gong sounded in the distance, and the young man raised an arm, indicating for them to follow the chief toward the beach and the tall tower.

As they walked, they saw half a dozen tribesmen in three small canoes paddling out of the grotto through the watery tunnels carved by the sea into its cliffs. Waves crashed against their small boats as the angry sea surged, and it took every ounce of strength and sheer will for them not to capsize.

"The creature will be lured from the sea by the scent of the rare herb," the young Wilder said. "When it gets close it should catch the scent of the knife and come all the way to the beach. You must be ready. It will want what you have to offer the moment it arrives. If you hesitate, the creature will take it and most likely you at the same time." The young man hesitated, and a frown contoured his brow. "The elf healer did not share her plans past this point. I'm sorry we cannot assist you more, but the chief has faith in all of you."

Vallaria noticed the way the Wilder's shoulders slumped and head hung as he walked away. Even he didn't believe they could pull this off. She glanced at Zane, who walked beside her, eyes straight ahead, mouth turned down into a frown.

As if he could feel her gaze, he said, "If we do survive and Faelin can make the elixir, the chief better free us, but I don't believe this is going to end well for any of us."

Panic rose in her stomach, clenching at the muscles and souring the food she'd consumed. The bitter sting of bile rose in her throat as the gong from the beach bellowed again. Desperate for anything to comfort, her she tried to will the cold magic to come forth, to give her an indication that it was there, at the ready, but her blood remained warm and the ice crystal silent.

She rubbed her fingers together. While her hands were cold from the winter wind gusting across the sea, they did not sizzle with the ancient magic.

Where are you?
As if the wind carried the answer, she heard a faint whisper.
We are here, waiting.

54
VALLARIA

The deep-throated bellow of drums echoed through the grotto as she and Zane stood atop the towering structure. The sky rolled overhead with dark storm clouds full of a winter precipitation that threatened to drop on them at any moment.

Vallaria shivered as the cold wind stung her skin.

"Where are they?" she asked more to herself than to Zane. The drums had been beating for quite some time, and the canoes had been gone almost as long.

Atop the cliff was a Wilder peering out to sea searching for the creature hunters. He was to signal their return to those who stood in the grotto.

"This is madness," said Zane. "These people intend to lure a creature of the deep into shallow water. It won't work. The creature will feel threatened, trapped by the caves. It will not enter this grotto, not for anything. It goes against the instincts nature gave the creatures of this world."

"The elf healer said it would come."

"She may have been grasping at straws. Luring any animal is a difficult task, but in these waters? A winter sea is tumultuous; nothing that lives in its depths comes near the surface this time of year."

As if to emphasize his point, a surge of heavy waves crashed through the tunnels. A roaring, swirling wall of water raced toward the shore engulfing the legs of the tower and shaking it. Vallaria teetered as the structure shuddered against the pounding surf, and she grasped Zane's arm.

His skin was strangely warm under her chilled fingers, and as she glanced at him she saw the same look in his eyes she'd seen a few times before. A softness in his dark brown irises, a depth that drew her in and a strength that empowered her.

"Let's hope the Wilders at least know how to build things," he said as the tower quieted and the foamy surf receded once again.

Before she could respond, the Wilder atop the cliff shouted. While the language was foreign to her ears, she didn't need a translator to read the panicked excitement of his body language.

"The boats are returning," she said, gripping the ceremonial knife. Glancing down at the beach behind her, she saw the chief and the young translator indicate to Faelin they should back away from the water.

Her stomach dropped and a thin layer of sweat covered her upper lip. The knife shook in her hand, and she took a deep breath, willing it and her pounding heart to calm.

The wind picked up and the dark sky, as if competing with the angry sea below, cracked with lightning.

Yells echoed through the caverns as the first canoe came into view. The occupants' eyes were wide as they strained against their oars, the natural surge of the sea helping to push them toward the tower.

One, two, three, Vallaria counted. All the boats had returned. But as the last canoe emerged from the shadowy cavern she noticed it had only one occupant. The Wilder struggled to keep up with the others, but his canoe, even with the help of the sea, lagged behind.

Her eyes darted to the swell of water emerging from the cavern behind him. Something was there, under the surface, and it gained quickly on the solo canoe. The displacement of the water indicated it was large, and Vallaria held her breath as the swell reached the Wilder's canoe and lifted it from the sea as it broke the surface.

The man's scream pierced the air as the canoe tumbled in the air, flipping him out and into the water below.

Zane swore beside her as the head of the creature emerged from the sea, but before she could get a clear view of it, thunder and lightning shook the sky and the clouds opened up, releasing a deluge of water upon them.

The drums stopped.

Vallaria shook her head, trying to clear the water from her eyes as the rain pounded down on them. A haze danced on the surface of the sea, and she cast her eyes around looking desperately for the location of the creature.

Screams drew her attention and she saw the Wilder who'd been thrown from his canoe splashing in the water.

"Quiet!" yelled Zane. "You will draw its attention." But his warning was swallowed by the hiss of the rain and the man's panicked screams.

Vallaria watched in horror as the swell of water moved toward the flailing man. The smell of seaweed and saltwater filled her nostrils and for a moment everything went quiet, muffled by the pounding of her heart and the rush of blood that exploded in her head.

Her shaking hand wiped the rain from her eyes as the creature breached the surface, closing in on the man. Dark green scales gleamed with water and small spikes protruded from its skin in a line down its spine, each connected to another by a flexible membrane of flesh. Its forked tongue flicked from its lipless mouth as it opened it wide, revealing rows of razor-sharp teeth.

A final wailing scream penetrated the stormy air as the creature swallowed the man whole and then turned toward the tower. Nostrils flared in its flat snout as it sniffed the wintery air.

Again, Zane swore, but this time his tone sounded different. It was as if he had a revelation.

"What?

"I should have known," he stammered, his eyes glued to the thrashing creature in the water.

"Known what?" Her voice cracked as the panic creating knots in her stomach swelled in her throat.

"The creature. It's a storm eel."

"How do you know that?"

"Because it's one of the rarest sea creatures in the world and one of the deadliest. They are dubbed storm eels because they only come to the surface during the beginning of the winter months when the sea is at its angriest. It all makes sense now."

"What does?" Vallaria asked, wishing she could look at Zane, but her eyes remained transfixed on the creature in the water below. It circled the remaining two canoes, which had been trapped by the receding surf and pushed away from the shore. Wilders on the sand were attempting to throw ropes to the canoes, but the wind flicked them in every direction making their efforts futile.

"Rare creatures have rare things—tusks, scales, claws, lifesaving fluid, apparently. The storm eel is a dubious creature, and many think of it as a myth because rare sightings have only been experienced by those from House Storm Eel of the Gold Coast."

"House Storm Eel?" she croaked, as tentacles emerged from the sea and wrapped themselves around one of the canoes, snapping it in two.

"The house of sea merchants, and the only ones crazy enough to travel the seas this time of year," Zane answered, cringing at the sight of the splintered boats.

Vallaria had studied the text of the Golden City and its reigning houses briefly before they left Mistenvale. From her recollection, there were seven houses, and although she couldn't recall all their titles, she remembered each had a specific role in the Gold Coast society—sea merchants, military—and the house she did remember, House Blood Viper, was the bloodline of rulers, the Mensah family. Firstborn males from this house had been emperors of the Gold Coast Empire for centuries.

Another bloodcurdling scream infiltrated her thoughts, but this time it came from the beach. Her eyes darted to the shoreline where a female Wilder had run into the water and pulled the upper half of one of the canoe's occupants into her arms.

The sea turned bright red as blood poured from his torso where he'd been severed in half by the creature's jagged teeth. Two other Wilders had waded in and were pulling her and the corpse back to the shore as the woman wailed. The eels head snapped toward the sound, and it again sniffed the air.

Vallaria glanced back at the group of Wilders struggling to get out of the water. Wrapped around the chest of the dead man was a dark green vine with slashes of white crisscrossing its large leaves.

"The rare herb. The one the creature desires, its wrapped around his chest," she screamed. "Zane, they're all going to die."

Without thinking she darted to the edge of the tower and began yelling, hitting the poles of the structure with the handle of the ceremonial knife. She felt him move in beside her and soon their voices pierced the air together. Their yells drew the attention of the storm eel, and it raised its head into the air and sniffed. Yellow eyes drew wide as it caught the scent of the concoction the Wilders had imbued the blade with. It reared back and dove under the water, surging toward them at a frightening speed.

Stepping back, Vallaria clenched her hand around the knife and waited. In moments it would rise from the sea, and she would most likely die.

A violent impact hit the base of the tower, and it shuddered beneath their feet. Zane grabbed her by the arm as she slipped on the rain-soaked platform. Steadying her footing she waited for the eel to emerge from the sea, but nothing but silence and the heavy hiss of the rain greeted them.

Her wet clothes clung to her, heavy and cold.

"Where is it?" she whispered. Seconds later another furious impact hit, and the tower shuddered again, followed by a resounding crack.

"It's trying to break the tower," Zane said. "Storm eels don't rise from the water. They hunt on the surface. Why in the name of the gods did the Wilder's think a tower would be effective? It will never come up here, but it will make sure we go down there."

Another blow and the tower began to tilt as the supports cracked more under the force.

Vallaria flailed as her boot heels slid on the wet wood and she fell on her back. The impact knocked the knife from her grip, and it clattered to the floor. Another snap and the tower began to tilt. Scrambling to gain a handhold, Vallaria dug her fingers into the floorboards as she slid. Pain sliced through the tips as slivers found their way under her skin. When the knife slid passed her, she reached out and tried to grab it, but a yank on her other arm pulled her away from its trajectory. Dread filled her chest as she dangled from Zane's hand and watched the knife slip over the edge into the foaming sea below.

"Hold on, Vallaria. We're going over," Zane yelled as the sound of splintering wood echoed below them. The tower jerked and then broke apart, sending them hurtling toward the water in an avalanche of broken timber.

As her body left the platform, Zane's hand still holding tight to her wrist, a comforting thought entered her mind. *At least we won't die alone.*

Freefalling into the water, Vallaria saw the sea beast swimming away toward the caverns. Seconds later she plunged into the frigid, murky sea. Brackish water filled her mouth and nose, and she clawed her way to the surface. Sputtering and coughing, she sucked in a deep cleansing breath.

Her eyes searched for the storm eel, but the surface of the bay was flat, no swells to indicate its location. The bay was deep until it inclined toward the beach twenty feet out. She turned in the water, scanning the surface. *It could be underneath you.* The sea churned around her as she began to twist, searching for the sea beast.

"Vallaria, calm down!" Zane's voice called from behind her. "It's drawn to movement. Try to remain still."

Inhaling deeply, she turned to face him and slowed her arms and legs. His head bobbed on the surface about twenty feet away, his dark eyes imploring her to remain calm.

Breathe.

The swell she'd been searching for appeared by the cavern and raced toward Zane. She raised a hand from the water and pointed. His eyes followed and he nodded. Debris floated around him, and he seized a splintered pole with a severed end.

Facing the oncoming beast, he waited and so did she, holding her breath.

Moments passed and as the swell neared she found herself muttering to the gods, their gods, begging for protection.

The swell rose and the eel broke the surface, mouth wide as it bore down on Zane. Raising her hands, she willed the ancient magic to come forth—but nothing.

The sea surged, the wind battered, the rain soaked, and she bobbed, helpless to do anything but watch him die.

The storm eel flicked out its forked tongue and sprang at Zane, who pushed through the water sideways, veering out of its path with inches to spare. When it swam passed, Zane lunged, and with a mighty thrust pushed the jagged tip of the wood pole directly into its eye.

The creature screeched, a high-pitched squeal of pain and anger that drowned out all the other sounds crashing around them. Vallaria cringed as the awful clamor buffeted her ears.

Tentacles lashed out and in one movement scooped up Zane and threw him toward the shore. Vallaria watched as he hit the water with such force it rendered him unconscious. Thankfully, the eel had tossed him into the shallow portion of the bay. Relief flooded through her as she saw Faelin, the interpreter, and two other young Wilders run into the water and retrieve his limp body.

Vallaria prayed he was unconscious and not dead.

Wounded, the storm eel thrashed in the sea about thirty feet from where she treaded water.

With what little strength she had left, she began to swim toward shore. Screams floated toward her on the wind as she swam, and she lifted her head. Three Wilders were frantically waving and pointing as they jumped up and down on the sand.

Vallaria turned her head and looked behind her. The eel was diving. The pole stuck into its bloody eye broke the water's surface as it swam toward her. She kicked with all her might, but the freezing water and the torrential rain had taken its toll. She was exhausted, and her leather tunic pulled at her body. Her arms and legs screamed in pain as the muscles, weakened by the elements, began to seize.

I'm going to die. The words flitted through her mind.

The wind roared and answered. *Not today. Revenge is ours and we want to take it.*

Hypothermia, delirium, sheer fatigue, her body was giving out and she was hearing voices, their voices. The sea surged around her as the waves pulled her under. She sputtered as salt water flowed down her throat.

Closing her eyes, she stopped struggling and waited for death.

A quiet surrounded her as the sounds of the sea disappeared. The wind, the hiss of the rain all slipped into the background and went silent.

Fight, one voice said.

Kill, said another.

A multitude of voices rose in her mind, a cacophony all repeating the same sentence. *Revenge, bring us our revenge.*

The quiet broke and the harsh sounds of the storm roared in her ears. Her eyes flew open as she felt the cold, salty sting of the sea rush through her veins.

The cold magic followed.

The familiar bitter chill burst under her skin, bringing with it a clarity, and a strength.

Vallaria stared into the yellow eye of the beast as it reared from the water in front of her. Icy shards exploded from her raised hands and hurtled toward the creature piercing its thick scales with ease. Again, it screamed, but the attack only seemed to infuriate it more, and it swung its thick tail out from the water, hitting Vallaria in the shoulder.

Pain rippled down her side as the impact snaked through her nerves. Spurred by the surging adrenaline, she turned on the beast and forced her hands and the magic under the surface. In response the sea froze. Ice crystals formed on the surface, turning the water into a thick layer of white ice that spread out in front of her and trapped the bottom half of the storm eel in the frozen surface.

The eel thrashed its thick body and swayed side to side as it tried to free itself. The bloody pulp of its mangled eye hung from its socket, and as Vallaria heaved herself up onto the ice, the pole and part of its eye fell to the surface.

Wincing at the pain in her shoulder, she raised her unhurt arm and sent more icy shards hurtling toward the eel. But this time, none penetrated the armor of its thick scaly skin. Instead, the spikes shattered upon impact, sending a cloud of ice dust floating languidly down around the creature.

One hand, half the power.

The beast swung a tentacle toward her, missing her head by inches as she ducked. Unfortunately, the backswing caught her in the side, knocking her to the ice and expelling the air from her lungs. Arching pain shot through her ribs as she gasped for breath.

The beast screeched again, and Vallaria struggled to her feet. Pain wracked her muscles, but from the corner of her eye she saw something bobbing in the water near the ice drift: the ceremonial knife.

She dragged her injured body toward the edge, fell to her knees, and scooped up the knife.

The sea beast thrashed as the ice cracked and began to tip.

Vallaria slid as the edge of the ice float rose from the water, hurtling faster as the ice cracked. As she slid, she flipped to her back, watching as she sped toward the sea creature who, as if seeing its prey getting closer, stopped thrashing and lowered its head to the ice.

Mage magic rifled through her veins, and she raised her hands, one clenched tight to the dagger. With a focus she didn't know she possessed, she shot a torrent of ice directly at the storm eel, hitting it between its eyes. It screeched in pain, and thrashed more violently, its gnashing teeth growing closer as she slid toward it.

The ice tilted again, and she spun and slid backward.

The pole, its wood covered in the remnants of the eel's eye, rolled toward her and she grabbed it.

When she reached the storm eel, Vallaria plunged the sharp tip of the pole into the soft flesh of its throat, and at the same time, slashed at the beast with the ceremonial knife. The sharp blade carved a long, thin slice across its skin. Blood dripped from the wound and within seconds the storm eel lay unmoving on the ice.

Cold rain stung at her cheeks as she pushed herself up onto wobbly legs and faced the eel. It blinked its one eye as she approached, knife at the ready. Fear widened its lidless eyes and its nostrils flared, but the storm eel remained paralyzed.

Limping, Vallaria walked to the side of the beast near its head. She raised her hand and cautiously touched the bulge below its jawline. A sac filled with fluid squished under her fingertips. With a trembling hand, she raised the knife and poked the skin with the tip. The creature did not react, but Vallaria could see a small droplet of water seep from its eye.

Vallaria grasped the wooden flask attached to her waist and

yanked it free. She raised the vessel and gently pulled the tip of the blade from the creature's flesh. A pale green liquid poured from the hole and filled her flask.

Cold magic simmered in her veins and as she raised her hand and placed it on the eel's open wound, a slow stream of frost left her palm and singed the edges of its flesh, sealing the hole.

The storm eel blinked as she backed away and a tremor rippled through its body. *The paralyzing agent must be wearing off.* Quickly she retreated to the far end of the ice float. Cracks in the ice began to form and chunks fell into the water, freeing the storm eel, who quickly slipped beneath the surface. A swell traveled away from her toward the caverns as the sea beast retreated to the sanctum of the deep water.

Exhausted, Vallaria dropped to her knees. She bent over and inhaled the cold winter air, trying to squelch the bile that burned in her throat. Her head swam as the familiar headache exploded behind her eyes. Blood dripped from her nose and a bright red bloom appeared on the ice.

She closed her eyes and listened to the sound of the waves lapping against the ice float as a whisper floated through her mind.

We will not forsake you, for you are one of us now.

55

FAELIN

A few hours had passed since they'd acquired the rare ingredient from the storm eel. The encampment had grown quiet as they waited for Faelin to finish the elixir. She held out a wooden vessel to the chief.

It had taken her three batches to get it correct but she finally finished the elixir that would hopefully help the Wilders back from the brink of extinction. While she was mixing the elixir Faelin had realized that her mother had combined a healing tonic with a fertility tincture. It was simple enough, but Faelin appreciated her mother's skill at effectively combining the two to address a very unusual problem.

"This should be enough to reverse the effects of the disease. It may take some time, but the tribe should be blessed with fertility again."

The young Wilder interpreter whose name Faelin discovered was Gohl took the container from Faelin and nodded. "The chief will be forever in your debt. If there is ever anything you need—"

"What will you do now that winter is upon us?"

"We will go back to the caves and the hot springs. We will hunt the migrating herds, fish near the calmer shores, and harvest what we can. The tribe has a few stores of supplies left, and if we ration appropriately, we will survive until the earth mother has blessed us with the warmer days of spring."

The chief grunted, gaining the young Wilder's attention. He whispered something to him and placed a small package wrapped in leather and a piece of twine into his outstretched hand.

"The chief wishes to return this to its rightful heir."

Frowning, Faelin took the small package he offered. "What is it?"

Gohl lowered his voice. "It was your mother's."

Her eyes darted to Vallaria and Zane, who stood down by the beach, thankfully out of earshot.

"My mother's?"

"Queen Gisele."

"How did you know?" Faelin's mother was careful not to identify herself as the elven queen when outside the borders of Mistenvale.

"That she was the elven queen? The chief has been around a long time and knows much. He assumes, when the time comes, that you will be as good a leader as she."

Tears threatened to fill Faelin's eyes, but she dug her nails into her palm and forced them back down. "Why did you not mention this before?"

"You are traveling under an illusion and with a mercenary from the Gold Coast. The chief surmised you did not wish for your travel companions to know of your true identity."

"Not at this time no. I thank the chief for his discretion."

"Please," Gohl said, indicating the leather-wrapped item in her hand.

Pulling the twine, she unwound the soft skin. When the last flap fell away, Faelin gasped. In her palm lay her mother's amulet, a white crystal wound with wire and surrounded by bright silver metal leaves known to her people as the elven heart.

"We thought this lost since it was not on my mother's person when we collected her body."

"We assumed it may be of great value to your people since your mother was the queen. The chief wanted to keep it safe until the time presented itself to return it. We hope having this back lessens the pain her death has caused you and your father."

"Thank you." Faelin rewrapped the necklace and tucked it into her tunic.

While the ire toward the Wilder tribe, which she'd held so close to her heart for so long had minimized, she still wasn't willing to fully trust the chief. The Wilders clearly cared for her mother, but for years they'd kept quiet about her death until a chance meeting in northern Ravenia had spurred their desperate kidnapping. Faelin still had reservations about their true motives.

"May I ask why you were still so far north this close to winter? Or was our encounter not by chance?"

Gohl spoke to the chief and then turned back to Faelin. "The chief grows weary and because of the disease he has no sons. While the meeting was by chance, it was not without merit. The chief had decided months ago to migrate west to Mistenvale to ask the elves for their assistance. When you dropped your illusion to show him your eyes, he knew the earth mother had blessed his plight. Elves have not been seen in these parts for a very long time. Your exile is well known amongst all the kingdoms of man."

"If you were going to Mistenvale to ask the king for help then why not do the same with me? Why the extreme measures?"

The Wilder nodded, understanding the unspoken words. "We are not a people who are typically violent, but your travel companions, the commander and his henchmen are known to our people. As is the dark queen they serve. None can be trusted."

Gohl glanced at Zane. "A mercenary from the Gold Coast cannot be either. Especially since your mother's murder was orchestrated by the emperor's son. You must be wary; he is hiding something."

Aren't we all? Faelin thought. "Are we free to go?"

He spoke with the chief, who nodded and then spoke animatedly for a few minutes, pointing at Faelin as he did.

The young interpreter moved in close to Faelin and lowered his voice.

"The chief wishes you safe travels but advises you to be careful. Not just of the mercenary but of the witch of Brulle as well. She is powerful but the magic in her veins is dark, vengeful. Magic of that type only brings sorrow and death."

Faelin stiffened. The similarity of the chief's warning to her father's was not lost on her. Since the Valley of Souls, something about Vallaria had changed. At times she was distant and unemotional. Since Pax's death she hadn't shed a tear, not even when in pain. Faelin had also caught her whispering, as if speaking to someone who wasn't there. When she'd asked Vallaria about it, the princess had shrugged it off as if it were nothing.

Faelin pulled Dagget Ra's death amulet from her pocket. "May I keep this?"

"Of course." Gohl hesitated and glanced warily back at the chief before continuing. "There is something else."

A brow raised at the young man's statement.

"I walk these lands mostly unnoticed and because of that I learn much." He leaned in closer. "There is a war coming. The Gold Coast, Zion, kingdoms who have allied with the emperor's son out of greed or fear will unite. But the kingdom of man is not who should be feared. There is a vengeful darkness coming, and it seeks to destroy all. Be mindful of what you cannot see, for the true threat lies in the shadows."

Without another word, Gohl and the chief left. Faelin stared after them until Vallaria came to stand by her side.

"Well?" she said.

"We are free to go."

"Thank the gods," Zane said as he too came to stand beside Faelin. "It is a long walk back to the kingdom and even farther to the city. If we leave now we may be able to reach the hot springs before nightfall."

"That won't be necessary," Vallaria said.

Faelin turned to her friend with a quizzical look.

"I can get us back to the kingdom much quicker." She raised her hand and flicked her finger. Frost formed on the tip, turning quickly into a long sliver of ice.

Zane let out a slow exhale.

"You have control of your powers," Faelin said as she raised a brow.

"It seems so."

"How?"

"I don't know." Vallaria's eyes slipped to the left, looking away from her companions.

Faelin caught a quick upturn of the corners of Vallaria's mouth and a small nod before her face relaxed and she turned back to them. There it was, that odd behavior. It was as if Vallaria was listening to someone, or something, that no one else could see or hear. "Then how do you propose getting us back to the kingdom?"

"I'm going to portal us out of here."

A slight inflection marred Zane's voice as he spoke. "What?"

"That's not a thing," Faelin said rolling her eyes. "You create portals, but you don't portal." She realized she was scolding Vallaria and sighed. "Anyway, portal jumping is achieved by the conscious mind. An individual can only open a portal from one place to another if they've been to both places. Wherever a portal leads, it goes there because its creator has been there before. And I'm not sure you want to open one to the city of Ravenia."

Vallaria's face darkened and she sniffed. "I can do this. There's a place close to the city where we won't attract any unwanted attention."

Faelin frowned and shifted her weight. Besides Mistenvale, the only places Vallaria had ever been would have been with her parents before their deaths, and she couldn't possibly remember much from when she was five. Certainly not enough to create a viable portal. "Where is this place?"

"Somewhere I haven't been in a very long time." A glossy look crossed Vallaria's eyes as she was momentarily lost in the memory.

"Then I say let's get out of here," Zane said enthusiastically. "Tagar will have made it back to the kingdom by now and given the queen the Dagger of Crusade. If you want into that castle time is running short."

Vallaria agreed and walked toward the pen to gather their belongings and a few supplies the Wilders had provided.

Faelin turned to the mercenary. "Why are you so eager to get back to the city of Ravenia? Do you not think your head will still be on the chopping block if the queen finds out you're still alive?"

"I'm sure of it, but Vallaria saved my life, and I promised to help her get into the castle. Anyway, there is nowhere else for me to go." The mercenary's dark eyes darted from Faelin's.

"You miss home," she said.

"Very much."

"Then why do you work for the dark queen? Why not stay in the empire?" Her voice had an edge of disapproval, and she noticed Zane tense in response. His eyes fell to his hands, and he paused for a second as if trying to find the right words.

"Besides the gold, I suppose a part of me feels a sense of loyalty. You know the queen is from the Gold Coast. She comes from a revered house."

Queen Cereli's background was no secret. The empire's hierarchy was well known throughout the lands. It was typical of a monarchy where birthright, wealth, and power separate the worthy from the poor and uneducated. The emperor and the families of the elite houses were deemed as the echelon of Gold Coast society and garnered respect, even if they didn't deserve it. But Queen Cereli had done what no female before her had. In a world ruled by men she'd risen to their equal—but made many enemies along the way, most of which were her own people.

Ignoring the odd influx in his voice, as if he admired the woman whom he spoke of, she said, "Yes, but that doesn't answer the question."

He shifted in discomfort. "I know what she is, the queen. I am not blind to her atrocities. I know better than most. But it's a complicated situation."

An eyebrow raised at the mercenary's curious admission. "You seem to know the queen well."

A dark shadow crossed his face. "Better than most, I suppose." Abruptly ending the discussion, he said, "I'll go help Vallaria."

Faelin gripped the hilt of her sword as she watched him walk away. Whether he was hiding something purposely or preferred to keep his business private, she thought it best to keep a close eye on him until he got them into the castle.

Thunder rumbled above as dark gray clouds churned. Faelin's brows knitted together. Zane was an unknown factor and the sooner they parted ways the better. The last thing she needed was a Gold Coast mercenary at their side when Vallaria revealed herself and challenged Queen Cereli for the throne. Especially one whose loyalties were suspect.

56
VALLARIA

With a crackling pop the portal closed behind Vallaria.

"Where are we?" Zane asked, looking around.

They stood at the edge of a small crystal clear pond surrounded by lush green grass, tall willowy trees, and cluster of tall rocks. The tranquility was strangely out of place, especially since the roiling clouds above them were anything but.

"Snow's coming." Zane said pointing skyward.

Without acknowledging him, Vallaria walked to the edge of the pond and scooped up some freshwater in her palm, taking a long sip. Her head pounded, but at least she didn't suffer the overwhelming nausea she had when wielding the magic before.

Wiping her upper lip with the back of her hand, she saw a red stain of blood. Frustrated, she rinsed it off in the water.

There will be consequences when using the ancient magic, Vallaria. There is always a price, but it takes a heavier toll on mortals.

Faelin had warned her more than once about the burden the mage magic may take on her, on her body. But Vallaria was not concerned. Why would the gods see fit to bless her with this destiny if they didn't think her worthy?

Zane's voice interrupted her thoughts as he crouched beside her. "Are you okay?"

"I'm fine," she snapped as she stood. She was tired of being treated as if she were weak and incapable.

Unfazed he asked, "The witches of Brulle, are they all as powerful as you?"

"What?"

"Your people."

Vallaria was also tired of being someone she wasn't. What if she told him the truth? Would he accept her as Princess Serifine Vallaria Ravenia? Would anyone?

Does it matter? She furrowed her brows. The voices were always listening to her thoughts.

Ignoring their defiant tone, she answered. More lies.

"The witches of Brulle possess different powers. I come from one of the oldest families in Brulle, but others possess powers more formidable than me." She hesitated and cast him a curious look. "Why are you not afraid of my magic?"

Zane crossed his arms. "One would think after the slaughter of the mages and the retreat into solitude by the elves that magic in this world would be an afterthought. Something of old. But it's not true. This continent and the next still have many who practice the arts. The Gold Coast emperor has his magi, the Shamans of Tet are known on the far isles off Brulle, and Ravenia of course has its dark queen. I've seen much in my travels so little surprises me anymore. I'd say I was wary, curious maybe, but not afraid."

Vallaria's blue eyes narrowed. "But you've never run into an elf or a witch in your travels?"

Zane shook his head. "Elves I can do without, and although I've traveled many times to the continent of Brulle, I've never ventured to its northern parts where the witches are rumored to live. Not because of their existence but because it was dark, cold, and gloomy, much like Ravenia. I prefer the southern hemisphere or the multitude of island ports dotting the south seas." He grinned. "There I can forget my troubles, enjoy the warm weather, local rum, and fresh fruit. I admit being from the Gold Coast has spoiled me for good weather."

He scooped up some cool water, closed his eyes, and drank down the liquid. With a satisfying sigh, he turned to face her, and with a sweeping motion, asked again, "Where are we?"

Blue eyes scanned the meadow. "A place from my childhood. I used to come here for picnics with my mother before she died."

Her eyes glazed momentarily as another image reared up in her mind. *The dream.* This was where she was in the dream. The reflection of herself was there and the raven sat atop the rock to the left. Her eyes scanned her surroundings looking for any indication of the place beyond the meadow. The place of darkness and sorrow, but there was nothing. Just the calm, peaceful atmosphere of her childhood.

She turned to Zane. "I'm surprised I remember it at all. I was so young. My mother loved it here. She said it reminded her of home."

"So your mother didn't come from the northern part of Brulle then."

"No."

"You don't speak of your parents much."

Vallaria tensed and looked at the ground. "They've been gone a long time." Walking away, she called over her shoulder, "The city of Ravenia is not far. We should make haste."

When they reached Faelin, who sat atop a tall boulder looking across the fields to the east, Zane said, "The light is dim and the cloudbank low, so it's most likely late in the day. If we leave now, we might be able to make it back to the city before nightfall, and if we stay off the main roads, we'll have less of a chance at being spotted by the patrols."

Faelin nodded in agreement.

The sky overhead cracked with fury, and lightning flashed behind the clouds as they left the meadow. The temperature had dropped considerably, and as they walked under the darkening sky,

Vallaria felt a new sense of confidence mixed with a simmering defiance. They were three people against an army and a queen who wielded dark magic.

The odds were stacked against them.

But that queen sat on a stolen throne.

A throne that belonged to Vallaria.

The cold magic sizzled at the tips of her fingers, and a whisper caressed her ear.

Take it back.

57
CERELI

Winter had brought the cold finger of death to her doorstep, but Cereli did not fear it, and if it chose to take her, she would accept her fate, but she wouldn't go willingly—not without a fight. She'd come too far by beating the odds, not accepting the hand she'd been dealt. If she'd accepted her lot in life, she'd be married to a Gold Coast merchant, one of several wives with a brood of children pulling at her skirts.

Thankfully she was much too cunning to submit to her cultural role.

And ruthless.

Yes she'd done some awful things in her lifetime but nothing that wasn't necessary or deserved. Men underestimated her and many paid with their lives for their narcissism. The boy who'd killed her cat when she was ten by drowning it in the sea found himself, six years later, tied to the bottom of a skiff as the tide came in, begging for his life. At seventeen she'd been raped in her bed by a drunk friend of her father's while he was passed out in the next room. Years later she skewered the nobleman like a pig as he cried. King Ryguard too had begged for his life when her forces invaded his home. He also begged for the lives of his wife and child. Unfortunately, he was already dead, his head impaled on a pike at the castle gates, when Tagar drove a sword through their guts.

Those memories were necessary, as were her actions. They reminded her of the world she lived in and how fatal one mistake could be.

A fire crackled in the hearth as she stood by the window watching the first flakes of winter fall from the sky. She looked forward to this time of year. Since her returned from the Isle of Haddes, the dark magic that had attached itself to her had inexplicitly seeped through the kingdom, turning the once-vibrant lands into a dreary, bitter, and gray place. She couldn't remember what the sun felt like on her face or recall the fragrant scent of spring flowers. Winter was the only time Ravenia had a color palette that wasn't a dull shade of gray.

Will this be the last winter I see? Or will fate grant me a reprieve?

Lost in thought, she didn't see the shadow pass the window until the raven landed on the windowsill and began tapping the glass.

Startled, she took a step back. Her heart thumped faster as she watched the large black bird. Suddenly it stopped pecking and lifted its head, its beady eyes locking on hers.

A shiver ran over her skin as if the cold hand of death itself, caressed it.

The bird cawed, its bellow so brash it shook the pane of glass.

Cereli jumped.

The raven raised its large wings, tapped once more at the glass, and flew away.

She stepped back to the window and peered toward the sky, watching as the large bird circled the castle towers and then flew out of sight. A raven of Ravenia had returned and no doubt more would follow. Her fingers turned white as she gripped the windowsill. The cold glass soothed the ache in her temples as she leaned her forehead against it.

You're out of time, Cereli. What is your next move?

A knock came from the door.

"Go away," she yelled, not caring who or why someone would bother her at this early hour. She needed to think. The signs were upon her and her hold on the throne of Ravenia was about to be threatened.

Her fingers drummed the sill. *By a young woman, no less.* She shook her head, trying to dispel the small voice of doubt.

"I'm the dark queen," she whispered. "I have bested kings, brought madmen to their knees, and struck fear into the hearts of all who stand beneath me."

A pounding in her head mimicked the knocking on the door.

She drew herself upright and smoothed the front of her gown. Her eyes drifted to the bedchamber door where the knocking persisted.

Who dares interrupt me at this hour?

Striding across the room, she flung open the door to find a young man on the other side. He lowered his eyes and stammered, "For you, Your Highness. He held out a piece of sealed parchment. "Yelin Barro asked me to deliver it to you immediately."

"Who are you?" she questioned as she glared at the young man.

A frown of confusion marred his young face. "I'm the castle messenger, my queen."

"No, you're not." Cereli glanced down the hall in both directions. "Who sent you?"

"Mr. Barro. The letter is from the Gold Coast."

Of course. Moricio had returned to Darrius and told him of her defiance. He'd sent a spy!

Before the young man could utter another word, Cereli had him by the throat, dragging him into her bed chamber and closing the door behind them. The dark magic in her veins surged. He struggled, dropping the letter as his hands clawed at hers.

"Did Darrius send you? My brother? Are you here to kill me?"

The young man's eyes were full of fear, but that only spurred Cereli on. Her mind, addled with suspicion, did not even register that the young man was dressed in the uniform of her castle staff. "Why are you here? Who sent you?" she repeated, her grip tightening around the boy's throat as the dark magic took hold.

Seconds later the young man stopped struggling and went limp. Cereli let go and he dropped to the floor in a heap. She stepped over his body and glanced at her staff leaning against the wall.

The smoke swirled. The darkness could sense death. She tilted her head back and forth from shoulder to shoulder. The words on the incantation flew through her mind as she leaned over the body and grasped his face, pulling his mouth toward hers. The pink in his cheeks disappeared and an ashen, mottled gray colored his skin. His eyes stared at nothing as his life force began to leave his body, finding its way into hers. Cereli watched with morbid satisfaction as the young man shriveled to a withered corpse at her feet.

Releasing him, she stood to full height and walked to the mirror that hung over the fireplace. Steaks of blood ran down her cheeks from her eyes. Black spider veins appeared under her skin, slithering from her hairline across her face and down her neck. She picked up her crown and placed it on her head, then pushed a stray hair back into place.

She smiled at her reflection.

Queen Cereli Damask Ravenia was not one to be trifled with.

YELIN BARRO ENTERED THE THRONE ROOM THE SAME AS HE ALWAYS DID, scurrying like a rodent.

Cereli watched in disgust as he came toward her. He looked ridiculous dressed head to toe in white, but it was the magenta slippers with black tassels that really set her off.

"Yelin, we really must discuss your wardrobe," she sniped.

The black mustache atop his lip twitched as he brought his hands together in front of him. "Your Highness?"

"This is Ravenia, and you dress like you live in the Gold Coast. Where do your loyalties lie, Mr. Barro?"

"Well with you, of course, Your Majesty."

Always the right answer, delivered in his unapologetic way. Everything that made Yelin Barro invaluable also made him untrustworthy. He'd served her well over the years, but it would soon be time to dispatch him from her service. The walls were closing in and there were few left she could trust.

"Did you get the letter?" he asked.

"What letter?" she asked, not really caring.

"I sent a messenger up to your room this morning after receiving the communication from the holy city. Did you not receive it?" He frowned. "I told the messenger boy to deliver the missive immediately."

Her heart skipped a beat as she thought about the young man whose life she'd taken. Closing her eyes, she rubbed her temples. She'd been so sure she hadn't recognized him, that he was somewhere he didn't belong. The pounding in her head returned, echoing his knock on her bedchamber door.

"I didn't know. I thought—"

"Your Highness, you look pale. Should I summon the royal physician?"

"NO!" Her eyes snapped open, and she glared at her advisor as the dark magic in her veins awakened. In a calm voice she said, "You will need to hire another messenger."

Yelin's face crumpled in horror as he saw the blood red tear that dripped from her eye. "Your Majesty, what have you done?"

"Just go deal with it, Yelin. And bring me the King Tirus's letter."

The small man turned and darted from the room without a backward glance.

Cereli gripped the arms of the throne. *I'm losing control.*

Ever since the ice moon rose in the sky, the dark magic had become erratic. It had become more difficult to keep at bay and feed it to its satisfaction. At times her mind was brilliantly focused, and at other times, a hazy confusion muddled her thoughts.

You've become paranoid. That voice, the hissing whisper, had returned. The apparition from her visions, and the Isle of Haddes was in her mind, taunting her. But now the entity was no longer faceless.

"Go away!" Cereli yelled.

A laugh floated through her mind. *I cannot. You made me and now the darkness joins us.*

It's all in your head, Cereli thought. Just your imagination playing tricks on you again. But she wasn't certain anymore what was real and what wasn't.

"You're not real," she screamed, holding her head and rocking back and forth.

Oh, but I am, and soon you will all be witness to my rise.

Moments later, Cereli felt the voice fade from her mind and the darkness calm inside her. Gasping for breath, she twisted on the throne. The darkness was taking over, consuming her and unless she found the Ring of Perpetuity to grant her immortality she may not live, even if she struck down Serifine Ravenia.

The door to the throne room opened and Yelin Barro reentered. His expression was grave, but he held the letter in his hand. When he reached the throne, his gaze dropped to his slippers and his hands shook, but not from fear. Cereli could feel the anger waft from him like waves lapping the shores of the Shimmering Coast.

She stood and took the letter he offered.

"That will be all," she said dismissively.

"He'd been in your employ for three years. His parents as well. His father is a soldier in your army and his mother works as a chambermaid. They have been loyal to you." Yelin's voice wavered, but his expression remained stoic.

"Give them a bag of gold for his funeral. And each a raise for their loss."

Dark eyes rose to hers and he flexed his left fist but remained silent, instead nodding in compliance. "As you wish, Your Majesty."

Cereli waited until he'd left before turning her attention to the letter. It was stamped with the white seal of the holy city—a cross and sword held by the hand of God. Breaking the seal, she read the text inside.

King Tirus of Kasmire requests the presence of your company along with the prince of Ravenia for the lighting of the Seven Halos.
After the sacred ceremony the king will announce to his people the upcoming union of Prince Zander to his daughter Princess Aerilla.

Cereli threw the missive to the floor and leaned back in her throne. The lighting of the Seven Halos took place on the last day of the holy week, which was in early spring. Tomorrow she would send a messenger to the Holy City of Kasmire with a letter, regretfully informing the king of the untimely and accidental death of the prince. Further, she would suggest still attending the sacred ceremony as a tribute to her fallen son.

Her index finger tapped the arm of her throne as she thought about the other two Myths of Three. The Pendant of Opulence granted untold riches and wealth. It was given to the elven king, King Elvander's father. But it was the Ring of Perpetuity that she desired to possess next. For it was said to have the power to grant immortality.

If the historical scrolls were correct, the Ring of Perpetuity was somewhere in the City of Kasmire, hidden from the ages. Of course, the mages would give the power of immortality to a devout king knowing he would never use it. Immortality belonged only to their god, not to any mortal man. To obtain the ring, she would need the king of Kasmire to allow her into the holy city, even without Zander by her side. It was the only way.

The Dagger of Crusade would then lead her right to the ring—for the Myths of Three, their magic connected, called to each other. The mages meant them to be a sign of peace, but once in her possession Cereli would use them as a sign of supreme power.

Neither Darrius Mensah nor a young girl who should have died years before would stop her from gaining the power she rightly deserved.

She'd sacrificed too much.

Her heart grew heavy as she thought of Zander. His betrayal had cost him his life. To align with the likes of Darrius Mensah was treason against the Crown, and the dark queen could not forgive any who betrayed her, not even her own flesh and blood.

But you sent him to the empire. Straight into the arms of the enemy because you were too afraid to look at his face. The way he tilted his head before he answered a question, how he flicked his wrist when raising his sword, the birthmark that could only be seen if the light caught his eye the precise way. It was all too painful. He reminded you too much of the past. Of him. You sent Zander to your brother and by proxy to Darrius. The Gold Coast was his home, not Ravenia. Why would he choose to be loyal to you when you made it painfully clear you cared little about him?

An oily black tear fell down her cheek as her voice of doubt spoke up.

All you have lost is your own doing, Cereli, and now you are truly alone.

58

ZANDER

It was dark when they entered the city. But an eerie glow cast down by the ice moon lit their way. Zander's eyes lifted to the sky. He'd heard of the ice moon, but he'd never seen one for himself. Many full moons had cast their soft light upon his face on the seas, but this moon was anything but comforting. Its size and hazy light instead sent shivers of foreboding across his skin.

He turned his attention back to the city.

All the stores and businesses were shuttered, and except for the odd stray dog and tavern drunk, the streets were mostly deserted. A low fog rolled across the cobblestone and a fine mist of icy rain fell from the black sky. Streetlamps glowed like orbs, and their candle flames flickered erratically as if they too were experiencing the effects of the moon.

Zander led them from the main gate to a small inn located near the slum in a part of the city farthest from the castle where Tagar's men did not patrol.

While Faelin went inside to acquire sleeping quarters for the night, Vallaria and he huddled under the overhang out of the cold wintery drizzle. Whatever strength remained in him had been sapped during the final walk from the meadow. He was sore and bruised, and his stomach growled constantly from the lack of nourishment. He stole a quick glance at Vallaria. Her eyes were closed, and her breathing was labored. A small bruise had appeared on her cheek, and he was sure that she felt no better than him. Sleep, food, and medicine was needed before they could even think of entering the castle.

He turned his attention back to the silent sky, black as pitch. Did he ever remember a time when the stars shone? Ravenia had been such a dark, unforgiving place for so long that if there were a time when he experienced joy here it had been washed from his memory long ago.

Goosebumps rose on his skin as a cold winter wind blew down the street. The temperature had plummeted since they'd been here days before and Zander suspected soon the first snowfall would be upon them.

As if the gods listened, the first flakes began to fall.

His eyes drifted toward the direction of the castle and a clench like a punch to the gut followed. He'd known the dark magic his mother possessed had been changing her for years. Paranoia, tense interactions with castle staff, and decisions made based on emotions more than well-thought-out plans. Queen Cereli had become terse, distant, and cruel. The mother he'd known had disappeared long ago, consumed by the greed, power, and darkness she so deftly wielded.

But to order the murder of her own son.

Zander felt a sudden desire to run directly into the castle and confront her. But he wouldn't get far. Tagar and the other guards would stop him long before he got near her chambers. And then he had no doubt the dark queen would finish what Tagar couldn't.

But why? Why did she want him dead?

Did she deem him unworthy of her lineage? Had the dark magic turned her mad? Did she perceive him as a threat? The image of Yelin

Barro's greasy face popped into his mind. What hand did he play in this?

Zander sighed as the cold wind whipped around him sending the first flakes of snow swirling and chilling his bones further.

He supposed it didn't matter, his mother's reasoning. Not anymore. Tomorrow he would get them into the castle and whatever destiny was meant to unfold would. But he prayed to the gods at the very least that his mother would know it was he who brought wrath to her doorstep.

The snow fell heavier.

"I've got us lodging for the evening," Faelin said, exiting the inn. "The rooms are around back."

Zander hadn't noticed that Vallaria's head rested on his shoulder. But now that he had, he didn't want to move. "We will be there momentarily," he said.

Faelin glanced down at the sleeping Vallaria and nodded before handing him two iron keys and disappearing into the shadows.

He gazed down at the woman who'd entered his life only days before. Where she'd come from and why, he would probably never know, but now that she was here, a part of him didn't want her to go.

She's not yours to keep, Zander.

He looked down at her beautiful face. *No, but maybe to hold onto for a little while longer.*

AN HOUR LATER ZANDER PACED THE FLOOR IN HIS ROOM.

A fire burned in the hearth, and its warmth seeped into his aching muscles, giving his tired body some relief. He rubbed the scar on his shoulder where the sword had penetrated the skin. Although Faelin had healed him, it still itched.

She too, like Vallaria, was a bit of a mystery. Sure, they all had secrets, everyone in Ravenia did. You keep your head down, don't talk too much, and maybe you won't attract the wrong kind of attention. But Faelin had an edge to her, a wisdom, that most women he'd met didn't possess at any age. It was as if she'd been hardened by time and a world long past.

Curious, he thought.

His mind drifted to Vallaria, and his breath hitched. She was quite the opposite. Naïve but not fearful, vulnerable but not weak. Her strength of character matched her strong will.

And she didn't bend to your charms like most.

Zander smiled. That was one of his favorite things about her: she was independent yet approachable. Vallaria was unlike any other who had come before.

His heart skipped a beat as he thought about what they were about to attempt. What he was about to do. What if he never got the chance to tell her how he felt? If his last breath came tomorrow, would she be his biggest regret?

Without hesitating Zander slipped out of his room, crossed the hall, and knocked on her door, hoping she hadn't already fallen asleep. His fist clenched and unfurled as he waited, but within seconds he heard movement and thankfully her door swung open.

Vallaria's ice blue eyes were full of curiosity when she saw it was him standing on the other side.

His breath caught in his throat as he took her in.

She was beautiful. Her long dark hair was pulled up into a messy bun at the nape of her neck and soft tendrils curled around her pale, perfect face. A faint smattering of freckles covered the bridge of her small nose and her crystal blue eyes danced with the light of the hallway candles. Dressed only in a long gauzy blouse that hung off her shoulders Zander's eyes traveled down to her long, slender, bare legs. His chest constricted and for a moment he couldn't find his voice.

"Zane?" she said, tilting her head to one side and frowning.

Had he woken her?

"I'm sorry to bother you." His voice was husky with desire. "It's just—"

She didn't let him finish. Grabbing his lapels, Vallaria dragged him into her room and kicked the door closed behind him.

Her lips were on his, and he kissed her back forcefully, his mouth hungry to savor every inch of her. The beating of his heart increased as she pulled him toward the bed.

"Vallaria," he whispered. "Are you sure?"

He felt silly for asking, but Vallaria was not just any woman. She wasn't one of the several faceless females he'd bedded over the years and then left behind without a second thought.

She was different.

The realization of what that meant struck him.

She had his heart. And for once in his life, he wanted to stay.

As he laid her gently on the bed, he hoped she felt the same.

At first, he took his time gently caressing her skin as he kissed her shoulders and neck, but soon the passion exploded, and he took her with a desperation unbecoming of a seasoned lover. Vallaria arched against him as he made love to her over and over. Soon they moved as one, and Zander prayed this night would never end.

Sated, he pulled her close and covered them with the thick wool blanket. She murmured something he couldn't make out and snuggled deeper into the crook of his arm. As her breath evened out and she drifted off to sleep, Zander knew Vallaria was the one he couldn't walk away from. But first, he would have to find a way to tell her who he really was and pray Prince Zander Damask would still be the man she wanted.

59
VALLARIA

The next morning Vallaria couldn't stop smiling after Zane left her room. Trembling fingers grazed her lips as she thought about his kiss. But then her stomach clenched when she thought about the secret she'd been keeping from him. He thought she was someone she wasn't. He accepted a witch from Brulle, but would he accept a princess of Ravenia? Her and Zane came from two very different worlds.

Her name floated through her mind. Princess Serifine Vallaria Ravenia. *Serifine.* Her birth name was so foreign to her, and it felt odd referring to herself in that way. After only being Vallaria for most of her life, *Princess* Vallaria *Ravenia* was unfamiliar enough.

Another thought entered her head. Faelin wouldn't approve of her and Zane.

Her friend had never liked the mercenary. Partly because of his unwarranted aversion to her race but mostly because Faelin had a difficult time trusting outsiders. Something in her past, long before Vallaria was born, had bred a wariness toward the kingdoms of man, but most fervently of the Gold Coast. Faelin had said as much when Vallaria studied them prior to their departure from Mistenvale.

"The empire is founded on cultural traditions. Many of which have not changed in centuries. Besides their misogynistic and societal differences, there are many practices still in place that other kingdoms outlawed decades ago."

"Such as?" she'd inquired.

"Slavery for one. Inhumane brutality has been a hallmark of the empire for centuries. Did you know they led the crusade against the mages? They twisted the minds of many rulers, fed them lies and fear until they turned on those who had been by their sides as allies, friends. The culling shaped the kingdoms of man that exist today, and greed, power, and treachery are still at the forefront. While the game may be played behind the guise of diplomacy, the shadows and the back alleyways are where things truly get done."

Vallaria sighed and leaned back on her bed, the last of the tingle from Zane's hands leaving her skin as the reality of today's events loomed. She would begin her quest for the throne in a back alleyway.

Irony meet destiny.

She, Faelin, and Zane had formulated a plan on the walk back to the city yesterday. Well, part of a plan anyway. Exhausted and defeated people didn't make exceptional tacticians. With Faelin not revealing her identity to Zane, the elf couldn't admit she'd walked the halls of the castle at Ravenia years before. To her the castle was an enigma, same as it was for Vallaria.

"We must trust that you can get us in without being caught," Faelin said. "Also, it's imperative to know the royal guard's stations, their patrol patterns, where the castle staff is at all times of the day, and any anomalies that could trip us up."

"There is a secret entrance at the back of the castle," he'd revealed. "The queen uses it when she wishes to leave without the guard's accompaniment. The castle has many secret passages hidden in the walls that open to the strangest of places. Only a privileged few even know they exist. This will be our best bet at getting into the heart of the castle undetected."

"And how are you one of the privileged few?" Faelin questioned.

Vallaria heard the accusation in the elf's words. Faelin didn't trust Zane and although they were all keeping secrets from one another, Vallaria too wondered how Zane knew so much about the inner workings of the kingdom.

"As I said before, I've worked for the queen for years." Zane hesitated. "Many times, being hired as private security for castle events or diplomatic visits. Knowing the landscape and every inch of that castle was part of my job."

Faelin's green eyes never left the mercenary as he spoke, and Vallaria felt the tension grow between them.

"We will also need to know where Queen Cereli will be," Vallaria added, hoping to bring the two of them back to the problem at hand.

Zane narrowed his dark brown eyes. "Why is entering the castle of such importance to you two, anyway? It can't be because you were cheated out of some gold."

Vallaria had opened her mouth to speak, but Faelin raised a gloved hand. A signal for silence. "I can promise you this," the elf said. "If we are successful in our endeavors, you will know the reason before the bells toll midnight tomorrow."

His dark gaze had turned toward Vallaria briefly before nodding and dropping the subject.

Zane hadn't asked again their reasons and hopefully he wouldn't engage her with questions today. Vallaria sensed there were more secrets between them than truths, and when all was revealed she prayed to the gods that she and Zane could find their way through.

She picked up her father's prayer beads and rolled the wood balls between her fingers. No longer could she rely on the help of her gods. Today she only had herself, the blade of an elf, the desire for revenge of a mercenary, and the magic that destiny had seen fit to bless her with.

The odds were against them.

Just get to the queen, Vallaria. Focus on that. The throne is yours. It is your birthright. If it's your destiny to be queen, you will find a way.

Vallaria stood and pushed the prayer beads deep into her black leather pants pocket. She wrapped her mother's wool travel cloak around her shoulders and pushed a stray hair off her face. Her mother's sword leaned against the door jamb, and she grabbed it as she left the room.

Today, one of two things would happen: she would avenge her family and take back what is rightly hers or she would join her parents in the afterlife.

60
VALLARIA

The castle sat atop a steep hill. Its mammoth towers rose skyward, their peaks hidden by the low, gray cloudbank swirling around them. High stone walls surrounded the perimeter, separating the castle grounds from the city it loomed over. Only three gates allowed access onto the grounds: the main gate, the side gate by the barracks, and the gate in the back used as a service entrance for deliveries.

They would use none of those.

Bile rose in Vallaria's throat as she recalled Zane's words.

"There is one way through the outer wall that is unguarded and easily attainable. You won't like it, but it is that or try your hand at overpowering the royal guard."

The city's sewage system.

She swallowed and inhaled the cool crisp air while shifting her focus to her surroundings.

It was late afternoon and torches burned beside the iron gates of the main entrance. A light snow had begun to fall, and Vallaria pulled her cloak's hood farther over her head. Guards posted at either side paid them no mind as she pushed the small cart of firewood in front of her. Zane walked ahead of her with a bundle over his shoulder. They were just another pair of peasants of which the guards cared little about.

Vallaria stole a glance through the iron gate as they passed. The city's cobblestone street ended at the castle's entrance, and a mix of white and black stone wound its way through the lawns directly up to the front courtyard. To the left a large stone building with two arched wooden doors stood open. Inside a black carriage waited. Ivy, its thick leaves covered in the new snow, crept up the walls, roofs, and spires. Stained glass windows, their panels a multitude of colors, stared like empty eyes toward the street.

Déjà vu crept cold across her skin as her gaze lifted to the large stone ravens that sat upon the ridge of the roofline. Movement caught her eye, and as she passed the main gate, she saw it—a large black raven perched atop the head of the stone one. Its glossy eyes blinked rapidly in its snow-covered head.

The wheel of her cart hit a rut, and it began to tip. Quickly she righted it and looked over her shoulder to see if she'd alerted the guards, but they were too busy helping a beautiful blonde traveler. They needed a distraction to enter the alleyway that led to the sewer grate undetected, and Faelin was it.

When the elf spoke to the guards, she twirled a piece of her long blonde hair around a gloved finger. Faelin was a beauty even under an illusion, and the guards instantly took notice. The winter wind carried her voice toward Vallaria as she stopped the cart at the mouth of the alley.

"Excuse me, kind sirs. I find myself somewhat lost in your grand city. I'm passing through on my way to the coast and was told you had a warm and inviting inn where I may find lodging for the night."

The guards stood tall as the one with the most stripes on his collar answered. "Welcome to Ravenia, madam. You must be looking for the Rosewater Inn. It's right next to the Boar's Tusk."

Their voices drifted off as Faelin steered their gazes in the other direction, giving Vallaria and Zane enough time to slip into the alleyway undetected. Faelin would circle around the block and meet them at the sewer grate. Even though the alley was a mere hundred feet from the main gate, the guards would not see Faelin slip through. As a shield, the elf's magic allowed her to move quickly and undetected for short periods of time.

Heavier snow fell as they walked down the alley toward the trough. Vallaria's bare hands tingled with cold, and as she rubbed them together, small puffs of crystallized ice fell from her fingertips. She wished she could put her wool gloves on, but her hands needed to be ready, in case she required more than her wit and the blade of steel at her hip. Although they walked into the unknown to face certain danger, she was happy that at least the ancient magic had not abandoned her.

Like your gods, said a taunting whisper at the edge of her mind.

Since the Valley of Souls, she'd heard them time and again. The mages of old—at least she assumed that's who they were. They spoke to her in whispers and although centuries had passed since they roamed these lands, their intent was clear. They desired vengeance for the betrayal enacted upon them by the kingdoms of man.

She'd not told Faelin of the voices, choosing not to be more of a burden to her friend than she already was. The king had tasked Faelin to be her guardian on this quest and much of that burden would lay heavy on the elf's shoulders in this moment. Keeping Vallaria alive to claim the throne was the future elven queen's destiny. Anyway, the voices were just whispers at the edges of her mind. Nothing more.

Lost in her thoughts, she almost ran into the back of Zane when he stopped suddenly.

"Down here," he said, following a set of stone steps that led down to the sewage trough.

Vallaria held her breath as the stench of excrement floated up toward her. The acidic odor burned at her nostrils, and she raised her forearm to cover her nose and mouth.

"Here." Faelin stood beside her, holding out a small tin of suave. "Just a dab inside each nostril."

Vallaria did as her friend suggested and thankfully the putrid smell lessened considerably.

She walked down the steps to join Zane at the metal grate. On the other side a stone trough about four feet wide ran parallel to the wall. A murky brown sludge flowed down its center and Vallaria's stomach heaved again at the sight.

"You want us to walk through shit?" she hissed as Zane used the tip of his knife to unscrew the bolts holding the grate to the wall.

"It's the only way. All the gates are guarded day and night, and we can't just walk through the front door." He held out his hand. "I'm sorry, but this *is* the only way."

Slapping away his hand, she stepped through the hole in the wall and landed ankle deep in human excrement. "They may not see us coming, but they'll damn well smell us," she grumbled as she took a few steps, each more laborious than the last as the sludge sucked at her leather boots.

Zane placed the broken grate back into the wall. "If no one looks too closely, they won't notice the bolts missing. If they do, well we will have the entire royal guard searching the castle and grounds for intruders."

"I thought you said the royal guards don't patrol down here," Faelin said, her brows furrowing.

"They don't, but maintaining a castle requires a large staff. It's unlikely it will be noticed, but there is always a chance." He shrugged and motioned for them to follow him. "Hopefully a porter or scullery maid won't be our downfall."

A hundred or so feet along the outer wall, the sewage trough tunneled into the base of a tower. They walked in the dark for a few hundred feet, listening to the echo of the squishing of their boots in the sucking waste and the squeak of rats as they scurried along the trough's edges.

Vallaria shivered in disgust, holding her breath for as long as she could, before gasping for air.

Using the blade of his dagger, Zane broke the rusty lock holding the sewer door closed at the far end. Carefully he opened it and peered out. "Follow me, but stay alert."

They exited the sewer on the castle grounds behind a large oak, its branches laden with a heavy snow. Vallaria gulped in the fresh air and knocked the crud stuck to her boots, off on the wall. Her eyes burned from the vapor rising from the excrement. Tears flowed down her cheeks, and she wiped them away in frustration, glad to escape the foulness of the sewers.

When they crossed the small courtyard, Vallaria noticed their footprints were left behind in the snow. What if someone saw them? This was becoming a calamity in the making.

"Zane," she said pointing to their footprints.

"No one uses this courtyard. It's too far from anything worthwhile in the castle. I believe at one point they used this area to bury the bodies of the royal hunting dogs." A crooked smile indicated Zane was teasing. "Trust me, no one's been out here in years."

Vallaria noticed Faelin assessing him with suspicion.

They followed Zane through another door in the wall and down rat-infested tunnels and out into the dungeons. Voices echoed from above and Zane raised a finger to his lips, pressing himself against the wall.

Footfalls drew near and Zane turned his head toward Vallaria and Faelin. "It's too early for patrol or for the prisoners to be fed," he whispered. "Stay here."

He crept out of the shadows and slipped around the corner. The footfalls got louder and soon a voice echoed back to them.

"Whose down here. Come forth."

Quick footsteps.

"Oh, it's you Pr—"

The man's words were cut short as a scuffling noise and the

sound of boot heels kicking the floor reached Vallaria's ears. Seconds later there was silence.

Zane's head peeked around the corner. His hair was disheveled and a thin layer of sweat glistened on his forehead. "Let's go."

They stepped out into the lit hallway, and Vallaria saw one of the cell doors was ajar. They passed an elderly man lying face down on the floor.

"He shouldn't be down here. He's a cook in the kitchen. There is no reason for him to be here," Zane said.

"Will they notice him missing?" Vallaria asked.

"Eventually, but they won't be too worried. He likes to take a drink on occasion. They'll most likely think he's napping it off someplace quiet."

Faelin glared at Zane. "I don't like this."

Neither did Vallaria. Their chances of getting to the queen undetected were flimsy at best, but if they accidently kept running into the help, they'd be lucky to get to the main floor without finding themselves marched back down here by the royal guard.

Quietly they exited the dungeons and climbed a narrow back staircase that emerged into the basement cellars of the castle. The smell of musty wine barrels reached Vallaria's nose, a welcome change from the pungent odor of excrement.

Zane turned and with a sheepish look said, "We have to go through the guard's quarters to get to the main floor."

Before Vallaria could even open her mouth, Faelin had the blade of her small knife placed against Zane's throat. "What type of game are you playing mercenary? You seem to know a lot about the inner workings of the castle and its staff. And now you lead us directly into the path of the royal guard."

Raising his hands, he said, "I told you I've worked for the queen for many years. The layout of this castle is not new to me I know it well. As for the chosen route, that is tactical. The guards will be at their posts or in the dinner hall. It's why I wanted to enter the castle now instead of under the cover of darkness. Much still happens in the castle this time of day and the royal guards are spread out. Later in the evening the patrols thin and many of the guards retreat to their quarters."

"If you do anything that I deem not in our best interest, you will not be leaving this castle."

"Understood," Zane said as Faelin released him from her grip. "But trust me, I am not deceiving you."

Vallaria knitted her brows and stared at Zane. Why did people always say "trust me" when it was clear that someone already did not. She placed her hand on Faelin's arm. "We are already in, and the castle is relatively quiet. Let's see where he takes us."

The elf cast her green gaze on Vallaria. "He might take us to our deaths."

"Do we have any other choice?"

Inhaling deeply, she sheathed her knife and looked back at Zane. "Cross us, mercenary, and I will kill you before the rope is slipped around my neck."

Zane extended a hand to Faelin. "Your intent was clear the first time, and I have no doubt you would certainly make good on your word. Shall we proceed in good faith?"

Faelin scowled and brushed by him.

Zane glanced at Vallaria and shrugged, dropping his hand back to his side.

He led them into another vacant courtyard.

The sky had darkened as night fell and a flat black canvas hung above the castle. A layer of snow covered the grass and a cross work of footprints were scattered across its white surface.

Zane noticed her concerned look.

"It's a small training ground for one-on-one combat. It's why I wanted to come this way. Our footprints will not be noticed."

Vallaria nodded and followed him, feeling a little less exposed in the shadows of the cypress trees as they crept to a small window at the far end of the castle wall.

"You're serious," Vallaria whispered, looking at the window that was slightly ajar. "You want us to crawl in, and what, tiptoe through the guards' quarters?"

"This is the bathroom," he said and pointed to the drainpipe on the other side of the window. "We are not going through; we're going over."

The pipe traveled thirty or so feet up the side of the wall and was anchored into the stone by thick metal bands that would make efficient hand and footholds. Near the top was a catwalk, a small iron walkway leading from one tower to the next. The side of the castle they were on was most likely nowhere near the throne room or the queen's chambers, so she assumed crossing to the other side would put them closer.

After a few choice words directed at Zane, Faelin scaled the drainpipe skillfully to the top.

"Your friend has a unique skillset," Zane commented as he watched her slither her way to the top.

If you only knew, Vallaria thought as he stepped up to the drainpipe and followed her up the wall.

The snow had softened again, and large flakes drifted aimlessly down to the ground as she reached up, grabbed the first metal bracket, and heaved herself onto the pipe. She was halfway to the top when one of the brackets securing the drainpipe snapped. The pipe shuddered causing her left hand to lose its grip. As she struggled to find a hand or toe hold, the damaged bracket fell and hit the stone foundation of the castle. A metallic ring shattered the quiet night, and within seconds a light spread out across the fallen snow.

"Whose there?" yelled a voice as the squeak of the window opening reached her ears.

Another voice joined in. 'What did you hear?"

"I don't know."

The light moved around, and Vallaria hoped they wouldn't look up and see her dangling precariously over their heads. She was far enough up that their torch light may not reach her, but the ice moon still lay low in the sky.

Her arm ached and her grip weakened, and her fingers were numb from the cold.

Don't let go.

Vallaria closed her eyes and bit her lip as she clung desperately to the metal band. The sharp edge cut into her flesh, and warm blood seeped from the gash and ran down her hand.

"Look it's a metal bracket. Must have fallen from the pipe."

The other guard grunted. "I'm going back to my ale. It's been a day."

A grinding squeak and a click was all Vallaria needed to hear before she threw herself around and grasped the pipe with her other hand. She shoved the toe of her boot into a crack in the castle wall and rested her head on the cold metal as she tried to slow her breathing.

"That was too close," Faelin said as she helped Zane haul Vallaria over the catwalk's railing.

She winced as Faelin looked at her cut hand. "I'm fine," she said, wrapping the strip of cloth her friend handed her around it.

They walked toward the other side of the catwalk, and Vallaria stopped to gaze over the kingdom. From this vantage point she had a broad view of the city below, but its sounds were muffled, and other than the occasional clop of a horse's hoof or a shout echoing from the street, the city lay quiet. Lamp lights dotted the streets, their orange glow casting wavering shadows on the dark silhouettes of buildings far below. Under the dominant presence of the dark queen's castle, the city felt small, as if it cowered in fear.

In the distance, torchlights moved as royal guards patrolled the perimeter. Further out, past the city gate at the outer edges of the realm, there was nothing but an inky blackness.

In the dim light of the waning ice moon, Ravenia looked every bit the dark kingdom.

61

FAELIN

Once inside the castle, Faelin's acute senses peaked.

Through the night's heaviness, she heard the normal activity humming inside the castle's walls. The skittering of mice, footfalls echoing through the shadows as guards patrolled hallways, and the low murmur of voices leaching out through closed doors. The castle was not yet asleep, but it was winding down.

The bells of the citadel rang out another hour.

Faelin counted the bongs—*eleven*.

At this time of night, most of the staff would be in their chambers or have already left the castle for their homes in the outlying villages. Only the guards on night duty would be walking the castle's corridors. If Zane could get them to the secret passages he claimed ran through many of the inner walls, maybe their presence would go unnoticed.

But if not.

She gripped the hilt of her sword.

Long shadows stretched down the hallways, dancing as they met the torchlight from the burning sconces attached to the walls. Faelin stepped into the darkness, her back pressed tight against the cold stone as she let Zane take the lead.

"We need to be two floors down," he whispered. "The throne room is located in the northernmost part of that wing."

Faelin tilted her head and frowned. "And this will be where the queen is?"

Shadows covered Zane's face, but she sensed him nodding. "Yes."

"How can you be so sure? The hour is late. What if she has already retired?"

"I have spent many a year in the service of the dark queen. She rarely sleeps, and when she does, it is late into the night. The throne room is the most likely place to find her at this hour."

An uneasiness gripped Faelin. His words were honest, but it was the way he said it that indicated he knew much more about the queen than a hired hand should. He claimed to have no stake in the kingdom's business, and while he certainly had a reason to want to exact revenge, mercenaries were opportunistic, and she couldn't trust him not to turn against them if an opportunity he deemed more enticing presented itself.

"The closest entrance to the secret passage on this floor is in the nursery. This way," he said and led them around a corner and down a dark hallway. Just as they reached the nursery door, the castle was suddenly filled with excited voices and commotion.

Zane gripped the hilt of his sword and placed his finger to his lips in recognition of the sounds echoing closer to their position. "There is too much ruckus. The royal guards must have been alerted to intruders in the castle."

Faelin pulled her sword. "We must take a stand here. Try to slow them down."

Zane pointed to Vallaria. "You want the queen, now is your only chance. Go through this door and look for the rocking horse. To the left is a tall bookcase. There's a small key under the big red book. It will unlock the bookcase so you can swing it open and enter the passageway behind it."

Vallaria looked at Faelin and then down the corridor, where footsteps echoed closer.

"Go!" Faelin hissed. "Take back what is yours."

Right after Vallaria slipped behind the nursery door, a handful of guards rounded the corner, coming face-to-face with two individuals who had no business being inside the castle walls.

Zane's sword flashed as he attacked the first guard, catching him by surprise. Two more, their mouths open in shock, looked quizzically at Zane before raising their swords in defense.

Faelin halted the downward thrust of a guard's sword as Zane fought the other two. She didn't have time to dissect the look on the men's face when they'd first seen Zane, but it seemed to be one of recognition mixed with surprise.

Her blade sang as it swiped through the air, deftly clashing with the other sword. She pushed the guard back against the stone wall and brought her knee up to his groin. In a howl of pain, he dropped his sword and doubled over. With one quick move she knocked him unconscious with the butt of her sword. Another group of guards hurried around the corner. The influx of men was larger this time, and she and Zane had nowhere to run. If they crossed the threshold into the nursery, the guards would surely find Vallaria.

They were trapped.

Another upswing caught a young guard off-balance, sending him teetering backward into another. Both fell to the floor. As she engaged a third, she saw Zane from the corner of her eye. He was about ten paces away. He moved steadfast on his feet, his sword arcing with precision as he twisted and turned, throwing guards off-balance with his agility. Two guards hesitated to raise their sword against the mercenary, confusion shadowing their features, but when Zane lunged, they reacted in kind.

Glancing back toward the nursery door, Faelin focused her hearing, hoping only silence would greet her, but a faint heartbeat reached her ears. Vallaria was still inside. She felt the tip of the sword at her neck before she saw it. The guard who held it was a grizzled old man barely able to hold the weight of the steel. She could have taken him with one swipe, but he'd bested her because she'd been distracted.

Why had Vallaria not done as she'd been told?

The familiar indignation at Vallaria's obstinance flared as another sword pointed to her ribcage and a third at her heart.

Faelin let go of her weapon, and it fell to the cold stone floor with a resounding clang.

"Surrender the sword or I'll have my men kill the girl." Tagar stepped from the shadows. His eye twitched as he stared at Zane, who'd stopped the assault but still held his weapon aloft.

Pushed to her knees, Faelin watched as the royal commander and Zane scowled at each other. One of the guards holding her pressed a small blade into her neck.

"Be a good boy, and drop the weapon," Tagar said.

Surrounded by seven guards and faced with Faelin's death, Zane laid his sword on the ground and raised his hands in defeat.

Tagar stepped up to Zane and punched him in the stomach. He doubled over clutching his abdomen.

"That's for not dying in the Valley of Souls," Tagar's husky voice echoed back to Faelin. "Although I must say I admire your resilience." The royal commander looked back at Faelin and sighed. "Where's the brunette?"

"Dead," Zane said, his voice a little more than a gasp.

Tagar grinned as he grabbed him by the hair and pulled back his head. "Why don't I believe you?"

Zane responded by spitting in Tagar's face, which garnered him another blow to the gut. This time the mercenary fell to his knees. Saliva hung from his mouth as he toppled forward onto all fours. He spit on the floor, inhaled deeply, then with a determination Faelin respected, he sat back on his haunches and smirked at the commander.

"Believe me or not, Tagar, I don't really care. Either way you are still a pile of cow dung."

The commander's boot came up fast, the toe catching Zane under the jaw. Zane's head snapped back and hit the stone wall. Blood dripped from his mouth, and he slumped to the floor, dazed.

Faelin struggled against the guards holding her. "Stop it. You'll kill him!"

The commander's cool gray eyes turned toward her as his upper lip curled into a snarl. "That was always the plan."

Tagar looked at his men mulling around. "You bunch, search the castle for the other girl, and you two take this one to the dungeon while I have a nice chat with Prince Zander."

Prince Zander. Faelin stared at the semi-conscious mercenary as the guards pulled her to her feet and pushed her down the hallway.

Queen Cereli's son?

While the guards dragged her away, one thought filled her mind: that lying piece of filth had led them into a trap.

62

VALLARIA

A musty smell saturated the nursery as Vallaria stepped over the threshold and closed the door behind her. The room was steeped in shadows, the only light coming from the ice moon's glow that breached the window on the far side.

Dust covered every surface in thick unyielding layers. Toys, long abandoned by their owners, filled painted boxes, were discarded on shelves, or tossed on the two small beds, their once frilly white covers now a dingy gray.

She stepped farther into the room, and dust clouds plumed around her boots.

The rocking horse sat silent in the corner next to the window; carved from wood, its mane twisted in a multitude of colors down its head and neck. Braided reins looped from a gold bit in its mouth up to the horn of a leather saddle strapped on its back.

The bookcase, which hid the secret passageway, towered over the room. Children's books were piled high, wooden building blocks littered the shelves, and a small tea set complete with two cups, a silver serving tray, and teapot sat on a small table in front.

Everything in this nursery was old. A snapshot of the past when a very different queen walked these halls. This must have been her bedchamber. The room where she played and dreamt.

A knot formed in Vallaria's stomach as she surveyed the childish items in front of her. Two stuffed bears sat perched on the two beds, two small pairs of white shoes sat neatly on the floor by the door. Two overstuffed chairs, two small writing desks, two dress racks, but only one held a small white dress embellished with delicate embroidery at the collar line.

Vallaria felt dizzy as she stared at the dress.

She'd seen that dress before.

In the dream. On her reflection in the meadow.

She grasped the back of a large wingback sitting in the middle of the nursery as a wave of nausea swirled in her stomach and a light-headedness caused her to feel faint.

Memories poked through the darkness, hazy and unclear. A dark-haired girl laughing as she ran around the nursery as if being chased. Squeals of delight filled the air and then she turned back and spoke to someone that Vallaria's memory wouldn't or couldn't manifest.

Was it Evinna? Her father?

She tried to make the memory clearer, but it faded, disappearing into the recesses of her mind before she could grasp onto the edges.

A light tapping attracted her attention. Another raven, smaller than the one perched at the top of the castle, pecked at the glass of the window. Moments later a second flew to the windowsill and began pecking at the glass. Relentless, they continued to strike the windowpane. The glass cracked and a swell of panic washed over her.

But it didn't belong to her.

Instead, she felt the fear of the others, those who existed long ago.

The whispers rattled her brain.

Ravens of Ravenia. No, it can't be.

She ran for the bookcase, her hands searching around the large red book. Her fingers fumbled to find the key.

The clamor filled the empty room as the birds' pecking intensified.

She had to get out of here. The chorus of voices in her mind intensified. They were afraid and wanted to get away from the ravens.

Her fingers touched cold metal, and she grabbed at the iron key. Searching the side of the yellow bookcase, its painted cracked and peeling, she found the keyhole tucked behind the wood trim. With shaking hands, she opened the lock and pulled the bookcase out. Without looking back, she hurried into the dark passageway and slammed the bookcase shut behind her deadening the sound of the incessant tapping.

The voices stilled.

Thankfully, a dull light filtered through the ceiling slats, giving her enough light to make her way through.

"Follow it to the end," Zane had directed. "There you will find a small winding staircase—take it down two levels. At the bottom follow the right passageway to the first fork, go left, and find the wooden door with the steel hinges. This will exit into the main library behind a painting."

Following his directions, she made her way to the staircase and hurried down to the floor below. When she turned the last corner, her eyes caught a glint of light. It was a torch flame, held by a royal guard standing at the bottom.

"Come all the way down," said a second guard, raising a crossbow in her direction. It was Faelin's weapon.

They've been captured.

Her heart sank as she raised her hands and descended the remaining stairs.

"Well, look here. It's the brunette the commander's looking for."

The other guard cracked a smile. "Smart of him to think to look in the secret passageways."

The one holding the crossbow nudged his companion. "That's why the commander has the queen's ear."

"And her bed," the other added.

They laughed as one pulled her from the bottom step. "I'll take that," he said, yanking her sword from its sheath. "You won't be needing it where you're goin'." He looked at his companion. "Do you think we'll get a reward for her capture? I could use a little jingle in my pocket to keep me in whores and ale."

They chuckled again and pushed her down the passageway.

As they walked in the gloom, Vallaria felt the cold sting of the ice crystal in her pocket. Moments later the cold magic surged through her veins. She raised her hand slowly and slipped the small dagger from her tunic pocket. The idiots had been too cocky to think of checking her for other weapons. *Or too dumb.*

Immediately after the blade was in her hand, a sizzling frost crept down its shaft. With a twirling slash she caught the man with the crossbow in the jugular. On reflex, he pulled the trigger, but Vallaria had already flattened herself against the wall and the bolt sailed by. The metal tip chipped the stone as it hit the wall and fell to the floor.

The guard grabbed his throat as the blood pumped from the wound. Red rivers of death spilled through his fingers and glided down his chest, soaking the front of his uniform in a gory stain. Still in shock from the violent assault on his friend, the other man fumbled to pull his sword from its scabbard. Her eyes locked on him, and his face crumpled in fear as she raised a hand toward him. A cold blast of air pulsed outward like a monstrous wave on the sea. The white searing cloud engulfed his outstretched arm as he raised it instinctively, attempting to protect himself. Eyes widened and his mouth formed into an oval. A second later, a primal scream shuddering from his throat as the man watched his arm turn black and shatter at the elbow. Frozen pieces of meat fell to the floor.

The royal guard wailed. "You damned witch," he screamed at her, cradling the stump of his arm with the other.

Vallaria stepped forward and plunged the knife up through his gullet, turning his wail into a gurgle as blood filled his mouth. Dark eyes glassed over and rolled back into his head as he fell to the floor dead.

A chorus of whispers rose around her, slithering sounds with no audible words. The cold magic exploded in her blood, surged through her pores, and coated the walls, the floor, and their dead bodies in a thin layer of frost.

Icicles appeared on the tips of her fingers and hung from the ceiling as a hollow ice wind began to swirl around her. The whispers became louder, and Vallaria felt as if she were drowning from within. Sucked into a vortex of cold magic.

She was losing control.

Desperate to make it stop she forced a shaking hand into her pocket and grasped the ice crystal. With every ounce of her being, she fought the magic's natural impulse and threw the crystal down the passageway. It clattered on the stones and slid across the slippery frost-covered surface. As it did, the waves of cold magic subsided and the chill dissipated.

Collapsing to the floor, Vallaria sunk into the exhaustion that followed. Her arms and legs felt too heavy to be hers. The pounding of her heart in her chest ached. A warm trickle of blood dripped from her nose and her eyes fluttered closed.

She's not ready, she heard as she drifted into oblivion.

How long she lay unconscious in the passageway she didn't know, but as her eyes fluttered open, Vallaria assumed she'd already wasted too much time. She pushed herself from the floor, and a wave of dizziness washed over her. The angry sting of bile rose in her gullet. She leaned her hand against the wall and bent over, retching the contents of her stomach onto the floor.

Wide dead eyes stared up at her as she wiped her mouth with the back of her hand. The guards' blood that pooled on the floor had turned black, and their skin had paled to a mottled blue.

With a trembling hand, she reached down and picked up her mother's sword and then the crossbow. Faelin would be glad to have this back.

On legs that wobbled too much for her liking, she walked slowly down the passageway in the direction of the library, stopping as she reached the ice crystal that lay silent on the floor. She picked it up and held it flat in her palm.

Mortals are not meant to wield magic. Faelin's warning sounded in her head.

A tear slipped down Vallaria's cheek as frustration and anger battled within. The mage magic was the only weapon she had worthy enough to challenge the queen's dark magic, and once again, she couldn't control it.

She shoved the ice crystal into her pocket.

Destiny was cruel. It was a burden and a curse.

Leaning against the wall, she closed her eyes. Did she attempt the overthrow anyway? Take her chances and accept the outcome would most likely be bleak?

A tingle on her inner wrist drew her attention, and she glanced down at the raven wings marring her skin. Ravenia blood ran through her veins. At one time that was enough.

She straightened. Whatever fate had in store this night, Vallaria Ravenia would not succumb to fear or cower in a corner. She'd waited a long time for a future, and an identity she could call her own, and now it lay in front of her for the taking.

Vallaria didn't need to have faith in her gods or the ancient magic. She needed to have faith in herself. Her destiny was her own and she would claim it or die trying, but whatever the outcome she would do it on her terms.

With a renewed determination, she slipped from the passageway and into the library, closing the portrait behind her. She glanced at the gilt-framed picture. It was an oil canvas of a man, bearded, bright blue eyes, a crown on his head. He was dressed in black leather and on his finger a large gold signet ring emblazoned with the letter R.

He sat upon a wood and leather chair with a tall back, and above his left shoulder, perched on the chair's top rail, was a large raven.

A shiver crept up Vallaria's spine.

It couldn't be her father. Queen Cereli would never let a portrait of King Ryguard hang in the castle, but the man looked too much like Vallaria for it not to be a relative. Maybe it was King Torrsen, her father's brother and Cereli's late husband.

A shiver crept up her skin as she stared into the portrait's bright blue eyes, and she quickly turned and hurried across the library. She pressed her ear to the door and heard echoes of voices, but they were distant, muffled. She reached for the doorknob and opened the door slowly, peering out.

The castle was quiet. *Too quiet.*

The double doors of the throne room loomed at the other end of the hall, and she was surprised to find it unguarded. Especially since the royal guard had been alerted to their presence.

Was it a trap? Had Zane or Faelin revealed her location and her destination?

Or maybe the queen wasn't there. Maybe she'd fled the castle altogether.

Her heart thumped. What if this was all for naught?

No. The signs were there. The prophecy had come to pass. Her destiny was meant to intersect with the dark queen's. Tonight, she would look into the eyes of the woman who'd had her parents murdered. Who'd stolen her childhood and her birthright. Tonight, under the glow of the ice moon, one of them would die.

Cautiously, she placed a hand on the door jamb and opened it wider.

The voices resonating through the castle had gotten farther away. As she stepped out into the empty hallway, a shiver of anticipation bristled over her skin.

The time had come for her to take back the throne of Ravenia.

It was now or never.

She gripped the hilt of her sword and set her shoulders. Her jaw tensed and her lips set into a firm line.

I am the rightful heir of Ravenia. I will prevail.

Faint murmurs drifted through her head as the ancient ones made their presence known.

The ice crystal burned cold in her pocket as the familiar surge of frost magic chilled her blood.

Kingdom of man, she heard one voice say. *Treachery* said another. The whispers reached a crescendo in her mind as she neared the throne room doors.

She could feel the mages' vengeance, their betrayal, their anger, swirl inside of her as if it were her own.

For Ravenia, she said as she gripped the handle to the throne room door.

We are with you, the mages said. *Take your revenge. Then take ours. Death to the kings. Death to all. The last mage has risen.*

63

CERELI

Commotion shook the halls of the castle as royal guards ran to their posts. Cereli sat clutching the arms of her throne. Fate had come for her.

The throne room door burst open and in came three royal guards, followed by a very flustered Yelin Barro.

The guards rushed to the dais, circling her.

"There are intruders inside the castle walls, Your Highness. We must get you to safety," Yelin said. His hands shook as he glanced at her and then to the guards. "These men will take you to the keep."

Cereli's eyes narrowed as she stared at the fidgeting little man in front of her who wouldn't meet her gaze. "There is something else. What is it?"

Yelin shuffled his slippered feet and stammered, "One of the intruders is your son, Prince Zander."

Queen Cereli's pulse quickened. So he wasn't dead. Tagar Garrate had failed in his task.

"He's been captured. Tagar has him locked in the dungeons along with the girl."

"Girl?"

"One of the two who accompanied him to the Valley of Souls, blonde, green eyes."

Not the princess of Ravenia then. "There was a brunette as well, no?"

Yelin nodded. "I believe Tagar mentioned a brunette with blue eyes accompanied them as well. And a small boy. An orphaned street rat. But neither of them have been seen in the castle." Yelin hesitated before his dark brown eyes locked on hers. "I thought there was an accident in the Valley of Souls and your son was killed."

Her blood boiled at the accusatory look she was receiving. He had no right to question her. She was the queen of Ravenia, and he would not question her authority.

"Get out," she said, her voice simmering with rage.

"But, my queen," he sputtered, his face reddening.

"I said GET OUT!" The power in her voice startled both Yelin and the guards. He turned and scurried from the throne room, but the look he gave her over his shoulder told her all she needed to know. His usefulness had come to an end. Once she dealt with the crisis at hand, she would cut his throat and send him back to the Gold Coast Empire where he belonged.

She waved off the guards. "Leave me. Clear the royal guards from this wing. Tell Tagar to keep searching the castle, but if there is any indication the other girl is here do not engage. Understood?"

The guards nodded dutifully.

"And you," she said, pointing at the young guard. "Fetch Amedus from his cage and bring him to me."

The young male swallowed and went pale. "As you wish, my queen."

The guards exited the room, and she leaned back on her throne.

It was rare that she let anyone else handle Amedus but her, but these were extenuating circumstances. The princess would come for her, she would come here, and Cereli wanted to make it as easy as possible. There would be no capture by the guards, no torture, no public hanging. No, she was nothing more than a mere girl. Young and inexperienced, and Cereli would deal with her directly.

If the prophecy was to come to pass this night, it would be under Cereli's terms. *Let's see if the young princess's sword and misguided determination can contend with my dark magic.*

"Come Serifine Ravenia and do your worst."

She thought about Zander sitting in the cold dark dungeon and smiled. He was nothing if not resilient. He'd outwitted Tagar somehow and aligned himself with the princess.

Did he know who she was?

Cereli doubted it. If the princess was smart, she would've kept her identity a secret until the very end. And if Zander did know, well could she blame him for trying to exact revenge?

The irony.

Her fate may not yet be sealed, but to have the path of her son cross that of the one person who could bring down her kingdom—

She thought of Zander's father. What would her life have been like had he lived? Her eyes filled with harsh tears.

You would have been happy.

The empire had taken everything from her, and in turn, she'd taken everything from Ravenia. Now it may all be taken from her again. Betrayal and revenge, such a vicious circle, creating a tightly woven web of deceit and loss where none ever truly won.

She sighed, reached down, and picked up the Dagger of Crusade, which lay on the seat beside her. The red liquid in the pommel twinkled under the torchlight. Her eyes tracked across the beautifully crafted pommel and the thin blade. She'd searched for years for one of the Myths of Three and now that she'd found one it was useless. Time was not on her side. Using the dagger to find the other Myths or to create a formidable army was not a simple overnight spell or trick. The mages had made the artifacts as a symbol of peace, not war. Cereli had deceived herself into thinking any of the artifacts would give her an immediate solution or a way to beat the prophecy. She'd been desperate, and her desperation had given her false hope.

But she still had the dark magic, and she was still the dark queen.

The harbinger's foretelling had come to pass, but it was not finite. She could still control the outcome of fate, bend it in her favor. Why would a young naïve woman be a grave threat to her?

She reached up and touched the crown on her head. She'd fought and clawed her way to power, to this throne, and she would be damned if it slipped from her grasp.

The throne room door creaked as it swung open, and she jumped, forgetting she had sent the young guard to retrieve her pet.

The guard came in, shuffling under the weight of the huge snake wrapped around his shoulders. When he reached the dais, he bent to a knee and lifted the snake from around his neck, placing it on the floor.

"Thank you," Cereli said waving the guard away. She bent down and caressed the snake's dark brown scales as it slithered up the steps to wrap itself around her leg. "Hello, my sweet boy."

Amedus flicked out his forked tongue and hissed. His dark brown scales shimmered as he gazed at her with bright green eyes.

Emperor Silvalas had gifted her the snake on her twentieth birthday. He'd been so small then, only twelve inches long. Now at nine feet he was not only her pet but her protector. Amedus was known to her people as a sand serpent and the representative of her family house. Adult sand serpents were predatory in nature but were highly intelligent, making them trainable. Their long muscular bodies were covered in a scaly hide that was almost impossible to penetrate. And they excreted a type of oil that allowed them to tunnel at high speeds through the sand. The military members of House Sand Serpent had used this snake in battles for centuries, breeding and training them to be an effective weapon in the emperor's army.

The snake hissed again and coiled up, raising his upper torso so he could look her in the eye. His tongue flicked outward as she stroked his head.

"We are going to have a visitor, my dear boy, and you will have to be on your best behavior."

The snake hissed again.

"Until I tell you not to be," she whispered.

"Come, Amedus," she said, sitting back onto her throne. "Let us wait for our guest."

Obediently the snake slipped over the arm and coiled itself around the top half of the throne. He placed his head gently on her shoulder and flicked his tongue in contentment.

The dark magic in her staff swirled—a warning.

Someone was coming. Someone the dark magic did not recognize.

It was time.

Time to end the Ravenia bloodline once and for all.

64

ZANDER

The sting of cold water hitting his skin made him gasp and he shook his head as the last of the dredges of unconsciousness left him. Zander swore as he looked up to see who threw the water in his face.

His eyes met the culprit, and he groaned and swore again. "Please tell me Tagar did not send you down here to torture me." He stared at the man in front of him, dressed head to toe in white satin, the cuffs and neck of his tunic embroidered with gold thread. "You're not much of a threat, Yelin."

"Shhh," the queen's advisor said. "I'm here of my own accord."

"Oh, this should be good," Zander said. "Why?"

"I thought you'd been killed."

Zander shrugged, shifting in the chair he was bound to. "I got lucky. Or Tagar got unlucky."

"No, I mean they said there was an accident and you died."

"Of course they did. Apparently the plot to relieve me of my life did not include you then?"

"Pray to the gods, no. You and I may not always see eye to eye,

Prince Zander, but I would not wish death upon you. Certainly not by betrayal."

Zander strained at the binds tying his hands behind his back. "Then why are you here if not to exact some type of punishment. To gloat?"

Yelin scurried around to the back of his chair, and Zander felt a tug on his binds and the distinctive sound of a knife sawing at rope. "Yelin, what are you doing?"

"Freeing you, Your Highness."

The rope gave way, and Zander brought his hands forward, rubbing at the chafed skin on his wrists. Yelin hurried back to the front and cut his legs free. Zander stood and brushed his dark hair off his face, narrowing his eyes to assess the small man in front of him.

Yelin's thick mustache twitched, and his eyes darted back to the open cell door. "You must get out of the castle immediately," he said, handing Zander the knife. "Your blonde companion is three cells down."

"Faelin," he said.

"If that is her name. I attempted to free her myself, but after I got one of her legs free she kicked me, called me a flurry of names I will not repeat, and spit on my tunic." He pointed to the spot to the left of his chest that still showed the damp stain.

"She is a feisty one," Zander said.

"It's probably best you release her."

"Is there anyone else down here?"

"No one that hasn't been imprisoned for months."

Zander prayed to the gods that Vallaria was safe, hidden in the passageways between the walls. "Yelin, why are you doing this?"

The man lowered his head and clasped his hands in front of him. "I have served your mother for many years. Providing a service that some may find distasteful at times. We can debate the necessity of my actions at a later time, but ensuring the balance of power, never allowing one kingdom to gain too much sway over another, has always been the end goal."

Zander raised a brow. "And to think I thought your end goal was always to fulfill Yelin Barro's personal agenda."

The black mustache twitched. "I will always watch out for my own neck, Your Highness, as I prefer my head to remain attached."

Nodding, Zander said, "You were saying . . . The reason you are helping me escape . . ."

"Yes, yes. Your mother has the Dagger of Crusade, but this is not what concerns me." Yelin lowered his voice and leaned in. "The darkness inside her has been slowly draining her for years, but she could always control it and keep it at bay by feeding it, but I'm afraid she can't anymore. It's consuming her and driving her mad." His voice cracked. "She killed young Barden."

"The castle messenger. Whatever for?"

"She thought he was a spy. She didn't recognize him. The dark magic muddles the queen's mind, and slowly your mother is disappearing. It won't be long before the darkness is all that's left."

He thought about his strong and insightful mother—cunning, calculated, dominate yes, but mad? "Is that why she ordered my death?"

"I'm sorry to say, but no. I believe I may have instigated that one." Yelin took a step back as Zander tilted his head and glared at the man. "Inadvertently of course." He flashed Zander a big, white-toothed smile. "Not my intention."

Zander took a step forward. "What did you do?"

The man withered under his stare. "I may have insinuated that you were aligning with Darrius Mensah to take the throne of Ravenia." His smile weakened and he took another step back. "I only expected her to banish you back to the Gold Coast. It is where you belong."

Zander lifted a hand to his head and ran his fingers through his dark curls. "I am sure there is a very good explanation as to why you would put such an asinine thought into my mother's head, but unfortunately I do not have the time for your long-winded excuses.

He pushed Yelin out of the way and strode out of the cell. "I'll deal with you later," he called over his shoulder.

Yelin hurried after him. "Zander, I freed you because only you can bring Ravenia and the Gold Coast back to heel. There is a war coming, and it will destroy all that we know if it is not prevented."

Zander whirled around and glowered at his mother's advisor. "You give me too much credit. I am a prince who has hidden in the shadows for years. I can't stop anything."

The man took a few steps toward Zander. "For centuries there have been prophecies, stories, whispers of heroes, saviors, and men who are destined to do great things. Reluctant or not, you are one of them. Magic is returning to this world, but it is dark and twisted, thirsty for revenge. Only those with the blood of the ancestral races can stop it. Only they have the power to unleash peace on this world."

"What are you speaking of?"

"It was the one secret I have held close to my chest for years. Never disclosed to your mother or anyone. You are more powerful than you think, Zander Damask. And when the time is right your destiny will be revealed. Whatever business you have here, make haste. You must return to the Gold Coast."

"I don't understand."

"You will in due time." Footsteps reverberated overhead. "I must go. Your mother has ordered all the guards to the far side of the castle."

"Why?"

"I don't know. Like I said, your mother's mind is no longer her own. You will find your weapons in the cell next to Fawlanes," he called as he ran to the stairs.

"Her name is Fae-*lin*," Zander yelled after him, but Yelin had already disappeared, his footsteps getting fainter as he ascended the dungeon steps to the upper floor.

The man was infuriating, but he'd given Zander a second chance, and this time he wasn't going to waste it. He had a score to settle with both the royal commander and his mother.

Quickly he turned and ran through the dungeon to the far cell. Pulling the key from the wall, he searched for Faelin, but the interior was shrouded in shadows.

He turned the key, opened the door, and stepped inside. Without warning, Faelin jumped from the gloom and punched him in the gut. He grunted and stepped back, ducking under the fist that swung toward his head.

"What did you do that for?" he asked, glaring at her as she stood there, hands on her hips, lips pulled into a tight line.

Her green eyes flashed. "Prince Zander Damask. Should I bow? I'm not sure of the protocol when in the presence of a lying treacherous fiend."

Zander sighed. "Maybe I should have told you who I was, but it's never been something I announce. Outside these walls, no one knows my true identity. I have been Zane the mercenary from the Gold Coast for so long, I don't know how to be anyone else."

Faelin frowned. "You have every right to live the life you want, but what doesn't make any sense is why your own mother would want you dead? I assume she knows who you truly are?"

He chuckled at the absurdity. "Yes, but sometimes I think she wishes she didn't."

"Why is that?"

Zander leaned against the bars of the cell and hung his head. "It's a long story and one I'm not sure I understand myself. Let's say my relationship with my mother has been complicated for a very long time. Anyway, enough about me. You are free to do whatever it is you and Vallaria wanted into the castle to do."

"Where is she?" Faelin asked. "Do you know?"

He shook his head. "Yelin said only you and I had been spotted. I assume she is still hiding in the passageways."

"Yelin?"

"The guy you kicked."

A perfectly sculpted brow raised. "I may have taken my ire at you out on him. "He's an easy target." Faelin shrugged. "Let's find Vallaria. But first we need to find some weapons."

Zander walked to the next cell and opened the door. He reached in, pulled out their swords, and handed Faelin hers. "I have other business to take care of first. The guards have been sent to the far side of the castle. I assume my mother is up to something, so you will have to be careful. I will direct you as best as I can to the throne room, but I can't go with you."

Green eyes locked on his. "I know the way."

"You do?"

She nodded. "We all have secrets. Promise me yours won't get us killed. If you betray me or Vallaria, I will find you and make sure you never betray anyone ever again."

"I took your warning to heart the last time we were in these dungeons and you threatened my life."

"I just wanted to be clear."

Zander couldn't hold back the grin that formed on his lips. There was never a question as to where you stood with Faelin. It was refreshing. Even knowing he was a prince didn't change how she treated him.

Hopefully Vallaria feels the same way.

"I assume your business is with the royal commander?"

He nodded and turned to walk away. "This time I can't let it go."

He and the commander had been clashing for years. The closer Tagar got to his mother, the more vitriol he pushed Zander's way. Frankly, Zander was surprised Tagar didn't kill him instantly in the Valley of Souls.

"Well, then, let's go." Faelin sheathed her sword and stood waiting.

"Why would you come with me?"

"Because I don't trust you. You are either telling me the truth and are going to find the commander and kill him, or all this is part of a larger ruse to flush out Vallaria. If it's the latter, I will not help you find her."

He was worried about Vallaria and really wanted Faelin to go find her. To help her. Whatever the reason she wanted to confront his mother, she should not do it alone. Her magic was strong but so was his mother's and he wasn't confident that Vallaria would come out on top. "Do you think she's all right?" His chest constricted as he asked the question.

Faelin's green eyes softened. "I have known Vallaria for a very long time. She may not be worldly, but she is tough and smart and determined. If she is not here in the dungeons with us and not with the commander, then sooner or later she will find the queen. When Vallaria sets her mind to something, she always follows through."

Zander didn't know if Faelin's assessment of her friend made him feel any better, but he couldn't worry about Vallaria right now. He had to deal with Tagar and trust that the gods would protect her. If this night didn't end with his own death, then Zander would find a way back to her.

His chest constricted. If anything happened to Vallaria, he wasn't sure what he would do.

65

FAELIN

Zander and Faelin almost made it to the commander's quarters at the far end of the undercroft without incident.

The poor stable boy found himself face-to-face with Prince Zander when he exited the back of the kitchen. He tried to run, and then scream, but Zander had him by the neck before the first sound emerged.

"Where is the royal guard commander?" he asked.

The young boy's eyes widened, and although he shook his head, his eyes drifted to the tall wooden door at the end of the hall. "Thank you," Zander said before knocking the boy unconscious and stuffing him in the cook's potato box.

"Did you really need to brutalize the boy?" Faelin asked.

"Iain is Tagar's nephew and just as much of an ass. The kid would sell his mother if it meant lining his pockets with gold. He was sent to Ravenia after his father died. His mother said he needed a male figure in his life, but what he got was the back of Tagar's hand when he screwed up. The kid's been molded into a smaller version of the commander. Stuffing him in a potato box is less than what the little shit deserves."

They stood in front of the tall door, Zander's ear pressed to the wood. He closed his eyes and held his breath. "Someone's in there." He tried the knob. "It's unlocked."

"Lead the way," Faelin said, but he shook his head and released the handle. "This is something I must do alone."

Her brow scrunched as she stared at the mercenary, trying to decide whether she should leave him alone with the commander.

"I know I haven't given you any reason to trust me, but I promise my intent is not to cross you." He glanced back at the closed door. "I have a long overdue score to settle."

Faelin's intuition told her he was being truthful. "I'll be right here."

He grasped the door handle again, sword in his opposite hand. "Do not enter, no matter what you hear on the other side. Promise me. This is not your fight."

She reluctantly agreed to stay outside and guard the door.

After Zander entered the commander's quarters and closed the door behind him, Faelin pressed her back against the cold stone of the undercroft's walls allowing the chill to penetrate the leather of her jacket. She welcomed the shiver that accompanied it, thankful for the jolt it gave to her weary muscles and even wearier mind.

Voices drifted through the door, and she pressed her ear against the wood to listen. Tagar's gruff voice was distinguishable from Zander's as he swore and said, "How the hell did you escape this time? You're like a goddamn rat."

"Coming from you I'll take that as a compliment."

The commander grunted and a scraping noise filled the room, like a chair being pushed across a stone floor. "What is it that you want, Zander? My men are on the other side of the castle, you know where the exits are. Why don't you leave? Run back to the Gold Coast. Maybe Darrius Mensah will employ you to clean the shit off his horses' hooves."

"Now why would I want to do that?" There was a challenge in Zander's voice.

"Because you aren't much good for anything else."

"I'm still alive. So that makes me good at surviving."

"Only because I promised your mother I wouldn't kill you." There was a goading tone to the commander's voice as he spoke.

"She's going to be angry with you, Tagar, once she sees I'm alive. No one disobeys the dark queen."

A laugh reached Faelin's ears. "Let me worry about your mother. But you, Zander, you surprise me. I didn't think you had the guts or the strength to go against the nightmares haunting the Valley of Souls. Perhaps I misjudged you."

"Or perhaps your perception of me was never correct to begin with. You do have a way of judging people without truly knowing them."

"I'm usually never wrong."

"That's a matter of opinion."

Faelin dropped her eye to the keyhole. She could see the commander standing behind his desk. Dressed in black pants and a black shirt open to the navel, there was a casual calm to him even with Zander standing in his chambers. His official tunic hung on the hook behind him, but he had not removed his sword.

Tagar walked around his desk toward Zander, his hand lowering to grasp the hilt of his sword. "Do you know why your mother wanted you dead?"

"Because she's a selfish, heartless, unholy bitch?"

A deep laugh bellowed from the commander's throat. "Well yes, but there is much more to it than that. You are the last piece of her past she wants to excise. Your mother is desperate to be rid of everything that tied her to the self she no longer is, nor wants to be. Much of her actions in life were necessary to unchain her from those who wished to keep her contained. Now with the Dagger of Crusade, she will be able to find the remaining Myths of Three and then Queen Cereli will be reborn into a ruler worthy of leading the kingdoms of Exile and the Gold Coast Empire into a new future. One ruler, one kingdom."

"So my mother looks at me as a burden of the past." Zander chuckled and shifted his stance. "Or a threat to her rule?"

The commander's eye's widened as he cocked his head and pursed his lips. "You've been speaking to Yelin Barro."

Zander shrugged. "My mother's aspirations are not a secret. She wants to rule with impunity and not be questioned. Every move she makes is calculated, part of a larger strategy to tighten her grasp on power."

Tagar emitted a gravely chuckle. "You are not a threat, boy. Just an inconvenient reminder of a man who ruined her life. Your mother was right to want to rid herself of you. You are nothing but trouble." The commander leaned back on his desk, a smug look contouring his face. "I never understood what your mother saw in your father. She was young, naïve, and easily manipulated, so he took advantage. Their union was blasphemy in the eyes of the gods and her punishment was your conception. A weak and insolent son who would rather run off and liberate the women of this great continent than stay in the kingdom and perform his royal duties and support his queen."

The tone in Zander's voice tightened. "You know nothing about my father."

"More than you." The commander's lips curled into a sneer and his eyes flashed with spite. "Who is it that you consider your father, Zander? The fat pig of a merchant who married your mother months before you were born and then abused her for years? Or maybe King Torrsen, the good and kind king who murdered his own brother in cold blood?"

Faelin could see Zander's body stiffen as she continued to watch the two men through the keyhole.

Tagar threw his head back and laughed. "Oh my, you still believe King Ryguard went mad and killed his wife and daughter, don't you? Well, since you have come into my quarters uninvited, let me enlighten you on your family history."

The commander crossed his arms and leaned toward Zander.

"Your mother's greatest tactical move and the one that secured her place in the kingdoms of men as an equal was convincing Torrsen that his brother was mad and not fit to rule. Torrsen killed Ryguard thinking it was best for the kingdom, but it was Cereli who ordered the execution of his wife Evinna, and daughter Serifine. Ryguard was dead before my blade cut them down."

Faelin's hand tightened around the door handle, trying to squash the longing to avenge Evinna's death by running into the room and ramming her sword through the commander's gut.

His gravelly voice continued. "For too long the elves had interfered in the affairs of man. The races weren't meant to be joined, but the elves thought themselves superior, always taking whatever they desired. I was more than happy to cleanse this world of an elf and her half-breed child."

Faelin could see only the back of Zander, but she could tell by the set of his shoulders and the tension in the muscles of his neck that he too was fighting the instinct to attack the commander.

"Your father was no better. He sullied your mother. Used some type of magic to make her think she was in love with him so he could coax her into his bed and infect her with his seed. The emperor was right to execute him. Even his own people didn't try to stop it for he'd betrayed them as well." The commander's face contoured into a mask of hate. "His death was better than the one he deserved."

Faelin pulled back from the keyhole as the words Tagar spoke resonated. The memory of that day resurfaced, snatching the breath from her throat and seizing her heart in a vice-like grip. Leaning against the cold stone of the wall, she tried to remain calm, but the damp, stagnant air caught in the undercroft only made the pressure in her chest more restrictive.

It all made sense now. All the suspicions she'd had of Zander. The familiarity she felt when he flicked his wrist before raising his sword or tilted his head before he spoke. His dark gaze had the same way of penetrating your very soul and making you feel small and uncomfortable. She'd thought it was because he'd been hiding something, but she'd ignored the obvious signs to the truth. Prince Zander Damask was his father's son and held many of Baladril's traits.

How could it be?

Her mind whirled as it replayed the events of the elf commander's execution. Helpless to intervene she stood in the crowd surrounded by guards as Emperor Silvalas read the charges against Baladril and invoked his sentence. She'd struggled against the strong arms of the emperor's men in vain. As her memory, clouded by the passing years, came into focus, she once again stared into Baladril's calm amethyst gaze. Only this time the memory was different, and she realized it wasn't her who held his stare.

Laboring for breath Faelin closed her eyes as the memory expanded and she found herself turning to scan the crowd behind her.

Who had held the commander's gaze in his final moments?

She was much younger then and not filled with hate, but the large dark eyes, silky black hair, and full lips were unmistakable. *Cereli Damask!* The woman who'd accused Baladril of raping her and sealed his fate with the executioner.

At the time, Faelin had been so filled with rage she could not see what was right in front of her. But now as she revisited that moment she saw the pain in Cereli's face as she stood behind her brother Moricio, peering in horror over his shoulder. When Cereli stepped out from behind him, tears streamed down her face, and she reached one hand toward the gallows while the other cradled her stomach.

In her mind, Faelin heard the words she refused to hear at the time—*I love you.*

Moricio had immediately pushed her back, his stern gaze silencing her before anyone in the crowd took notice. Faelin's gaze shifted back to Baladril as the sword severed his neck and a blood-curdling scream pierced the air.

Faelin's fingers dug into the cold stone of the undercroft's walls.

All these years she thought the scream came from her, but it had been Cereli. She'd blocked out part of the day's event, refusing to see the truth. Instead, she punished herself for years thinking her actions were responsible for his death. Baladril was a sentient, same as Thaneil. It's what made them exceptional warriors. His magic was powerful, and if unleashed he could have easily saved himself, but he chose to die, to keep peace between the elven kingdom and the empire.

No. He chose to confess to a crime he did not commit to protect the woman he loved and the child she carried and—

And you.

The emperor should have killed Faelin as well. It did not matter her lack of involvement in the alleged crime. She'd entered the city with the commander on a diplomatic mission to mend the fractures between the elven kingdom and the empire. Any infraction by one could have easily been conveyed to the other. But instead, the emperor had ordered Faelin's immediate expulsion from the Golden City with a warning never to return.

Elevated voices drew Faelin's attention back to the present. The clash of metal rang out behind the closed door. She gripped the hilt of her sword.

Do not enter, no matter what you hear on the other side. Promise me. Zander's words echoed through her mind as her hand hovered over the door handle.

"Damn it," she hissed and stepped away.

Prince Zander Damask was Baladril's son, identical in many ways, stubborn, independent, proud. She hoped that he wouldn't get himself killed. She didn't need his death on her conscience as well.

66

ZANDER

The commander flashed a cold smile as he spoke of Zander's father.

Who Tagar was describing confused him. His mother had always told him his birth father was a military captain lost on the high seas shortly before Zander was born.

"Your father was no better. He sullied your mother, used magic, we had to execute him." The high-pitched buzz in Zander's ears muffled most of Tagar's words. His mind twisted, searching to understand what the commander claimed.

That your real father was an elf.

The room began to spin. Heat rose in his face and his heart palpitated. He found it difficult to hold his sword as his hands turned clammy. The commander's mouth still moved, but Zander could no longer hear his words above the roar in his ears.

He's lying, playing games. Nothing he says is the truth. He's doing what Tagar does best, manipulate. Trying to push you off kilter. Don't listen to him.

Zander took a deep breath, inhaling through his nose and

releasing it out his mouth. As he did, the pulsing in his head diminished and the commander's words once again became clear.

"She needs a real man to rule by her side."

Swallowing the lump forming in his throat, Zander calmed his shaking hands. He refused to play the commander's game or be deceived by his lies. Locking eyes with the man, he said, "And I suppose that man is you, Tagar?"

The royal guard commander's eye twitched as a sly smile formed on his lips. "I have been at your mother's side for years. I have also warmed her bed when your stepfather could not. I know what she needs, what she desires."

Zander chuckled. "Then you should know the one thing she doesn't need is a man. To her men are a means to an end. Don't inflate your position in my mother's eyes, Commander. If you wish to keep your head, I suggest you take heed and don't ever become irrelevant. You are nothing special, no matter what hangs between your legs."

Muscles tensed in Tagar's jaw, as the smile slipped. The man's gray eyes burned.

Zander had hit a nerve.

Tagar Garrate was a man of questionable honor, willing to follow unscrupulous orders or bend the law if necessary. Although unwaveringly loyal to Queen Cereli, he was still a military man at heart, proud of his strength and capabilities and would not take kindly to anyone thinking he was the queen's plaything.

Zander's cheek twitched as he tried to stop the smile that quivered on his lips. "Once my mother gets what she wants from you, your throat will be slit, and another will warm her bed."

The commander lunged. A furious roar exploded from his mouth, sending spittle flying. His sword carved through the prince's flesh as the blade swept by his forearm. Zander cursed and quickly sidestepped a second attack. He'd been too focused on taunting Tagar, and he'd let his guard down, forgetting how quick the commander was in a fight.

Retaliating, Zander's blade sang as steel connected with steel. He pushed Tagar back and carved an arc in the air, the sharp edge of the blade barely missing the commander's face.

The two men battled back and forth. Sweat and blood covered their exposed skin and each labored under the exertion. Zander, void of proper nourishment, felt his limbs become heavy. Each parry, lunge, and pivot took a toll on his tired and aching muscles.

A glint flicked in the commander's eye as he noticed his fatigue. "Do you need a rest, boy?"

The tang of blood filled Zander's mouth and he spat onto the floor. "No, old man. I'm good."

Tagar flipped the sword in his hand in one movement and thrust upward. The square pommel caught Zander in the bridge of the nose. Tears filled his eyes, and a warm fluid fill his nasal passage. He staggered backward as pain exploded in his head and blood dripped from his nose. Blackness threatened his sight, and in a blind response he swiped at where Tagar last stood.

An arrogant laugh burst from the commander. "So pathetic," he spat. "A pampered prince who plays with a sword and thinks he's a warrior. You're weak and an embarrassment to our people. Certainly not worthy of carrying the name of one of the greatest houses in the Gold Coast."

Filled with hatred for the man, Zander yelled, "Screw you, Tagar, you jealous shit. You will never be one of us no matter how many times you bed the queen or do the emperor's dirty work. Your skin is too white, your muscles are too big, and your brain and balls too small."

Tagar Garrate's face exploded with crimson. "I'm going to kill you, and then I am going to gut you and hang your limp, lifeless body from the bell tower for all the kingdom to see. You are nothing but a dirty little half-breed who will never be more than a sad excuse for a man."

Half-breed. The insult rang in Zander's ears. "The only one gutted here today will be you," he countered. With a burst of energy fueled by a deep-seated rage and a primal instinct to survive, Zander fought the commander with every ounce of determination and strength he had left.

Muscles screamed when he lifted the steel of his sword and swung it low toward the commander's leg as he ducked under his advance. The edge caught Tagar above the boot top. ripping through his trousers and slicing through layers of flesh.

Commander Garrate bellowed as he was thrown off-balance. With a renewed purpose, Zander went on the offense, hacking and slashing in succession. Tagar did all he could to block his attacks.

Zander circled the man, sword at the ready. The commander growled, lunged, and swung his sword downward, but Zander anticipated his move, pivoted, and carved his weapon through the air. The sharp edge sliced through the flesh, sinew, and bone of the commander's wrist.

With a gut-wrenching howl, Tagar staggered backward. His sword clattered to the stone floor, his hand still clutching the hilt. Grasping his severed limb, he fell to his knees. Blood pumped from the appendage as he stared in utter disbelief at the bloody stump.

With a slow and steady gait, Zander walked to where the commander crouched and lifted his sweat-drenched head, using the tip of his sword. He stared into the man's gray eyes, expecting to see fear, hear him plead for his life, but the commander's face was like stone. Zander wanted to feel pity for him, but all he felt was empty.

Coughing up blood, the commander gasped, "Do it. Unless you're too much of a coward."

Without a word Zander shoved the tip of his blade through Tagar's throat. Those distinctive gray eyes widened in surprise and his mouth opened in a silent scream. Swollen and discolored, his tongue flicked from his mouth as the fingers on his uninjured hand clawed at the blade embedded in his neck.

With a vicious yank, Zander pulled it out.

The commander's eyes hazed, and a gurgling noise escaped from his lips as blood bubbled from the sucking wound in his throat. He continued to slap at the gash in his neck, and for a second, Zander mused if maybe the commander might be too stubborn to die.

The pallor of his skin changed, and his hand went limp and fell to his side. His gray eyes rolled back in his head until all Zander could see were two globes of white. His head lolled to the side, and as he began to teeter, Zander raised his boot and kicked him in the shoulder. The commander fell to the cold stone floor, *dead*.

Using the back of his hand, Zander wiped the blood from his nostrils and upper lip. He stood for a moment, staring into Tagar's glassy, unseeing eyes. He felt no remorse. The empty void inside only grew.

With a shaking hand, he drew the blade back and forth across the dead man's pants, cleaning it of blood and then sheathing it.

Zander took a deep cleansing breath.

Justice had been served.

"Now to find mother," he whispered. As he walked away from the body, he kicked the commander's severed hand across the room.

THE LOOK ON FAELIN'S FACE WHEN ZANDER EXITED TAGAR'S QUARTERS TOLD him all he needed to know—he looked as bad as he felt.

His nose ached at the bridge and his left eye had begun to swell. His forearm, which he bandaged with a strip of his shirt, stung where Tagar's blade had found its mark.

"He's dead." He thought the words would be more difficult to say, but he found himself relieved instead.

Her green eyes scanned his wounds. "Sit and rest."

Zander shook his head. "There is no time. Vallaria needs our assistance. The queen knows she is here and plans on facing her one-on-one. That is why she sent the royal guards to the far side of the castle."

"You won't be any good to Vallaria if you can't stand on your own two feet." She pushed him toward the wall and without much resistance he slid down it and sat heavily on the floor.

"Most of them are superficial, contusions and small cuts. Your nose may be broken, but it's the cut on your forearm that worries me. It's deep and could get infected. I don't have any suave or gill weed but—"

Through half-closed eyes he looked at the young woman whose expression seemed pained. "But what?"

"I can heal you if you let me."

Zander heard the uneasiness in her voice. There was something different about the way Faelin looked at him. Her green eyes were softer, yet they flitted back and forth from his as if she was uncomfortable looking him in the eyes for too long. "What are you not saying?"

Faelin shifted and let go of his wounded arm. "I heard what Tagar said."

"Which par?" He grimaced as he tried to sit up.

"The part about your father."

Zander's head began to throb, and he pulled up one leg so he could rest his forehead against his knee. "Don't believe anything that man spews. It's all lies. He knows nothing of my father."

Her next words rattled him.

"But I do."

He raised his head and ran a hand across the back of his neck. "How old are you, twenty? Twenty-one? I don't know who you think my father is, but he died shortly before I was born, so I doubt you ever knew him."

"His name was Baladril," she said. "I don't know what story Queen Cereli concocted, but Tagar was right. Your father was one of the greatest commanders to ever lead the elven army."

A rush of blood pounded in his ears, and he scrambled awkwardly to his feet. Glaring at Faelin, he grabbed her arm and yanked her forward until her face was inches from his. "I don't know who you are or what game you are playing, but my father was not an elf."

He released Faelin and placed his head in both hands, trying to calm the pounding.

"I know this is hard to hear and maybe even harder to accept, but your mother lied to you. I knew your father. At one time he was my commander."

Zander dropped his hands and raised his head and quickly jumped back away from the stranger that now stood in front of him. Where a blonde-haired, green-eyed female had stood seconds before, now stood a young woman with smooth unblemished skin, a tinge of pink at the cheeks. Her silver hair was swept up at both sides falling in a mane of silky strands halfway down her back. But it was the lilac eyes and pointed ears that had the adrenaline coursing through his body.

Swearing, he yelled, "Stay away from me."

"You don't need to be afraid."

He jabbed a finger in her direction. "You are a damn elf."

Faelin nodded as she morphed back into the green-eyed girl he was used to seeing. "Yes. And I did know your father. I am fifteen hundred years old."

"Curses," he said as he moved slowly down the hall away from her. A flurry of emotions overwhelmed his senses and his mind blurred. Without thinking he began to run.

"Zander!" Faelin yelled after him, but he didn't stop, didn't turn back. At first he ran blindly, not caring where his legs took him, but suddenly he found himself running toward the throne room.

For his entire life he had stood on the outside looking in. Always wondering why his mother didn't love him and what he'd done to deserve her judgment.

Is this why? Was my father this Baladril? Am I truly a half-breed?

So many questions and the only one that had the answers was his mother.

As his boots pounded on the stone floor, he clenched his fists. He would make her talk, make her tell him the truth. To tell him it was all a lie, that his father was a military captain for the Gold Coast Empire, and he really was Prince Zander Damask of House Sand Serpent.

But his sinking stomach told him the answers he seeks may not be the ones he wanted to hear. For somewhere in the deepest part of his heart, he knew Tagar, and the elf were right.

67
VALLARIA

S ilence greeted her as she entered the throne room. Shadows
stretched across the stone floor and flames danced in the
torches attached to the walls. Long-lost memories were
nudged from the recesses of her mind by the familiarity of the room.

Her parents used to let her play here.

But it was a happier place then, full of life and warmth. Now the
throne room, like the castle and kingdom, was cold, lonely, and
wrapped in despair.

"Welcome."

A voice echoed from the shadows at the far end. Vallaria gripped
her mother's sword tighter. "Who's there?"

A torch sparked and the flame grew, lighting up the dais upon
which Queen Cereli sat on a black metal throne. She looked the same
as the day in the square when Vallaria had watched her execute
Alagarn—black gown, tall crown, ebony kohl lining her dark eyes.

Vallaria swallowed and took a step toward the front of the throne
room. The queen didn't say another word, just watched as Vallaria
approached.

Halfway to the dais Vallaria felt the familiar surge as the cold magic awakened. Relieved, she straightened her shoulders and continued toward the queen.

The flames in the torches lining the walls flickered as the whispers rose in her mind. *Betrayal, revenge, betrayal, revenge,* the mages chanted.

Stop! Vallaria thought and the voices went silent. Her fingertips sizzled with cold, sending a sheen of frost down the hilt of her sword. The closer she came to the queen, the more her magic took notice.

Blue eyes flashed as Vallaria assessed her opponent. The dark queen sat quietly on her throne, the staff at her side, the smoke in its glass ball swirling languidly. At Cereli's feet, coiled as if ready to strike, lay a large snake. Its bright green eyes followed Vallaria's movement, and it hissed with each step she took.

"Hush, Amedus. Don't be rude to our guest." Queen Cereli stroked the snake's head with a finger heavily laden with silver-banded rings that coiled from fingertip to knuckles.

As Vallaria reached the bottom of the dais, the queen smiled. It wasn't warm or welcoming—it was malevolent and cold. Black eyes void of emotion stared directly into Vallaria's.

"I have been awaiting your arrival, Princess Serifine. It seems our paths were destined to cross."

Vallaria stiffened. *How does she know who I am?*

"Dark magic has a way of unlocking secrets that others desperately try to conceal," she said as if reading Vallaria's thoughts. "Although I admit at first I did not know it was you the harbinger spoke of."

Prophecy? Harbinger? Did she know of the last mage prophecy as well?

"Those who cross the barriers between here and the after world are so unclear in their forewarnings." Cereli waved her hand. "Anyway, it doesn't matter. Fate has finally brought us together."

"And now fate will be your undoing." Vallaria's voice was low and calm as the ice crystal burned cold in her pocket, giving her the confidence to confront the dark queen.

"Maybe so, but fate like revenge, always finds its way back to where it began. Your mother found that out the hard way."

Vallaria tensed, willing the cold power surging under her skin to calm. "My mother did not deserve to die. She was a good person."

"Your mother was a fool," she spat. "I never understood why she would give it up all for your father."

"Because she loved him." Vallaria clenched her fist as her ice blue eyes sparked with fury.

The queen scoffed. "Love is weakness, my dear." Her eyes drifted to Amedus. "It will make you blind, vulnerable, and eventually it will be your downfall. Just as it was Evinna's. In the end, love changed her for the worse. A mother's love is unmatched. Evinna was willing to sacrifice the life of an innocent child to preserve yours." The dark queen tilted her head and frowned. "I wonder whose child died in your stead?"

The queen's words hit Vallaria like a blacksmith's hammer. She felt sick. Someone's little girl had died that day so Vallaria could live.

"You don't know do you?" The queen laughed and leaned back in her throne. "I suppose I shouldn't gloat. I only realized it myself recently."

Lifting her chin, Vallaria eyed the queen. What was she talking about?

Cereli waved her bejeweled hand. "I suppose it makes no difference now. It was such a long time ago. Anyway, the history of the Ravenia family is so complicated, I wouldn't expect you to be aware of all your ancestor's dirty secrets."

The queen eyed Vallaria. "The kingdom used to be Gold Coast territory. Did you know that? But after your ancestor stole the land, centuries of kings have sat on this throne blessed by the mages of old to hold the north. Your grandfather waged war on a small kingdom between Ravenia and Mistenvale because he wanted to extend his territory. The poor kingdom didn't stand a chance against the

Ravenia army; they were a bunch of artisans and bakers ruled by a self-appointment king." Cereli tapped a finger to her temple. "Silly place, can't even remember its name."

She glared at Vallaria. "For generations your family continued to betray those around them for their own self-interest. Your father broke his oath with the emperor and betrayed me in turn. Your mother did unspeakable things to ensure the throne for another generation. Your Uncle Torrsen overthrew your father and killed him in cold blood. But I stopped the callous trajectory of your family when I poisoned your uncle and took the throne for myself."

"You were never Ravenia's true queen. The kingdom was never rightfully yours," Vallaria said. "A stolen crown, a stolen throne, does not make you a ruler. It makes you a murderer and a thief."

The queen laughed. "And you think you would be a just ruler. That your blood entitles you to this throne. What do you know about being a queen? The world of man is cruel and unyielding and not for the weak of heart or mind. What chance would a young woman like you have of surviving it?"

"You know nothing about me," Vallaria said.

"I know it is best you leave this kingdom right now and go back to wherever you came from," she said in a dismissive voice.

"The throne is mine."

The smoke swirling in the queen's staff became erratic. Cereli leaned forward and raised a dark brow. "Then come and take it."

Before Vallaria could decide what to do, the throne room doors flung open and a breathless Zane ran in, followed moments later by Faelin. The elf's green eyes cast Vallaria a stern look and she shook her blonde head, lifting an index finger to her lips as she indicated the mercenary.

Zane walked toward the dais, and as he glanced quickly in Vallaria's direction the corner of his mouth lifted. A sense of relief flooded through her as she realized how happy she was to see him. Although he looked dreadful. The skin under his left eye was swollen and discolored. Dried blood covered the bridge of his nose, and a red bloom marred the white cloth wrapped around his arm.

The queen frowned as the two uninvited quests entered her domain. "Well, I see Tagar didn't do his job." She directed her statement toward Zane.

"That won't be a problem from now on," he responded.

The queen raised her brow.

"He's dead."

For a moment the queen's stoic demeanor seemed to slip, as if the news of her royal commander's demise upset her. But just as quickly she regained her composure and spat at Zane. "What do you want?"

He glared at her. "You owe me answers."

The queen tilted her head and drummed her fingers on the throne's arm. "And what answers do you think I can give?"

Before he could answer Vallaria blurted out, "Let's start with why you ordered your royal commander to kill Zane in the Valley of Souls."

The queen straightened in her seat and leaned forward. "Zane?" she said as a slow smile crept over her lips. "You two are acquainted?"

"Yes," Vallaria replied, pointing at him. "I went with your mercenary on the quest to retrieve the Dagger of Crusade."

"My mercenary?" Her laugh was low and full of mockery as she turned her gaze on Zane. "I never understood: why a mercenary? It's so beneath your stature."

"What do you care? You sent me to my death. You betrayed me!" he snapped.

Queen Cereli's eyes narrowed as she shifted her attention back to Vallaria. "And who, may I ask, does my mercenary think you are?"

Vallaria felt her face flush as she lowered her gaze, before quickly glancing at Zane."

"As I thought. It seems you two have misled each other." Cereli stood, bringing herself up to her full height. Her black eyes flitted back and forth between them. Amedus hissed as he glided off the throne. Beady green eyes fixed on Vallaria as his pink tongue flicked in and out.

"Quiet my pet," the queen said, stroking its head. "It seems I need to make proper introductions." Cereli stepped off the dais and the snake slithered back to coil like a serpent king on the seat of the throne.

"Vallaria, this is my son, Prince Zander Damask, master of House Sand Serpent of the Gold Coast Empire and heir to the throne of the Holy City of Kasmire. Well, once he marries the Princess Aerilla, that is."

Vallaria's mouth slackened, and she blinked rapidly, trying to force back the stinging tears that threatened to spill from her eyes.

Prince? Getting married?

Her stomach lurched as she watched the queen smirk and turn to Zane.

"And this young lady, Zander, is Princess Serifine Ravenia. Back from the dead to claim her family's throne."

The queen's dark eyes flitted to the back of the room where Faelin stood. "You, I don't know."

A peculiar smile spread over the elf's face. "Since we are being truthful and making proper introductions, my name is Faelin, daughter to King Elvander and future queen of the elven kingdom."

The queen's brow raised, and she crossed her arms. Her gaze flicked quickly to Zane and then back to the elf. "Oh my. This is rather interesting."

A band tightened around Vallaria's chest, and she found it difficult to take a breath. Turning her head, she glanced at Zane. He met her gaze, but he no longer looked at her the same way. His eyes were cold, haunted, accusing.

Vallaria's heart broke.

Zane was no longer an ally; he was the enemy.

68

ZANDER

Vallaria had lied to him. She was no witch from across the sea; she was heir to the throne of Ravenia.

But you lied too.

He shook his head, ridding himself of the voice of reason.

That was different; he didn't hide his identity to further his own agenda.

Didn't you?

Not in order to steal a throne!

Vallaria had played him for a fool. Used him to get to his mother. How long had she known who he really was?

He glanced back at Faelin. Had they both known? Did they orchestra all of this so he could help them gain access to the castle?

Was he nothing more than a pawn? Were they the same as every other woman in his life? His mother who tossed him aside when he was a young boy. The girls who claimed to love him because he was a prince but only desired stature within the empire. They all drove him to hide his identity, to keep people at a distance, to distrust and hide his heart. And now Vallaria . . ."

A tightness gripped his stomach as logic battled with his frayed emotions. Was her omission really any different than his? For years he'd kept people at arm's length. Outside the castle, he lived another life. There'd been no reason to tell Vallaria who he truly was, so why expect any different from her?

We all have secrets.

He glanced in Vallaria's direction. Streaks of blood marred her pale skin and strands of her black hair fell randomly from her thick braid. Her knuckles were white from gripping her sword and her black tunic was streaked with dirt and dust. Those ice blue eyes—

Zander's breath hitched and he tore his gaze away, looking back to his mother. Her eyes assessed him. He recognized that look. She was scheming. Trying to find the best way to control the situation to divide them, turn them against one another.

Finally, she broke the unrelenting silence that hung over the throne room.

"You're in love with her, aren't you, Zander?"

Her voice mocked him, but he didn't dare break her gaze for fear he would look at Vallaria, and she would see what his mother said was true.

"You have no idea what love is, Mother."

"I loved your father."

"Did you? Is that why you never told me the truth? Never spoke his name?"

The queen's face darkened, and she bit her lower lip.

"Tell me his name, Mother." Zander stepped closer to the dais.

Cereli tilted up her chin and inhaled. "It doesn't matter."

"No, not to you. You are a heartless bitch who never cared about anyone unless they could help you achieve what you desired."

Amedus hissed and rose as if getting ready to strike. Zander looked at the snake with disgust. *Mother's beloved pet.* The reptile was large, deadly, and very protective of the queen—the perfect intimidation tactic.

From the corner of his eye, he saw Vallaria raise her sword and he willed her to lower it.

The queen's dark eyes flicked in Vallaria's direction, but she didn't acknowledge the perceived threat. "Don't push me, Zander. You don't know of what you speak."

"Then tell me. Who is my real father?"

A dark shadow passed over the queen's features as she struggled to stay composed. He was testing her patience, but he couldn't stop. He had to know if Tagar and Faelin were telling him the truth. He had to hear it from her.

"Tell me!" His voice cracked with emotion.

"His name was Baladril," the queen said. "He served as the high commander of the elven army. He was killed, executed, for loving me."

For a moment Zander saw a brief glimpse of the mother he used to know. A woman with a heart who knew how to love. But as if she realized he was watching, it quickly disappeared behind the wall of darkness she now used as a shield.

"But that was a long time ago and it no longer matters," she continued.

Cold.

"Where does your allegiance lie, Zander?" The queen jerked a finger in Vallaria's direction. "With a Ravenia orphan? Or maybe with the elves who turned their back on the empire and betrayed us?"

He couldn't listen to this anymore. "I no longer swear a covenant to you or any who sit on the throne of Ravenia. I am a citizen of the Gold Coast Empire and that is the only allegiance I acknowledge."

"You're a fool, Zander. Our customs and culture wouldn't have looked kindly on your birth if they'd known who your father truly was. Your conception was an abomination, and they would have drowned you in the central fountain if my secret had been revealed. If I were anyone else but a daughter of the most powerful House in the city, things may have been different, for us both. I will not apologize for saving your life. Hate me if you must, but I did what I needed to for both of us to survive. Maybe someday you will understand."

"I understand you all too well," he spat. "You tried to kill me as you have many others who got in your way."

His mother flexed her fingers, and her face, normally a mask of cool reserve, began to slip. "Being a queen is not for the weak. It requires sacrifice,"

"Just not yours." Zander's dark eyes burned. "You are no true queen, and I will die before I see you keep a throne tainted with the blood you spilled."

Years of frustration poured out of him as he challenged her. He, like Vallaria, was an orphan; the only difference was his mother still lived. But he no longer felt the need to try and please her. The deception had all become too much. The woman who stood before him was nothing more than a stranger, a broken shadow of the mother he once knew. He would no longer bend to her demands.

"As you wish, my son," she said, gripping her staff and pulling it toward her. The fire in the sconces flickered and a hollow wind whistled in the rafters. The smoke in the glass ball swirled as the dark magic awakened. "You can die with the Ravenia scum and the elven royal."

Suddenly, Faelin was at his side, sword raised, but he couldn't force himself to look at her. Not now that she'd been proven right.

"I hope antagonizing your mother wasn't the wrong thing to do," she whispered.

His mother raised her arms and began to chant in a tongue he did not recognize. Black tears pooled in her dark eyes, falling like oil down her cheeks. A network of dark spider veins appeared at her temples and extended down her neck. "It probably wasn't one of my better ideas," he responded.

Queen Cereli's irises flashed red and gold as she continued to chant louder. Within seconds, a funnel of black smoke swirled up from the stone floor. One to her left and another to her right. As the funnels grew larger and the smoke thicker, others began to appear, swirling in different places around them.

Like a spark in a fireplace, red eyes appeared in the smoke.

Shadow demons, Zander thought as the smoke funnel shifted and took the shape of the under-demon. Like much of his knowledge of the creatures of the night, King Torrsen had spoken of these too. But only of their existence and appearance, nothing more.

He glanced quickly at Vallaria who stood some ten feet away. Her feet were planted shoulder-width apart, and she held her sword to her right side, tip pointed toward the floor. A thin layer of frost covered the blade, and Zander silently thanked the gods.

No matter how good a swordsman he was or what tricks the elf may have up her sleeve, there was no way they could hope to defeat his mother without the powers Vallaria possessed. Wherever they came from.

"I call upon the shadows of the dark realm beyond. Hear me and do my bidding. Destroy those two." Queen Cereli pointed at him and Faelin, and with a growl that sounded like it came from directly under their feet, the half dozen or so shadow demons turned and glided toward them.

"Do you have any magic that can stop them?" he asked Faelin. It was worth a shot. Even if he cared little for their race—

Your race.

He clenched his teeth, pushing the thought from his mind.

"I'm a healer and a shield. Neither of which is appropriate in this type of situation."

"A shield?" he asked.

"I can use the elements to create an invisible barrier around myself. It's a protection gift."

He changed his stance as the demons closed in on them. "Only around yourself?"

Faelin raised her sword. "I can project it, but it saps my magic and my energy. I'm sure you would rather have my strength and skill set in this moment. Anyway, it only works well in combination with a sentient like your father."

Another unearthly growl interrupted their conversation and Zander was glad for it.

The shadow demons drew closer, and he heard his mother say to Vallaria, "You, I will gladly take care of myself."

Zander slashed at a demon, but his blade passed right through. Without the density of flesh and bone to stop his momentum he stumbled forward. The demon's form shifted and a smokey hand complete with razor-sharp claws ripped through his shirt and carved four bloody lines into his chest. A searing pain exploded on his skin, and he cursed, stumbling backward before the demon could strike again.

Faelin swung her sword at another, but she too had little success. These creatures couldn't be killed by steel alone. Only magic could defeat magic. They continued to thrust and jab while sidestepping the demons as they formed mouths full of sharp teeth or smoke-swirling limbs complete with claws. Zander caught movement in his peripheral vision. Turning he saw a long winding column of smoke stretching toward Vallaria. It flowed from his mother's staff. Vallaria didn't see it coming because she was busy evading Amedus, who Cereli had sent as a distraction.

Before he could yell a warning the long rope of smoke wrapped around Vallaria's neck like a noose. Realizing the prey was caught in his master's trap, Amedus slid back into the shadows.

My mother is toying with Vallaria. Like a cat with a mouse.

More shadow demons advanced, and Zander was drawn back into an unwinnable fight. From the corner of his eye, he watched as Vallaria struggled with the smoke tightening around her neck. Her face reddened and she grasped at the coil, but her hands slipped through the translucent object as if it weren't there.

"Do you still think you can take the throne?" his mother asked, her voice mocking the young woman who she held in her grasp. "Your death will come at my hand. Destiny will favor me this night."

Vallaria fell to her knees as his mother jerked on the staff, pulling at the smoke noose. Her dark kohl-rimmed eyes found Zander. "Death to the Ravenia bloodline. Long live the true queen."

More shadow demons closed in around him. He swiped at one,

pushing it back until it could reform and slither forward. This was an endless pursuit. The shadow demons did not swarm him and Faelin. They came one at a time. His mother had planned it this way.

Like Amedus they too were a distraction.

She wants me to watch Vallaria die.

Helpless to do anything else, he continued to slash at the shadow demons. A primal scream erupted from his mouth as his burning muscles lifted his sword again. But this time when he attacked he swung his blade in an arc, watching as it cut through four of them.

As the steel passed through their forms, the demons were violently pushed back. But the smoke shifted and reformed, and Zander noticed that when the demons advanced again, they stopped, like an invisible wall now existed between them and the shadow demons.

"Go," Faelin said, indicating the struggling Vallaria. "I won't be able to hold them off for long."

Even though he heard the words, his legs wouldn't move.

"I know you love her, Zander, but if you're happy to watch her die, then do nothing." The elf's voice wavered, and her hands shook as a shimmering sweat appeared on her forehead.

Before he could react, Amedus struck. He'd slithered from the shadows and hit Faelin in the stomach with his muscular tail. She sailed through the air and crashed into a metal statue headfirst. The elf slumped at its base, eyes closed. A trickle of red slipped down her face from her hairline, but the slight rise and fall of her chest indicated she was still alive.

Suddenly an unholy chill saturated the throne room. The air he drew into his lungs stung as it touched his warm insides. His breath came out in puffs of white, and ice crystals formed on the metal of his sword. The steel became so frigid it burned the skin of his hands, and he dropped the weapon in pain.

Blisters appeared on his palm and fingers where the skin had adhered to the metal. Cradling his hand, he looked to where Vallaria stood. Her sword crackled with ice as she held it aloft. It dripped icicles onto the floor, but it was the darkness shadowing her blue eyes that reminded Zander of someone else.

The shadow demons shrieked and disappeared into the floor. He turned toward his mother, who stood facing Vallaria twenty feet away. She reeked of power. Not just from the dark magic dimming her eyes, but also in the way she held her head, the regal slope of her shoulders, and that staff—

When he was a little boy he'd discovered the staff behind the throne and picked it up. He'd run around the dais pretending to be a great magician, using his magic to fell dragons and foe.

His mother had been furious when she'd walked into the throne room and caught him. It was the last time Zander had ever touched the staff, and as he aged, he'd begun to understand the dark power it controlled and why the queen protected it so.

Because without it she is nothing.

A thunderous crack pierced the air. Turning he saw Vallaria had shoved the tip of her sword into a fracture in the stone floor. Frost began to spread and snow crystals glistened under the firelight as the ice twisted and turned like a meandering river, covering the floor, walls, tables—anything in its path.

From the other side, dark magic swirled around his mother. A smoky haze crept across the floor like that of a mist-covered bog. Her eyes, the color of the midnight sky, locked onto Vallaria. A single black tear slipped down the queen's cheek.

Zander's stomach lurched as he watched the two women. He ran to Faelin, grabbed the unconscious elf, who still lay slumped against the iron statue, and dragged her toward the throne room door. There was nothing more they could do but get out of the way.

The temperature in the room dropped considerably as the two women moved toward one another. Waves of smoke rolled by. He coughed. His fingers were numb with cold, and his eyes stung from the acidic furl of the smoke.

Using the back of his glove, he wiped his eyes and watched the scene unfold before him. Their magic may be different, but the intent was the same. To destroy. He shuddered at the thought, his mind taking him back to the night he lay with Vallaria. She'd been so warm and full of life, but now as the ice magic exploded around her, he knew she mirrored his mother—cold, ruthless, and detached from everything around her.

In a flash of steel, smoke, and ice, the queen and the princess brought all their magic to bear as they battled for supremacy.

Only fate would determine the outcome.

But what Zander knew, his heart heavy with the realization, was that although Vallaria thought differently, in many ways she was much like his mother. A woman driven by power and cursed by ancient magic.

While he watched her stalk toward the queen, two things became certain. He loved Vallaria like he'd never loved another. And if at the end of this night he was still alive, he had to walk away.

From this place *and* from her.

69
VALLARIA

The smoke wrapped its inky warm finger around Vallaria's throat as she watched the snake slither back into the shadows. She tried to pull the offending noose from her neck, but her hands slipped right through.

Where is my magic?

As if they listened, a chorus of voices rose in her mind and the ice crystal swiftly burned cold in her pocket. Mage magic surged through her veins and saturated her blood with a bone-chilling cold. Instantly she sensed the presence of those restless spirits whose only sense of peace lay in their magic being once again born into this world.

Voices rose in unison and fragmented words and sentences drifted through her mind.

Betrayal. Pay for their sins. Revenge. Come home. One of us. Death.

The familiar swell entered her hands and instantly ice formed on her palms, freezing the smoke noose around her neck, and shattering it. She stumbled, gasping for breath.

"NO!" she heard Cereli yell.

Vallaria turned in the direction of the queen's voice, picking up her sword as she stepped forward. The magic flowed down the handle and into the blade, covering it with ice and frost. The metal crackled as she lifted it, driving the tip into a fissure in the floor. When the blade touched the stone the magic expanded, in a wave of frost across its surface. Tentacles of ice crept up walls and over tables. The power of the ancient magic surged through her body and her mind. But this time she felt one with its strength.

It was intoxicating, exhilarating.

She felt invincible.

Breathing in she smiled. The time of her destiny was now.

She could sense Zander's dark eyes upon her, but she didn't care. She'd been a fool to trust him, to fall for him. Prince Zander Damask was very much like his mother. A liar and a user. She could understand him not telling her who he truly was—she hadn't been truthful either—but taking her to bed knowing he was to marry another—

Another betrayal. Whatever was between them had been lost with a few cruel words of truth from the dark queen. Well, Vallaria would have her revenge. She would take back the throne of Ravenia and wage war on any who didn't accept her rule. No one would ever deceive her again. And if they did, the icy hand of revenge would soon find them.

Cold magic pulsed around her, and the mage's voices whispered.

Revenge. Death to the kingdoms of man.

The throne room grew cold as the magic seized the air in its icy grasp.

Her blue eyes locked on Queen Cereli, and she found herself amused by the way the queen's face contorted in disbelief. *You expected an inexperienced and delusional young woman but instead you are faced with someone as powerful as you.*

With a flick of her wrist, and before the queen could react, Vallaria lifted her hand and splayed her fingers. Ropes of frost-covered ice flew across the distance between her and the queen, twisting themselves like tentacles around Cereli's body at a frightening speed, pinning her arms to her side.

The queen screamed, struggling to hold onto her staff.

Shadow demons reappeared and advanced on Vallaria, but with a wave of her hand, she encased their lower halves in ice.

Her powers came easier now.

Cruel laughter filled her head. The mages were pleased.

Kill.

Silence, she thought, sending the whispers back into the recesses of her mind.

Vallaria had begun to understand the frost magic. She could control it better when the voices didn't rise. The magic was triggered by them, but it also became chaotic when they also became unruly. In time she would understand the magic better and she would learn to adapt to its power, and hopefully the magic would become innate.

Vallaria approached, and Queen Cereli looked up, her dark eyes questioning. Her chest heaved and her voice was nothing more than a tortured whisper. "What are you?"

Her ice blue eyes crackled with the mage magic, a strange feeling as if Vallaria's irises were flecked with flakes of frost, but her vision now was so precise. The beginnings of a smile danced on the edges of her lips as she reached where Cereli stood. "You have not heard of the prophecy of the last mage?"

Confusion clouded the dark queen's eyes. "The last mage is nothing more than a story. There is no truth to it."

"So your eyes deceive you?" Vallaria held up her hand and summoned an ice spear from her palm.

The queen struggled against her binds. "It's a curse. The magic we possess. It wasn't meant to be ours. It will consume you. It always takes more than it gives and then wants more. Eventually it will consume your soul and then take your life." A shadow crossed the queen's irises as black tears began to seep down her face. "As it will take mine."

"It will not be the dark magic that takes your life."

"Have mercy," Queen Cereli croaked, coughing up a black oily liquid. "For my son."

Vallaria's stomach clenched at the mention of Zander. He stood at the back of the room but didn't interfere.

"You ask for mercy, but I have none to give," she whispered.

The queen struggled against her binds, but the ice ropes held tight. "Release me," she snarled as her eyes turned into thick black globes. The smoke in the glass ball at the top of the staff swirled. "NOW," she bellowed, in a voice not her own.

For a moment Vallaria paused. The voice coming from Queen Cereli seemed familiar, as if it was tucked away somewhere in the recesses of her mind. Shaking off the uneasiness she stepped back, lifted her sword, and brought it down on the staff in one swift motion. A shower of glass and smoke rained down on the floor, a shriek filled the throne room, and somewhere within the piercing sound Vallaria heard her name. Another wail erupted as the shadow demons writhed, struggling against their ice prisons. Their forms ebbed in and out as they were pulled from this world, and into the one beyond.

Lowering her sword, Vallaria leaned close to Cereli's ear. "Maybe the gods will be more forgiving."

"Maybe, but I won't be," Cereli hissed.

At first it was a burning sensation her lower abdomen, but as Vallaria's brain registered what happened it turned into a searing pain. She gasped and pulled back, dropping her sword. Looking down, she saw blood leaking from the tear in her tunic. Vallaria gaped at the queen, whose hand still gripped the dagger that she must have had hidden in her skirts.

Pressing her hand against her stomach, Vallaria bit her lower lip. How could she have been so stupid? To let Cereli stab her with the damn Dagger of Crusade. Gingerly she lifted her tunic and shirt, grimacing as a stinging pain exploded from the wound. Thankfully, the puncture was not deep. With the ice ropes pinning down the queen's arms, she had no ability to plunge the blade any deeper than the tip.

Clenching her teeth, Vallaria released a small amount of frost onto the wound. The ice hit her skin and she cried out. Pain washed over her torso in agonizing waves. But immediately, the gash stopped bleeding and the searing pain subsided to a dull throb.

A fury roiled in her blood as she glared at the woman standing in front of her. Ripping Faelin's birthday gift from its sheath on her thigh, she held her own dagger aloft and snarled, "This is for my parents, my lost childhood, and the kingdom you stole and then destroyed."

Without another word, she drove the dagger into the queen's gut and twisted it as far to the right as it would go.

Cereli wailed, convulsing as she fell to the floor. The ice binds shattered against the stone.

Blood, the shade of a deep red wine seeped from the wound, but it wasn't enough to kill her. No, Vallaria wanted her to die slowly. She wanted the dark queen to feel her life leaving her body and experience the suffocating fear of knowing she would soon die. "May you burn in the underworld for eternity," Vallaria whispered, staring down at the queen.

Cereli's dark eyes blinked rapidly as the blackness left them. She opened her mouth and gulped in air. Looking broken and defeated, the dark queen managed to pull herself up into a sitting position, her back against the steps of the dais.

Vallaria turned and found Zander at the back of the room. Even though part of his face was hidden in shadow she could see his clenched jaw and the thin line of his pursed lips. Yet he stood unmoving, watching.

Her eyes flitted to Faelin, who sat on the floor rubbing the back of her head. Suddenly, her head tilted as if she heard something, and her green eyes darted toward the window.

The ravens are here. The ravens have returned. Don't let them in.

The whispers raged in Vallaria's head.

Do they know? We can't be seen. Don't tell them. Don't let them in.

And then there was silence, an aching hollow silence.

Moments later a rumble erupted outside, and the thunderous sound of flapping wings echoed though the throne room. Screeches and caws filled the night air. Large black birds appeared at the windows, tapping, tapping. Within seconds the glass broke, and dozens soared into the room, circling, their wings flapping furiously as they dove to peck at the snake slithering across the floor.

A trail of blood followed the wounded reptile as the relentless attack continued.

Amedus hissed. The fangs protruding from his mouth dripped with thick toxic saliva. He lunged at the birds, but there were too many and their beaks too sharp. They penetrated the thick scales, tearing chunks from the snake's body. Thrashing, Amedus flicked his tail into the sky. The tip caught a raven as it flew by, knocking it from the air. Feathers scattered as the bird landed injured on the floor. The snake managed to kill another and injure two more, but the ravens were too numerous, and soon, weakened and bleeding profusely, Amedus lay unmoving on the floor.

"Amedus," the queen croaked, her voice little more than a gasp as she watched the reptile's green eyes close for the last time.

Cereli turned her dark gaze toward Vallaria and coughed, black blood spurting from her mouth. Rivers of dark red blood seeped through her fingers as she clutched at the knife wound in her stomach. "Your destiny has been fulfilled. You have the throne. The Ravenia bloodline will once again rule this kingdom, but you must heed my words." She closed her eyes for a second and winced. Drawing in a shuddering breath, the queen said, "There is another. One who calls from the grave. She's in my head, she's everywhere, and she's coming for you, Serifine. You will not reign in peace." The dark queen reached out a bloody hand and grasped Vallaria's wrist. "It is not the throne she desires, only revenge, for you lived while she died."

Cereli's eyes widened, and her hand dropped to her lap. With a small gasp she took her last breath. Dark eyes stared unseeing at Vallaria. Without her staff and the dark magic encased within, the dark queen was nothing more than a mere mortal.

Like me. Vallaria quashed her thoughts. They were nothing alike. She'd done what the prophecy demanded. She avenged her parents and put their kingdom's rightful ruler back on the throne. She didn't take what wasn't hers; she took what was hers *back.*

Ravens perched on desktops and sconces, others pecked at the floor. Dozens of sets of blinking eyes watched with curiosity as Vallaria took the Dagger of Crusade from the dark queen's limp hand.

She watched the birds with curiosity. Texts in the elven library detailed the stories of the infamous ravens of Ravenia, protectors of the kingdom and of the Ravenia royals. But none had been sighted in Ravenia since her parents' deaths.

Until now.

A Ravenia had come home, and the ravens had returned.

The aching creak of hinges drew Vallaria's eyes to the back of the room in time to see the throne room door swing slowly close.

Faelin stood to one side, but Zander was gone.

70

ZANDER

As Zander stood concealed by the shadows, he felt empty. Shouldn't he feel something for his mother's plight: distress, empathy, *relief*? A desire to assist in her time of need? Instead, he remained frozen, eyes transfixed on the scene unfolding before him. The well of hollowness in the pit of his stomach grew. Any feelings toward the woman he called mother were gone.

Lives had been ruined because of her selfishness and thirst for power. And now fate had come to collect.

Fate. Wrapped in the body of a young woman thought dead.

Vallaria deserved her revenge, but at what cost? Would she too become tainted by the darkness?

His hand clenched around his sword, and he glanced down at Faelin. His hand went to his ear and his fingers skimmed over the smooth round edge at the top.

Exhaling, he thought about all he'd learned recently.

So many secrets, so much deceit, so many lives touched by the gods' wrath. By his mother's madness.

Before he left the throne room he glanced for the last time at the two women. Propped up at a grotesque angle by the base of the dais was his mother's body. Her dead eyes seemed to stare at him accusingly. A large raven perched on the throne's arm pecked at the tips of her crown that sat askew on her head.

Standing over the queen's corpse, Vallaria's blade sizzled with cold magic. He sensed the power swirling around her because he knew it well. In many ways that magic was like his mother's: dark, unforgiving, and soulless. Ancient magic, reaped from the past, the type mortals were never meant to possess. It didn't matter if it came from the depths of a cursed isle, the mages of old, or the hands of the gods themselves. No matter who wielded it, man or elf, shaman or witch, magic was dangerous.

Vallaria turned her blue gaze his way, and for a moment, he thought he saw a dark shadow pass through her eyes.

He shuddered and his mouth went dry.

Faelin looked up at him. "Zander?" she croaked, rubbing her hand across the back of her head.

"Take care of Vallaria. She needs you," he whispered as he slipped through the throne room door.

THE SOUND OF HIS FOOTFALLS ECHOED OFF THE STONE WALLS AS HE WALKED away. He kept his feet moving, afraid if he stopped he may not be able to leave.

Shouts echoed around corners and down corridors, and he slipped into the shadows as a handful of his mother's royal guards ran toward the throne room.

He leaned his head against the cool stone.

Would the guards remain loyal to the dark queen? Would the army? Would they hold Vallaria accountable or bend a knee to the new queen? Many of the royal guard and much of the army were men who'd served King Ryguard. Did they secretly remain loyal to the Ravenia bloodline?

Queen Cereli had cultivated a culture of respect from fear inside and outside of her realm. Fear of her dark magic and fear of the Gold Coast to which she was irrevocably linked had kept allies at bay. But once news of her death breached the castle walls, Zander wondered if that fealty would still hold. Would the people of Ravenia accept their new queen? Would Ravenia's allies? It wouldn't surprise Zander if the kingdom and its people were ready for change, but there were others who would see this as an opportunity. To challenge the young queen. Vallaria could not let her guard down.

Voices faded as the guards dispersed to the far reaches of the castle. He only needed to make it to the stables and he would ride out of the kingdom forever. He stepped from the shadows and headed toward the back stairs that would lead to the kitchen.

When he crept around the corner, he heard a loud whisper.

"Prince Zander."

He recognized the whine in the man's voice. *Yelin.*

Zander began to walk quicker. He had no desire to speak to his mother's advisor. While Yelin had released him from the dungeon, he certainly hadn't done it out of the goodness in his heart.

The corrupt little man didn't have a heart, not a good one anyway.

Always playing an angle, pitting everyone against each other to further his end game. Zander had always disliked him, but he recognized the man's shrewdness. And if he hadn't left the castle yet, there was a reason, because Yelin Barro's survival was always his primacy.

"Please, Zander, wait."

There was something different in Yelin's tone that made Zander slow. Desperation, concern, he couldn't quite put his finger on it, but it seemed genuine and that was not something Yelin Barro was known for.

Stopping, he turned toward the voice, hoping he wouldn't regret his decision.

Yelin's head poked out from a door.

"Are you in the closet?" Zander asked, raising a brow.

"Come," Yelin said, flicking his fingers and looking down the hallway. "Quickly."

Shaking his head, Zander stepped into the small room and Yelin closed the door behind him. The space was cluttered, filled with buckets, mops, and brooms. Yelin in his black wool pants, leather boots, and gold tunic stood out in the dismal space like a swollen teat on a cow.

"What is it you want, Yelin, and why are you in traveling clothes? Are you going somewhere?"

"Yes, back to the Gold Coast."

"But what of your precious queen?"

"She's dead." A pained expression flitted across the man's features.

"So you know."

Yelin nodded and wiped at his mustache with a shaking hand.

"It was your mother's fate."

"To die. Not much of a fate. We all die eventually."

"No, to die by the hand of the last living heir of the Ravenia throne. The one touched by the gods." He lowered his voice and leaned in. "The last mage."

Zander drew himself up to his full height and glared at the little man in front of him.

"You try my patience, Barro. Tell me what you speak of and not in riddles."

Yelin's fingers fidgeted with the buttons on his tunic. "There is a prophecy that has been whispered through these lands for centuries. While much has changed with the retellings, the gist is the same: a new age of darkness, of magic, will emerge, when the shift of power changes the face of Exile forever. It begins with the rise of the last mage, a young girl of royal blood chosen by the gods to wield the powers of the ancient frost mages. Her act of revenge will be the beginning of the end. The catalyst that pits kingdom against kingdom and ushers in a new and destructive time."

For a moment, Zander found it difficult to breathe in the small and stuffy closet that seemed to be closing in around him. Did Yelin speak of Vallaria?

Not a witch of Brulle, but the last mage? He didn't want to admit it to himself, but somewhere in his heart he'd known her powers were darker, similar to his mother's.

How had he never heard of this prophecy? In all his travels, never a whisper.

Maybe Yelin was full of it. Just moving another piece across his considerably large game board.

"It sounds like every other time of war that has fractured this great continent."

"There is more, something the prophecy doesn't foretell."

"And what is that?" Zander was getting bored.

"It is your place within it."

Zander took a step back and knocked over a mop. "I have no place in any prophecy."

"But you do, Zander, which is why we must get you out of Ravenia and back to the Gold Coast."

"Your little mice, the ones who scurry around listening in corners and whispering in your ear, did they tell you this? Are they filling your head with nonsense?"

"I have proof, and all will be revealed when I get you home."

Home. That concept had become foreign to him over the past few days. Ravenia had never been his home, and the Gold Coast—

His mind drifted to the warm sandy beaches and the clear blue of the sea, and suddenly his mother's voice rose in his mind. *Your conception was an abomination, and they would have drowned you in the central fountain if my secret had been revealed.*

The chill of the castle walls seeped into his bones. "The Gold Coast is no longer my home." Zander lifted his hand and absently grazed the top of his ear.

Yelin scrutinized the gesture. "So you know."

Zander frowned at the man's odd statement. "Know what?"

"Who your father is." Yelin shrugged as if it wasn't significant.

"You knew." Zander felt his face burn, and he clenched his hand, willing himself not to punch the man.

"I suspected."

Footsteps ran down the hall outside the door and Yelin held up a chubby finger to his lips.

When the sound of running had faded, he said, "We must leave, Your Highness. I cannot guarantee your safety inside the city walls."

"You can't guarantee my safety in the Gold Coast either."

Yelin Barro pulled himself up to his full, yet condensed height, and looked Zander directly in the eye. "Do not underestimate me, Zander Damask. I do not do things without forethought. The Gold Coast *is* the one place I can keep you safe. You must trust me. I will explain all once we arrive in the east."

Carefully he opened the closed door and peered out. "Come, the kitchen will be empty and we can use the service entrance to cross to the stables. I have two horses at the ready."

While following Yelin Barro through the darkened halls, he wondered, *why*. Trusting this man was foolish. But he had nowhere else to go. He would still need to enter the Golden City to find passage to Brulle even if he wished to escape the continent. Maybe his Uncle Moricio would know what to do. What choice did he have?

Exiting the kitchen into the cold night air, Zander pulled up the leather hood on his coat. The ice moon no longer hung in the sky, and the night had turned black.

As they rode through the city's vacant streets, Zander noticed a flock of black birds circling the kingdom. Some descended to perch on rooftops, others soared and then dipped above the castle walls, others landed on the cobblestone streets pecking at crumbs left behind.

A large bird sat atop a lamppost, its beady black eyes trained on Zander as he passed. A shudder ran down his spine as the bird's deep resounding caw splintered the quiet of the night sky.

The ravens of Ravenia had returned to herald in the new queen.

But how long would that reign last?

Zander had no doubt once Darrius learned of these happenings, he'd feel compelled to try and overthrow Vallaria, and there was a good possibility he'd want Zander to sit on the throne when he did. It would be the easiest way to bring Ravenia back into the empire's clutches. He was Queen Cereli's son after all, her heir apparent and next in the line of succession. But a Damask had no right to sit on the throne of Ravenia, and he was a prince in name only. He was not born of royal blood. And this was not his fight. He wanted nothing to do with the struggle for dominance that was sure to come. After years of an unstable peace, the continent of Exile would once again see blood stain its soil.

The Gold Coast had many allies, and Darrius Mensah was not one to lose.

But Vallaria Ravenia had an ungodly power, and the elven king would surely align his kingdom with hers.

Zander glanced back at the city of Ravenia as he rode out its gates on his steed. The city wall cast a stalwart shadow across his back, and he shivered.

War was inevitable and eventually he would have to choose a side.

71

FAELIN

Faelin hurried down the castle corridor.

Months had passed since Queen Cereli's death. Just as Alagarn had predicted, most of the army and royal guard were still loyal to the Ravenia bloodline, and once Vallaria had revealed her mark, they'd quickly bent a knee in fealty to King Ryguard's rightful heir.

Justice to those who refused was swift. Over a hundred men had been convicted of treason, executed, and their corpses burned. Mostly acolytes of the Kingdom of Zion or military transfers from the Gold Coast.

Vallaria had opened the royal coffers, ensuring every single subject received a small bag of gold and a week's worth of supplies. For days Faelin and the castle guards had distributed money, food, and medicine to the hundreds of people who lined the streets around the castle walls. Riders had been sent to the rural villages and farms to assist with repairs and to announce the queen's declaration that the Crown would forgo collecting taxes until the farms were once again producing profitably. As the destitute again regained their dignity, the darkness hovering over the kingdom lifted, and for the first time in years, the dark clouds parted and the sun appeared. And the citizens rejoiced their beloved new queen.

Faelin nodded at the guards stationed outside Vallaria's bedchamber.

Knocking on the door, she waited for a few seconds and then entered without waiting for a reply.

Vallaria stood on the balcony, her back to the room.

"He's here, my queen."

Vallaria stiffened but didn't turn around. "Thank you. I will meet you in the royal crypt momentarily."

"As you wish." The elf bowed and exited the room.

Vallaria had not been the same since Pax died. While Faelin didn't understand why Vallaria became so attached to the young orphan boy, she did know his death affected her deeply. Losing Zander added to that pain.

Walking down the shadowy hallway, Faelin took note of the changes Vallaria had implemented. The dark kingdom had risen like a phoenix from the ashes of Cereli's rule. Its people were happier, and the sun shone in a vast blue sky; still, against Faelin's advice, Vallaria had decided to embrace the dark kingdom moniker.

"Are you sure, Vallaria?" Faelin had asked when the new queen had first told her of her plans. "The dark kingdom has become a term associated with fear of its leader and the dismal atmosphere of the realm. You are changing Ravenia for the better."

"I do not want those who think because I'm young, I must also be weak, and therefore easily manipulated."

"And how does ruling a realm nicknamed the dark kingdom persuade them otherwise?"

"It creates an ominous representation out in the world, Faelin, and fills the mind and heart with trepidation. It will make them think before they cross me."

"Isn't that the world Cereli created?"

Vallaria's eyes had flashed. "Cereli Damask's kingdom leeched darkness and cruelty. My darkness is only an illusion."

"Is it? And where does the illusion end and reality begin? Don't you want to show those who think you too young and inexperienced that a queen can be good, kind, *and* powerful? That retribution is not the only way."

"Is that the way of the elves? To allow others to dictate their existence in the world? You retreated once before because of the actions of those who saw you as a threat. But only managed to make yourselves look weak. I won't do the same."

The conversation had ended in that moment. There was no getting Vallaria to see how much she'd adopted Cereli's attitude and way of thinking. For her, same as it had been for Cereli, it would always be her against everyone else. As the commander of the queen's forces, it fell to Faelin to ensure no enemy threatened the Crown's sovereignty.

Even if that meant the new queen herself.

When Faelin exited the castle, she caught a whiff of a sweet blossom scent. The apple trees had begun to bloom as an early spring had arrived in the kingdom. A warm breeze tickled her cheek, and her eyes caught the movement of the flags proudly displaying the new royal crest of Ravenia as they flapped lazily on the peaks of the tower roofs.

The ravens of Ravenia circled above—a sentry of black birds always watching, always alert.

Everything was as it should be.

For now.

The peace which had captured the kingdom in its fragile web would not last. Sooner or later, chaos would once again come calling.

As instructed, Faelin's men lined the pathway leading to the royal crypt. Their black armor gleamed in the sunlight and the black feathers adorning the combs of the helmets swayed in the spring breeze. Melded into the breastplate were sculpted wings, the royal insignia stamped in the center. The pauldrons had been expertly crafted to take the shape of the raven's claws. Made of black plate, the armor was a nod to the ravens of Ravenia, and like the birds, the metal was light yet incredibly strong. Neither blade of sword nor tip of arrow could pierce its exterior.

Faelin quickened her step as she saw two of her men enter the crypt with a small form wrapped in burlap.

"In here," she said, directing them through the open door.

Bringing Pax back to Ravenia was the only thing Vallaria had insisted upon after she regained the throne. Faelin had sent her best men to retrieve his body and bring it back to be buried in the royal cryptic.

The service was to take place a few hours before the coronation.

Vallaria insisted having Pax near would be a reminder of the good in the world and the reason she'd fight any who threatened her reign. But Faelin feared Pax may be a symbol of vengeance for Vallaria. A reminder of all that had been taken from her.

Faelin entered the crypt, and King Elvander stepped from the shadows.

"Father." Her voice conveyed the surprise she felt at seeing the elven king unannounced in the kingdom. "What are you doing in here? I didn't expect you in the kingdom until later." She looked around. "And where is Thaneil?"

"He's in your quarters. I hope you don't mind, but it was imperative I speak with you in private."

The king smiled, but the look in his eyes told her he'd seen a future that hadn't yet happened.

Taking his arm, she led him to a small room off the main entrance. Bottles of embalming fluid, burlap casings, and surgical tools lined the shelves. Her father looked uncomfortable as his eyes scanned the room. He'd never understood why humans were so vulgar in their death rituals.

"Father, did you have a vision?"

The king's gaze came back to his daughter, and he nodded. "But first there is something you should know."

The king's shoulders sagged, and he suddenly looked much older than his three thousand years. Faelin felt his hand tremble.

"What is it? What troubles you?"

The smile that appeared on his lips was weak. An attempt to lessen her concerns. But the quiver in his voice as he began to speak only made them worse. "Long before Vallaria was born, Evinna realized the power her daughter would eventually wield and the path to destiny she would walk. In turn, she made the ultimate sacrifice to protect the one person who could save the world from ruin."

The king's gaze dropped to the floor and his voice lowered to a whisper. "Regrettably, it was never clear exactly which daughter that would be."

Faelin frowned, thinking her father had misspoken. "I don't understand."

"Evinna sacrificed everything for Vallaria to live. It was a heavy price to pay so destiny could be fulfilled. You see, there was another. A girl younger by only minutes."

Faelin's heart skipped a beat and the blood in her ears roared. "Vallaria had a twin?"

As she spoke the words aloud, a long-lost memory resurfaced. The last time she'd been to the Kingdom of Ravenia, it had been for Vallaria's celebration of birth. But there had also been another. A private baptism performed away from prying eyes. She'd paid little attention then as it was only Kelena, Queen Evinna's advisor, and a priest in attendance.

Suddenly it all made sense. "She was the little girl Cereli's invading forces killed with Queen Evinna when they sacked Ravenia."

Her father hung his head, but Faelin could tell he was happy to be free of his burden.

"Yes," he answered. "For years King Ryguard and my sister tried everything in their power to avoid what would soon come. But no matter what they did, fate always found a way to correct its path back to the one they were desperate to avoid. In the end, it was inevitable. Only one of her daughters was meant to live."

Faelin felt ill. "The child was dead before she'd ever been born."

A heavy silence filled the small room. Faelin's mind spun. "What was her name?"

"Sashia Vivienne Ravenia."

The princesses' names echoed in Faelin's mind. *Serifine Vallaria Ravenia and Sashia Vivienne Ravinia.* She looked at her father. "How did I not know about her? How could anyone not? Evinna kept a second daughter, a twin, secret from the entire realm. From our family. How?

"Foresight is often a heavy burden to bear. Evinna's vision coming so soon before the twins' birth allowed us time to plan. After they were born, Sashia was hidden away under an illusion and raised as an orphan by Kelena. Those of us who knew of her existence ensured her identity remained a secret at all costs. With the passing of your mother, Kelena and I were the only ones who remained with that knowledge."

Faelin took her father's hand. "This is the burden you carried with you all these years. Every time you spoke of Vallaria's birth, it was the memory of Sashia that weighed heavy on your mind."

"A decision that left us all scarred but none more so than Evinna. My only solace is that Sashia died in her mother's loving arms."

"Why are you telling me this now? What does Sashia have to do with your vision and the reason you are here?"

"After Cereli killed Evinna and her child, she took their bodies to the Isle of Haddes, leaving them at the bottom of the tarry pits. Whatever darkness Cereli found on that isle somehow infected Sashia's soul, providing her vengeful spirit with a passage into this world."

The king's shoulders sagged.

"I have seen her rise, Faelin. It is only a matter of time. Sashia does not want the crown; she seeks only revenge for the life that was stolen. She's coming to destroy Vallaria and all who knew of her life and death."

Faelin inhaled sharply. "Vallaria must be told of this, Father. She must be made aware that she had a twin sister and the threat she now poses."

A sigh escaped the king's lips. "Yes. It can remain a secret no more."

Faelin dropped her father's hand and leaned against the small table at the room's center. A frown pushed her perfect brows together. "Vallaria's changing. It's not visible yet, but I sense it. She carries a bitterness she didn't before. I fear recent experiences have shaped her perception of how a queen should rule."

The king placed a hand on his daughter's shoulder. "Every young ruler has a growth period. Mistakes will be made, but in time, Vallaria will find herself and become the queen we know she can be."

Emitting a small laugh, the king looked at Faelin and tilted his head. "I know you dread the day you will take my place. You feel inadequate in your own abilities, and fear that those in our race will think you unworthy. None of your misgivings are warranted. Because there hasn't been an elven queen in hundreds of thousands of years does not mean you won't make an exceptional ruler, Faelin. Like you, Vallaria will find her way."

Faelin nodded. Her father understood her all too well.

"Something else weighs on your mind," he said.

Faelin thought about the time she saw Vallaria in the castle library speaking as if someone else was in the room. She'd been agitated, pacing, and frost had covered her fingertips. But it was the words Faelin overheard that chilled her to the bone. *You shall have your revenge. The kingdoms of man will fall under the cold magic I wield. You must be patient and bid your time. They will pay for the sins of the past.*

The memory dispersed, but the chill lay present under Faelin's skin. "I fear Sashia may not be the only vengeful spirit who has attached itself to this world."

"What do you mean?"

"I believe she hears them, the mages of old. Speaks to them. The ancient magic somehow linked her to the mages' vengeful spirits when we were trapped in the Valley of Souls. They want revenge—on all of us."

"I was afraid of this. When you told me of your time there I feared the magic would call to those who created it. It will be their darkness that she may not be able to control one day."

"But Vallaria is strong. She will keep them at bay."

"Powerful magic can be very seductive and can easily destroy a person. Look what it did to Cereli Damask."

Faelin shook her head. "There were many things in that woman's past that shaped the person she became."

"As there are in Vallaria's."

What her father said was true. Cereli's and Vallaria's pasts were very much alike. But Faelin hoped Vallaria's future would not emulate the dark queen's.

"One thing is for certain. The future encompassing Vallaria holds death and destruction. Therefore, you must never leave her side. You must be the one to curb her worst instincts should any arise. Exile will be lost if the darkness takes her."

"And if I can't?"

"Then it must be you who ends her life."

The finality of the king's statement gripped at Faelin's heart. If destiny demanded it of her, could she kill Vallaria?

72
VALLARIA

Her jangled nerves calmed as Vallaria entered the royal crypt. The burial chambers were on the backside of the chapel, and the priest had already begun the ceremonial draping of Pax's small body.

The room was empty except for the priest, the two royal guardsmen who'd escorted her, Faelin, and King Elvander. Vallaria raised a brow at seeing the elven king standing beside his daughter. While she expected him at her coronation, she'd not been notified of his early arrival.

Their eyes met and for a moment his lavender irises darkened.

"Your Majesty," the priest murmured, drawing her attention back to Pax. He bowed and motioned for her to come forth.

When she approached, Vallaria tried to catch Faelin's eye, but the elf respectfully stared straight ahead, her hands clasped behind her back. She no longer wore a mask of illusion to hide her pointed ears, bright lilac eyes, and long silver hair, and it gave Vallaria a sense of comfort to look upon a face she knew so well.

Faelin and King Elvander would never have to hide behind an illusion while she wore the crown.

The prayer beads in her hand felt heavy, awkward. She hadn't picked them up in weeks, hadn't prayed to the gods, or thought about them either. Not since Zander—

Closing her eyes against the memory of the grim look contouring his handsome face the last time she saw him, Vallaria knelt at the altar, bowed her head, and began to pray.

She prayed to her gods for Pax's salvation.

She prayed to them for forgiveness.

And she prayed for strength, but most of all, Vallaria prayed that the next time she laid eyes on Prince Zander Damask, it would not be her undoing.

SHE WAS BACK IN THE MEADOW, BUT THIS TIME EVERYTHING WAS DIFFERENT. The breeze blew sluggish across the land, and the green grass had withered and faded to a dull brown. The pond's surface, now covered with thick green algae, reeked of rot.

Vallaria's reflection in the unseen mirror had also changed. No longer did a little girl look back at her. Now the reflection was of a young woman, long black hair tucked neatly into a black glass crown.

A slithering cold ignited on her skin, and she turned to see the raven, its black eyes bleeding blood. Its ebony feathers had lost their burnished surface and were frayed, falling to the ground as the raven shook its wings.

Her legs felt weak, and she couldn't catch a breath.

The bird opened its beak and released a strangled caw.

From the corner of her eye, she saw her reflection move, and when her gaze drifted back, the mirrored image had changed. Her hair was now long and white, reaching past her feet and spreading out like tentacles across the dead grass. Black orbs replaced blue eyes and when she opened her mouth to speak a black oily substance dripped from her lips.

Vallaria moved closer, and unexpectedly the reflection reached out and grabbed her by the throat.

"Hello, sister."

Vallaria gasped for air as she sat up in bed, frantically clawing at her throat. The candle on her fireplace had burnt down to almost nothing, but it still cast enough light to see she was alone in her bedchamber.

Just a nightmare.

While she thought about the dream, something inside her mind opened and a deluge of memories surged into her consciousness.

Two little girls dressed in white playing in a sunny, flower-filled meadow. A beautiful, tall, silver-haired woman sat on a blanket by the pond. A basket of apples next to her. *Her mother.*

"Serifine, wait for your little sister." It was Kelena's voice.

Vallaria's heart raced, and she felt faint.

Little sister. But only by a few minutes.

Vallaria had a twin. *Sashia.* The name drifted through her mind. Princesses Serifine and Sashia Ravenia.

Although their faces resembled one another, Vallaria had been brave and bold, always exploring and finding mischief, while Sashia was shy and reserved, content to have her nose in a book.

A wave a nausea washed over her, and her abdominal muscles clenched. Quickly she leaned over the side of the bed and threw up on the floor.

Tears slipped from her eyes as more memories flooded her senses. Birthday parties, carriage rides, picnics in the meadow, but then they turned five and everything had ended.

Pulling her knees up to her chest, she wrapped her arms around them as the last memory, clearer than all the rest, ricocheted through her mind.

It was dark and screams rang throughout the castle. Vallaria had been scared, and she'd held tight to Kelena's shoulders as her mother pushed them toward the bookcase in her bedchamber. Sashia, wrapped in a blanket, lay on the bed asleep. "Goodbye," Vallaria had whispered as tears filled her eyes, and they slipped through the secret doorway.

Her mother had closed the door behind them.

It was the last time she'd seen either of them.

When they'd run through the dark passageway and out into the waiting arms of King Elvander, Vallaria had closed her eyes so tight she'd made her memories of her life before the elves vanish into the far reaches of her mind.

THE SUN'S EARLY-MORNING RAYS CASCADED ACROSS THE SKY. BRIGHT splashes of orange, yellow, and red welcomed Vallaria as she gazed across the kingdom from her balcony.

After last night the warmth felt good on her skin and calmed her frazzled nerves. Ravens perched on the castle rooftops spreading their wings to the sun, others took flight, swooping and gliding through the warm morning air.

Her gaze drifted to the east.

Somewhere far beyond the horizon, on the shores of the Shimmering Coast, lay the Golden City. *And Zander.* Closing her eyes, she let old memories surface. Vallaria could still feel the way his fingers caressed her skin, warm and gentle. The pressure of his lips on hers and the salty scent of his skin as he kissed her.

A firm knock on her chamber door interrupted her thoughts.

"Come," she called walking inside from the balcony.

Faelin entered, a small white scroll in her hand. She looked at Vallaria and frowned. "Something troubles you."

Vallaria tensed. No matter how hard she tried to hide her emotions, the elf could always discern when something was wrong. "It's nothing."

"You're thinking of him."

"I'm thinking of them."

"Them?" Faelin raised a brow.

Vallaria sat on the chair by the bed. "The Gold Coast, Darrius, General Moricio, and yes, Zander. Do you think they will come?"

"I do."

"And try to kill me and possibly take back the throne?"

"No doubt."

Vallaria sighed. "Revenge is a vicious circle, Faelin."

The elf nodded. "That it is." She handed Vallaria the scroll. "A missive from the holy king of Kasmire."

"Whatever could he want?" Vallaria asked, her thumb sliding over the red wax seal that bore the insignia of the holy city.

"The holy city has long been a solitary entity. Concealed behind its high walls and dangerous sea cliffs, it's not known for its interaction with the other kingdoms of Exile. It may be a positive sign that the holy king has reached out to a new queen. Maybe he's inviting you to the lighting of the Seven Halos. Spring is upon us and holy week is not that far off."

Breaking the seal, Vallaria unwound the parchment. Blue eyes glazed as she read the scroll's contents.

"Vallaria. What is it?" she heard Faelin say.

"It's an announcement."

Faelin frowned. "Regarding?"

Vallaria's hand shook as she handed the parchment to the elf. "The marriage of Princess Aerilla Amorian to Prince Zander Damask." As she spoke the words aloud, her voice wavered, and a black fog slipped over her vision. The room began to spin, and for a moment, she thought she'd lose consciousness.

Gripping the arm of the chair, she inhaled deeply pushing the air out through her mouth. Her heart ached. Nothing that happened between them had been real. At least not for him anyway. A wave of anger made her see red. *How could you be so stupid? So naïve. He didn't want you, at least not the way you wanted him.* Even after all that had happened, a small part of her still hoped he'd come back.

Now he never would.

"Vallaria, I'm sorry." Faelin said, stuffing the announcement into her pocket. "Your army awaits to officially pledge allegiance to their queen. I can tell them you've taken ill?"

Tears welled up in Vallaria's eyes, and she angrily wiped them away and shook her head. "No, I'll be along in a minute." She refused to let this interfere with her royal duties. Vallaria had reclaimed her parents' kingdom and yesterday her coronation had made it official.

The people of Ravenia needed her.

Prince Zander had made his choice and now she would make hers.

The crown of black glass, its points ascending inches above her head, suddenly felt heavy as a weariness set into her bones. But she pulled back her shoulders and swallowed the pain.

Being Queen Vallaria Ravenia was the only thing that mattered. She raised her hand and willed the frost to come forth. As the familiar tingling cold surged down her arm and into her fingertips, she rotated her hand back and forth, watching as the frost covered her skin.

Calling the magic had become second nature. It had become a part of her and she it.

"Do you not fear it?" Faelin asked.

"What?"

"The ancient magic."

"No."

"You should." Elven eyes glinted in the sunlight that poured through the open balcony doors. "And what of your gods? Do you fear them?"

Vallaria's face burned with heat as she thought about the prayers, the sacrifices, the loneliness, and uncertainty.

Sashia. Zander.

The silence was deafening. For the gods had abandoned her. Betrayed her.

"The gods be damned," she said through clenched teeth. "They don't carry this burden. They've thrust this destiny upon me and sit in silence while I suffer."

In a fit of rising anger, she ripped her father's prayer beads from the table and broke the leather string, sending the wood and glass balls scattering across the floor in a flurry of snow. The flat piece of metal stamped with the letter R skidded across the room and disappeared into the floor grate. A tinny sound rang out as it fell and hit the pipe.

Vallaria was her mother's daughter, kin of the elves, queen of Ravenia, and the last mage. No more would she hide behind the mountains of Mistenvale or cower behind the Ravenia army. And she had no intention of showing mercy to her enemies or any who sought to dethrone her. For a queen was only as strong as the weakness her enemies uncovered or that which she herself succumbed to.

Cold sizzled at her fingertips, and a wicked smile contorted her lips.

And Vallaria Ravenia was anything but weak.

Continue the story with Book 2, Crown of Shadows.

Sign up for my newsletter and get a free short story. The Mercenary's Debt is a prequel that focuses on Zander's time as the mercenary, Zane.
https://dl.bookfunnel.com/7fx8apl4qu

ABOUT THE AUTHOR

Jaci Miller is a dark and epic romantic fantasy author. She is the author of the Scrying Trilogy, a contemporary portal fantasy, and The Dark Kingdom trilogy and the first in the Endless Sea universe, an epic fantasy world that will expand with future books.

Jaci currently lives in sunny Florida with her husband and their tuxedo cat, Draco.

Sign up for Jaci's newsletter at www.jacimiller.com/contact and receive a short story from the world of The Dark Kingdom.

And follow her on social media.

ACKNOWLEDGMENTS

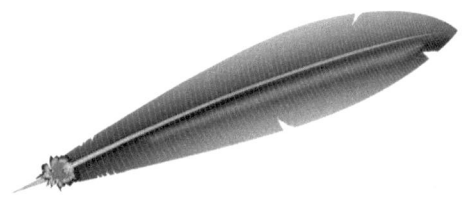

To say the least, 2020 was a trial in perseverance that tested our sanity like never before. I started this book at the end of November 2019 with the intention of having the final draft completed and to my editor for final copy edits by end of April 2021. But, like everything else, this too went into lockdown. Dealing with some personal issues I ended up hating my first draft and had a difficult time seeing past its shortcomings. Taking a break for a month, I came back to it with a fierce determination to turn the draft around. I scheduled a developmental edit and went back to the drawing board. Now, almost a year later, this book is not only something I love, but something I am very proud of. This was a world I had wanted to create since ending my last trilogy. It had characters who whispered to me at night, begging me to tell their stories.

The words on these pages were worth every page torn in frustration, every tear shed, and every moment of late-night hysteria when I didn't think I would ever complete it. But complete it I did, with the help of some very amazing people.

A big thanks to my editor Tiffany White at Writer's Untapped. You were there for me when I was stuck and felt like giving up. You not only pushed my creativity, but also gave me immensely helpful feedback and heartfelt encouragement. This book would not be what it is today if not for you.

To Jake at J Caleb Design who created the original covers for this trilogy and to the design team at Miblart who created the new 2025 versions.

To my friends and family. Thanks for being my cheerleaders, my support group, and standing steadfast behind my dream, especially my husband, Dale.

And to the two halves of my heart, my sixteen-year-old Parson Russell Terrier, Ike (now my angel), and to Draco my ninja tuxedo cat —one curled up under my desk, one lays on it.

And lastly, to my readers, thank you so much. I hope you enjoy the journey of reading my books as much as I do in creating them.